Catherine Jane Hamilton

Women Writers

Their Works and Ways. Second Series.

Catherine Jane Hamilton

Women Writers
Their Works and Ways. Second Series.

ISBN/EAN: 9783337386269

Printed in Europe, USA, Canada, Australia, Japan

Cover: Foto ©Andreas Hilbeck / pixelio.de

More available books at **www.hansebooks.com**

WOMEN WRITERS:

THEIR WORKS AND WAYS.

SECOND SERIES.

BY

CATHERINE J. HAMILTON,

AUTHOR OF

'MARRIAGE BONDS," "THE FLYNNS OF FLYNNVILLE," "DR. DELTON'S
DAUGHTERS," &C.

"What good is like to this,
To do worthy the writing, and to write
Worthy the reading, and the world's delight?"

WARD, LOCK, & BOWDEN, LIMITED,

LONDON: WARWICK HOUSE, SALISBURY SQUARE, E.C.,

NEW YORK, MELBOURNE, AND SYDNEY.

1893.

PREFACE.

THE First Series of *Women Writers: their Works and Ways* has been so favourably received that I am encouraged to offer the Second Series, in the hope that it may be found equally interesting. My object is the same—to give the life-stories of some celebrated authoresses, to tell how they gained success, and how they enjoyed it.

As we advance farther into the nineteenth century, we do not find that gaiety, that intense joy of living which are so characteristic of Fanny Burney and Lady Morgan. Our women writers have become less amusing ; they are terribly in earnest, much impressed with the seriousness of life, and with difficult social problems.

I am well aware that many notable names have been unavoidably left out, so many that, in course of time, it may be necessary to add a Third Series of *Women Writers: their Works and Ways.*

I have taken great pains to ascertain correct dates. In almost all the short biographical notices of Mrs. Hemans the date of her birth is given as 1794, on the sole authority of Mr. W. F. Chorley, who only knew her during the later years of her life. Her sister, Mrs. Hughes, in her memoir of Mrs. Hemans, says distinctly 1793. She had the best opportunity of knowing, as the sisters were brought up together, so her authority seems to me quite conclusive.

The difference between the ages of Robert and Elizabeth

Browning is usually said to be six years, but as he was born in 1812, and she, according to the best authorities, in 1809, the difference in their ages could only be three years.

I am deeply indebted to Miss Gaskell, not only for revising my sketch of her mother, but also for several valuable notes. She has also entirely re-written the translation of her letter to Madame Mohl about the Lancashire distress. Our knowledge of Mrs. Gaskell's private life has hitherto been so very scanty that I am glad to be able to offer this slight but, I am glad to say, thoroughly accurate account of one of our best and purest women writers. Miss Gaskell has also most kindly allowed me to reproduce Richmond's portrait of Mrs. Gaskell, which is the best likeness that exists.

I am much indebted to Mr. Cross for allowing the portrait in his second volume of *The Life of George Eliot* to be copied. From his interesting book I have gleaned most of the information about George Eliot and her works. From the *Life, Letters, and Journals of Louisa Alcott*, edited by Ednah D. Cheney, the information about the author of *Little Women* has been chiefly collected.

I am under deep obligations to Miss Helen Blackburn, editor of the *Englishwomen's Review*, for lending an engraving of Hayter's picture of the Hon. Mrs. Norton, from which the likeness in this volume has been taken. She has also lent Richmond's portrait of Harriet Martineau, and has supplied many useful hints about the other portraits.

CONTENTS.

I.

II.

III.

CONTENTS.

FELICIA HEMANS.

BORN SEPTEMBER 25TH, 1793; DIED MAY 16TH, 1835

WOMEN WRITERS:

THEIR WORKS AND WAYS.

SECOND SERIES.

—••—

I.

MRS. HEMANS.

1793–1835.

Birth at Liverpool—Childhood at Gwrych—Early love of reading and marvellous memory—Bronwylfa—Conway Castle—*Early Blossoms*— Meets Captain Hemans—Marriage—Dislike to Daventry—Birth of her son, Arthur—Return to Bronwylfa—Prize Poem—*Vespers of Palermo*—*Siege of Valencia*—*The Forest Sanctuary*—Rhyllon—*Records of Woman*—Settles at Wavertree—Visit to Abbotsford—At "The Dove's Nest"—Wordsworth—Goes to Dublin—Declining health— Death.

A RE the poems of Mrs. Hemans quite forgotten? Are they never read? We often hear that this is the case, but some obstinate facts seem to tell us the contrary.

The tide of years is rolling on, and yet two leading publishers issue cheap editions of her works. Her poem of *Casabianca* is the first taught to us in childhood; *The Graves of a Household*, the *Stately Homes of England*, *The Better Land*, and *Oh ! call my brother back to me*, are found in every school reading-book, and at least three

2

of her pieces—*Richard Cœur de Lion*, the *Lady of Provence*, and *The Ballad of Roncesvalles*—are frequently
on the list of favourite selections for recitation. There is,
too, a Mrs. Hemans' *Birthday Book*, published as late as
1884. With these facts staring us in the face, how can it
be said that the poetry of Mrs. Hemans is quite neglected ?

She was no Sappho ; she gave us no passionate love-
songs ; she was the poet of the affections. Nature, too,
spoke eloquently to her soul ; the romance of war and
chivalry, the glitter of steel and the waving of banners
kindled her imagination. Some of her shorter poems do
and will live, notwithstanding the ebb and flow of modern
opinion. Without profound insight, they have a directness
and pathos which nothing can destroy. We need not look
for "obstinate questionings," for involved reasoning and
passionate yearnings in Mrs. Hemans. The unrest which
troubles so many at the close of the nineteenth century
had not begun. She is plaintive, but never passionate ; she
is subdued, but never rebellious or defiant. Carlyle once
said that there is " a thin vein of true poetry in Mrs.
Hemans." He is right ; the vein *is* thin, but it is there.
By virtue of this "thin vein of true poetry" Mrs. Hemans
takes rank amongst the singers of the century. She is not
a deep teacher, but she has a sweet voice of her own. Let
us take a brief glance at her life.

Felicia Dorothea Browne was born in Duke Street, Liverpool, on the 25th of September, 1793.[1] By descent she
was only half Irish. Her father, a wine merchant in good
business, was a native of Ireland, but her mother (whose
name had been Wagner) was of mingled Italian and German
descent, and was the daughter of the Tuscan Consul at
Liverpool. Felicia, the fifth of seven children, was remark-

[1] Mr. H. F. Chorley, in his *Memorials of Mrs. Hemans*, gives the date
of her birth 1794, but Mrs. Hughes, her sister, says 1793, and she must be
the best authority on the subject. This date is also given in *The Dictionary
of National Biography*.

able from her birth for extreme beauty and precocious talents. Before she had reached the age of seven, her father, having suffered commercial losses, broke up his establishment at Liverpool and removed with his family to Wales, where for the next nine years they resided at Gwrych, near Abergele, in Denbighshire. Their house, now almost entirely pulled down, was a large, solitary old mansion, close to the sea, and shut in by a chain of rocky hills. In the calm seclusion of this romantic region, with a large library at hand, little Felicia spent a happy childhood, and in after-life her thoughts travelled back to it with regretful tenderness. Here she drank in that ardent love of Nature and that warm attachment for the green land of Wales, its true-hearted people, its music and its traditions, which never left her. Gwrych was supposed to be haunted, and Felicia, having heard a rumour of a fiery greyhound, which kept watch at the end of the avenue, sallied forth, by moonlight, quite alone, to encounter the goblin. She had such a charm about her, that the old gardener used to say, " Miss Felicy would 'tice you to do anything." Her eldest sister died young, and Felicia's education was undertaken by her mother. Felicia repaid her with a love more than usually strong. Her first lines, when she was only eight years old, are addressed to her mother, and in one of her last sonnets (to a family Bible) she acknowledges that the teaching of her early years had been a seed—

" Not lost, for which in darker years,
  O Book of Heaven ! I pour with grateful tears
  Heart blessings on the holy dead and thee."

Felicia's quickness in acquiring knowledge was only equalled by her amazing memory. Her sister says that she could repeat pages of poetry from her favourite authors after having read them but once, and a scarcely less wonderful faculty was the rapidity of her reading. When she was quite a child a bystander would imagine that she was only

carelessly turning over the pages of a book ; in reality she
was taking in the whole sense as completely as another
would do who pored over it with the closest attention.
"Why, Felicia, you can't have read that," one of her friends
used to say. " Oh ! yes, I have," was her answer, "and I
will repeat it to you." And so she would. One of her
earliest tastes was a passion for Shakespeare, which she
read as her chosen recreation at six years old. "In later
days," says her sister, Mrs. Hughes, "she would often refer
to the hours of romance she had passed in a secret haunt of
her own, a seat among the branches of an old apple-tree.
There, revelling in the pages of her cherished volume, she
would become completely absorbed in the imaginative world
it revealed to her." The following lines, written at eleven
years old, show something of her youthful enthusiasm :—

> " Led by Shakespeare, bard inspired,
> The bosom's energies are fired.
> We learn to shed the gen'rous tear
> O'er poor Ophelia's sacred bier ;
> To love the merry moonlit scene,
> With fairy elves in valleys green ;
> Or, borne on fancy's heavenly wings,
> To listen while sweet Ariel sings."

Her beauty was of a very delicate and fragile kind : her
complexion brilliant, her hair long, curling, and golden.
One lady remarked in her hearing, "That child is not made
for happiness, I know ; her colour comes and goes too fast."
She never forgot this observation, and used afterwards to
say it gave her great pain.

At the age of eleven she passed a winter in London
with her father and mother, and the visit was repeated the
following year. During one of her London visits she was
taken to see a sculpture-gallery, and she involuntarily exclaimed, "Oh ! hush ! don't speak." At another time, her
mother used to tell of the interest she excited in a party
who were visiting the Marquis of Stafford's collection of

pictures; she not only expressed great delight, but knew
all about the classical subject. She never visited London
again. The contrast between the confinement of a town
life and the happy freedom of her own mountain home
was, says her sister, even then distasteful to her. Plays
and sights soon ceased to interest. She longed to rejoin
her younger brother and sister in their favourite amusements, in their excursions to the nutting-wood, in their
visits to the beloved apple-tree, to the old arbour with its
swing, to the post-office tree, in which a daily interchange
of family letters was established; and to the pool, where
fairy ships were launched, generally painted and decorated
by Felicia herself. Dearer still were the wild rambles on
the sea-shore, or the mountain expedition to the Signal
Station, or the Roman Encampment.

In 1809 the Browne family removed from Gwrych to
Bronwylfa, near St. Asaph, in Flintshire. Here, though
in less seclusion than before, Felicia's mind continued to
develop, and her tastes and pursuits grew wider in their
range. She began to study Spanish and Portuguese, along
with the already-acquired French and Italian. She also
read German, though it was not till some years later that
she entered into the spirit and soul of the grand Deutsch
tongue, and wrote of it as having opened to her a "new
world of thought and feeling, so that even the music of
the Eichenland, as Korner calls it, acquired a deeper tone
when she had become familiar with its noble poetry."
The powers of her memory became more and more extraordinary, so as to be sometimes made the subject of a
wager by those who could hardly believe in them. To
satisfy the incredulity of one of her brothers, she learned
by heart the whole of Heber's poem of *Europe* in one
hour and twenty minutes, and repeated it without a single
mistake or a moment's hesitation. She had never read
the poem before, and it consisted of 424 lines. Her cor-
rectness of eye and the length and clearness of her vision

were as proverbial among her friends as her wonderful
memory. Music was one of her great pleasures. She
played both harp and piano with feeling and expression,
and her sister says that certain melodies are completely
identified with the recollection of her peculiarly soft and
sostenuto touch, which gave to the piano an effect approaching to the swell of an organ. Even in her joyous days she
loved melancholy music. Welsh and Spanish airs were her
favourites—Jomelli's *Chaconne*, Oginsky's *Polonaise*, and
a little touching air called *The Moravian Nun*. In one of
her letters she says, " What a deep echo gives answer within
the mind to that exclamation of Richter at the sound of
music, 'Away! away! Thou speakest of things which
throughout my endless life I have found not, and shall not
find.' All who have felt music must at times, I think, have
felt this, making its sweetness too piercing to be sustained."
So in her poem, *The Voice of Music*, she says it is—

> " Something that finds not its answer here—
> A chain to be clasped in another sphere."

"I do not think," she wrote in her later years, "that I
can bear the burden of my life without music for more than
two or three days." Some of her happiest hours were
spent during her visits to friends at Conway. The charms
of water, wood, and ruin are enough to awaken poetry
in the most prosaic ; with little Felicia they roused the
most vivid enthusiasm. Sometimes she entered with
child-like delight into the joys of a mountain scramble,
or a picnic water party, but often in a graver mood she
would dream away hours amidst the grey ruins of that
noblest of Welsh castles Amongst the ruins of Conway
Castle, Felicia read Joanna Baillie's play of *Ethwald* and
on this account had a peculiar admiration for it. Here
also she first made acquaintance with Froissart's romantic
Chronicles. Her own little poem, *The Ruin and its
Flowers*, was written during an excursion to the old fortress

of Dyganwy, which is situated on a bold promontory near the entrance of the river Conway. Its ivied walls, now fast mouldering to decay, once bore their part bravely in the defence of Wales.

In 1808 a collection of Felicia Browne's poems was published in a quarto volume under the title of *Early Blossoms.* It was thus criticised in the *Monthly Review :* " We hear that these poems are the genuine productions of a young lady between the ages of eight and thirteen, and we do not feel inclined to question the intelligence ; but although the fact may insure them an indulgent reception from àll who have children dear, yet when a little girl publishes a large quarto, we are disposed to examine before we admit her claims to public attention. Many of Miss Browne's compositions are extremely jejune ; they contain some erroneous and some pitiable lines, but we must praise the *Reflections on a Ruined Castle,* and the poetic strain in which they are delivered." The reviewer goes on to say that if the youthful author were to content herself for some years with reading instead of writing " we would open any future work of hers with pleasure, though we must observe at the same time that premature talents are not always signs of future excellence, and that the honeysuckle attains maturity before the oak." The effect of this criticism was that the little author had to go to bed for several days, weeping and heartsick with vexation and disappointment. Fortunately for her, this was her first and last adverse criticism ; reviewers ever afterwards were singularly merciful to her, and she never had the thorny honour of a " cutting up " in the *Quarterly. Early Blossoms* was reprinted in 1841, and I now hold the tiny volume in my hand : the poems are perhaps rather better than those of most clever children, but certainly not worth the dignity of print.

Two or three years after the appearance of her first book she was introduced to Captain Hemans ; she was then only fifteen or sixteen years of age, and in the first flush of that beauty which was destined to fade so early. "The mantling bloom of her cheeks," says Mrs. Hughes, " was shaded by a profusion of natural ringlets of a rich golden-brown, and the ever-varying expression of her brilliant eyes gave a changeful play to her countenance which made it impossible for any painter to do justice to it." No wonder that the susceptible captain in the 4th was vanquished at once, and vowed eternal devotion. As for Felicia at this time, her fancies had taken a warlike turn. Two of her brothers were in the army, one serving under Sir John Moore ; she was full of British devotion and Spanish patriotism, and had written a poem on England and Spain. To her Captain Hemans seemed a hero, and she clothed him with a romantic veil of her own. But marriage did not immediately follow. Captain Hemans was obliged to rejoin his regiment in Spain, and meanwhile Felicia wrote on industriously, and published her *Domestic Affections*. In 1812 Captain Hemans returned, and the marriage took place when the young poetess was in her nineteenth year. The newly-married couple took up their residence at Daventry, in Northamptonshire, Captain Hemans having been appointed adjutant to the Northamptonshire Militia. They remained at Daventry about a year, and their eldest son, Arthur, was born there. Mrs. Hemans missed her " own mountain land," and found the country about Daventry tame and uninteresting. The only place she liked was Fawsley Park ; the woods and lawns, the old Hall, with its quaint gables and twisted chimneys, and the venerable ivy-mantled church, always kept a place in her memory, and is celebrated by a sonnet, *On an Old Church in an English Park*. The militia having been disbanded, the Hemanses returned to Wales and took up their abode at Bronwylfa with the rest of the Browne family. Here they remained, and here their four sons were born. It is needless to say that their marriage was a failure. Given two certain quantities, and a necessary result is sure to follow. A middle-aged man, remarkably matter-of-fact, accustomed to the regular routine of military life, and a dreamy, pensive, enthusiastic young poetess. What could they have in common? Officers who have retired from active service generally find their time hang heavy on their hands, and are often exacting about trifles. Captain Hemans returning to dinner rather peevish from his bad state of health, which had suffered from the hardships of a soldier's life, was but too likely to find his wife surrounded by heaps of books, her eye in a "fine frenzy rolling," her fingers smeared with ink, and quite oblivious of mundane things. She had been a petted child; her mother and sister managed the house, so she was utterly ignorant of domestic matters. Captain Hemans was once heard to declare that it was the curse of having a literary wife that he could never get his stockings mended. And so the little rifts came, and all music between this ill-matched pair was utterly mute.

In 1816 Mrs. Hemans published *The Restoration of the Works of Art to Italy,* and *Modern Greece,* and in 1818 her *Stanzas on the Death of the Princess Charlotte* appeared in *Blackwood's Magazine,* and awakened universal attention. She was not only an enthusiastic poet, but she was also a laborious worker. She explored every book she could find, she gathered materials from every source, and this course she pursued, we are told, "in season and out of season, by night and day, on her chair and sofa and bed, at home and abroad, in rambles and journeys and visits, in company with her husband and at hours usually devoted to domestic claims, as well as in the solitude of her study." Alas! for practical, commonplace Captain Hemans, thrown by the "cessation of war into forced inactivity, and possessing a larger share than usual of the cool, calculating utilitarianism of everyday life."

In 1818, after six years' experience of matrimony, he took his departure for Rome, under the plea that his health required a warmer climate. Nothing like a permanent sepa-

ration was then contemplated, but he and his wife never
met again. It has been said that literary women do not
make good wives, but facts prove that occasionally they do.
Mrs. S. C. Hall, Mary Howitt, Mrs. Stowe, and last, but not
least, Mrs. Browning, show that the strongest affection has
existed between women of great intellectual gifts and their
husbands. But it requires, on the woman's side, rare tact,
meekness, self-surrender, and common sense. Mrs. Hemans
did not understand the art of uniting the nectar and
ambrosia of genius with the dry bread of everyday duties.
Yet, strangely enough, in her writings she was specially
given to exalt the beauty of a happy domestic life. In
one of her best poems, *Corinne Crowned at the Capitol*,
she cries—

> " Radiant daughter of the sun,
>   Now thy living wreath is won,
>   Crowned of Rome, oh ! art thou not
>   Happy in that glorious lot ?
>   Happier, happier far than thou,
>   With the laurel on thy brow,
>   She that makes the humblest hearth
>   Lovely but to one on earth."

But happiness cannot exist without sympathy, and between
Mrs. Hemans and her husband there was none. In a letter
to Mary Howitt she congratulated her, with a mournful
reference to herself, in possessing in her husband a kindred
spirit and a friend. She was fated to have that saddest of
all sad fates—to be an unloved wife, separated from the
person whose name she bore, the lawful partner of her joys
and sorrows. In one respect she showed singular delicacy
and refinement of feeling. She had every temptation to
follow Lord Byron's example, to take an admiring public
into her confidence, and to relate all the grievances she had
had to endure ; but, on the contrary, she never cast a
reproach on her husband. It was truly said, " No sharp or
scornful speech is on record against her." She was a most

devoted mother to her five sons : "You will smile," she writes, "when I tell you that I have stolen time to-day for the important purpose of making garlands for my little boys to dance with, as it is the birthday of the youngest."

In 1819 a member of the Highland Society, wishing to raise a national monument to the memory of Wallace, offered prizes for the three best poems on the subject of Wallace inviting Bruce to the Scottish throne. There were fifty-seven competitors, and amongst them James Hogg, the Ettrick Shepherd. The task of the judges was no joke, for one of the poems was as long as *Paradise Lost!* The first prize of £50 was unanimously given to Mrs. Hemans' poem, *Wallace's Invocation to Bruce.* It begins—

" The morn rose bright on scenes renowned,
    Wild Caledonia's classic ground."

Without being a first-class poem, it has considerable force and beauty of expression, and Hogg, though a defeated competitor, says that the prize was justly awarded to Mrs. Hemans, her poem being vastly superior to the others in elegance of thought and composition. "My heart," he says, "never warmed to any author so much for any poem that was ever written." She also obtained in June, 1821, the prize awarded by the Royal Society of Literature for the best poem on Dartmoor. "I wish," she writes to one of her friends, "you had seen the children when the prize was announced to them yesterday. Arthur sprang up from his Latin exercise and shouted aloud, 'Now I am sure mamma is a better poet than Lord Byron.' Their acclamations were actually deafening, and George said his pleasure had given him a headache." The two elder boys, Arthur and George, were sent away to the house of a clergyman, and the day when Mrs. Hemans went to fetch them home was, she said, one of the white days of her life. The village at which they were staying was embosomed in mountains, and only approached by a narrow lane. The glorious summer day,

the quiet beauty of the hill country, the luxuriance of the
ferns and foxglove, were all felt and enjoyed ; and then the
two happy boys rushed down a green slope, flapping their
pinafores in ecstasy at the sight of the carriage. They did
the honours of the village, the church, and the bridge, and
in the evening drove home to the gladsome meeting with
grandmamma and the three merry little brothers.

Amongst Mrs. Hemans' Welsh friends was the Bishop of
St. Asaph, Dr. Luxmore. In him she found a never-failing
friend and counsellor. Her children talked of him as their
own bishop, and in a letter from Chiefswood she says, "I
have been much at Abbotsford, where my boys run in and
out as if they were children of the soil, or as if it were the
Palace." Reginald Heber was the first literary celebrity
with whom she was personally acquainted. He admired her
tragedy, *The Vespers of Palermo*, so much, that he advised
her to offer it to Charles Kemble. The critics of the green
room thought well of it, and after three years' delay and disappointment it was produced at Covent Garden on the 12th
of December, 1823. Mrs. Hughes gives a pretty picture of
the excitement at Bronwylfa ; the post-office was besieged
at twelve o'clock at night, and the boys had worked themselves up into an uncontrollable state of excitement to hear
about mamma's play. It was a bitter mortification to Mrs.
Hemans to tell them that all these bright visions were
dashed to the ground, and that the performance was a
failure. Though Mrs. Hemans is best known by her short
poems, yet this tragedy, and her dramatic sketch, *The Siege
of Valencia*, show the extent and variety of her powers
more than her shorter pieces do. *The Vespers of Palermo*
tells the fatal story of the Sicilian conspiracy whose signal
was the vesper bell. The midnight scenes and the fury
of the oppressed conspirators are dramatically brought out ;
so is the fortitude of Raimond di Procida, who refuses to
join in an underhand plot, even against the tyrant Eribert.
Then comes the unjust accusation against Raimond, and his

death in battle in the arms of Constance, Eribert's sister and his betrothed bride. In spite of the failure at Covent Garden, which was put down to Miss Kelly's bad intonation, the play was afterwards acted at Edinburgh and went off in a way that exceeded every one's expectations. "The scene in the judgment-hall," writes a friend to Mrs. Hemans, "carried off the audience, and handkerchiefs were out in every quarter. Mrs. H. Siddons (Constance) searching the faces of the judges was perfect. She flew round the court, went from judge to judge, paused before Procida, and fell prostrate at his feet. The effect was magical." Sir Walter Scott wrote the epilogue, stuffed, he writes to Mrs. Hemans, "with parish jokes and bad puns." Murray had given two hundred guineas for the copyright, and Mrs. Hemans' merits as a poet were universally recognised.

In *The Siege of Valencia*, she went to Spain for her story. Gonzalez has to give up his two sons to be slain by the Moors in order to save the city entrusted to him, and the struggles of his wife, Elmina, between maternal love and patriotism, are finely told. The speeches of Hermandez are more than eloquent. Here is one of them :—

> " By my side the stripling grew,
> Last of my line, I reared him to take joy
> I' the blaze of arms, as eagles train their young
> To look upon the day king. . . . His quick blood
> E'en to his boyish cheek would mantle up
> When the heavens rang with trumpets, and his eye
> Flash with the spirit of his race. . . . Around my steps
> Floated his fame like music, and I lived
> But in the lofty sound."

The play has a spirited flow and a martial ring which those who have not read it would hardly give Mrs. Hemans credit for. The fault of both plays is unrelieved gloom. They are all shade. There is no humour, no gaiety ; early death, separation, loss, misfortune, hang like a dark cloud over everything.

In the autumn of 1824 Mrs. Hemans began *The Forest Sanctuary*. The title was suggested by one of her brothers, and tears often flowed as the poem was read out to the little circle during the winter evenings. Here, again, she took a melancholy subject. A Spanish Protestant in the time of Phillip II. suffers persecution, and at last escapes to an American forest with his child. The *auto-da-fé* and his imprisonment in a vaulted cell furnish Mrs. Hemans with many a pathetic touch. " The damp roof's water drops, intensely heard amidst the silence," calls back to his sick soul "a clear spring, whose side with flowers o'ergrown,

> " Fondly and oft my boyish steps had sought."

Woe succeeds woe. The captive is released ; he rejoins his wife, but he sees her fading gradually before his eyes, and he exclaims—

> " Oh ! could we live in visions, could we hold
> Delusion faster—longer—to our breast,
> When it shuts from us with its mantle's fold
> That which we see not, and are therefore blest ! "

Leonor dies at sea, and the wanderer reaches the American forest, " lifts to Heaven a sad heart, and learns the might of solitude," while his child "breathes low on the breast of night." Mrs. Hemans always considered *The Forest Sanctuary* her best poem. Passages of great pathos and beauty are strewn through it, but the prevailing melancholy leaves an oppressive feeling on the mind. " *Toujours perdrix*," we are ready to exclaim. Let us have melancholy in reason. A little sadness is all very well, but not whole courses of it served up in succession. Though finished early in 1825, it was not published till the following year, when it was brought out along with *Lays of Many Lands*. In this volume are found *Casa Bianca* and *The Treasures of the Deep*, two of Mrs. Hemans' best-known poems. Many in the collection had already appeared in the *New*

Monthly Magazine and in various annuals. From the editors of these annuals Mrs. Hemans was constantly receiving overtures. "These appeals," says Mrs. Hughes, "were beginning to be half tormenting, half amusing, but nothing to the Vallombrosa-like showers of these autumnal leaves which came pouring down in after-years, when the annual fever reached its height."

In the spring of 1825 Mrs. Hemans, with her mother and sister and four of her boys (the eldest was put to school at Bangor), removed from Bronwylfa to Rhyllon, another house belonging to her brother, not more than a quarter of a mile from the former place. Rhyllon was a bare, tall brick house, while Bronwylfa was a bower of roses, yet at Rhyllon some of her happiest days were passed. She joined in the games of her boys, as they trundled their hoops and let their kites loose. Roses and honeysuckles were trained on the house, and she spent many hours in the dingle, on what the boys called "mamma's sofa," a little grassy mound under a beech-tree. Here she read the *Talisman*, and here cowslips grew as cowslips never grew before. Many years afterwards, in the sonnet, *To a Distant Scene*, she addresses her well-remembered haunt—

> " Still are the cowslips from thy bosom springing ?
> O far-off grassy dell ! "

" The rustling of the trees," says her sister, " spoke to her in tones full of meaning. It was one of her favourite fancies that each tree had its peculiar language suited to its character for majesty, solemnity, or grace, and that she could distinguish with closed eyes the measured tones of the oak or elm, the funereal sighs of the cypress, or the sensitive murmurs of the willow or poplar. She took great delight in seeing the waving boughs of trees through a church window. All legends relating to trees or flowers were peculiarly dear to her. One of her favourites was the Welsh legend regarding the trembling of the aspen, which, with a like superstition about the spotted arum, is mentioned in the *Wood Walk and Hymn.* The howling of the wind at night had a peculiar effect upon her nerves ; not fear, but it worked upon her imagination to a degree which was always succeeded by fatigue and weariness. These influences are alluded to in many of her poems, especially *The Song of Night* and *The Voice of the Wind :*—

" Oh ! many a voice is thine, thou wind, full many a voice is thine,
　From every scene thy wings o'er-sweeps, thou bear'st a sound and sign ;
　A minstrel wild and strong thou art, with a mastery all thine own,
　And the spirit is thy harp, O wind ! that gives the answ'ring tone."

The pleasant home at Rhyllon was darkened by the death of her mother in 1827. Mrs. Browne was a bright, sympathetic woman, and her loss was irreparable. On the evening of her death, after long watching, Mrs. Hemans went downstairs to see her boys. They were all sitting, hushed and awe-struck, round the fire. They looked at her sad face with sorrowful wonder, and little George entreated to be allowed to read her a chapter in the Bible—"he was sure it would do her good."

The *Records of Woman* came out in 1828. These poems illustrate the depths of woman's heroism, constancy, and tenderness. *The Switzer's Wife*, *Properzia Rossi*, and *Juana*, are good specimens of Mrs. Hemans' style, and drew forth strong praise from Jeffrey in the *Edinburgh Review.* "It may not be the best imaginable poetry," says this king of critics, "but it is infinitely sweet, elegant, and tender, touching, perhaps, and contemplative rather than vehement and overpowering . . . finished throughout with an exquisite delicacy, and even severity of execution, but informed with a purity and loftiness of feeling which must satisfy all judgments."

Mrs. Hemans' fame was now established, her portrait was taken, and she was celebrated as Egeria by Miss Jane Jewsbury. "Egeria," says the description, "was totally

different from any other woman I had ever seen, either in
Italy or England. She did not dazzle, she subdued me.
She was lovely, without being beautiful, her movements
were features, and if a blind man had been privileged to
pass his hand over the silken veil of hair, that when un-
braided flowed round her like a veil, he would have been
justified in expecting softness and a love of softness, beauty
and a perception of beauty. Her gladness was like a burst
of sunlight. She was a muse, a grace, a variable child, a
dependent woman."

After the marriage of her sister, in 1828, Mrs. Hemans
left Rhyllon and went to Liverpool, partly for the sake of
educating her sons and partly for society. She settled in
the suburbs, at Wavertree, in a small house, the third of
a row. She soon became acquainted with the brothers
Chorley, all enthusiasts for German literature, and with
Mary Howitt. She often complained of many things
pressing on her heart, amongst them the want of hills, the
waveless horizon wearying her eyes, accustomed to the
mountains. She was besieged by curious visitors, who
came to see what the poetess was at home, and to bring
a few compliments as incense to her shrine.

"They found a lady neither short nor tall, no longer
youthful or beautiful in appearance, yet with hair of the true
auburn tinge, and as silken, profuse, and curling as it had
ever been, with manners quiet and refined, though a little reserved. She had no ear for the news of the day, and the
ladies when they departed had to tell that the room was
in a sad litter with books and papers, that the strings of
her harp were half of them broken, and that she wore a veil
over her head like no one else."

One of her visitors advised her to wear a fur cloak,
another a flannel dressing-gown, a third proposed woollen
comforters for the wrists and throat, or a piece of hare-skin
next the chest. All were armed with albums, so that Mrs.

3

Hemans said she trembled to see a muff enter her little parlour lest it should contain an album. An American girl was particularly anxious to see her; she said, " they would think so much more of her in America if she had seen Mrs. Hemans." It was summer when Mary Howitt met her, and once, as they were sitting together, little Charles Hemans ran into the room holding a dark Bengal rose, and exclaiming, " Oh! mamma, the red rose of glory!"

In July, 1829, she visited Sir Walter Scott at Abbotsford, and took walks with him over moor and woodland, listening to song and legend, till, she says, " my mind forgets itself and is carried back to the days of the slogan and fiery cross and the wild gathering of border chivalry." The " mighty master," as she calls him, took her to Ettrick and Yarrow and Newark Tower, and they walked through the Rhymer's Glen together, up wild and rocky paths, over rude bridges, and along bright windings of the little haunted stream. He repeated snatches of mountain ballads and showed her the spot where Thomas of Ercildoune

> " Was aware of a lady fair
> Came riding down the glen."

When some tourists made a precipitate retreat as the Abbotsford party approached Newark Tower, Sir Walter said, smiling, " Ah, Mrs. Hemans, they little know what two lions they are running away from!" "I shall never forget," writes Mrs. Hemans, " the kindness of Sir Walter's farewell, so frank and simple and heartfelt, as he said, 'There are some whom we meet and should like ever after to claim as kith and kin, and *you* are one of them.'"

A visit to Wordsworth, at Rydal Mount, was another delightful experience.

" My nervous fears," wrote Mrs. Hemans to her sister, "at the idea of presenting myself to Mr. Wordsworth grew upon me so rapidly that it was more than seven o'clock before

I took courage to leave the inn at Ambleside. I had indeed
little cause for such trepidation. I was driven to a lovely
cottage-like building, almost hidden by a profusion of roses
and ivy, and a most benignant-looking old man greeted me
in the porch. This was Mr. Wordsworth himself, and when
I tell you that, having rather a large party of visitors in the
house, he led me into a room apart from them, and brought
in his family by degrees, I am sure that little trait will give
you an idea of considerate kindness which you will like and
appreciate. There is an almost patriarchal simplicity about
him, an absence of all pretension ; all is free, unstudied—
' the river winding at its own sweet will '—in his manner
and conversation ; frequently his head droops, his eyes half-
close, and he seems buried in quiet depths of thought. I
have passed a delightful morning walking about with him
in his own richly-shaded grounds and hearing him speak of
the old English writers, particularly Spenser, whom he
loves, as he himself expresses it, for his earnestness and
devoutness. I must not forget to tell you that he not only
admired our exploit in crossing the Ulverstone Sands as a
deed of ' derring do,' but as a decided proof of taste. The
Lake scenery, he says, is never seen to such advantage as
after the passage of what he calls its majestic barrier. I
seem to be writing to you almost from the spirit land. All is
here so brightly still, so remote from everyday cares and
tumults, that sometimes I can hardly persuade myself that I
am not dreaming. It scarcely seems to be the light of
common day that is dotting the woody mountains before
me ; there is something almost visionary in its soft gleam
and ever-changing shadows. I am charmed with Mr.
Wordsworth, whose kindness to me has quite a soothing
influence on my spirits. Oh ! what relief, what blessing
there is in the feeling of admiration when it can be freely
poured forth ! There is a daily beauty in his life which is in
such lovely harmony with his poetry that I am thankful to
have witnessed and felt it. . . . He gives me a good deal of

his society, reads to me, walks with me, leads my pony when I ride, and I begin to talk with him as with a paternal friend. The whole of this morning he kindly passed in reading to me from Spenser, and afterwards his own *Laodamia* and many of his noble sonnets. His reading is very peculiar—slow, solemn, earnest. When he reads or recites in the open air his deep, rich tones seem to proceed from a spirit voice and belong to the religion of the place. Yesterday evening he walked beside me as I rode on a long and lovely mountain-path, high above Grasmere Lodge. I was much interested by his showing me, carved deep in the rock, the initials of his wife's name, cut there many years ago by himself, and the dear old man, like Old Mortality, renews them from time to time. No wounded affections, no embittered feelings have ever been his lot; the current of his domestic life has flowed on bright, pure, and unbroken. He has treated me with so much consideration and gentleness and care. They have been like balm to my spirit after all the false flatteries with which I am *blasée*. His daily life in the bosom of his family is delightful, so affectionate and confiding. I cannot but mournfully feel in the midst of their happiness, still—still I am a stranger there. But where am I not a stranger now ? "

Wordsworth lamented Mrs. Hemans' ignorance of housewifery, and said she could as easily have managed the spear of Minerva as her needle. He purposely drew her attention to household affairs, and told her he had bought a pair of scales as a wedding present for a young lady! After spending a fortnight at Rydal Mount, Mrs. Hemans took a "sweet little retired cottage called Dove's Nest," on Lake Windermere. Her three boys joined her, and she says, "Harry is out with his fishing-rod, Charles sketching, and Claude climbing the hill above the Nest. I cannot follow, for I have not strength yet, but I think in feeling I am more a child than any of them." The summer passed pleasantly, and, after a second visit to Scotland, she made up her mind to leave Wavertree and to settle in Dublin, in order to be near her brother, Major Browne, who had been appointed Commissioner of Police. Here she made many new friends, especially with the Whately family and the Archbishop himself. Never a lover of towns, her greatest pleasure was in making excursions to the County Wicklow, to the Devil's Glen, and to Glendalough, where the guide told her she was "the most courageousest and lightest-footedest lady" he had ever conducted there. She also spent a day at Woodstock, and saw the grave of Mrs. Tighe, the authoress of *Psyche*, with its monument by Flaxman. She had made it the subject of her poem, *The Grave of a Poetess*, and now, after her visit to the spot, she wrote the lines beginning :—

> " I stood where the lip of song lay low,
> Where the dust had gathered on Beauty's brow,
> Where stillness hung on the heart of Love,
> And a marble weeper kept watch above."

Mrs. Hemans' health was rapidly failing, and she had three moves—from Pembroke Street to Stephen's Green, and from Stephen's Green to Dawson Street—all in one year. She was soon obliged to keep to her sofa, but still she went on writing. In 1834 the *Hymns for Childhood* came out, and were soon followed by *National Lyrics*, and *Scenes and Hymns of Life*, which was dedicated to Wordsworth.

In the summer of 1834 she was attacked by scarlet fever, and then caught cold from reading too late in the gardens of the Dublin Society. The end approached gradually but surely. Even a stay in the country, at the Archbishop's place, Redesdale, could not bring back her strength. Her two sons, Charles and Henry, were her constant companions. She used to say that she lived in a fair and happy world of her own, among gentle thoughts and pleasant images. " No poetry could express, no imagination could conceive, the visions of blessedness that flitted across her fancy." She often said to her faithful attendant, Anne Creer, "I feel like a tired child, wearied and longing to mingle with the pure in heart."

. On Saturday, the 16th of May, 1835, she sank into a gentle slumber which continued almost unbroken during the day, and at nine o'clock in the evening she passed away, without pain or struggle, at the age of forty-one. Her remains were laid in a vault under St. Anne's Church, Dublin, close to the house where she died. A small tablet was placed in the church, with her name and age, and the following lines from a dirge of her own in *The Siege of Valencia :*—

> " Calm on the bosom of thy God,
>   Fair Spirit, rest thee now !
> E'en while with us thy footsteps trod,
>   His seal was on thy brow.
> Dust, to its narrow house beneath !
>   Soul, to its place on high !
> They that have seen thy look in death
>   No more may fear to die."

Mrs. Hemans led a dreamy, contemplative life, and her poetry bears the impress of this life. She is ideal, picturesque, melodious, and devout. A mother's love, the fidelity of a child, the beauty of spring, the sadness of early death, and the hope of heaven, are her most congenial themes. She varies her metre with ease, for music of sound came naturally to her ; she brings in romance and legendary surroundings ; but the subjects are frequently the same. As Mrs. Jameson truly says, her poems could not have been written by a man ; their love is without selfishness, their heroism without ambition. During her later years, when she was an invalid, she relapsed more than ever into that passive state when the mind seems rather a spectator than an actor. One of her last sonnets, *The Sabbath Sonnet*, is an example of this passive reflectiveness :—

> " How many blessed groups this hour are wending
>   Thro' England's primrose meadow-paths their way
> Tow'rds spire and tow'r, midst shadowy elms ascending,
>   Whence the sweet chimes proclaim the hallowed day.

> . . . I may not tread
> Like them those pathways ; to the feverish bed
> Of sickness bound, yet, oh, my God ! I bless
> Thy mercy that with Sabbath peace hath filled
> My chastened heart and all its throbbings stilled
> In one deep calm of holiest thankfulness."

Here is the true spirit of resignation ; the heart, after life's fitful fever, was lulling itself to rest. Some time before her death, a stranger called on Mrs. Hemans and told her that her poem of *The Sceptic* had been the means of converting him to Christianity. Nothing could have given her so much satisfaction, for her aim in life had been to consecrate her talents to God. A higher testimony could hardly have been paid her than that given in Wordsworth's lines, in which he laments her as " a holy spirit " :—

> " Sweet as the spring, as ocean deep,
> Who ere her summer faded
> Has sunk into a breathless sleep."

It was well said by L. E. L. that : " Mrs. Hemans was spared some of the keenest mortifications of a literary career. She knew nothing of it as a profession, which has to make its way through poverty, neglect, and obstacles. The high road of life, with its crowds and contention, its heat, its noise, and its dust that rests on all, was for her happily at a distance ; yet even in such green nest the bird could not fold its wings and sleep to its own music." In answer to such laments as these from the "bay-crowned" L. E. L., Elizabeth Barrett, then a young woman of twenty-six, eagerly replies in her *Stanzas on the Death of Mrs. Hemans*:—

> " Would she have lost the poet's fire for anguish of the burning ? "

And finally concludes with the lines :—

> " Albeit softly in our ears her silver song was ringing,
> The footfall of her parting soul, is softer than her singing."

Thus wept, honoured, and sung, the favourite poetess of that day passed away.

MRS. JAMESON.

1794–1860.

THERE are many classes of writers. First, we have those who create, those whose imaginations are strong enough to give " to airy nothings a local habitation and a name." After these comes another class of writers : those who can pleasantly and graphically convey their own impressions to others ; those who can appreciate and explain the great works of genius and thus teach the public what and how to admire. To this latter class of writers Mrs. Jameson belonged. Hers was emphatically a busy and a useful career. Without being a genius, she had a vast amount of talent and energy, she was always an entertaining and often an instructive writer, she had a great deal of reading and culture, and had educated her powers up to the very highest point. During her life she enjoyed much popularity, and since her death no one has been found exactly to fill her place. Though she died in 1860, no account of her life appeared for many years. Her niece, Mrs. MacPherson, struck by some remark in Miss

MRS. JAMESON.

BORN 1794; DIED MARCH 17TH, 1860.

(*From a Bust at the National Portrait Gallery, 70, Mortimer Street, London, W*

Martineau's Autobiography, resolved to vindicate her aunt's memory and to write her memoirs. This she accordingly did, but while the work was passing through the press, Gerardine MacPherson herself died. Thus an additional interest is given to it. From its very interesting pages we learn that Anna Brownell Murphy was the eldest daughter of a young miniature-painter of considerable talent and popularity. She was born in 1794 in Dublin. Her father was a patriot and an adherent of the United Irishmen, whose desperate attempts at revolution met with such an untimely end. Fortunately the young artist was called to England by professional engagements, and thus escaped the tragical fate of Lord Edward Fitzgerald and the Sheareses. Brownell Murphy had an English wife and three small daughters ; before the last struggle began in '98 he came over to Whitehaven with his wife and their eldest child, Anna, leaving the two younger behind at nurse near Dublin. The young artist and his wife remained four years at the quiet Cumberland watering-place, and here a fourth little daughter was born. An anecdote is told of Anna that when the bedroom in which she slept beside her mother and baby sister took fire in the night she fled to her usual hiding-place, an antiquated clock-case, and there fell asleep with a sense of perfect safety.

"In memory," says Mrs. Jameson, "I can go back to a very early age. I perfectly remember being sung to sleep, and can remember even the tune which was sung to me—blessings on the voice that sang it ! I was an affectionate, but not, as I now think, a lovable or an attractive child ; I did not, like the little Mozart, ask of everybody around me, 'Can you love me ? ' The instinctive question was rather ' Can I love you ? ' With a good temper there was the capacity of strong, deep, silent resentment, and a vindictive spirit of rather a peculiar kind. When my governess inflicted what then appeared a most horrible injury and injustice, the thought of vengeance haunted my fancy for months, but it was an inverted sort of vengeance. I imagined the house of my enemy on fire, and I rushed through the flames to rescue her. She was drowning, and I leaped into the deep water to draw her forth. She was pining in prison, and I forced bars and bolts to deliver her. If this was magnanimity it was not the less vengeance, for I always fancied evil and shame and humiliation to my adversary, to myself the *rôle* of superiority and gratified pride. There was in my childish mind another cause of suffering ; it was fear—fear of darkness and supernatural influences. I had heard other children ridiculed for such fears, and I held my peace. At first these haunting, stifling, thrilling terrors were vague, afterwards the form varied, but one of the most permanent was the Ghost in *Hamlet.* There was a volume of Shakespeare lying about, in which was an engraving I have not seen since, but it remains distinct in my mind as a picture. On one side stood Hamlet, with hair on end, literally like 'quills on a fretful porcupine,' and one hand with all the fingers outspread. On the other strode the Ghost, encased in armour with nodding plumes, one finger pointing forwards, and all surrounded with supernatural light. Oh, that spectre! for three years it followed me up and down the dark staircase, or stood by my bed—only the blessed light had power to exorcise it. How it was that I knew, while I trembled and quaked, that it was unreal, but never cried out, never expostulated, never confessed, I do not know. In daylight I was not only fearless but audacious, inclined to defy all power and brave all danger that I could see. I remember volunteering to lead the way through a herd of cattle (among which was a dangerous bull, the terror of the neighbourhood), armed only with a little stick, but first I said the Lord's Prayer fervently. In the ghastly night I never prayed. These visionary sufferings pursued me till I was nearly twelve years old."

In 1802 the family went to the more important town of
Newcastle-on-Tyne ; here the young painter's prospects
became more secure, for the little girls left in Ireland were
sent for, and the family was reunited. The two children,
still very young, came from Dublin under the charge of
Miss Yokely, the daughter of one of the Duke of Leinster's
secretaries ; she was clever, accomplished, and an efficient
if an over-strict teacher. She gained her eldest pupil's
(Anna's) respect and esteem, but never won her love. The
miniature-painter and his belongings settled down in a
modest set of rooms over the shop of the chief bookseller of
the place, a Mr. Miller.

An incident belongs to this period of Anna's life dimly
recollected by her youngest sister. Anna was the leader of
the little troop of girls, and evidently used her power with
unquestioned sway. They had all gone with their governess to a village called Kenton, while their father and
mother were absent in Scotland. Miss Yokely also accepted
an invitation to visit some friends, and the little girls were
left alone for two or three days. Their temporary guardian
interfered to prevent some delightful composition of mud-
pies on which the younger children had set their hearts.
The wail that followed came to Anna's ears. Without a
moment's hesitation she proposed a plan of escape from the
landlady's tyranny. The plan was that all four should
instantly start to join their father and mother in Scotland.
They must eat all the bread-and-butter they could at
tea, and stow away as much as possible in .their pockets.
As the eldest and strongest, Anna arrayed herself in a many-
caped gig-cloak belonging to Miss Yokely, under cover of
which the little party could, she said, sleep at night under
the hedges. As for food, when their own slices of bread-
and-butter gave out, they need only knock at some cottage
door and announce that they were on their way to Scotland
to find their father and mother, and they would be sure to
get a crust of bread and a drink of milk. Each provided

with a tiny bundle containing a change for Sunday, the
little girls stole softly out under the charge of their nine-
year-old leader. Their steps broke into a run as they passed
down the village street. The villagers wondered to see the
little Murphys running off by themselves, and, much to Anna's
vexation, pursued and caught them. The fugitives had not
met a single adventure, except the loss of Camilla's red shoes,
which fell out of her bundle into the dirty water of a ditch.

In 1803 the Murphys came to London ; their first resting-
place was at Hanwell, one of the prettiest spots near
London. Here the governess who had ruled her small
pupils so strictly became their aunt, having married Mr.
Murphy's brother. In the year 1806 their quarters were
shifted to the busy region of Pall Mall. Anna worked hard
at French, Italian, and even Spanish. The works of Sir
W. Jones were then appearing, and she was seized with a
craze for the romances of India and Persia. A map of
India hung in hers and her sister's sleeping-room, and it
was a favourite fancy to keep her three little sisters tracing
different routes from town to town across the map, while
she herself travelled in imagination along the Eastern roads
and read aloud passages from a book, describing the various
parts of the journey.

She began to write a story on Eastern subjects which she
called *Faizy*, and which soon became the absorbing interest
of the nursery. Besides this story, which brought her under
the notice of Mr. James Forbes, author of the *Oriental
Memoirs*, she wrote heroic lines to Collingwood and Nelson.
A hatred of falsehood, a high spirit, and a passion for independence were Anna's early characteristics. Her sister
Camilla remembers how she would declaim, with her head
erect and her blue eyes glancing, the well-known lines :—

> "Thy spirit, Independence, let me share,
>   Lord of the lion-heart and eagle eye.
> Thy steps I'll follow with my bosom bare,
>   Nor heed the storm that howls along the sky."

There were many talks about economy in the struggling household at Pall Mall, and Anna, after listening to some of them, resolved on a mighty plan. She had heard of the lace-making of Flanders, and her spirit was stirred within her at the idea of her father and mother striving hard to make the two ends meet, while the four girls, from twelve downwards, were eating the bread of idleness. Another baby had been added to the band, a tiny Charlotte in her cradle, too young for dreams of work and independence. Anna's plan was that she and her sisters should set out for Brussels, learn the art of lace-making there, work at it successfully, and earn a rapid fortune. Their course was to be along the banks of the Paddington Canal as far as it went; then they were to inquire the nearest road to the coast, and from thence take ship for Belgium. Eliza, however, declared that she could not be spared; the mother and baby required all her attention, and she must stay behind. Camilla, whose little red shoes had been lost in the last adventure, was timid and wavering; but Louisa was firm. The sisters, dressed in their white frocks and best ribbons, came down to dessert for what was to be the last time. The father put some wine in his glass for his pet Louisa. "There's no telling when we may be together again, my darling," he said, and poor Louisa's heart failed. She threw her arms round her father's neck, and cried, "Oh, papa! papa! I will never, never leave you." So Anna's second plan fell through. Camilla gave in on the spot, and the "eldest" could not hold out alone. But at sixteen her dream of independence was realised; not Brussels and lace-making, but governessing, was fated to be the order of the day. Mr. Murphy, from his calling as a miniature-painter had many aristocratic connections, and it was in the family of the Marquis of Winchester that Anna began her career as a governess, and she remained in the same situation four years. Her picture, taken at this stage of her life by her father, is an attractive one. The expression is eager and

listening—"the rapt soul sitting in the eyes"—while the
uplifted hand seems as though some divine harmony of
the Beautiful or Heroic was faintly heard. Lady Byron's
lines on this portrait describe it admirably :—

> " In those young eyes, so keenly, bravely bent
>   To search the mysteries of the future hour,
>   There shines the will to conquer, and the pow'r
>   Which makes that conquest sure, a gift, Heav'n-sent,
>   The radiance of the Beautiful was blent
>   E'en with thine earliest dreams."

In the winter of 1820–21 Anna Murphy was introduced
to a young barrister, Robert Jameson, a native of the Lake
country, and a *protégé* and favourite of Wordsworth. Anna
was at the time living with her parents, and these two
clever, capable young people immediately fell in love with
one another. But difficulties clouded the course of true
love, and the engagement was broken off. Anna, disgusted
and disappointed with her life, again left her home and
went to Italy as governess to a beautiful girl, almost grown
up, who is only spoken of as Laura. The matron of the
party was still young and attracted many admirers, while
Laura's charms drew down storms of *confetti* as the ladies
drove up and down the gay Toledo during the Naples
Carnival. Through picture-galleries and *musées* the young
governess wandered, brooding, perhaps, morbidly on her
own sorrows, on her absence from her lover, and the gloomy
prospects of her romance. She took refuge in writing a
diary, in which she put down all she saw, her opinions,
scraps from her reading, sketches of character and of the
beautiful landscapes which often drew her out of herself.
These little locked volumes were always kept on her table,
and were the confidant of many an unspoken grief. Here
is one of the opening sentences : " I leave behind me the
scenes, the objects so long associated with pain, but from
the pain itself I cannot fly ; it has become a part of myself.

. . . But I will not weakly yield, though time and I have
not been long acquainted. Do I not know what miracles
He, the All-powerful Healer, may produce? Who knows
but this dark cloud may pass away? Continued motion,
continued novelty, the absolute necessity for self-control,
may do something for me." Then follow some verses, which
have since been set to music :—

> " It is o'er, with its pains and its pleasures,
>   The dream of affection is o'er.
> The feelings I lavished so fondly
>   Will never return to me more.
> With a faith, oh ! too blindly believing,
>   A truth no unkindness could move,
> My prodigal heart has expended
>   At once an existence of love.
> And now, like the spendthrift, forsaken,
>   By those whom his bounty has blest,
> All empty, and cold, and despairing,
>   It shrinks in my desolate breast."

And yet there were gleams of sunshine in this foreign
tour. At Paris, Anna marvels at her own versatility ; she
wonders how soon her quick spirits were excited by this
gay, gaudy, noisy place. She made a solitary pilgrimage to
a church which possessed the figure of a Virgin of miracu-
lous powers, who was dressed in a real blue silk gown,
spangled with tinsel stars, and the simple piety of one of
the women-worshippers made her return home rejoicing in
kinder, gentler, happier thoughts. At Rome, before any
one was ready for breakfast, she ran up a gigantic flight of
marble steps leading to the top of a hill. " I was at the
summit in a moment," she cries, " and there lay Rome
before me in innumerable domes, and towers, and vanes, and
pinnacles, brightened by the rising sun. I gazed and gazed
as if I would drink it all in with my eyes." One of her first
pieces of art criticism was singularly unfortunate. Michael
Angelo's *Holy Family in the Tribune* she thought a dis-

agreeable and hateful picture, and "fire will not burn this opinion out of me." She was afterwards one óf Michael Angelo's most abject worshippers. After her return to England, she changed her situation and became governess to the children of Mr. Littleton, one of the members for Staffordshire (afterwards Lord Atherton), and remained in that family four years. And now happiness seemed to dawn again, her affection for Mr. Jameson revived, and in the year 1825 she was married to the man who seems to have been her first and only love. But—

> "Oft expectation fails, and most oft there
> Where most is promised."

The newly-married pair began life in lodgings at Chénies Street, Tottenham Court Road, and they had hardly passed the threshold of matrimony when discord commenced. The ceremony took place on a Wednesday, and on Sunday Mr. Jameson announced his intention of spending the day with some friends at whose house he generally spent his Sundays. The young wife was struck dumb at the proposal. "But," she said, "they do not know me : they may not want to know me. Would it not be better to wait until they have time at least to show that they desire to make my acquaintance ? " " That is as you please," answered the husband ; "but, whether you come or not, I shall go." So the bride of four days put on her white gown and set off, but rain began, and, under pretence of saving her gown, she declared it impossible to go farther. " Very well," answered the bridegroom, " you have an umbrella. Go back, by all means, but I shall go on." So he did. To the great surprise of his friends, he calmly ate his dinner, spent the evening, and went home, while his young wife, alone in lodgings, was speculating as to her future with such a stoical mate.

Among Mr. Jameson's friends was a man of the name of Thomas, who had begun life as a cobbler, but had gradually worked himself up to be a bookseller, with a strong inclination

towards the study of the law. He had, besides, a love for
music, and could play well on the guitar. One evening, at
the Jamesons, Mrs. Jameson's visit to the Continent was
spoken of, and, by her husband's wish, the green-covered
volumes of the Diary were brought out, and parts of it were
read aloud. Thomas asked for the MS., and declared that
he was ready to run the risk of publishing it. The idea was
new and amusing. "You may print it if you like," said Mrs.
Jameson, " and if it sells for anything more than will pay
the expenses, you shall give me a Spanish guitar for my
share of the profits." Thomas accepted the condition, and
the MS., somewhat altered, was given into his hands. It
was to be published anonymously, and a final fictitious paragraph was added, which stated that the writer died on the way
home at Autun, in her twenty-sixth year, and had been buried
in the garden of the Capuchin monastery near that city.
Thomas advertised the work as *A Lady's Diary*, and Mr.
Colburn bought the copyright of it from him for £50, so a
ten-guinea guitar was duly handed over to Mrs. Jameson.
As *The Diary of an Ennuyée* the book met with great
success, and was followed by two more, *The Loves of the
Poets* and *Celebrated Female Sovereigns*, both now out of
print. The Diary gained its author many friends ; among
them were Mr. and Mrs. Basil Montagu and their daughter,
Mrs. Procter, wife of the poet usually known as Barry
Cornwall. At the Montagus' house at Bedford Square
Fanny Kemble met Mrs. Jameson, and says : "While
under the spell of the fascinating Diary it was of course very
delightful to me to make Mrs. Jameson's acquaintance,
which I did at the house of our friends, Mr. and Mrs.
Montague. At an evening party there I first saw Mrs.
Jameson. 'The Ennuyée,' one is given to understand,
dies, and it was a little vexatious to behold her sitting on a
sofa in a very becoming state of blooming plumpitude, but
it was some compensation to be introduced to her." And
so began a close and friendly intimacy. Fanny Kemble

4

describes Mrs. Jameson as an "attractive-looking young woman, with skin of that dazzling whiteness which generally accompanies reddish hair such as hers was. Her face, which was habitually refined and *spirituelle* in its expression, was capable of a marvellous power of concentrated feeling, such as is seldom seen in any woman's face, and is peculiarly rare in the countenance of a fair, small, delicately-featured woman, all whose characteristics were extremely pretty. Her hands and arms might have been those of Madame de Warens" (Rousseau's love).

After five years of matrimony Mr. Jameson looked out for a colonial appointment, and in 1829 was made puisne judge in the Island of Dominica. His success was uncertain, the climate was unhealthy, and there never seems to have been a thought of his wife going with him. The two parted amicably, and Mrs. Jameson returned to her father's house. Not exultantly happy had been her life, but still not utterly wasted with melancholy, and her buoyant spirit kept her up and promised better things. Shortly after her husband's departure she went to the Continent with her father and his friend and patron, Sir Gerard Noel. She was not now playing the Ennuyée; she abandoned herself to the quickening influence of new objects. Not now self-engrossed or looking for sympathy, she was keen to observe with all the strength of an awakening mind. The party consisted of two ladies and two gentlemen. "We travelled *comme un milor Anglais*," Mrs. Jameson says, "a *artie-carrée* in a barouche hung on the most approved principles, double - cushioned, rising and sinking on its springs like a swan on the wave."

In 1832 Mrs. Jameson published her *Characteristics of Women*. The object of this book was to illustrate, by Shakespeare's women, what various modifications the female character is capable of. Mrs. Jameson thought that women of the present age did not rise to their higher destinies, did

not recognise what they might be. Madame de Staël
defines vulgarity as the reverse of poetical, "so vulgarity,"
says Mrs. Jameson, "is the negative of all things. In
literature, it is the total absence of elevation and depth of
ideas, and of elegance and delicacy in the expression of
them ; in character, it is the absence of truth, sensibility,
and reflection. The vulgar in manner is the result of
vulgarity of character ; it is grossness, hardness, or affecta-
tion." In contrast to this low standard she brings forward
characters of intellect—Portia, Isabella, Beatrice, Rosalind ;
characters of passion and imagination—Juliet, Viola, Helena,
Perdita, Ophelia, Miranda ; and characters of the affections
—Hermione, Desdemona, Imogen, Cordelia. "A woman's
affections," says Mrs. Jameson, "however strong, are sentiments when they run smooth, and become passions when
opposed. In Juliet and Helena, love is depicted as a
passion properly so called, there is a natural impulse throbbing in the heart's blood and mingling with the very
sources of life, a sentiment more or less modified by the
imagination, a strong abiding principle and motive, excited
by resistance, acting upon the will, animating the other
faculties, and again influenced by them." The book shows
a great amount of thought and study, much beauty of
language, and a deep appreciation of Shakespeare. It was
dedicated to Fanny Kemble—"her dearest Fanny"—and
the frontispiece was designed by Mrs. Jameson herself. It
represents a female figure seated dejectedly beneath a tall
lily, a tiny bark vanishing away into a stormy distance.

Mr. Jameson returned from Dominica early in 1833 and
rejoined his wife ; then, having procured a better appointment in Canada, through the influence of his wife's friends,
he set off there, intending to make a home for her. Meanwhile she went to Germany, and found that her book had
made her welcome with many literary people. Her acquaintance with Mr. Noel, Lady Byron's cousin, was the
means of introducing her to the family of Goethe at

Weimar and to the great poet himself. The friendship
between Ottalie, Goethe's fascinating daughter-in-law, and
the "liebe Anna," lasted for thirty years. These pleasant
German wanderings, which extended to Munich, were put a
stop to by a severe paralytic seizure which attacked Mr.
Murphy. His daughter hurried to London, fearing she
might not find him alive ; but his speech had returned, and
"Such a gleam of joy came over his face," she says, "when
he saw me." He was never restored to health, but lingered
for years in a semi-paralysed condition, partly dependent
on his daughter's earnings. She made her home with her
sister Louisa, now Mrs. Bate, the wife of an artist, and
lavished all a mother's tenderness on her niece Gerardine.
Her Essays on various subjects were collected, revised, and
published in four volumes. Topics of all kinds were
touched upon in them, sketches of German society alterna-
ting with dissertations on the genius of Mrs. Siddons.
Amongst Mrs. Jameson's friends were now numbered Mrs.
Opie, Joanna Baillie, and Lady Byron, who seemed to have
exerted an extraordinary power of attraction over some
minds. After Mrs. Jameson's first interview with her, she
was asked what impression Lady Byron had made on her.
"Implacability," was her answer, and she afterwards found
the truth of her remark.

From Toronto letters now came from Mr. Jameson
urging his wife to go out to him. He complained that he
had not heard from his dearest Anna for months, and " as
he prunes his tree he feeds his fancy with the idea that
before the leaves disappear she will be walking by his side."
The relations between this couple seem to have been of the
most peculiar kind. Mrs. Jameson, on her part, sometimes
says that " she never hears a word from Jameson. In the last
sixteen months I have had two letters." This complaint
was made during her Weimar visit ; and then followed a
letter addressed to Mr. Jameson himself, in which she says,
" A union such as ours is a real mockery of the laws of God

and man." Yet, if summoned, she expresses herself willing to go to Canada.

Early in August, 1836, the summons came, and in September she set off for Toronto, further urged by pressing letters from her husband, who seemed all impatience to welcome her. The puzzle was to reconcile his words and his actions. When she arrived at New York early in November she found no sign that she was expected. Neither her husband nor his friend were there to meet her ; not even a letter to tell her how she was to travel. For nearly three weeks she was alone in a New York hotel, while her usually buoyant spirits sank down to zero. At last a letter from Mr. Jameson, telling her to proceed to Toronto, arrived. A winter journey to Canada was then beset with horrors. In November the roads were smothered with snow, the navigation was frozen, and there was only a night boat on the Hudson. However, she set out, and the spectacle of the Catskill Mountains, " left behind in the night, robed in a misty purple light," astonished her as something new and beautiful. The steamer, its prow armed with a sharp iron sheath, crashed its way through solid ice four inches thick. Six days and nights of such travelling made the poor lonely wanderer sink with fatigue. She at length arrived at the ferry of the Niagara River at Queens-town, about seven miles below the Falls. The little boat was tossed in the darkness along the foaming waters, guided by a light on the opposite shore, while the deep roar of the cataract filled and shook the atmosphere around. Mrs. Jameson found, contrary to expectation, a steamer on Lake Ontario. Once on board she fell into an exhausted sleep. When the steamer reached Toronto she hurried on deck, and when she stepped out of the boat she sank ankle-deep in ice. Half blinded by sleet driven into her face and by the tears that filled her eyes, she walked through the " dreary, miry ways of the unknown town, never much thronged, and now by reason of the impending snowstorm

nearly solitary. I heard no voices, no quick footsteps of
men or children; I met no familiar face, no look of
welcome. I was sad at heart as a woman could be, and
these were the impressions, the feelings with which I
entered the house which was to be called my home." This
dreary arrival was followed by dismal days to match it.
"I am like an uprooted tree," she says, "dying at the core,
yet with a strange, unreasonable power of working at my own
most miserable weakness." She went to bed in tears one
night after saying her prayers for those far away across that
terrible Atlantic. The battle with physical discomfort, too,
with chill and frost and ague, made her long to be a dor-
mouse or a she-bear to sleep away the rest of the cold, cold
winter, and to wake only with the first green leaves. Yet
she still had a cheerful faith, a desire to know, an impatience
to learn, and a readiness to please and be pleased. She was
even able to criticise and reflect on Goethe and Eckermann,
on art and literature.

In all the sublime desolation of winter she set off for
the Falls of Niagara, and was disgusted to find that she
was disappointed in them. "I have no words for my bitter
disappointment," she cries. "Oh! I could beat myself.
What has come over my soul and senses? I am meta-
morphosed; I am translated; I am an ass's head, a clod,
a wooden spoon, a fat weed growing on Lethe's bank, a
stock, a stone, a petrifaction."

But though disappointed with Niagara, she was in love
with Lake Ontario. "I look on it as mine," she says. "It
changes its hues every moment; the shades of purple and
green flitting over it are now dark, now lustrous, now pale,
like a dolphin dying, with every now and then a streak of
silver light dividing the shades of green." Mrs. Jameson's
stay at Toronto was short. "If I found in Jameson anything
I wished!" she cries, bitterly; "but as it is, to remain would
be only a vain and foolish struggle, a perpetual discord
between the outer and inward being." And again she

cries, "If God had only given me children I think I could have been blest." Her husband seems to have been a cold, self-sufficing man, to whom his wife never appeared necessary. This to a woman of her temperament was torture. Perhaps she herself was better fitted for literary work than household cares. Before she returned to England she explored the depths of the Indian settlements as far as Lake Huron, and published the results of her visit in a book called *Winter Studies and Summer Rambles.* Arrangements were made by which her husband, now Attorney-General, allowed her £300 a year. He wrote that, in leaving Canada to reside with her friends or elsewhere, she carried with her his most perfect respect and esteem. "My affection," he adds, "you will never cease to retain." During the delay caused by legal business she went to the States and paid a visit to Mrs. Sedgwick. The two authoresses became life-long friends and constant correspondents. After a stormy passage across the Atlantic, Mrs. Jameson returned to the house of her sister, Mrs. Bate. She soon became busier than ever. She not only prepared her travels in Canada for the press, but she compiled an elaborate catalogue *raisonné,* or companion and guide to various art collections in London—the Ellesmere and Grosvenor Galleries and the collections of the Queen and Sir R. Peel. In a letter from the Hon. Amelia Murray, dated Buckingham Palace, August 2, 1842, we are told how Mrs. Jameson's *Guide* was received by the Queen : "Although much hurried, the Queen saw me for a few minutes, and listened with evident pleasure to the little explanation which you wished made respecting the catalogue, and read your few words on the title-page with one of her sweetest smiles. She then said, ' Pray thank Mrs. Jameson for me very much.' . . . Making a graceful kind of half-bow, half-curtsey, which she sometimes does when she is pleased, she ran lightly off with the book in her hand, as if she were going to show her treasure to the

Prince." The following year Mrs. Jameson contributed to the *Penny Magazine* a series of papers on the early Italian painters, which, when republished, became one of her most popular works. Her responsibilities increased with her work, for her father died, leaving her 'mother and two sisters dependent on her. One of her fugitive papers, *The House of Titian*, brought on an intimacy with Elizabeth Barrett, who lived next door (50, Wimpole Street) to the house where Mrs. Jameson was staying, and numerous notes in the poetess's tiny handwriting were written to Mrs. Jameson. "First, I was drawn to you," writes Elizabeth Barrett, "then I was, and am, bound to you." Mrs. Jameson soon began her great work—the work of her life—*Sacred and Legendary Art,*—and went to Italy to gather materials for it. She was accompanied by her niece, Gerardine, who was to her as a daughter. On the journey, she met the Brownings on their wedding tour, and a pretty incident is told how at Vaucluse, at the source of the fresh clear water, Mr. Browning took his wife up in his arms, and carrying her "across the shallow water, seated her on a rock that rose, throne-like, in the middle of the stream." Mrs. Jameson's life—first at Florence, then at Rome—was devoted to the study of her beloved Art. Her favourite haunt was the Church of St. Clemente at Rome. Her rooms were over Spīthover's shop, and had little balconied windows. Her large old-fashioned drawing-room, hung with dim, long mirrors, and possessing a deep-mouthed fire-place, which had martial figures in brass for the firedogs, was the meeting-place for Gibson, the sculptor, and Father Prout, the wit. Here, too, the little tea-maker, Gerardine, was wooed and won by her Scotch artist-lover, Robert MacPherson.

After her niece's marriage Mrs. Jameson went to Ravenna, Padua, and Venice, to study the paintings there ; and whilst her book was coming out she went to Ireland, where she met Maria Edgeworth. She had worked hard with her pencil as well as her pen, and had copied many a mediæval saint from the Italian art galleries. In the beginning of '51 her name was put on the Pension List for £100 a year. She now took up her residence at Bruton Street, in London, with her sister Camilla, Mrs. Sherwin. Here she was able to have her friends round her and to enjoy literary society. She had Wednesday evenings, such as she had had at Rome, and her all-absorbing friend, Lady Byron, was often to be seen at them ; she was, of course, a most interesting personage, and the Bruton Street drawing-room was the scene of lively talk and animated discussion. Mrs. Jameson's *Common-Place Book* came out in '54, and found many readers. She had always been in the habit of putting down stray thoughts, and marking passages in books which roused her sympathies or antipathies. So the little volumes grew, and gave interesting peeps into a most cultivated mind. Her rupture with Lady Byron was one of the great sorrows of her life. She accidentally became acquainted with a secret about one of Lady Byron's family which Lady Byron herself did not know. When Lady Byron heard of this, and of Mrs. Jameson's previous knowledge of it, her stern temper was roused, and, in spite of their great friendship, she and Mrs. Jameson never met again. Mrs. Jameson, sensitive and proud, suffered acutely ; she frequently said that Lady Byron had " broken her heart."

In 1854 Mr. Jameson died in Canada. His wife had given up the papers that secured her allowance of £300 a year, and when his will was opened no provision was made for her. She was thus suddenly deprived of her income. Her friends collected a sum by which £100 a year was secured to her for life. She soon began another ramble to Paris and Rome, collecting materials for *Legends of the Madonna.* This book was the result of intense thought and anxiety. It was with broken spirits and weary energies that she began in 1857 to collect materials for the *Life of our Saviour.* It was during this visit to Rome that she met

Nathaniel Hawthorne, and he gives us, in his Note Book
for 1858, his impression of her. He says she was " a
rather short, round, and massive personage of benign and
agreeable aspect, with a sort of black skull cap on her
head, beneath which appeared her hair, which seemed once
to have been fair, and was now almost white. I should
take her to be about seventy years old. She began to
talk with affectionate familiarity, and I was equally gracious
to her. In truth, I have found great pleasure and profit
in her works, and was glad to hear her say she liked
mine. We talked about art, and she showed me a picture
leaning up against the wall of the room, a quaint old
Byzantine painting. She seems to be familiar with Italy,
its people and life as well as with its picture-galleries.
She is said to be rather irascible in her temper, but
nothing could be sweeter than her voice, her look, and
all her manifestations to-day." He says again, May 9th :
"Mrs. Jameson called this forenoon to ask us to go and see
her this evening. She invited me to take a drive of a few
miles with her this afternoon. She suffers from gout, the
affection being in her foot. Her hands, by the way, are
white, and must have been, perhaps are, beautiful. She must
have been a perfectly pretty woman in her day, a blue or
grey-eyed, fair-haired beauty. I think that her hair is not
white, but only flaxen in the extreme. We came to the
Basilica of San Sebastiano, where we alighted ; we walked
round glancing at the pictures in the various chapels. Mrs.
Jameson pronounced rather a favourable verdict on one
of St. Francis. She says she can read a picture like the
pages of a book, and it was impossible not to perceive that
she gave her companions no credit for knowing one single
simplest thing about art. We drove homewards, talking
of many things—painting, sculpture, America, England,
spiritualism, and whatever came up. She is a very sensible
old lady, and sees a great deal of truth, a good woman, too,
taking elevated views of matters."

She felt that her vital powers were fast giving way, and only hoped that her strength might hold out till she finished this her last book. But it did not. She returned from the Continent to attend a Social Science meeting at Bradford. Her paper, " On the employment of Women," made a deep impression. When she rose to speak a silence fell upon the crowded assembly. " It was quite strange," says Miss Parkes, " to see the intense interest she excited. Her singularly low and gentle voice fell like a hush on the crowded room, and every eye was eagerly fixed on her— every ear drank in her thoughtful and weighty words." Up to the day of her last illness she worked hard. Return- ing from the British Museum in a snowstorm (March, 1860) she caught a cold which settled on her lungs, and in a few days she had breathed her last in her sixty-sixth year.

So " that great heart, that noble human creature," as her friend, Mrs. Browning, calls her, passed away after a life of labour. " I have love and work enough," she said after her return from Canada. Thus, to her dauntless spirit it seemed, no outcry came against the decree which had marked out her life's history. She was one of the first to claim for women that higher education and those wider opportunities which they now enjoy. In her day colleges and degrees for women were unknown, and she had to carve her own way through enormous obstacles and prejudices. She had to educate herself in art before she could write about it, and in the end she succeeded in becoming one of the great authorities on the subject. To her, and to those like her, the women of the nineteenth century owe a large debt of gratitude.

III.

FREDRIKA BREMER.

1801–1865.

Born in Finland—The Bremers go to Stockholm—Strict discipline—The old house at Årsta—"The Ugly Duckling"—Poems and practical jokes—"The gay, good, and handsome lieutenant"—An imprisoned spirit—Sketches of everyday life—*The H—— Family*—*The Home*—*The Neighbours*—Visit to America—*Hertha*—Nathaniel Hawthorne—A tea-table in Rome—Margaret Howitt—Death at Årsta.

THE glowing South has furnished us with many a heroine for a stormy five-act tragedy. Cleopatra, Lucrezia Borgia, Catherine de Medici, Juliet, and hundreds of others, all belong to the favoured "climes of the sun." But if we wish to find a home-angel, true as steel and constant as the day, such women flourish to perfection in the cold and churlish North—in the country of the Vikings— where the pine forests show dark among the snow-clad mountains, and where the iron mines lie hidden beneath the frost-bound earth.

It was in such a region as this, in the chilly climate of Finland, that Fredrika Bremer, the future biographer of the joys and sorrows of Northern domestic life, first saw the light. Her father, Carl Frederic Bremer, belonged to a Swedish family that had settled in Finland; he was an iron-master, and had inherited large ironworks which employed several hundred people and brought him in a consider-

44

FREDRIKA BREMER

BORN AUGUST 17TH, 1801; DIED DECEMBER 31ST, 1865.

able income. The Bremers lived in the manor-house of Tuorla, near Åbo, beside a market-place; here Fredrika was born on August 17, 1801. She had an elder sister, Charlotte, who has given us an interesting account of the Bremers' family life. Their residence in Finland was of short duration. Fredrika's father hearing that that country was soon to be annexed to Russia, sold his estates near Åbo, and removed to Stockholm with his wife, mother-in-law, and four children, for, besides Charlotte and Fredrika, there was now another daughter, Hedda, and a little son, Claes. The education of the two elder daughters soon began. When Charlotte was six and Fredrika only four they were handed over to a French governess, Miss Frumeric; they had the greatest love and respect for her, and Charlotte says, " She laid the foundation of all that is good in us." After a couple of years the two children were able to speak and read French, and to recite fluently some of Madame de Genlis's plays, *L'Ile Heureuse, La Rosière, Les Flaçons,* and many others. Fredrika frequently knew a whole act by heart, and poor Miss Frumeric, or Bonne Amie as she was called, often lost patience and cried, " *That* Fredrika ! she is perfectly intolerable with her recitations ; there is never an end to them ! " To this Bonne Amie the Bremer children came in all their troubles, and whenever they heard the voices of their parents they ran to hide themselves in their governess's room or in that of their nurse, old Lena.

During the first years of their residence at Stockholm the elder Bremers were constantly out in the fashionable world, and their children only saw them at stated times of the day. Discipline of the severest, strictest kind was rigorously kept up, and it is amazing to us, with our modern English notions, to read of the court which these little Swedes had to pay to their exacting parents. At eight o'clock in the morning they had to be ready dressed, and had to go in to say good morning to their mother, who sat in a small drawing-room taking her coffee. She looked at them with a scrutinising glance during their walk from the door up to her chair. If they had walked badly they were obliged to go back again to renew their promenade, to curtsey, and kiss her hand. If their curtsey had been awkwardly performed, they had to make it over again. Poor little Fredrika could never walk, sit, or stand to the satisfaction of her mother, and had many " bitter and wretched " moments in consequence. Then they had to go and " salute " their father. When they entered his outer room the footman laid down a large square carpet and placed on it a chair ; on this the formidable master of the house sat down, after having been enveloped in a large white cloak which reached down to the ankles. Then came the hairdresser, Mr. Hagelin, and the great business of hairdressing and powdering began, of which the children were secretly amused spectators. When they had curtseyed to their father, they went to Miss Frumeric from nine till one o'clock. Everything was to be done by rule, and plummet, and line.

Madame Bremer had laid down three principles for her children's education : the first was that they should be kept in perfect ignorance of everything evil in the world. They were never allowed to remain in the drawing-room when there were visitors, and they were strictly forbidden to speak to the servants except their old nurse, who was ordered never to tell them anything. Thus they breathed an outward atmosphere of purity for which they were afterwards thankful. The second principle was that they should acquire as much knowledge as they could. With the carrying out of this there was little difficulty, but the third principle was rather more unwelcome—the children were to eat as little as possible ! Madame Bremer had read vast quantities of novels, and her hope was that her daughters would grow up to be " delicate, zephyr-like heroines of romance," not strong, stout, tall women, for of this type of her sex she had a positive abhorrence. At eight o'clock in the morning the children each had a small bowl—poor Charlotte plaintively

observes that she had never seen such small bowls—of cold
milk and a small piece of *knäckebröd*—a kind of very thin
brown clap-bread. If they were ever so hungry they never
dared to ask for anything more, and their old nurse was not
permitted to give them as much as a piece of dry bread.
At two o'clock dinner came, and this was a glorious time for
the famished children, for they were then allowed to eat as
much as was thought necessary. Of four or five dishes they
might taste three, and Charlotte adds, with much gusto,
they tasted wonderfully good. Then the children went to
the drawing-room to watch their parents drinking coffee ;
at four precisely the punctual father disappeared to his own
room to take a nap, and the little ones went with their
Bonne Amie to write, cipher, and work. At six they went
again to the drawing-room ; the elders drank tea, and the
youngsters looked on, occasionally, by great good fortune,
getting a rusk. They had no more regular meals except a
small glass of cold milk and a small piece of *knäckebrod.*
After this scanty repast, at eight o'clock they went to the
dining-room, curtsied, kissed their parents' hands, and said
good-night. But Fredrika's energetic spirit, which had been
kept in all day, found some little vent during the process of
undressing. She preferred running about the room and
dancing with her old nurse, Lena. Poor Lena's patience
often gave way ; she got red in the face and burst out with,
" Ah ! *that* will be a nice one when she gets older, for
certain it is that the older people live the worse they
become."

Fredrika says of herself that the first juvenile feelings she
could remember were an immoderate greediness for sweet-
meats (no wonder ! when she was half-starved) and an
intense desire to distinguish herself and be spoken of. This
desire was fated to be kept down for many an irksome year.
Fredrika's father had bought the large estate of Årsta,
twenty English miles from Stockholm, and in the summer
of 1806 the whole family removed there. The house is

described as a "large palace-like edifice, with projecting turrets, a tall sloping roof, high lattice windows, and dark walls, from which the plaster had fallen off in many places." To the children this dilapidated "Castle Rackrent" seemed rather awful, but they were soon delighted at the spacious vaulted hall, rising through three stories, with its high stone pillars and double staircases. For a wonder, they were allowed to run up and down these stairs while the carriages were unloaded. It was in this old house that Fredrika was to spend the better part of her days, here she was to dream dreams and see visions, here she was to yearn for freedom, and here, at last, she was to fold her hands and pass into the "Silent Land." All the rooms at Årsta were nineteen feet high, every step awoke an echo; the largest saloon was forty-eight feet square, with nine high windows, and there was a large garden, where the imprisoned children—who had hardly ever been allowed to go out when at Stockholm—might pick flowers and fruit and hear the birds sing. But to be as happy as the curate's children, whom they saw digging with their wooden spades, that they soon saw they never could be. Fredrika was a queer child, full of freaks and oddities. One of these was for throwing pocket-handkerchiefs, nightcaps, stockings, &c., into the fire, and all the excuse she could make was that it was so "delightful to see the flames." Another unpleasant failing was for cutting a piece out of a window-curtain or a round or square hole in the front of her dress. Once she locked herself in the drawing-room, and when she opened the door it was found that she had cut a large round hole in the silk cover of an armchair, and had poked a piece of her own dress, cut out of the front breadth, into the hole. She never tried to disguise or excuse her handiwork. When she and her sister got presents of two beautiful pieces of French porcelain, she broke them directly. One was thrown on the stone flags, the other on a load of firewood. But the next day she offered her mother a penny, the only one she had left, and asked forgiveness for having also broken a decanter and three wine-glasses.

Another brother, August, and a baby sister, Agatha, had been added to the household. Charlotte—the good, orderly Charlotte—who took as much care of her dolls as if they had been little children, was her father's favourite. Fredrika was not the favourite with any one except with her sisters, to whom she loved to give the presents which had been given to her. She had "inquiring days," when she tormented the family by asking puzzling questions, and during their country rambles she was sure to lose her gloves or her garters, to tear her dress, or come home late for dinner. When her father scolded she gave saucy answers, which made him excited and angry. Yet in poor Fredrika's little body there dwelt, as she says, "a boundless capacity to love and sacrifice herself with joy for the good of those she loved, a desire to give, to make happy, and to comfort." She was like "The Ugly Duckling" in Hans Andersen's story. In vain people said to her, "Do as others do, be as others are." She could not follow their advice, and they could not make out why she had such a good memory for learning and such a bad memory for every-day things. In consequence she was either curbed by severity or her thoughts and feelings were ridiculed. She passionately loved and admired her mother, who was very elegant in her manners and dress. She longed to please her, but she failed completely. In spite of her best efforts she walked badly, stood badly, curtsied badly, and then, in despair, she was constantly forming plans to drown herself or put out her eyes, so that her mother might repent her severity. But all ended in her standing by the edge of a lake or feeling the pricking of a knife on her eyeballs. Sometimes patriotic and warlike feelings stirred within her. The war with Napoleon was then raging. She wept bitterly at not having been born a man ; she longed to fight for her native country. She would go to Germany, disguise herself,

5

perhaps be made page to the Crown Prince. Fired by these
romantic ideas, she actually took her little shawl on her
arm and set out for Stockholm, but she only got as far as
the "red gate" of Årsta. She made another attempt, and
walked on for about a mile, hoping that some family would
meet her and take her up. After waiting for half an hour,
she returned home quite dispirited. "No carriage—not
even a car—had she seen."

A passionate love of nature was one of her early characteristics. The snowy rocks, the blue lakes, the rushing rivers
of her native country, roused her to enthusiasm. Once, in
a walk through a beautiful park, she was lost for some hours.
Shouts were of no avail, and just as the family were returning to the hotel in despair, she ran up to her father crying
out that she had seen Pan, the wood-god, playing on his
flute. This incident seems to have made a great impression
on her, for she brings it in at length in the beautiful story
of *The Home*, Petrea, the big-nosed heroine of the adventure,
being a faithful portrait of Fredrika herself. She soon began
to use her pen. At the age of eight she wrote her first verses
to the moon, beginning, "O corps celeste de la nature."
Then, two years later, came a ballad, the first verse of which
is—

> "In the fine palace Elfvakolasti,
> Situated in some parts of Sverge,
> Once resided little Melanie,
> Only daughter of Count Stjernberge."

A more ambitious poem, *The Creation of the World*, was
then commenced, but, like a similar effort of Petrea's, it was
doomed never to emerge out of chaos. It seemed, even
then, as if she were going to be the champion of her sex,
for she wrote some doggerel lines without capitals or stops :—

> "can man not learn the art of saving
> could not our stronger sex be taught
> not from their poor wives all help craving
> to save their wages as they ought."

Later on, Fredrika composed theatrical pieces for birthday *fêtes*, and Charlotte and she played pianoforte overtures, and shone with applause in *The Battle of Prague.* She had a peculiar taste for practical jokes. Her favourite victim was her brother's tutor, and one evening she slily put a heavy leaden pincushion into his dress-coat pocket while he was playing chess with Bonne Amie.

When Charlotte was fifteen, novel-reading for half an hour a day was allowed. Amongst other attractive volumes Miss Burney's *Evelina, Cecilia,* and *Camilla* were eagerly devoured ; and now Charlotte and Fredrika were constantly imagining themselves the heroines of some romantic adventure. Every evening, one autumn, Charlotte expected to hear a ladder being raised to the window of her room, while Fredrika was certain that they would both be carried off in broad daylight on Sunday during their drive from church. Week after week she eagerly looked first to the right, then to the left, to see whether any horseman would be rushing out of the forest, commanding the coachman to stop. When every Sunday they came back to Årsta without having met any adventure, she was much disappointed.

As Fredrika grew up, she says that religious enthusiasm and worldly coquetry struggled within her—feelings for which she could not account, but which seemed to burst her young bosom. " Like two all-consuming flames, the desire to know and the desire to enjoy were burning in my soul, without being satisfied for many long years. The mere sight of certain words in a book, such as Truth, Liberty, Glory, Immortality, roused within me feelings which vainly I would try to describe." At the age of seventeen, Fredrika was taken out to balls and suppers at Stockholm. She was fond of dancing, but was not always asked to dance, and she enjoyed herself most at the theatre, where she says her soul was thrown into a state of topsy-turvy. She tells us that in company she frequently behaved in a ridiculous manner, because it was utterly impossible for her to keep her body or

soul quiet. Her eyes were remarkably handsome, full of
thought and vivacity, but her head was large in proportion
to her small, slight figure, and her nose—was a stumbling-
block to beauty! During her childhood she was always
making experiments to improve it, and the end was that it
swelled out larger and larger, and was often very red. She
was more successful with her forehead, which was naturally
low, but by cutting away the hair at the roots, and then
twitching out the hair as it grew with a pair of tweezers, she
produced a fine high forehead, much more becoming, her
sister says, than the low one. But what availed the forehead when the nose was so obstinate? "My nose," laments
poor Fredrika, "naturally large, used to become illuminated
in hot places, darkening my prospects of pleasure and keeping admirers at a distance." In spite of the nose, however,
Fredrika *had* admirers. One young gentleman, nowise
handsome, but rich, saw her for a couple of hours when she
was paying a visit, and—fell in love with her. "With his
hand upon his heart," she says, "he whispered his agony,
but the door was forcibly shut upon him by my father, who
would willingly have got all his daughters married, but
would never tolerate the face of a suitor in his house."
Another time, at a watering-place, she met a "gay, good,
and handsome lieutenant." He began to sigh for her, and
she to respond. "It was a pastoral moment," she says,
"when once in the green fields I was wiping and scraping
some tar off one of my shoes, when he, with half-words and
sighs . . . Well! nothing more came of it. We left at last,
and he accompanied us back to the town. I remember, not
without a pleasant sensation, this first silent harmony of my
soul with another's. I gave him a carnation and a curl-
paper, and he gave me a few sprigs of lavender. I cried the
whole night after our parting, and for a long time afterwards
sighed his name in my heart, but very calmly."

The convent-like life at Årsta was now resumed, and a
dull and joyless business it was. After the age of fifteen

Charlotte and Fredrika were allowed to eat as much as they pleased, but this seemed to be the only liberty they enjoyed. The Bremer parents wished their four daughters to be of the same opinion as the Swedish poetess, Anna Langren, when she says, " *Our* household, that is our republic ; our politics, the toilet ; " they had the girls taught cookery, and wished them to spin, weave, and sew. But the household affairs did not sufficiently occupy the four sisters. Charlotte had a real liking and aptitude for them ; but Fredrika began to be more and more hampered with her humdrum life. It was like a prison, a cage, to her soaring spirit. " What use to dress and undress," she cries in *Hertha*, "just to do nothing ? " The mere fiddle-faddling of piano-practising and flower-painting could not satisfy the demands of her energetic mind, and she often exclaimed, "The worst destiny of all is to have no destiny at all ! " The long autumn evenings were especially irksome. After tea, at six o'clock, the whole family assembled in Mr. Bremer's sitting-room while he read aloud in German or English. He chose *The Thirty Years' War*, or Robertson's *History of America*, and as his hearers did not understand German or English well enough to follow him, they yawned and nodded over their sewing and embroidery. Without, the snow and rain beat against the windows, and the storm howled its mournful song. After supper, at ten o'clock, there were compulsory conversations, and as no topics but the gossip of the house or neighbourhood were allowed, it was hard indeed to " make talk." Fredrika's father was a just, upright man, but he thought " tedium was good for young maidens." Chess-playing was worse than all. Fredrika detested it, especially when her father laughed and chuckled as he captured her unguarded pieces. After such evenings she often wept bitterly, and complained that no one understood her.

Here are some of her stray thoughts written down at random during these monotonous years :—

" 24th November. Why burns within thee the desire to become famous and renowned ? When thou art laid low in thy cold grave dost thou then hear thy name mentioned on earth ? "

" Love and thou shalt be happy ; love all mankind, press the whole world to thy heart. Some one will thank thee with equal love, but if none should thank thee, should love thee in return, oh ! still I must love mankind or I should be deeply unhappy."

" 1st March, 1823. How stagnant, like a muddy pool, is time to youth, dragging on a dull and inactive life ! Watch, pray, struggle, and hope. I am only twenty-two, and yet I am often tired of this world and wish I was taken from it ; but then we do lead a very dull life."

" 10th April. In vain, young enthusiastic girl, in vain dost thy fiery heart beat for all that is great and noble. In vain thine eye looks forth into a world where everything appears to be great and noble ; where the temples of honour and virtue, raised amongst rocky heights and precipices, seem to thee so easy of access. Poor young girl ! soon, very soon, shall thy bold step be arrested by opinion and the etiquette of everyday life ; soon shall thy feelings be damped, thy thoughts be lowered to trifles, enthusiasm die away in thy soul, and soon shalt thou find everything around thee as weak and wretched as thou art thyself."

In August, 1821, the whole family—six children, father, mother, and servant—set off from Stralsund in covered carriages for a long journey. They went to Darmstadt, through Switzerland, to Geneva and Paris, but the prison was only changed for one on wheels. Fredrika says that for all the treasures of the world she would not again make the journey in the same way. Her father's gout made him un-usually irritable, especially if the family were not ready to start exactly at the appointed time. When there was any compulsory talk of this pleasure trip after it was over, Fredrika remained silent. Her love for her sisters—for the contented Charlotte, for the kind Hedda, for the vivacious Agatha—was intense. They had become more than ever united during the common sorrows of their journey, but Fredrika's ardent spirit yearned for knowledge, for liberty, for fuller and freer life. "I suffered like Tantalus," she says ; "embroidering a grey kerchief, I became more and more benumbed. The flame in my soul was flickering fearfully, and wanted only to be extinguished for ever." She was like a growing plant placed in a pot too small to contain it, or like a rapid current which chafes its narrow bed and struggles for a larger, wider outlet.

"Years rolled past," she says, "and everything remained in the same state ; physical pains, caused by inward pains, seized me, an eruption covered my face, my eyes became yellow, I felt both in body and soul a sense of utter frost— a sensation as if I was becoming mouldy ; I had a fear and horror of any one looking at me. The fate of women in general, and my own in particular, appeared frightful. I was conscious of being born with powerful wings, but I was also conscious of their being clipped, and I thought they would always remain so."

Trust and hope seemed tottering. When her sister Agatha returned from Paris, where she had been under orthopædic treatment, she hardly knew Fredrika, she was so altered in two years. But there is a proverb which says that "much corn grows in the winter time," and so it was with Fredrika. Unconsciously these years of dreary apprenticeship were training her for her real work. She had tried several times to find a fitting channel for her energies. The calling of an artist attracted her ; she had a peculiar talent for catching likenesses, and she painted miniatures of the Crown Princess and the King, and sold them in secret. Within a year she earned nearly two hundred rix-dollars for charity. Another time she resolved to be an hospital nurse, and was determined to tell her parents of her intention. She industriously doctored the poor people about, once giving essence of cloves (a toothache remedy) for weak eyes. To her great relief, however, the mistake had no bad results, and the patient came to beg for some more of the "blessed drops." But her real powers were soon to assert themselves. Without imagining that she had any literary genius, she wrote, during a solitary winter spent at Årsta with her two younger sisters, the first volume of *Sketches of Everyday Life.* Her only motive was to get a little money to assist the poor ; and when her brother August wrote from Upsala to say that Mr. Palmblad, the publisher, was willing to pay one hundred rix-dollars for the little book, she and her sisters danced with delight. This first volume included "Stockholm Suppers" and "Axel and Anna," a correspondence between two lovers living in different stories of the same house. In both of these the lightness and grace of touch, the peculiar ease and "nature" which afterwards distinguished Fredrika Bremer's writings, are faintly but distinctly shown. The edition only consisted of three hundred copies, and the name of the author was not given. The reviewers gave the book a measure of praise ; one said that it was the work of a lady, a young lady (Fredrika was now twenty-eight), and hoped that when her talents were more matured, he might be able to give her works more unlimited praise. On the margin of this review Fredrika wrote, "Yes, dear critic, that rests in the hand of God."

After the publication of the first volume of *Sketches* Fredrika's horizon seemed to clear. Mentally and physically she recovered ; lukewarm baths had a healing effect on her body, the eruption on her face disappeared, her complexion became clear, and she was bodily as one new-born. One day as she walked across snow-covered fields just as the sun was setting, her eyes turned to the flood of purple and golden glory in the western sky ; there came, too, across the wide expanse of snow a breath of air, delicious and full of spring. She looked round, and, turning her thoughts to herself, asked, "Would I now wish to die?" For the first time for many years she could answer "No!" A new resurrection awoke within her, though she could not explain why or how it had come. When she went to Stockholm, with her improved complexion and calmer soul, she received two offers of marriage, one from a "major with arms and crest on his seal, and an estate in the country," but both these offers she refused. Her ideas on marriage were of the very highest kind. As to her calling as an authoress, it had not yet attained that dignity and importance which it after-wards did. She looked upon it as a sort of pastime. Still, encouraged by an occasional word of praise, she began a second volume of *Sketches*. Among these is *The Solitary One*, which, though morbid and melancholy, has a silver lining to the clouds ; and the first part of *The H—— Family*. In this last story the bright, innocent, playful humour which is one of Fredrika's peculiar gifts came out in full force ; it is not merely to be seen here and there—it pervades the whole and breathes its perfume in every page. The discovery of it, Fredrika says, was quite unexpected to herself ; it started out from those gloomy Årsta years like a crimson flower from a grave. This volume was offered to a Stockholm publisher, who refused to have anything to say to it ; but the faithful Palmblad undertook to print it, little guessing its future fame, and that it would be translated into almost all the European languages.

Family events, too, came quickly during this eventful year of 1830. Fredrika's father died in the summer, after long sufferings, and in the following November, Charlotte, the good, peaceful "eldest," was married, and this was one of the happiest days spent in the family—full of innocent joy and harmony. And now at last came to Fredrika the distinction for which she had pined so long, and to which she had become half indifferent. "Go where you will," writes one puzzled correspondent, "you hear nothing spoken of

but a Lady Bremer or Miss Bremer who has written," &c.
The Swedish Academy awarded her their large gold medal
for "Genius and Taste." One critic, Brinckmann, writes
that it is humiliating to think that the first volume of
Sketches should have vegetated for more than two years,
and not one of the critics should have discovered its merits.
"I am acquainted with the choicest literature of most
countries," he adds, " but I defy them to be able to produce
in the *genre* which you have chosen more beautiful or true
pictures, not only of reality but of the ideal world which
lives and breathes around us, and all this with such genuine
unmistakable womanliness. I have heard some silly maidens
say, 'She must surely have been assisted by some *man—*
some scholar.' Pardon me, they know not what they say."
To all this unlooked-for praise Fredrika cries, " It is absurd,
absurd, absurd ! I believe that some kind fairy has pronounced some hocus-pocus on me and my little book ; the
sensation which it creates is quite ridiculous. It is now the
ton to read it ; it is spoken of everywhere, and so is its
authoress, who cannot hope now to remain anonymous. I
am obliged to listen to so many fine things that I am half
astonished they do not make me quite giddy. *The H——
Family* especially gets the most splendid encomiums."

And then Fredrika tells her sister of an animated evening
at home in Stockholm, when Franzen, the poet, and an old
friend, brought Brinckmann, the critic, to visit her. The
latter, she says, was half crazy ; he quoted her book continually, and said she had not *read* it properly herself.
Then Franzen, anxious to show off his *protégée*, asked to
see her paintings. After going through them, Brinckmann
heard that she was also a *musicienne.* " Indeed I begin to get
quite tired now," he exclaimed. He finished by going down
on his knees before poor astonished Fredrika.

She now threw herself into her new calling with heart
and soul, and her intellectual being grew and strengthened
every day. A portrait of her, taken after she had entered

on this higher stage of her existence, gives us an interesting peep of what she was. There is a wonderful charm of humorous sadness in the face; those yearning, thoughtful eyes have wept, but they have also laughed ; there is an arch piquancy in the expression, and an undercurrent of penetrating loving insight which looks into the world with something between a smile and a sigh. Fredrika Bremer's books are like nothing else in fiction ; they have a flavour of their own. To compare her with Miss Austen, as is often done, is not fair to either. As a story-teller, she is inferior to Miss Austen, but she has a broader outlook on human nature. She has a more poetical soul ; she has a larger sense of the " soul of goodness in things evil." She sees the weaknesses, the oddities of others, but she does more than see—she feels that underneath all these may lie a nobler nature than is dreamed of.

While at Stockholm she made the friendship of a Miss Frances ——, who introduced her to the writings of Bentham. She now saw that the more her intellect could be trained, the greater would become her capability of labouring for the benefit of mankind and of being happy herself. The old childish desire for living awoke within her. " I beheld," she says, " a new sun, and in his light a paradise. I saw the road I ought to follow—how I would and could rise higher and higher to light and truth, and every step would bring with it some fruit for my fellow-men. My soul rejoiced."

Another offer of marriage was refused about this time. The wooer wrote with so much warm anxiety, goodness, and real excellence of soul that Fredrika was deeply touched, but she felt that she had placed a barrier between herself and marriage, " that one cannot unite the vocations of wife and authoress without failing in both," and that as an authoress she could make herself as useful as her powers allowed.

After the second part of *The H—— Family*, *The President's Daughters* came out. The story is related by Made-

moiselle Ronnquist, the governess, and the first chapter
begins with her introduction to the president, who is a
widower. He does not wish his daughters to be prodigies,
neither does he wish them to be brilliant, vain, learned, or
pedantic ; he wishes them to be capable women, good
housewives and mothers. They may read, but any sort of
book-learning is not allowed, as that would take them out of
their sphere. This system, however, has its faults, as
Mademoiselle Ronnquist soon perceives when her two elder
pupils, Edla and Adelaide, return from a ball. Edla is
gloomy, austere, and forbidding ; Adelaide is lovely, radiant,
and swanlike. Edla is miserable at being forced into
society for which she does not care ; she moves like a dark
shadow beside her beautiful, admired sister, and her strong
and vigorous intellect is allowed to find no scope whatever.
The cast-iron rules of the President's " blessed wife " treat all
girls alike, whether they are beautiful, or unattractive, clever
or stupid ; no allowance is to be made for individual
peculiarities. Edla is not likely to be married, and the
repressive system is working injuriously on her mind, which
is like a millstone that will grind corn if it has corn put into
it, but if not, will grind itself. Fredrika Bremer has a rare
faculty for grouping a variety of characters round her
principal *dramatis personæ*, and these are not turned off as
if by machinery : they have all a life of their own. She
takes us to a *soirée*, and we get intimate with the noble
Count Alaric, with the commonplace Otto—both Adelaide's
admirers—with the young artist Angelika and her glowing aspirations, and we have to like even the crotchety, well-mean-
ing President himself. We know all about the supper, too,
the oysters and heathcocks, the plovers' eggs and mushrooms,
the cold pike and crabs' claws, the delicate lamb cutlets and
green peas. In spite of the President's protests, Edla's imprisoned intellect finds free scope, and the dark clouds are
rolled away from her spirit, which demands a larger outlet
than housekeeping cares alone can give. The latter are not

undervalued—far from it—but Fredrika Bremer felt acutely
that girls should be treated according as their peculiar tem-
peraments and tendencies dictate. No mere outline of plot
can ever give an idea of the peculiar charm of her writings ;
the style is everything with her ; *c'est le ton qui' fait la
chanson ;* the dainty humour, the delicate touches of light
and shade make every page attractive. There is something
quite inimitable in her way of putting things. The chapter
called " Unlucky Days," when Mademoiselle Ronnquist in
an evil hour cuts the President's hair so short that he is
ashamed to be seen, is a marvel of innocent playfulness.

After the *President's Daughters* came *Nina*, a sequel to
it, and this was followed by *The Neighbours*, which is
generally considered to be Miss Bremer's masterpiece. Her
writings were now not only known in Sweden, but had
penetrated to Germany, France, England, and America.
She had also gained a larger knowledge of life, she had
spent much time at Christianstadt, in the south of Sweden,
with her sister, and in Norway with her friend the Countess
W. In *The Neighbours* she has attained the very summit
of easy naturalness, that art of concealing art which is one
of her special characteristics. Fransiska, the heroine, tells
her own story in letters, but *such* letters, such graphic,
inimitable, soul-discovering letters ! Take the opening
paragraph for instance : " Here I am, dear Maria, in my
own house and home, at my own writing-table, and sitting
beside my own Bear. And who is Bear ? you will probably
ask ; who should he be but my own husband, whom I call
Bear, because it suits him so well ? " The newly-married
Fransiska and her Bear have just arrived at Rosenvik, their
future home, and she has been introduced on the way to her
husband's stepmother, a tall eccentric Generalska, whom
she found playing the violin while her servants dance. The
two half-brothers and their wives, the prim Jane Maria and
the spoiled childish Ebba, soon come to the front—in fact,
we get acquainted with no end of " neighbours "—with the

gingery old maid, Miss Hellevi Husgafvel, and the pure and
lovely Serena Dahl. Fransiska and the Bear have their
quarrels ; he is fond of smoking in the house, which she
forbids ; he makes grimaces, and she stops his mouth with
her sugar-cakes ; sometimes she gives in to him, as, for
example, in the following passage :—

"Again a little strife. It is dangerous to wake the
slumbering lion. The scene is over our dessert.

HE. My dear friend, what bonnet do you think of wearing
this afternoon ?

SHE. My little straw bonnet with lilacs.

HE. *That !* Oh no ; wear the white crape bonnet, it is
so lovely.

SHE. That ! My only state and gala bonnet ! What
can make you think of that, my angel ? To sit in the
cabriolet in the dust, and it may perhaps rain——

HE. Then it would not get dusty.

SHE. How witty you are ! but then the rain would not
improve it.

HE. My dear Franskin, it would give me great pleasure
if you wear that bonnet.

SHE. Then, dearest Bear, I *will* wear it even though it
rained and were dusty at the same time.

And thus I go to put on the white bonnet. What would
Madame Folcken say if she saw me driving on a country
road in it ? Our little gardener youth serves on this extraordinary occasion as footman in a grey jacket with a green
velvet collar."

So the Bear and his Bearess set off on their tour of visits,
but alas ! the rain does come down, and the poor bonnet is
completely spoiled. Darker shades than these came into the
story. *Ma Chère Mère*, Bear's stepmother, has a son of her
own, Bruno, who when a boy committed a theft ; with the
spirit of a Roman matron she cursed him, and, stung with

shame, he ran away and was heard of no more. He returns now under an assumed name; his is a dark, gloomy, Byronic nature with flashes of light underneath. He falls in love with Serena, and *Ma Chère Mère* is at length reconciled after he has saved her life. For even the most hopeless there is seen to be light and trust; the torch of mutual love burns unquenchably. The character of *Ma Chère Mère* is remarkably well brought out; she belongs to the grand old race of the Vikings, she has a store of pithy proverbs, and is true and just to the core, though at times rough and stern. As to Fransiska, we get to know her as well as an intimate friend. After reading *The Neighbours* Charlotte Brontë said she thought everybody would fancy that she had taken her conception of Jane Eyre's character from that of Fransiska, and persisted in saying that Fransiska was Jane Eyre married to a good-natured Bear of a Swedish surgeon. Some resemblance there may be, but Charlotte Brontë, with all her power, could never have touched off individual traits with half the delicacy and lightness that Miss Bremer has shown. "*The Neighbours,*" says Miss Bremer, modestly, "has many faults, but I have good hopes for future sketches."

She made much use of her two years' stay at Tomb, in Norway; the scenery and manners of the people had a particular charm for her. "I notice," she says in one of her letters, "greater simplicity than in Sweden; the housekeeper prepares the dinner and other meals, and then goes with La Comtesse to pay visits and to balls. She says 'thou' to the daughters of the house, and her voice and opinion is listened to on all matters. The steward at Tomb goes to dine with Baron W. without being invited, he occupies as a guest the seat of honour at table, the host converses with him as with one equal in rank. They show him the young ladies' embroidery; they chat with him, and he dances with them when there is an opportunity." Miss Bremer's story *Strife and Peace* is a study of Norwegian life. Susanna, the bright capable housekeeper of the Lady Astred, stands up most amusingly for her native country, Sweden, while Harald, the steward, takes the part of Norway. " God loves Sweden the best," says Susanna. " Norway say I," answers Harald ; and so the strife goes on, till at last the whole party are lost in a snowstorm ; Susanna saves Harald's life, he marries her, and finally there is peace, and she agrees to give him his favourite Norwegian dish of "fruit-soup with little herrings." Along with all these humorous scenes there are capital descriptions of the beautiful valleys and rock shapes of Norway, its snow-fields and woods.

It was in the steamer, on Miss Bremer's return from Norway, that Hans Christian Andersen made her acquaintance. He was then poor and unknown, and hearing she was on board, he had a great wish to make her acquaintance. One morning, at sunrise on the great Wener lake, he saw a lady, neither young nor old, wrapped in a shawl and cloak, coming up from the cabin. He ventured to speak to her. She answered him coldly, and asked his name. The name at that time carried no magic with it, but he happened to have a copy of his first book, the *Improvisatoire*, with him, which he lent her, and when she returned it to him in the afternoon, her face was beaming, and she was full of cordiality. They became intimate in Stockholm, and corresponded for years. " She is a noble woman," he says. " The great truths of religion and poetry in the still circumstances of life have deeply penetrated her."

Great changes happened in the Bremer family ; August, the younger son (the cornet of the H—— family), died in 1832 ; and Hedda, the good Hedda, her mother's and sisters' darling, five years afterwards. *The Home*, one of Fredrika Bremer's best and longest works, was produced in 1839, when her powers were fully matured. There is not, perhaps, quite so much variety as in *The Neighbours*, but we are made most intimate friends with a family circle : Judge Frank, the master of the house ; Elise, the house-mother ; Louise, the good, useful " eldest " ; Petrea, the flighty eccentric one ; Eva, the beauty ; Leonore, the invalid ; and Gabrielle, the pet. Then there is Henrik, the only son, his mother's summer-child. How well we learn to know every one of these can only be seen in the delightful pages of *The Home.* The family drink coffee, eat sugar-biscuits, and laugh at the tutor ; Elise writes a novel in secret which her husband calls " trash " ; she is in despair that she has no " roast " when her husband brings in his old flame Emilie to dinner, and embraces the friendly Mrs. Gemilla when she produces two chickens out of her voluminous bag. So the life is lived till Louise marries the tutor and Petrea turns out an authoress. In the end the whole party, including Louise's eight berserkers, drink a skal for peace on earth. There is little plot in *The Home,* and yet it is so charming, so original, and so life-like, that few books of the kind can be compared to it. Another point of interest is the character of Petrea. When Fredrika Bremer says, " That which was a fountain of disquiet in Petrea is now become a fountain of quiet," we feel that she is speaking also of herself. The home is not always a Paradise on earth, there is sometimes " sour paste," but as the judge says, " Want and care, disturbing, nay, even bitter hours may come, but they will also go, and the bonds of love and truth will give consolation—nay, even will give strength."

Miss Bremer now began to feel a longing for strange scenes. She knew her own country well ; she knew the pine forest of Nordland and the mountain of Avasaxa, where, on St. John's Eve, the sun is never seen to set ; she knew the wondrous falls of Trollhatta and the blue waters of the Wener Lake, but she wished for something different. She determined to go to America, where her books had already procured her a warm welcome. In the summer of 1849 she travelled by way of London to New York. What her impressions were of Washington and Florida, of Cuba and of Concord, where she visited Emerson, are given in her *Homes of the New World*. In October, 1851, she was in London, on a visit to the publisher, Mr. Chapman, and George Eliot, then assistant editor of the *Westminster Review*, was a boarder in the same house. She writes: "All the world is doing its *devoirs* to the great little authoress." She found Miss Bremer equally "unprepossessing to eye and ear. I have to reflect every time I look at her that she is really Fredrika Bremer." In a subsequent letter to Miss Hennell, she says, "I wish you could see Miss Bremer's album, full of portraits, landscapes, and flowers, all done by herself. A portrait of Emerson, marvellously like, one of Jenny Lind, &c. To-night we had quite a charming *soirée*. Miss Bremer was more genial than I have seen her. She played on the piano, and smiled benevolently. Altogether I am beginning to repent of my repugnance."

All Miss Bremer's tales had been translated into English by Mary Howitt, and this, of course, brought on an intimacy with the Howitt family. On Fredrika's return she was greeted by the unexpected news of her sister Agatha's death —that sister whom she called "her innermost." She now resumed her old occupations at Stockholm. Since her visit to America she was more than ever an apostle for the "emancipation of women"; she had studied the condition of her own sex in different countries, and she was now perfectly certain that in Sweden there were many grievances which ought to be redressed. There was at that time a law by which every unmarried woman of any age was declared a minor during her parents' lifetime. The only way in which she could obtain her freedom, or receive any property that might be left to her, was by going before a court of law and demanding a legal document by which she was declared to be freed from the guardianship of her parents. Such a step few unmarried women cared to take, and the consequence was that they remained in the state of pupilage nearly all their lives—unable to act for themselves, unable to marry without their parents' consent, and completely fettered by a cruel and unjust law which "God never made." Fredrika with her additional experience now began to wage war against this state of bondage. *Hertha,* her last novel, is written with a purpose—written to show how fatally the law of treating women of seven or eight-and-twenty as minors would work on a powerful, impetuous, and yet affectionate nature. Hertha shrank from exposing her avaricious father (who had appropriated her mother's fortune, rightly due to herself and her sisters) before a court of law, yet she bitterly felt her dependent condition. Her eager aspirations were cramped and ridiculed, and her weariness at the dull, meaningless days before her fell on her soul like a mist. "How happy are men," she cries, "who can study the arts and sciences!—who can penetrate into the secrets of the beautiful and the true, and then go out into the world and share the wisdom they have learned, the good which they have found! I would have lived on bread and water, and have thought myself only too happy if I could have learned what young men learn at schools and colleges, if I had enjoyed freedom to choose my own path by my own struggles." Hertha's touching love for her dying sister Alma, and her successful rescue of the father who has injured her from a fire by which his house is destroyed, shows her character in another light. Her conversations with Yngve Nordin, the young engineer, and her opening of a school for the higher education of women, give Miss Bremer many opportunities for unfolding her ideas respecting her own sex. The end is sad, for Yngve, after waiting seven years for Hertha, dies when they have been married a few months. But Miss Bremer cannot help being humorous, and the wooing of Dr. Hedermann, when he asks Jugsborg Uggia if she has ever called him "a dromedary," is as amusing as anything in *The Neighbours.*

There are many extravagances in *Hertha*, but there is much that is good and noble. We feel better as we read it; we feel the influence of an exalted nature which longs to see women rising higher and higher, and joining with their brother men in one common aim—the purifying and ennobling of the world. Her views on the subject of women's rights were so advanced that she thought women ought to prepare themselves in the public schools to be lecturers, professors, judges, and physicians. One grievance she lived to see removed : a new law was passed by which unmarried women in Sweden attain their majority at the age of twenty-five. A school was also formed in Stockholm for the education of female teachers. Up to that time no women teachers in schools had been allowed. When the cholera broke out Fredrika Bremer was the president of a ladies' association for the relief of the sufferers ; she also visited the prisons, helped to establish a deaf and dumb school, an asylum for the infirm, and to build a better class of labourers' cottages.

The influence which she exercised on literature was a most important one. When she first began to write, French novels of a most injurious tendency were spreading their poison far and wide on the Continent, but when her *Sketches* appeared, their simple original charm was at once felt ; they were read and re-read ; edition after edition of all her books was called for, especially in Germany. She makes her readers feel at home wherever she takes them, whether amongst the passengers on a Nordland steamboat, in the little gossiping town of Kungsköping, amongst the brothers and sisters of a family circle, or with the sightseers in the iron mines of Dalecarlia. A fresh air, a fragrance as of pine forests comes with her—she brings an atmosphere of brightness, innocence, and joy. The Swedes used proudly to say, " Our two greatest women are Jenny Lind and Fredrika Bremer."

She took another long journey alone. She went to

Greece, Italy, and Palestine, and wrote *Life in the Old World*, which gives her impressions of these five years, and has been translated into English by Mary Howitt. While she was in Rome, in 1858, Nathaniel Hawthorne gives us a vivid word-picture of her in his Note Book :— " Miss Bremer," he says, " called on us the other day. We find her very little changed from what she was when she came to take tea and spend an evening at our little red cottage amongst the Berkshire hills, and went away so dissatisfied with my conversational performances. She is the funniest little old fairy in person whom you can imagine, with a huge nose to which all the rest of her is but an insufficient appendage, but you feel at once that she is most gentle, kind, womanly, sympathetic, and true. She talks English fluently, in a low, quiet voice, but with such an accent that it is impossible to understand what she says without the closest attention. . . . At seven o'clock we went by invitation to take tea with Miss Bremer. After much search and lumbering painfully up two or three staircases in vain, we found her in a small chamber of a large old building, situated a little way from the Tarpeian Rock. It was the tiniest and humblest domicile that I have seen in Rome, just large enough to hold her narrow bed, her tea-table, and a table covered with books and photographs of Roman ruins, and some pages written by herself. I wonder whether she is poor. Probably so, for she told us that her expense of living cost only five pauls a day. She welcomed us with the greatest cordiality and lady-like simplicity, making no allusion to the humbleness of her environments. There is not a better bred woman, and yet one does not think whether she has any breeding or no. Her little bit of a round table was already spread with her blue earthenware tea-cups, and after she had got through an interview with the Swedish minister, and dismissed him with a hearty pressure of his hand between both her own, she gave us our tea and bread and a mouthful of cake. . . . There is no better heart than hers, and not many sounder heads, and a little touch of sentiment comes delightfully in, mixed up with a quick and delicate humour, and the most perfect simplicity. There is also a very pleasant atmosphere of maidenhood about her ; we are sensible of a freshness and odour of the morning in this little withered rose, its veins purer for never having been gathered and worn, but only diffusing fragrance on its stem. God bless her good heart ! She is a most amiable woman, worthy to be the maiden aunt of the whole universe."

After her return, "Tante Fredrika," as she liked to be called, lived by herself in an *étage* at Stockholm. Margaret Howitt gives a very interesting account in her *Twelve Months with Fredrika Bremer*, of her visit to the same house in the winter of 1863–4, and of Tante Fredrika's good works. She adopted a charming young artist, Hulda ; she visited the hospital and the " Silent School," as the deaf and dumb institution was called. Altogether she led a happy, busy, useful life, was welcomed in the palace by the Queen, as well as in the poorest cottage, and was beloved by everybody. Margaret Howitt mentions reading to her *Silas Marner*, which, she says, "Tante Fredrika considers one of the most beautiful and perfect stories ever written." The last few months of her life were spent at Årsta. Her old home had passed into other hands, but she found that the inmates were glad and happy to receive her amongst them. In the spring of 1865 she went to them, and never had she been so calm and happy. Christmas passed joyfully. Tante Fredrika celebrated it with thirty poor children belonging to the estate. She danced with them round the tree, gladdened them with nice presents, partly prepared by herself, and spoke many " precious words " to them about Christmas. Then there was music, and she listened to the daughters of the house as they played, finishing up with organ preludes. After tea she read aloud two of Hans Christian Andersen's stories—*The Christmas Tree* and *How the Nightingale Sang to the Emperor.* That night she dreamed of hearing the most glorious music. She caught cold from coming out of church on Christmas morning, but seemed to get better. Inflammation of the lungs, however, set in, and her sister and brother-in-law were sent for. She had a dream once that she would die at the age of sixty-six, and she said, smiling, to her sister, "You know it is not my death-year yet." But her illness increased. She went, leaning on the arm of her nurse, from window to window, as if she were taking leave of the country she loved so well, and often exclaimed, in broken sentences, "Light, eternal light!" She said she would have liked to remain a little longer to finish the work she had begun, but, later on, she whispered, "Now I am so tired that if God were to call me, I should be content." He *did* call her, at three o'clock in the morning of the 31st of December, 1865.

Innumerable wreaths of green leaves and white everlastings were put on her coffin, but the most beautiful of all, made of white camellias and long feathery grass, was from the children of the "Silent School." At the head of her grave, shaded by two lime-trees, stands a cross, with her name and the dates of her birth and death, and underneath, according to her own wish, are the words—

"WHEN I CALLED UPON THE LORD, HE DELIVERED ME OUT OF ALL MY TROUBLE."

IV.

HARRIET MARTINEAU.

1802–1876.

Birth at Norwich—" Dull, unobservant, slow, and awkward "—At school in Bristol—Deafness begins—" V " of Norwich—Writes Penny Stories for Houlston—Three Prize Essays—A rift in the clouds—Success of Political Economy tales— *Green glass bottles, soap and sweets !— Deerbrook—The Hour and the Man—The Knoll*—Writes leaders for the *Daily News*—Visits from George Eliot and James Payn—Death.

CARLYLE once said to Harriet Martineau, "You are like a Lapland witch on her broomstick, going up and down as you will. Other people, without broomsticks, drop down and cannot come up when they would, and that is the difference between you and them." Nothing could have given a better idea of her inexhaustible activity. As Hartley Coleridge declared, "She was a *monomaniac* about *everything*." The practical side of life pressed closely upon her. Her question always was, "What use can I do here ? What end can I serve?" She saw distinctly what she could do, and she did it thoroughly well. Life was to her a tremendous fact, or rather a series of facts. It was given to her to seize upon the popular needs of the day, and to supply them. Her father belonged to a French Huguenot family, who emigrated to Norwich in 1688. For some generations the men of the Martineau family were surgeons; but Thomas Martineau set up as a bombazine and camlet manufacturer,

HARRIET MARTINEAU.

BORN JUNE 12TH, 1802 ; DIED JUNE 27TH, 1876.

(From a Painting by RICHMOND.)

and married Elizabeth Rankin, eldest daughter of a Newcastle sugar-refiner. Harriet was the sixth of their eight
children, and was born at Norwich on the 12th of June, 1802.
Naturally a puny, delicate child, from bad nursing, and then
from being fed on a milk diet, which always disagreed with
her, she became more and more weakly. She had a horrid
lump at her throat for hours every morning, and the most
dreadful oppression at night. Nervous terrors haunted her.
The dim light of the windows in the night seemed to advance
till it pressed upon her eyeballs; the starlight seemed always
coming down to crush and stifle her; and she could not
even cross the yard to the garden without flying and panting,
and fearing to look behind, because she thought a wild beast
was after her. One of the children's walks was up to the
Castle Hill at Norwich. On a piece of waste ground at
the side of the hill, feather beds were brought out and
beaten with a stick, and the sound—a dull thud—made little
Harriet's heart stand still. She hated that walk, but her
parents knew nothing of all this. Her mother especially
seemed in total ignorance of the nervous child's fears. Perhaps she could not understand them, or was too busy to
attend to them.

"The child is father to the man," and so one of
Harriet's early propensities was towards a sort of practical
philosophy of her own. When she was two or three, she
used to nod her head and say, "Never cry for trifles,"
" Dooty first and pleasure afterwards," and sometimes she
got courage to edge up to strangers, and ask them to
give her a maxim. She had a little book, made of folded
paper, in which her beloved maxims were copied. She was
soon anxious to teach others, and remembers taking her
baby-brother, James, out of his crib, putting him in the
open window, and talking religiously to him, as she looked
out on a gorgeous sunset. Fretful, self-conscious, love-needy,
with a keen sense of justice, disturbed by strange dreams,
terrified at the prismatic colours of the lustre on the mantel-

piece, jealous that her sister Rachel should be petted, and
given a copy of Gay's Fables, altogether she must have been
a puzzling child.   The usual impression of her was that
she was dull, unobservant, slow, and awkward.   She often
cherished thoughts of running away from home; if she could
only get to a farmhouse, wear a woollen petticoat, and milk
cows, she would be safe.   Her first journey was to Newcastle.
Four of the children, including herself, were dressed in
nankeen frocks, and accompanied by their mother and aunt,
were packed into a post-chaise.   On the way, Harriet's
curiosity was excited by being told to guess what she would
find standing in grandpapa's garden.   The first thing she
said was, "I want to see what that thing is in the garden."
It was a heavy stone sun-dial.   Here, raising herself on
tiptoe, with her eyes on a level with the plate, she watched
and pondered day by day, forming conceptions of time.
Years after, when she built a house at Ambleside, her first
thought was to have this very sun-dial; but it could not be
removed, and another was given to her.

During her childhood she wept, she prayed, she wrote
sermons.   She enjoyed going to the Unitarian chapel with
her parents, though she was often puzzled at the injustice of
the preachers when they spoke of the duties of inferiors to
superiors.   What about the other side? she thought.   Much
time was spent in sewing; the three girls made all their
clothes, plaited bonnets, knitted stockings, and covered silk
shoes.   They could make shirts and puddings, iron and mend,
but still Harriet felt herself dismally awkward about little
things, and acutely remembers upsetting a basin of moist
sugar over a giblet-pie.   Her mother had a "setting down"
way, terrible to a sensitive child; she ordered everything,
right and left, and had no patience with slowness or stupidity.
Her little daughter, with cheeks pale as clay, flat, white
forehead, over which the hair grew low, eyes light, large,
and full, generally red with crying, stood in awe before her.
She remembers coming home from chapel with a dreadful

pain in her ear ; she laid it against a piece of cool iron ; it
seemed unbearable. When her mother came in, and said
something in a tone of pity, Harriet rested against her soft
muslin handkerchief with a sense of relief. " Oh ! if things
could be like this always ! " Another time a fly got into
her eye. " Harriet," said her mother, " I know that you
have resolution, and you must stand still till I take it out."
When the operation was over Harriet ran to the great gate-
way near the street, and beckoned to a companion to tell
her what her mother had said. It was the first encouraging
word she had ever heard. This stern repression of sympathy told upon her ; she felt herself to be the pariah of
the family, yet all the time she was capable of intense affection, and was the companion and caretaker of her brother
James, who was an irritable child. When she heard that a
new baby-sister was born, she was in raptures at the idea of
seeing the growth of a human mind from the very beginning. But once her sense of justice was roused she grew
intolerable. Jealous of her sister Rachel, she once said that
her mother always *did* agree with Rachel against her. Her
mother asked what she meant by that ? " I looked her full
in the face, and said that everything Rachel said and did was
right, and everything I said and did was wrong. Rachel
burst out into an insulting laugh, and was sharply bidden to
be quiet." Harriet was then told to go and practise her
music. She went ; her hands were clammy and tremulous,
her fingers stuck to each other, her eyes were dim, and there
was a roaring in her ears ; still she opened the piano, lighted
a candle, and began with a steady hand. She had never
played so well, and she went on for an immense time, till
her mother sternly ordered her to go to bed.

" With my candle in my hand, I said, ' Good-night.' My
mother laid down her work, and said, ' Harriet, I am more
displeased with you to-night than I have ever been in your
life.' Thought I, ' I don't care ; I have got it out, and it is

all true.' 'Go and say your prayers,' my mother continued,
'and ask God to forgive you for your conduct to-night, for I
don't know that I can. Go to your prayers!' Thought I,
'No, I sha'n't,' and that was the only night from infancy to
mature womanhood that I did not pray. I detected mis-
giving in my mother's manner, and I triumphed."

Such treatment did much to make Harriet hard and
relentless. Her mother never said, "My child, I never
dreamed that such terrible thoughts were in your mind. I
am your mother. Why do you not tell me everything that
makes you unhappy?" Silence and reserve reigned, and
Harriet complained that she had no spring in her life. Her
education went on for two years at home. Her eldest
brother taught the two girls Latin; their next brother,
writing and arithmetic; and their eldest sister, French,
reading, and exercises. But a phœnix of a schoolmaster
turned up in the person of Mr. Perry, who had been an
orthodox Dissenting minister, and had kept a large boys'
school. He now became a Unitarian, and Harriet and her
sister were sent to his school every day. He had powdered
hair, and a pointing, see-sawing finger. Under his care
Harriet's education went on swimmingly, and she felt that
she was really making progress. He took special interest in
the girl's compositions, and Harriet generally got credit for
her themes. But her nervous depression was so great at
this time, that one day when she heard that Mr. Perry had
called on her father, her heart utterly failed. Surely some
terrible delinquency must have been found out! She cried
desperately from sheer relief when her father announced
that "Mr. Perry says he never has a fault to find with
Rachel and Harriet; and that if he had a school full of such
girls he should be the happiest man alive."

Mr. Perry went to Ipswich, and Harriet's health became
bad, and her mind ill at ease. The great calamity of her
deafness, too, was slowly opening before her. Her family in-

sisted first that it was all her own fault; that she was absent, that she never cared to attend to anything that was said; that she ought to listen; that none were so deaf as those who won't hear, &c. When it got worse, she was blamed for not asking about everything that was said. A sorry way out of the difficulty! She resolved that she would not get out of temper, and as she had rather a violent one, the strain was very great. She had a horror of being like a distant relation, who had also become deaf in her childhood, and whenever she came up the steps the Martineaus would cry, "What *shall* we do? We shall be as hoarse as ravens all day. We shall be completely worn out." When Harriet herself was becoming deaf all this came back to her, and one of her questionings was, "Shall *I* put people to flight as —— does? Shall *I* be dreaded and disliked in that way all my life?" Her beloved hour was when she stole away from dessert, and read Shakespeare by firelight in winter. The newspaper which was taken in was *The Globe*, and from it she gleaned information about Political Economy, the National Debt, and the Funds. Considerable time was spent in sewing and music-copying, and her indolence was such that she had great difficulty in getting up in the morn- ing, and had a positive detestation of the daily walk. Up to the age of twenty she wrote a vulgar, cramped, untidy scrawl, which afterwards developed (take comfort, bad scribes!) into a bold legible hand. At sixteen she was sent to her aunt's school at Bristol for more than a year. Here her heart warmed and opened under genial influences. She was in raptures with the beauty of the Leigh Woods, Kingweston, and the Downs; she pored over Milton and Wordsworth, and had a great admiration for the well-known Unitarian minister, Dr. Carpenter.

She returned to Norwich in 1819, less morbid and de- sponding than before. Her eldest sister married, and now there sprang up a genuine cordial feeling between her mother and herself. They began to understand one another. It

was not then the fashion for young ladies to be literary ; a
woman who wrote or read much was thought to be a *half-
man !* So Harriet was at the work-table regularly after
breakfast, making her clothes or the shirts of the household,
or engaged on fancy work.   She studied almost by stealth,
meeting her brother James at seven in the morning to read
Latin with him, or translating Tacitus, that she might learn
to compress her thoughts.   She contrasted a translation of
hers from Tacitus with another done by Dr. Aikin, and
naïvely says that she found her own translation incomparably the better of the two.   It is sometimes well to have a
" gude conceit " of oneself, and Harriet never scrupled to say
what she honestly thought.   At this time of her life she was
pale and thin, rather above the ordinary height, with abundant dark-brown hair.   " I never had but one civil speech
about my looks," she used to say, " and that was a compli-
ment to my hair."   She had a very grave face, with no
light in it, no expression to redeem her features ; the low
brow and rather large under-lip increased the effect of her
natural seriousness.   People asked, " What has offended
Harriet that she looks so glum ? "   " Nothing," was the
answer ; " she is not offended, it is only her way."   " How
ugly all my aunt's daughters are, Harriet in particular ! "
was said by a satirical cousin, and she never doubted her
ugliness after *that.*   The fact was, her soul still slept and
had not yet shone out to dignify and glorify her face.

In 1821 she made her first appearance in print.   Her
brother James was leaving for college, and she was so
miserable at the thought of parting with him that he advised
her to write something out of her own head, and try her
chance with the *Monthly Repository*, a Unitarian periodical
which the Martineaus took in.   She acted on the suggestion.
Her paper was, " Female Writers on Practical Divinity," and
she carried her packet to the post-office herself to pay the
postage of it.   The letter " V." was put at the end of the
little MS., and her heart beat fast when she saw her article

in the next number of the *Repository*, and in the notices
to correspondents, a request to hear more from " V." of
Norwich.

" There is, certainly," she writes, " something entirely
peculiar in the sensation ot seeing oneself in print for the
first time. The lines burn themselves in upon the brain in
a way of which black ink is incapable in any other mode."
But her surprise was still greater when her eldest brother
returned from chapel to tea, and held out his hand for the
Repository. "They have got a new hand," he said. "Listen."
After a paragraph or two he repeated, " Ah ! this is a new
hand. They have had nothing as good as this for a long
time." At length, he said, "Harriet, what is the matter ?
I never knew you so slow to praise anything before."

So Harriet confessed, " I never could baffle any one. The
truth is, that paper is mine."

Her brother laid his hand on her shoulder, and said,
gravely, " Now, dear, leave it to other women to make
shirts and darn stockings. Do you devote yourself to this."

" I went home," says Harriet, " in a sort of dream, so that
the squares of the pavement seemed to float before my eyes.
That evening made me an authoress."

She now began her first work, *Devotional Exercises*, and
her brother (who soon afterwards died) gave her a great
many hints and much judicious praise. After writing this
book she gave up the practice of copying her MSS., but
wrote on straight without care or anxiety, only glancing to
see if a word was omitted or repeated, and never altering
a single phrase. In this she differs from almost all good
writers. Miss Edgeworth wrote her Tales over and over
again ; Charlotte Brontë corrected and revised repeatedly,
and so did Miss Mitford. But no dissatisfaction, no ques-
tioning that there could be a better way of expression, ever
crossed Harriet Martineau's mind. She herself knew per-

fectly what she meant to say. She said it, and that was enough.

Troubles soon came to the Norwich household ; one commercial crash was followed by another. Mr. Martineau's manufacturing business began to totter, and in 1822, worn out by anxiety, he died. He had done his best for his family, but they were now comparatively poor. Harriet had an attachment to a gentleman, who in prosperous days believed her rich ; he now generously came forward, and they were engaged. She was ill, she was deaf, but still under this gleam of sunshine she grew almost happy, and enjoyed the thought of the new life that opened before her. But her intended husband became suddenly insane, and after months of illness of body and mind, he died.

"It was happiest for us both," adds Harriet, "that our union was prevented by any means. I am, in truth, very thankful for not having married at all. My strong will, combined with liberty of conscience, makes me fit only to live alone, and my taste and liking are for living alone. I am provided with what it is the bane of a single life, in ordinary cases, to want—substantial, laborious, and serious occupation. My business in life has been to think and learn, and to speak out with absolute freedom what I have thought and learned. My work and I have been fitted to each other, as is proved by the success of my work and my own happiness in it."

An acquaintance of hers had put her in the way of corresponding with a "solemn old Calvinistic" publisher, Houlston, of Wellington, in Shropshire. He accepted the first two little eightpenny stories she sent him, and gave five pounds for them. Then he wrote to ask for more. Machine-breaking seemed a good subject, and a little story of *The Rioters* was written on it ; its success was such that some hosiers and lacemakers of Derby and Nottingham wrote to ask for a tale on *Wages*, which was, accordingly, written and called *The Turn-out*. Miss Martineau also wrote a good many tracts for Houlston, which he sold for a penny, and for which he gave her a sovereign apiece. For him was also written a long tale, *Principle and Practice*, and later on, a sequel to it was added. The new editor of the *Repository*, Mr. Fox, now made an appeal for literary aid, and Harriet sent him essays, reviews, and poetry ; he could give no money, but he gave her useful hints and criticism. Then a member of the Diffusion Committee asked for a Life of Howard the Philanthropist, and promised £30 for it. The Life was written, but no satisfactory answer could be got, and years afterwards the manuscript was found, dirty, marked, and snipped, at the bottom of a chest. An aunt now came to live with the Martineaus, and she was hardly settled, when a fresh misfortune took place. The manufactory in which the money of the widow and daughters had been placed, failed, and they never recovered more than the merest pittance. Harriet was left with precisely one shilling in her purse. The effect was like that of a blister upon a dull, weary pain. She rather enjoyed it, for there was necessity for action. One sister went out as a governess, the youngest taught the children of a relative until her marriage. Harriet's deafness shut her out from teaching, and she, her mother, and aunt lived on at the old house. She inquired about her Life of Howard without success. She had not enough now to pay for the postage of a thirteenpenny letter. Mr. Fox, the editor of the *Repository*, offered the only sum at his command, £15 a year, for as much reviewing as he required. To work Harriet went with needle and pen. Besides studying German, a few tales were written ; she brought them to London, made a volume of them, and called it *Traditions of Palestine*. But the book was not published till the following spring. She had no literary friends or connections, she could not get anything even looked at, so

7

that everything went into the *Repository* at last. Her
relations urged her to keep to fancy-work, by which they
thought she could alone earn money, so at fancy-work
she toiled all day, and after tea she went upstairs to her
literary work, and wrote till two or three in the morning.
She was thinking of remaining in London to undertake
proof-correcting or other literary drudgery, but her mother
sent for her to return to Norwich, and take the place of her
youngest sister. Back she went without prospects, with only
a piece of news, that the Central Unitarian Association had
advertised for three prize essays, in which Unitarianism was
to be presented to Catholics, Jews, and Mahometans. Ten
guineas were offered for the Catholic, fifteen for the Jewish,
and twenty for the Mahometan essay. Mrs. Martineau said
it might be well to try for one. "If I try at all it shall be
for all," answered Harriet.

The Essays were to be sent in by the 1st of March, and
Harriet wore herself thin writing, and dreamed of the
destruction of Jerusalem and the burning of the Temple
every night. One hot day in May, she came back to
London from a short visit in Kent. She had been eating and talking for an hour, when a daughter of the
house called out, "Oh! I forgot . . . I suppose . . . I
suppose you know about those Essays—those prize Essays,
you know?" "No, not I. What do you mean?" "Oh,
well! we thought . . we thought you knew." "Well,
but what?" "Oh! you have—why, you have got *all* the
prizes!"

So it really was. The secretary of the association had
called with a message from the committee, and soon came
a public meeting, at which Harriet heard little beyond
the beating of her own heart. With her prize money, she
went to Dublin to her brother, and now she planned out
her tales to illustrate different points of Political Economy.
Property, strikes, wages, banks, were to be the pivots on
which some of the tales were to turn. They were intended

to tell ordinary people about knotty questions which had
hitherto been kept for the wise and learned. The tales
were needed, so Harriet thought, and she was right, for
there was no easy popular way of teaching such subjects.
But the time for new ventures was unpropitious ; the
Reform Bill was pending, the cholera was at the door,
and men's hearts were failing them for fear. Harriet
visited Messrs. Baldwin and Craddock on her way home
through London. She opened out her scheme while they
sat "superb on their armchairs in their brown wigs." They
half consented to publish the series, and had even engaged
a stitcher for the monthly volumes, but the risk was too
great, and they withdrew their consent. Another publisher
was tried without success ; then Mr. Fox suggested a third.
Again Harriet went to London. It was the beginning
of December, foggy and sleety ; again she heard of the
Reform Bill and the cholera ; again came shakings of the
head and the ominous words, " No chance ! " Day after
day she came back to the brewery, where she was staying,
weary from trudging through the clay of the streets in the
gloomy December fog, but still wearier from disappointment.
She returned only to work, for the first two numbers of the
series must be ready in case of a publisher turning up. At
length, Mr. Fox brought a prospectus of terms from his
brother Charles. The work was to be published by subscription ; five hundred copies must be taken before it came
out, and if a thousand copies were not sold in the first
fortnight the publication was to be stopped. Hard terms
indeed ! Harriet was stunned at them. She took the prospectus to town, however, and then had to walk back four
miles and a half to the brewery. On the road, not far from
Shoreditch, she became too giddy to stand without support.
She leaned over some dirty palings, pretending to look at a
cabbage-bed, but saying to herself, with closed eyes, " My
book will do yet." She wrote her preface that evening,
and finished it as the brewery clock struck two. At four

o'clock she went to bed and cried herself to sleep ; but at half-past eight she was up again, preparing and sending out her circulars. Thin, yellow, and coughing with every breath, she returned to Norwich. The publisher's weekly letters were gloomy, and sometimes rude. " There is no chance of the work succeeding unless the trade takes it up better ; we have only one considerable bookseller's order for a hundred copies." But the turn of the tide was coming. The sale went up with a rush. A happy thought of Mrs. Martineau's had been acted on ; a circular had been sent to every member of Parliament, and soon two thousand, three, four, and five thousand copies of the Political Economy Tales had to be struck off. On the 10th of February, 1832, Harriet walked down the grass plat of the Norwich garden, and felt that her pecuniary troubles were over for ever !

At the age of thirty, Harriet Martineau had found her work. It pressed so much upon her that she decided to live in London, and she took lodgings at a tailor's shop in Conduit Street. The lodgings were up two pair of stairs, and she arrived at them on a dark foggy November morn- ing. But the fog had cleared away from her life, and the tide of success was flowing in full and strong. She made her coffee at seven o'clock, and wrote till two. She first made a skeleton plan of her whole course, and divided it into four—Production, Distribution, Exchange, and Con- sumption ; then she embodied each leading principle into a character. If she chose a foreign scene, she sent to the library for books of travel, then she reduced her materials into chapters. After that the rest was easy, and the story went off like a letter. She wrote twelve pages a day. Whoever takes up these tales now is filled first with intense dis- appointment, and then with utter amazement at their success. They are dry and heavy ; the descriptions are sometimes good, but the people resemble wooden blocks on which clothes are fitted at drapers' shops. They have no life, no individuality about them. They seem as if they were pinned and tacked together.

In the first tale, *Life in the Wilds*, a small body of South African settlers are stripped of their all by savages, and are left without even a hatchet or a nail—left with nothing but their clothes, the seeds in the ground, and their wits. From this we learn the elements of wealth and the division of labour ; dull conversations press the story down and make it almost unbearable. In *Ella of Garveloch* the scene is laid on a Scotch island ; here we see how rent increases with the value of the land. In *Weal and Woe in Garveloch* the question of over-population is touched, too many children are shown to be a positive evil, and Ella herself, instead of talking like a Scotch peasant, delivers long speeches full of Malthusian philosophy about the horrors of large families. Miss Martineau says she wrote this tale with the perspiration streaming down her face. She was quizzed in the *Times* by Moore for it, she was caricatured in *Fraser*, and ridiculed in the *Quarterly* by Lockhart, who found out many errors in her system though she could not see them herself, for she was so certain that she was right that it never occurred to her that she could be wrong. Her power of describing countries which she had never seen was certainly remarkable ; by a few hints gathered from books she conjured up a very successful idea of a foreign land. This is especially seen in *The Charmed Sea*, in which Siberia plays a part. The object of this tale is to show the origin of currency in place of barter. "The Siberian market," says Lockhart, "was carried on briskly for a whole day on *five* mouse-skins! These being carried off by the cat or by a travelling fur-trader, the colonists had recourse to a new kind of money, consisting of mammoth-bones." In *Cousin Marshall* alms-houses and lying-in hospitals are denounced as most injurious. The tale on Ireland is weak and flabby. Lockhart truly says that Political Economy is far better taught by Miss Edgeworth in *Castle Rackrent* and *The Absentee*.

Berkeley the Banker is a tale in which some of Miss Martineau's own experience is brought in. There is really a powerful bit when Hester, the innocent wife, is sent out to pass forged notes without knowing them to be such. Her dismay at the discovery, combined with her affection for her husband, might be worked up into a tragedy. But tragedy had no part in Miss Martineau's plan, and as for wit or humour, in both she was singularly deficient.

Smuggling was dealt with in *The Loom and the Lugger.* Not knowing whether there was a lighthouse at Beachy Head, she set off with a letter of introduction to a farmer, whose daughters proposed a walk to the Head before dark. Carrying a new loaf and a bottle of beer, they set off, and the indefatigable authoress learned "all about" the doings of smugglers. Next morning she flew off to Pevensey Castle and back to London in the coach, writing on her knees to avoid jolting. After her arrival, fourteen notes had to be written before she hurried off to dine with Lady S——.

Her mother and aunt had joined her, and a small house was taken at Fludyer Street, Westminster. Here she gave literary *soirées*, which were crowded to the doors. In spite of her deafness, which obliged her to use a trumpet, she dined out every day but Sunday. Visitors poured in, and floods of invitations, blue-books, and suggestions came from all quarters. Sydney Smith said that she might have managed the business of calling, by sending round an inferior authoress in a carriage to drop the cards! Carlyle was not one of her admirers; she often went to his house at Cheyne Row, but her self-sufficiency and self-assertion jarred on him. He remarks in his *Reminiscences* that her talent might have made a " quite shining matron of some big female establishment, mistress of some immense dress-shop, but was totally inadequate to grapple with deep spiritual and social questions, into which she launched, nothing doubting."

When she had finished one series of Tales she began

another—*Illustrations of Taxation.* It seems amazing to hear that the Chairman of the Excise Committee sent to say that he would be obliged for her suggestions, and Mr. Wickham, who had been struck by the mischief of the duty on starch, cried out when he met her in the street, " Oh ! Miss Martineau, starch, starch ! " But she had found her subject and stuck to it—*Green glass bottles, soap and sweets!* She is very happy in her titles. *The Farrers of Budge Row,* though it is a dull story about annuities, piques one's curiosity strangely, and the names of some of her chapters—" Midsummer Moonlight," " Fasters and Feasters," " A Harvest Eve," " Nothing but a Voice," are striking and attractive.

The Queen, then Princess Victoria, was a great admirer of *Ella of Garveloch,* and ran to her mother with a hop, skip, and a jump, to show the advertisement of the Taxation Series. In 1834 this series was finished, and Harriet went into St. James's Park for the first thoroughly holiday walk she had taken for two years and a half. Walking, to her, felt very like flying ; the grass under foot, the sky overhead, the trees around, were wholly different from what they had appeared before. The circulation of the series had reached ten thousand in England, and she had received a little more than two thousand pounds for the whole work. Best of all, she had got popularity and a hearing. One gentleman who took up *Demerara* before dinner could not lay it down till it was finished, and the little books were on every one's table, and the talk of the town. At a dinner at Rogers's she related how a letter addressed to the "Queen of Modern Philanthropists" had been sent to her, with " Try Miss Martineau " in the corner.

She now resolved on a visit to America, and left Liverpool for New York early in August, 1834. In America she was fêted, caressed, almost worshipped by the antislavery party. Sonnets were written to her ear-trumpet, six carriages were offered at Charleston for her use, and cambric handkerchiefs were worked with emblems of her

character and fame ! Her former plainness no longer
existed. She had a face of simple, cheerful strength, with
light and sweetness in the play of feature, and eyes steadily
alert, as if they were seeking something. A certain Mr.
Loring asked his Caroline if she were not jealous of his
growing too fond of Harriet Martineau; his "glorious wife"
answered, "Oh no, take all the comfort you can out of
her." When she ran the risk of being lynched at an
Abolitionist meeting, and actually spoke at it, the adula-
tion knew no bounds.

Back again in England, her arrival was announced in the
Morning Chronicle, and no fewer than three publishers
competed for the honour of bringing out her travels. Two
of them ran against one another on the stairs, and finally
Mr. Saunders carried off the prize for £900. *Society in
America* was followed by a work of a lighter kind, *Retro-
spect of Western Travel*. In 1837 an Economical Magazine
was contemplated, and Miss Martineau was to be editor
of it, but her brother James was against the plan, and she
gave it up, and was at liberty to think of her novel of *Deerbrook*. This book is certainly her masterpiece. She admired
Miss Austen, and it is something in Miss Austen's style. It
deals with middle-class society; she would have nothing to
do with the "silver fork" school ; the hero, Edward Hope,
is a village doctor, and the Misses Ibbotson are young
ladies from Birmingham. The story opens when their
cousins, the Greys, are expecting them on a visit to the
country village of Deerbrook. Dr. Hope falls in love with
Margaret, the second sister, while Hester, the elder and
prettier, is smitten with *him*. He is told of her liking, and
considers himself bound to marry her. After the marriage
Margaret lives with the Hopes, and the struggles of the
doctor against his affection, Margaret's love for Mr. Enderby,
and Hester's uncomfortable temper are capitally told. At
last, victory comes. Dr. Hope conquers his affection for
Margaret, and she, in spite of a village mischief-maker, is

married to Philip Enderby. Everything in *Deerbrook* is good ; it is thoroughly interesting and true to life, and full of noble sayings. For instance—

" I believe half the misery in our lives is owing to straining after happiness. What have we to do ? To rest the care of each other's happiness upon Him whose care it is ; to be ready to do without it. Depend upon it, this happiness is too subtle and divine a thing for our management. Men say of it, 'Lo ! it is here,' but never has man laid hold of it with a voluntary grasp."

" If the temper of the hour is right, nothing is wrong."

Charlotte Brontë might well say that in reading *Deerbrook* she tasted a new and keen pleasure and experienced a genuine benefit. While engaged on *Deerbrook* Miss Martineau also wrote the little manuals called *Guides to Service*. She had the great good fortune to be present at the Queen's coronation in June, 1838. Dressed in pearls, blonde, and crape, she went to Westminster at four o'clock in the morning, took her seat in the gallery, and watched the wonderful sight of peers and peeresses in their robes, and Prince Esterhazy in his diamonds. She admits that the homage of the peers, the self-coroneting of the peeresses, and the acclamation when the Queen was crowned were very animated, but she does not forget to observe the old hags with their dyed or false hair, and their necks and arms so brown that they made her sick. She had little enthusiasm, and calls the festival a highly barbaric one. After attending a meeting of the British Association at Newcastle, she went to the Lake district, to Scotland, and then abroad. Walking up a hill in Germany, one of her companions observed that she was on the brink of a terrible illness. So it turned out. She was brought home by the shortest way and was laid on a sick bed, first at Newcastle, and then at Tynemouth, for six long years.

Deerbrook had come out in the spring of '39, and she now began *The Hour and the Man.* Miss Nightingale thinks it the finest historical romance in the language ; but few will agree with her. It is vastly inferior to *Deerbrook* in life and interest. Miss Martineau had not enough imagination to create an historical romance, though her hero was Toussaint l'Ouverture. Her children's books—*The Settlers at Home, Feats on the Fjord,* and *The Crofton Boys*—were all written from the sick-bed at Tynemouth, and have found great favour with the child-world. *The Crofton Boys* is specially good : the style is admirably simple and clear, and there is a realisation of the character of the boys which we do not find in the Political Economy Tales. George Eliot mentions reading it, and having some delightful crying over it. *Life in the Sick-room* was written faster than any of Harriet Martineau's books. To use her own words, " It went off like sleep. I was hardly conscious of the act, so strong was the need to speak."

About this time she had the honour of refusing a pension from Earl Grey ; it was a period of public adversity, and she preferred sharing the poverty of the many to be helped out of the public purse. Three Prime Ministers—Earl Grey, Lord John Russell, and Mr. Gladstone—proposed giving her a pension at different times, but she always refused, as it was against her principles to burden the State. A subscription was, however, raised for her, and brought in £1,400. Comforts flowed in from all sides, and Sydney Smith said that every one who sent her game, fruit, or flowers was sure of heaven, provided they punctually paid the dues of the Church of England. She was at length advised to try mesmerism, and the consequence was—a perfect cure ! She even mesmerised others, and succeeded in curing them.

A year after she had been lying a helpless sufferer on her sick-bed, she was walking out in a snow-storm looking for lodgings at the Lakes. Her mother had settled with her married children at Liverpool, and so

Harriet was free. Seeing a rocky knoll with a charming view, she bought it for five pounds, and began to build a house on her own plan. It was built of dark grey Westmoreland stone, with large bay-windows, gables, and clustering chimneys. It was soon covered with ivy, roses, and passion-flower, and the porch was a bower of honeysuckles. Her "farm of two acres" was flanked by an oak copse and enclosed by a fence of larchwood entangled with rose-bushes. Farther down was the farm-servants' cottage and the little roothouse with its young pine-trees and pollard willows. The village of Ambleside was below. Beyond the church spire, rose the Furness Fells, and through the branches of an oak-tree a gleam of Lake Windermere was seen. The Knoll was a perfect poem—sunny within and without. The costly sun-dial, the gift of a friend, was made of grey granite in the shape of a Gothic font; it caught the eye like a gleaming spark. The motto, "Come, Light, visit me," was approved by Wordsworth, who was one of Harriet Martineau's neighbours.

She was now forty-five, and considered herself settled among the rushing of mountain streams and the soothing sough of the wind in the valley of the Rothay. But on a visit to Liverpool to her friends, the Yates's, they proposed a tour to the East, Mr. Yates finding the piastres. She consented to join them, and the party set out for the Nile and Egypt—to Judea and Hebron. The result was a bulky volume on *Eastern Life.* Miss Martineau's *Forest and Game Law* had been a failure, and she took special pains with *Eastern Life.* When she came home she began to give lectures on her travels at Ambleside, first to the school-children, then her audience extended to the workpeople about, but no gentry were admitted. She lectured on sanitary subjects, on the history of England and America, and instituted a building society. Her next book was a *History of the Peace*, which took her a whole year of industry. She rose at six and took a walk, returning to her solitary breakfast at half-past seven.

Her household affairs, indoors and out, were settled by half-past eight, and she worked on till two. Among her visitors was Charlotte Brontë, who says, "She is a great and good woman—not without peculiarities. She is both hard and warm-hearted, abrupt and affectionate. I believe she almost rules Ambleside. Her house is very pleasant both within and without, arranged with neatness and comfort. Her visitors enjoy the most perfect liberty. I pass the morning in her drawing-room, she in her study. We meet at two, talk and walk till five."

Here is another view of her from Hawthorne's Note Book :—

"I saw Miss Martineau," he says, "a few weeks since. She is a large, robust, elderly woman, but withal has so kind, cheerful, and intelligent a face that she is pleasanter to look at than most beauties. Her hair is of a decided grey, and she does not shrink from calling herself old. She is the most continual talker I ever heard ; it is really like the babbling of a brook, and very lively and sensible too. All the while she talks she moves the bowl of her ear-trumpet from one to another so that it becomes quite an organ of intelligence and sympathy between you and herself. It seems like the antennæ of some insects ; if you have any remark to make you drop it in. All her talk was about herself and her affairs ; but it did not seem like egotism, because it was so cheerful and free from morbidness."

Ever since her cure by mesmerism her religious beliefs had been undergoing a change, further developed by her friendship with Mr. Atkinson, a freethinking philosopher for whom she had an unquestioning admiration. Between them they wrote *Letters on Man's Development*, sometimes called the H. M. Letters, in which their confession of faith, or rather *un*faith, is fully given to the world. It is a lamentable fact that Harriet Martineau's strong mind should have been so darkened by this shallow thinker, who, as Charlotte Brontē says, " serenely denies us our hope in immortality, and quietly blots from man future heaven and the life to come." This chapter of Harriet Martineau's life, though she looked upon it with complacence, seems almost incomprehensible. Her brother James wrote, " Nothing in literary history is more melancholy than that Harriet Martineau should be prostrated at the feet of such a master, should lay down at his bidding her early faith in moral obligation, in the living God, in the immortal sanctities." Yet, marvellous to relate, she was serenely convinced that she was right. Carlyle quotes Lady Ashburton's words, and applies them to Harriet Martineau's profession of atheism. " A stripping of yourself naked, not to the skin only, but to the bone, and walking about in that guise." Whatever concerned herself she immediately confided to the public. She was deaf, she wrote her *Letter to the Deaf;* she was sick, she wrote *Life in the Sick Room;* she became an atheist, and she joined in writing the H. M. Letters, to announce the fact to the world. She was never disturbed from her self-complacency. She was disappointed in Wordsworth, she lamented Carlyle's unpopularity, Miss Mitford's flattery, and Charlotte Brontë's touchiness, but she was never disappointed in herself. She always seems to be saying, " What fools other people are, and what a wise, sensible woman I am ! "

Her next work was to translate the French philosopher Comte's book on Positive Philosophy—a herculean task, as she had to condense a great part of it. The execution of it was excellent, but it added another stone to the denial of her faith. Then came her connection with the *Daily News.* She wrote for this paper above sixteen hundred leading articles, at the rate, sometimes, of six a week, and there was something remarkable in the " patness," clearness, and ᵗforce of her papers. She was the first lady journalist, and one of the very best there has ever been. She had all the qualifications for journalism, prompt-ness, decision, and a capacity for grasping and condensing facts. She thought clearly, she wrote clearly, she spoke clearly. In 1851, being asked to write stories for *Household Words*, she refused to do so, from sheer inability to write fiction well ; she proposed instead to try her hand at describ-ing some of the Birmingham manufactures. Here again her peculiar happiness in the choice of titles was seen. The paper on electro-plating was called " Magic Troughs at Bir-mingham "—the papier-mâché works " Flower Shows at a Birmingham Hothouse "—the flour-mills " The Miller and his Men "—Coventry ribbons " Rainbow-making"—the slate works at Valentia, " Hope with a Slate Anchor." These articles were all reprinted. Her contributions to the *West-minster Review* brought on an intimacy with George Eliot, who, in one of her letters, says : " Miss Martineau is the only Englishwoman that possesses thoroughly the art of writing." In October of the same year (1852) George Eliot paid a visit to the Knoll, and says: " Miss Martineau was at the gate with a beaming face to welcome me. She is charming in her own house, quite handsome from her animation and intelligence. She came behind me, put her hands round me, and kissed me on the forehead, telling me she was so glad she had got me here."

Another of her visitors was James Payn, the novelist, then a very young man, who came to see her with an introduc-tion from Miss Mitford. In his *Literary Recollections* he describes her as a " lady of middle age, with a smile on her kindly face, and her trumpet at her ear." The acquaintance ripened into intimacy, and when he settled at Ambleside, a year afterwards, he went in and out of the Knoll as he pleased. Though she says in her *Autobiography* that, with the exception of Mrs. Marsh's *Two Old Men's Tales*, she never once succeeded in getting a manuscript published for anybody, Mr. Payn believes that he owes his appearance in the *Westminster Review* (an article on Ballads for the People) to her influence. "I wish," she writes to him, "I could have done a twentieth part of the good I wish you." He tells a story of how she used her ear-trumpet as a weapon of defence against a bull in a field.

One satirical philosopher said she had no need for ear-trumpets, she talked so much herself. "Does she mean to say that she ever wore one ear-trumpet out in all her life in listening to what anybody had to say?"

In 1854 she had repeated attacks of illness, but during a stay at Upper Norwood she wrote frequent articles for the *Westminster Review*, and gave herself little rest. She had constant sinking fits, and thought she might die in the night, so she sent for her executor, made her will, and prepared to die. "I find death in prospect," she said, "the simplest thing in the world." To her it was nothing but extinction. Then she wrote her autobiography, and waited for death ; but it did not come for twenty years. Her busy life still went on. She wrote leaders for the *Daily News*, and a *Guide to the English Lakes*, she worked cushions in Berlin wool, and entertained numerous visitors. She died in the summer sunset of her Ambleside home on the 27th of June, 1876.

Her biographer, Mrs. Chapman, has done her best to make her ridiculous ; she compares her to Joan of Arc, to Deborah, who sat under a palm-tree for forty years judging Israel ; and informs us that her initials, H. M., stood with the Abolitionist party for Her Majesty ! Harriet Martineau was, in fact, a woman with a strong mind, a vigorous brain, great personal influence, and much nobility of character. The great popularity she enjoyed during her life will not follow her. Her *Political Economy Tales* are quite forgotten, her *History of the Peace* is seldom read ; no one looks at the H. M. Letters. When we think of her it is well to forget the disciple of Mr. Atkinson ; she is best remembered as the useful practical writer, full of shrewd common sense, and as the author of *Deerbrook*, *The Crofton Boys*, and *Settlers at Home*.

V.

LETITIA ELIZABETH LANDON
(MRS. MACLEAN).

1802-1838.

Birth at Hans Place—The laurel-tree—Trevor Park—Affection for her nurse—At Old Brompton—The poetess of love—Death of her father—Miss Spence's literary *réunions*—*The Improvisatrice*—Cruel attacks—*The Troubadour*—*The Golden Violet*—*Romance and Reality*—*Francesca Carran*—Rupture of her engagement with Mr. Forster—Marriage with Mr. Maclean—Tragic death at Cape Coast Castle.

THERE was once a magic in the three initials " L. E. L." which we of the present day can hardly understand. The melancholy, melodious poetry which belonged to those initials set young people weeping, and made the old feel young again. Since that time poetesses have become as plenty as blackberries, but none have ever sung with that peculiar sweetness and plaintive grace which belongs to L. E. L. alone. She was welcomed at first with a burst of praise ; by contemporary critics she was even compared to Shakespeare, and her poems had a circulation only equalled by that of *Lalla Rookh*. When the news of her tragic end arrived, there was a nine days' wonder, then came speculations as to who would now fill the pages of the *Literary Gazette* and the *New Monthly*, who would edit *Fisher's Drawing-room Scrap-book* and supply a new volume to Longman's list. In a few years the authoress,

LETITIA E. LANDON.

BORN AUGUST 14TH, 1802; DIED OCTOBER 15TH, 1838.

her genius, her sorrows, and her fate, were almost forgotten; we just know that she lived, and that is nearly all. Yet she still takes a place in the history of literature, and her sister poet, Elizabeth Barrett Browning, has not forgotten to throw a flower on her grave.

Letitia Elizabeth Landon was born on the 14th of August, 1802, at 25, Hans Place, Chelsea. Her father was the eldest of a large family, and belonged to the Landons of Herefordshire. At the time of his daughter's birth he was a partner in the house of Adair, a prosperous army agent in Pall Mall. Mrs. Landon had been a Miss Catherine Jane Bishop with a fortune of £14,000, " a horse and a groom." She was a personal friend of the great Mrs. Siddons, and she used to say, " Sally Siddons worked the first cap ever put on my Letitia's head when she was a baby." The house in Hans Place had two pleasant drawing-rooms, and a third which made a sort of conservatory boudoir, and looked out on a garden full of roses. There was also a laurel-tree.

" How well I remember it," says L. E. L. in her *Traits and Trials of Early Life*, "that single and lonely laurel-tree! It was my friend, my *confidante*. How often have I sat rocking on the one like pendent branch which drooped even to the grass below! I can remember the *strange pleasure I took in seeing my tears fall* on the bright shining leaves; often while observing them I have forgotten the grief which led to their falling. I was not a pretty child, and both shy and sensitive; I was silent, and therefore not amusing. No one loved me but an old nurse. Why she should have been fond of me I know not, for I gave her much trouble. She was far advanced in years, but still strikingly handsome. Her face, with its bold Roman profile and large black eyes, is still before me as I used to see it bending over my crib, or rather crooning me to sleep with the old ballad ' Barbara Allan.' Never will the most finished

8

music be so sweet in my ears as that untaught and monotonous tone."

Letitia had a brother, Whittington, some years younger than she was. She went alone to learn to read from an invalid neighbour, who used to scatter letters on the floor, and tell her pupil to name them after her, and then form them into words. " She must have been very quick," says her brother, "for she used to bring home many rewards, and I began to look eagerly for her coming back."

If she had been unsuccessful she crept up to her nurse to be consoled. At five years of age she went as a day scholar to a school in Hans Place—No. 22—the very same to which Mary Russell Mitford had been sent a few years before. Miss Rowden was now the head of it, and as fond of poets and poetry as ever. L. E. L. was the youngest child in the school, and it was said that the only fault that could be found with her was that she could never " walk steadily from joyousness of spirits." Her disposition must have been like an April day, full of tears and smiles. When she was seven years old her father removed to Trevor Park, East Barnet. Here her first great grief, parting with her nurse, who chose to marry, came ; and she vividly describes the acuteness of her sorrow as she watched the coach pass along the windings of the green hedges and stop at the gate. She clung to her nurse ; she implored her to let her go with her. " Make me your own child ! " she cried. But the only answer she got was, " How tiresome the child is ! I shall have to see the coach go without me." Poor crushed Letitia says : " How often have I since exclaimed, ' I am not beloved as I love ! ' " " I walked slowly away from the gate," she adds, " without looking back. I heard the horn echo in the air, and flung myself down on the grass, the words, ' How tiresome the child is ! ' still ringing in my ears." A severe attack of illness followed. Her nurse had left her a present of *Robinson Crusoe ;* at first she could not bear to look at

it, but when once she opened it, enchantment began. "I
went to sleep with the cave, its parrots and goats, floating
before my closed eyes. I wakened in some rapid flight
from the savages landing in their canoe." A large curly-
coated dog, Clio, became her man Friday; with this companion she wandered about the "large, old, somewhat
dilapidated place, where the flowers grew in the luxuriance
of neglect over the walks, and the shrubs drooped to the
very ground, heavy with leaves and bloom." There was a
large deep pond, too, with a little island on it.

"One side of the pond was covered with ancient willow-
trees whose long pendent branches drooped for ever over
the same mournful mirror. One of these trees, by a natural
caprice, shot out direct from the bank a huge straight
bough, so that a rapid spring enabled me to gain the island,
where I would remain hidden in the deep shades of these
gloomy trees."

Misfortunes seemed always hovering about her. Her
favourite dog, "the only being that missed her," was bitten
by an adder, and had to be shot, and Lucy, the beautiful
little girl who helped her to plant flowers on its grave, died
young. The history of her childhood she sums up in four
words—Sorrow, Beauty, Love, and Death.

She once went to a juvenile ball. She was dressed with
special care, and turned to leave the nursery with an unusual glow of complacency, one of the servants smoothing
down a rebellious curl. "As I passed, I heard the other
say, 'Leave well alone!' and I heard the rejoinder, 'Leave
ill alone, you mean! Did you ever see such a little plain
thing?'" At the ball she had the melancholy satisfaction
of sitting unnoticed in a corner, and when the lady of the
house insisted on her dancing, she fancied that every one
was laughing at her. When she had to advance by herself
the room swam round, her head became giddy, she left her

partner, sprang away, and took refuge in a balcony and a burst of tears. " For music I had no ear, for drawing no eye, and dancing was positively terrible to my timid temper." Still she found a sort of happiness in talking to herself, with what she called " her measuring stick " in her hand. If any one spoke to her, she said, " Oh, don't talk to me. I have such a delightful idea in my head." As she grew older she became devoted to Walter Scott, and knew the *Lady of the Lake* by heart. In her poem to the Great Unknown she tells how she peopled all the walks and shades

" With images of thine ;
This lime-tree was a lady's bower,
This yew-tree was a shrine ;
Almost I deemed each sunbeam shone
O'er bonnet, spear, and morion."

She had a remarkably generous nature. Her brother tells how he once asked her father for three shillings. By way of compromise, Mr. Landon proposed that his son should learn the ballad, " Gentle river, gentle river, lo, thy streams are stained with gore," and that if he did so he should have a new eighteenpenny-piece. The thirty verses seemed a terrible task to young Landon, but Letitia came to the rescue, repeated them correctly, and got the three shillings. She then tried to teach her brother the ballad. " I don't," he says, " remember whether I ever said it, but I do re- member that she gave me the three shillings." Another of her self-imposed tasks was teaching the gardener to read. He was thirty years old when he began, but he profited so well by his instructions that when he set up as a milkman he was able to keep his own books. During the Trevor Park days another daughter was born, who died early from consumption. Mrs. Landon gave up all her time to this new charge, and Letitia was left more than ever to herself to dream dreams and see visions as she might. Troubles, however, soon came. Mr. Landon took a farm, and lost

large sums by the mismanagement of his bailiff ; then the
failure of Adair's house plunged him into further difficulties,
from which he never recovered. The Landons now left
Trevor Park, and went to Old Brompton. Here it was
that a certain well-known journalist, Mr. W. Jerdan, editor
of the *Literary Gazette*, chanced to look out of his window
one morning, and saw a little girl trundling a hoop with one
hand and holding a volume of poems in the other. This little
girl, who occasionally peeped into her book as she ran, was
no other than the future poetess of the initials, then somewhat of a romp. Brompton wore at that time rather a
rural aspect. "Haymaking," we are told, "went on
in Brompton Crescent, monthly roses and honeysuckles
flourished in Brompton Row, Michael's Grove *was* a grove
though one might count the trees, and farther on were
lanes which penetrated beyond Old Brompton and termi-
nated in the country."

The mature man of letters began to take an interest in
the round-faced, poetry-reading, hoop-trundling little girl.
Some of her poems were shown to him, and he was amazed
at their promise. When she was only eighteen, a Swiss
narrative poem, *The Fate of Adelaide*, was published, and,
though she reaped no profit from it, the sale was very large.
In 1823 a great many of her short poems appeared in the
columns of the *Literary Gazette*, then a weekly journal of
considerable importance, edited by Mr. Jerdan. Her initials
became, as Mr. Blanchard says, "a name," critics began to
admire and praise, to talk of genius, and to wonder what
new star was this which had risen in the poetical firmament.
The late Lord Lytton (then Mr. Bulwer) tells how, when he
was an undergraduate at Oxford, there was always a rush
in the reading-room of the Union every Saturday for the
Literary Gazette, and an impatient anxiety to hasten at
once to that corner of the sheet which contained the three
magic capitals, L. E. L. "All of us," he says, "praised the
verse, and all of us guessed at the author. Was she young ?

was she pretty? and—for there were some embryo fortune-hunters amongst us—was she rich? The other day, in looking over some boyish effusions, we found a paper superscribed to L. E. L., and beginning, 'Fair Spirit!'"

L. E. L.'s early poetry is remarkably simple and natural; it flows without strain or effort. She is never diffuse or obscure, never tiresome, as Mrs. Hemans occasionally is. She is the poet of feeling, and her true womanly thoughts go at once to the heart. There is, too, a songfulness about the poems which is peculiar to herself. They seem to sing themselves. Here is part of one, written before she was twenty-one :—

> " Another day—another day,
>   And yet he comes not nigh,
> I look amid the dim blue hills,
>   Yet nothing meets my eye.
>
> I hear the rush of mountain waves
>   Upon the echoes borne,
> I hear the singing of the birds,
>   But not my hunter's horn.
>
> The eagle sails in darkness past,
>   The watchful chamois bounds,
> But what I look for comes not nigh,
>   My Ulric's horse and hounds.
>
> Three times I thus have watched the snow
>   Grow crimson with the stain
> The setting sun threw o'er the rock,
>   And I have watched in vain.
>
> I love to see the graceful bow
>   Across his shoulder flung,
> I love to see the golden horn
>   Beside his baldric hung.
>
> I've waited patiently, but now
>   Would that the chase was o'er!
> Well may he love the hunter's toil,
>   But he should love me more.

Why stays he thus ?   He would be here
    If his love equalled mine ;
    Methinks had I one fond caged dove,
    I would not let it pine."

L. E. L. delighted in melancholy, and love—"the dearest theme that ever waked a poet's dream "—love, unrequited, unblest—was the favourite subject of her muse. She dwelt upon every phase of it, much to the gratification of her female readers. Sometimes she becomes morbid, there is a tone of despair, an utter want of hope, which seems strange in one so young, and, as some say, so naturally joyous. Hers was essentially a love-needy nature. We are per-petually reminded of the forlorn child clinging to her nurse, and begging to be taken off in the stage-coach. All her life she seemed to be wandering through dry places, seeking rest and finding none, craving for love which always disappointed her. She used sometimes to say, " I believe there is a sort of curse hanging over us," and this idea she puts into verse when in one of her poems she addresses an imaginary being and says :—

    " I would not be beloved by thee,
        I know too well the fate
    That waits upon the heart which must
        Its destiny create ;
    A spirit passionate as mine
    Burns only to consume its shrine.
    I was not born for happiness,
        From my most early hours
    My hopes have been too brilliant fires,
        My joys too fragile flowers.
    Love still and deep as mine must be
        Content with its idolatry."

L. E. L. had a keen sympathy with Nature. Her descrip-tions of flowers and woods have a truth and pathos of their own that can only spring from a thorough love of her sub-ject. How simple is the following little song ! In its sweet-

ness, in its sentimentalism, it is essentially L. E. L.-ish.
It belongs to Miss Landon's earlier period before she had
learned that strength which came in after-years :—

> " Violets ! deep-blue violets !
> April's loveliest coronets.
> There are no flowers that grow in the vale,
> Kissed by the breeze, wooed by the gale,
> None by the dew of the twilight wet,
> So sweet as the deep-blue violet.
> I do remember how sweet a breath
> Came with the azure light of the wreath
> That hung round the wild harp's golden chords
> Which rang to my dark-eyed lover's words.
> I have seen that deep harp rolled
> With gems of the East and bands of gold,
> But it never was sweeter than when wet
> With leaves of the dark-blue violet."

About the time of L. E. L.'s first introduction to the
public her father died. The bond which held the family
together was snapped, and this young sensitive girl was left
without a protector at a most trying period of her life.
What her career might have been had her father been
spared would be a curious speculation. It is certain that
his loss to her was irreparable. For his memory she always
preserved great veneration, and in her poem of *The Troubadour* she thus alludes to him :—

> " My page is wet with bitter tears,
> I cannot but think of those years
> When happiness and I would wait
> On summer evenings at the gate.
> Then run for the first kiss and word,
> An unkind word I never heard.
> My father ! though no more thine ear
> Censure or praise of mine can hear,
> It soothes me to embalm thy name
> With all my love, my pride, my fame."

To make her father's loss still heavier, Letitia did not, as the phrase is, get on well with her mother. There was no sympathy between them, and there could be little love. Occasionally there seemed a sort of regretful fondness, but their tempers and dispositions clashed, and they could not agree. Poverty, too, in its grimmest and harshest aspect, threatened them, and the young poetess was now compelled to turn her rhymes and sonnets into hard cash, or else earn her bread in some other way. She made up her mind to go and live with her grandmother, Mrs. Bishop, in Sloane Street, and to work at her pen harder than ever she had done before. She soon fell in with a number of celebrities, great and small, who looked upon this new prodigy of the *Literary Gazette* as a sort of white elephant to be exhibited for their amusement. William Howitt says, " We have met L. E. L. She is a pretty, merry, fidgety, little damsel." One of her patronesses was Miss Spence, then known as the authoress of *Dame Rebecca Berry*, a production which had the honour of being attributed to the beautiful and witty Miss Rosina Wheeler, afterwards the first Lady Lytton.

L. E. L. has described these *bas-bleu réunions*, Miss Spence doing the honours in a velvet toque ; she was a little woman, almost as broad as she was long, and full of talk and flattery. Her "humble abode" (as she always called it in her notes of invitation) consisted of two rooms on the second floor of a house in Quebec Street, Marylebone. Tea was made in the back bedroom, and in the drawing-room the guests assembled. Amongst them was the rising author, Mr. Bulwer, handsome, courtly, and fastidious, very much in love with Miss Wheeler, who was one of the principal attractions of these *soirées*. Lady Caroline Lamb sometimes dropped in for half an hour, and took a great interest in L. E. L., who was at this time about twenty-two, and is described as a comely girl with a blooming complexion and very beautiful deep grey eyes — laughing eyes—with dark eyelashes. Her hair, never very thick, was of a deep brown, and as fine as silk. Her forehead was white and clear, and her eyebrows arched and well defined ; but oh, horror ! her nose was *retroussé*. She was also rather inclined to be fat—a crying sin in a sentimental poetess. As years went on her figure became slighter, and ended by being "neat and easy, if not graceful." Her mouth was arch, and well proportioned to her face ; and her feet and hands were small. People were almost startled when they saw how lively and vivacious this writer of lovelorn lyrics could be ; she was fond of dancing, liked gay talk and girlish ways, and scorned the idea that she wrote from her own experience.

In an account of a Christmas spent with her uncle at Aberford she tells how it was given out that she was the great London author ; she was, consequently, placed next the only young man of the company. She amazed him not a little by asking for a mince-pie, a dish of which she had been surveying for some time with longing eyes. His start discomposed a "no-age at all, silk-vested spinster," whose plate was thereby deposited on his lap ; and, to make matters worse, poor L. E. L. had to do without her mince-pie, for the astonished beau forgot to help her.

In 1824 Miss Landon's first long connected poem, *The Improvisatrice*, came out, and awakened a chorus of enthusiasm amongst her admirers. The *Literary Gazette* spoke in raptures of its originality of conception, fineness of imagination, generous feeling, glow of expression, and pathos. In one of the poems there was an allusion to the Greek poetess Sappho, and now L. E. L. was called another Sappho, with all Sappho's fire and power of song, and a purity that was all her own. *The Improvisatrice* is, of course, an Italian, who knows not which she "loves most, pencil or lute." Then comes the usual enchanter, and she begins to sing in good earnest :—

> " It was not song that taught me love,
> But it was love that taught me song.

I owned not to myself I loved,
No word of love Lorenzo breathed,
But I lived in a magic ring
Of every pleasant flower wreathed.
A brighter blue was on the sky,
A sweeter breath in music's sigh,
The orange-buds all seemed to bear
Fruit more rich and buds more rare.
There was a glory in the noon,
A beauty in the crescent moon,
A lulling stillness in the night,
A feeling in the pale star-light,
A spell in Poetry's deep store
That I had never marked before."

Some of L. E. L.'s isolated expressions are peculiarly happy. For instance, "Silence is love's own peculiar eloquence of bliss." Along with *The Improvisatrice* were included a variety of minor poems, *The Covenanters*, *The Bayadère*, *The Minstrel of Portugal*, *The Guerilla Chief*, &c., and all show how this young girl's fancy exulted in romantic and legendary scenes. One of her poems, *Good-night*, is a fair specimen of her easy versification, and has a graceful charm of its own :—

" Good-night ! what a sudden shadow
Has fallen upon the air !
I look not round the chamber—
I know he is not there.

Sweetness has left the music
And gladness left the light,
My cheek has lost its colour,
How could he say good-night ?

And why should he take from him
The happiness he brought ?
Alas ! such fleeting pleasure
Is all too dearly bought

If thus my heart stop beating,
My spirits lose their tone,
And a gloom like night surround me
The moment he is gone."

It was about this time that the first attempt to injure Letitia Landon's character was made in the *Sun* newspaper. Her name was coupled with that of Mr. Jerdan, her first literary friend. Such an attack was peculiarly cruel and unjust. "My soul writhes under the powerlessness of its anger," she says. "Because I am poor, unprotected, and dependent on popularity, I am a mark for gratuitous insolence and the malice of idleness and illnature." Circumstances had made her very much indebted to Mr. Jerdan, who was old enough to be her father. She was very grateful to him.

"I have not a friend in the world but himself," she writes, "to manage anything of business, whether pecuniary or literary. Place yourself in my position; could you have hunted London for a publisher, endured all the alternate hot and cold water thrown on your exertions, canvassed, nay, quarrelled over accounts the most intricate in the world?"

Her intercourse with Mr. Jerdan had been slight, ten or five minutes being the usual time for his visits as he called to look over papers and MSS. on his way to town, and they hardly ever met in the round of winter parties. But what can be easier than to "frown a reputation down"? A look, a nod, a whisper, and the thing is done. As Hamlet said to Ophelia, "Be thou chaste as ice, pure as snow, thou shalt not escape calumny." "The more I think of my past life," says L. E. L., "and of my future prospects, the more dreary do they seem. I have known little else than privation, disappointment, unkindness, and bereavement. From the time I was fifteen, my life has been one continual struggle in some shape or other with absolute poverty."

On account of her grandmother's death she had now to look about for another home. She would not return to her mother, because she disliked to be worried and annoyed, so she decided on taking up her quarters at Hans Place, in the very house where she had once gone to school. The Rowden *régime* was now over, and three maiden ladies, the Misses Lance, lived with their father, kept the school, and received two or three boarders. Amongst these boarders L. E. L. was now numbered. She dined with the school, and slept in a small attic looking out on the square. Here, too, she wrote, often without a fire in the middle of winter. If she did not "get on" with some people, others were enthusiastic in their admiration of her generosity, her vivacity of manner, her winning smile, her charming voice in speaking, and her willingness to appreciate others. She always had a welcome from Sir Edward and Lady Bulwer, and from Mrs. Wyndham Lewis (afterwards Mrs. Disraeli); and "Lady Emmeline Stuart-Wortley sought her out and introduced her to the Marchioness of Londonderry, at whose sparkling assemblies the young poetess was the star of the evening." In one of the long, low rooms at Hans Place, with a dim, dark paper, L. E. L. once gave a fancy ball, which was attended by the Bulwers and a host of literary friends.

She was often thoughtless and imprudent. Once she made a wreath of flowers for Mr. Jerdan, and rushed with it into a "grave and numerous party" to place it on his head. Another time, when she was sent a volume of Bernard Barton's poetry, she wrote him a full account of a ball she had been at, particularising all the dresses, and quite forgetting that she was writing to a sober Quaker. Yet nothing positively wrong could ever be brought against her. Reports of all kinds circulated briskly. One was that she had had two hundred offers of marriage. To this she answered that it was very unfortunate that the offers should resemble the passage to the North Pole and Wordsworth's *Cuckoo*, which were talked of, but never seen. Comments on her dress, which was sometimes fanciful, abounded. To this she replied, "That it was easy for those whose only trouble on that head was to change to find fault with her, who never in her life knew what it was to have two new dresses at a time."

The Improvisatrice was soon followed by *The Troubadour.* L. E. L.'s fancy exulted in the stirring scenes of a minstrel's life. Raymond wins the troubadour's prize and the favour of Eva, but he goes away and plights his troth ,to a high-born lady, Ellinor. On his return he finds Eva dead ; and the pyre is described struggling with the fierce winds of night :—

> " Red was the battle, not in vain
> Hissed the hot embers with the rain."

A vivid glow and fire of words bring out scene after scene ; we have an armed array .

> " Winding thro' the deep vale their way,
> Helmet and breastplate gleaming in gold,
> Banners waving their crimson fold."

A ruined castle is thus described :—

> " The hall was bare,
> It showed the spoiler had been there,
> E'en upon the very hearth
> The green grass found a place of birth."

And a stream is

> " So fierce, so dark, the torch's glare
> Fell wholly unreflected there."

But *The Troubadour* was almost put in the shade by the publication, in 1826, of *The Golden Violet,* which was said to be a " glorious triumph for the fair sex of England, and to show the possession of masculine powers along with womanly tenderness and pathos." The story was taken from Warton's mention of the Provence poetical competition for the prize of a golden violet. L. E. L. brings the minstrels of every country forward, and their various tales, romances, and ballads are recited to the lady who presides at the festival which is held on the 1st of May. The lot is first drawn by Vidal, who sings *The Broken Spell*, *a Provençal Romance of a Disenchanted Prince ;* then comes *The Falcon*, by a Norman knight, *The Child of the Sea*, by a Scottish minstrel, and so on. *Erinna* concludes the whole, and was considered by Lord Lytton L. E. L.'s best poem. There is not a doubt that she had gained in power immensely since her first poems ; there was now a fulness, a distinctness of tone which she had never had before. *The Venetian Bracelet*, her last published volume of poems, is one of her best. In a dramatic sketch, called *The Ancestress*, she rises to a height that she never attempted before. There is a mournful prophecy in the following :—

> "She had a strange sweet voice, the maid who sang,
> And early death was pale upon her cheek ;
> And she had melancholy thoughts that gave
> Their sadness to her spirit. None knew
> If she had loved, but always did her song
> Dwell on love's sorrows."

There is more than musical words—more than sweetness —there is force and fire in some parts of *The Ancestress.* The following passage has the intensity of feeling that belongs to the Juliets of the South. Every word has power in it :—

> "O, Jaromir, it is a fearful thing
> To love as I love thee, to feel the world,
> The bright, the beautiful joy-giving world,
> A blank without thee. . . .
> I have no hope that does not dream for thee,
> I have no joy that is not shared by thee,
> I have no fear that does not dread for thee.

The book drops listless down, I cannot read
Unless it is to thee ; my lonely hours
Are spent in shaping forth our future lives
After my own romantic fantasies :
He is the star round which my thoughts revolve
Like satellites."

Till 1831 L. E. L. had confined herself entirely to verse,
but in that year her first novel, *Romance and Reality,*
appeared, and showed powers of wit and satire that no one
had previously given her credit for. Lord Lytton calls it a
novel of great merit, and the author a lady of remarkable
genius. The heroine, Emily Arundel, is introduced to us
at a country house, and Lady Alicia Delawarr, who brings
her out in London society, is thus admirably described :—

"Few women think, but most feel. Lady Alicia did
neither. Nature had made her weak and indolent, and she
had never been placed in circumstances either to create or
call forth character. As an infant she had the richest of
worked robes and the finest of lace caps. The nurse was
in due time succeeded by the nursery governess, whose
situation was soon filled by the most accomplished person
the united efforts of fourteen countesses could discover.
Pianos, harps, colour-boxes filled the schoolroom, but Lady
Alicia had no ear for music, for dancing no time, and French
and Italian were somewhat unnecessary for one who considered her own language a needless fatigue. At eighteen
she came out. Beautiful she certainly was, accomplished,
for Lady F., her mother's intimate friend, had several times
confidentially mentioned the names of her masters, while
Lady C. expressed her approbation of the reserved dignity
which led the daughter of one of our oldest families to shun
that display which might gratify her vanity, but would
wound her pride. All was prepared for a ducal coronet,
at least ; when the very day after her presentation her father
went out of town and the Ministry together, and three long

years were wasted in the stately seclusion of Etheringham
Castle, where the mornings in summer were spent at a little
table by the window, and in winter by the fire cutting out
figures and landscapes in white paper. The middle of the
day was devoted to a drive if fine ; if wet, in wondering
whether it would clear. Dressing came next—a mere
mechanical adjustment of rich silks and jewels where vanity
was out of the question with no one to attract, and still
dearer hope, no one to surpass, for vanity is like those
chemical essences whose only existence is when called into
being by the action of some opposite influence. During
dinner, the earl lamented the inevitable ruin to which the
country was hastening, and after grace had been said, the
countess agreed with him, and observed that dress alone was
destroying the distinction of ranks, and that at church silks
were as common as stuffs. Here the conversation ceased,
and they returned to the drawing-room, the countess to
sleep, Lady Alicia to cut out more paper landscapes. Twice
a year there was a great dinner, to which she was regularly
handed down by the old Marquis of Snowdon, who duly
impressed upon her mind how very cold it was, and in
truth he looked like an embodied shiver. At one-and-
twenty an important change took place. Lady Alicia was
summoned from the manufacture of a little paper poodle
to the earl's own room, where she found her lady mother
sitting on an erect chair. What could have caused such
a change in the domestic economy of the castle ? What
but a circumstance that has caused many extraordinary
proceedings ? What but an offer of marriage ? "

Romance and Reality, though witty and sparkling,
wanted connection, and *Francesca Carrara*, L. E. L.'s
next novel, was considered an advance on it. It was dedicated to Mrs. Wyndham Lewis as " a slight remembrance
of her kindness." The story opens in Italy, proceeds to
France, describes the Parisian revels of the early days of

9

Louis Quatorze, and finally terminates in England when
Charles II. ascends the throne. Cardinal Mazarin, Christina
of Sweden, Charles, Buckingham, stern Puritans and reckless Royalists, are introduced with brilliant touches of
description. Some of the observations show a keen knowledge of human nature. For instance—

"Audacity, oddity, and flattery are the three graces which
make their way in modern society."

" Be necessary, let men have aught to hope from you,
forward in any way their interests, and it matters not how
you do it. Be harsh, abrupt, insolent, and it will only be
your way. People would, to be sure, rather attain their
object by trampling upon you, but sooner than not attain it
they will let you trample on them. . . .

" Climax of feminine indifference, she did not care how
she looked. . . . "

" When we recall how feverish, how wretched, how incomplete the life of mortality has been, we feel that the
present owes us a future. . . . "

"So much for anticipation in this life ! Had Francesca
been asked that morning what would give her the most
perfect happiness, she would have replied unhesitatingly,
her meeting with Evelyn. They had met, and she was
sorrowful even to weeping. Ah ! hope fulfilled is only
another word for disappointment."

Miss Landon's last prose works were *Traits and Trials of
Early Life*, and *Ethel Churchill*, by some considered her
best novel. In it Lady M. W. Montagu and Pope are
introduced at Strawberry Hill, and there are some well-
described scenes between Walter Maynard, the dramatic
author, and Ethel Churchill, the successful actress. L. E. L.
worked hard ; often she had to finish the concluding lines
of a poem as she rose from her bed, while the printer's boy
was waiting. She contributed to almost every magazine

of note, and wrote for no end of Keepsakes, Forget-me-nots, and albums. The profits of all her books amounted to about £2,500, the largest sum being £600 for *The Troubadour*. Out of her yearly income of £250 which she had realised, she devoted £100 to her mother and to her brother, who had taken his degree at Oxford.

She was in the height of her fame when Mr. Forster (the biographer of Dickens), then a young barrister, and the editor of the *Examiner*, made her an offer of marriage. No sooner had she accepted him than a host of kind friends came forward, and repeated those tales which are so easy to tell and so hard to disprove. *" Have you not heard this ? "* *" Oh, you must know that ! "* These tales Mr. Forster mentioned to his betrothed ; she referred him to those who knew her best. " Ask *them*, the married, respectable, trustworthy friends whom I see every day." All were unanimous in declaring these tales to be unfounded slanders. Mr. Forster was satisfied, but L. E. L. was too proud to consent to a marriage after being once doubted. " No ! " she answered, "I will never marry a man who has once distrusted me." The engagement accordingly came to an end. If any one suggested that it might possibly be renewed, she begged that the subject might never be mentioned, and declared that she was not really attached to Mr. Forster. But any one that knows a woman's heart, would doubt these vehement assertions, and would put them down to the struggles of a wounded spirit that vainly tries to hide what is working within. In giving up Mr. Forster, she gave up sympathy, protection, a happy home, literary society, everything that was necessary to her existence. Illness, too, she had to bear.

"I have suffered," she writes to Mr. Forster, "for the last three days a degree of torture that made Dr. Thomson say, 'You have an idea of what the rack is now ' ; it was nothing to what I suffered from my own feelings. Again I repeat that I will not allow you to consider yourself bound to me by any possible tie. I do every justice to your own kind and generous conduct. I am placed in a most cruel and difficult position. Give me the satisfaction of having, as far as rests with myself, nothing to reproach myself with. The more I think, the more I feel that I ought not—I cannot—allow you to unite yourself with one—accused of—I cannot write it. The mere suspicion is dreadful as death. Were it stated as a fact, that might be disproved. Were it a difficulty of any other kind, I might say, look back on every action of my life, ask every friend I have. But what answer can I give, or what security have I against the assertions of a man's vanity, or the slander of a vulgar woman's tongue ? I feel that to give up all idea of a near and dear connection is as much my duty to myself as to you. Why should you be exposed to the annoyance, to the mortification of having the name of the woman you honour with your regard coupled with insolent insinuations ? You never could bear it. I have just received your notes—God bless you—but . . . After Monday I hope I shall be visible, at present it is impossible." The letter ends with, "Under any circumstances, the most grateful and affectionate of your friends, LETITIA E. LANDON."

This certainly seems like the language of wounded pride, and love that would be trusted "all in all or not at all." No one could ever trace these fatal reports ; like some noxious night-bird they shrank from daylight and could never be discovered. It is an old truism that hearts are often caught in the rebound, and many a high-minded woman's first impulse is, "Since I cannot marry the man I like, I will take the first one that asks me." Thus it was with L. E. L.

One evening she went to a party at a friend's house in Hampstead. Among the guests was Mr. George Maclean, governor of Cape Coast Castle. He was considered a hero in a small way, he had put down an insurrection of natives, and the party was specially invited to do him honour. L. E. L. had got up such an enthusiasm about this very poor specimen of a warrior that she wore a Scotch scarf over her shoulders, and a sash of the Maclean tartan. She had now left the Miss Lance's establishment, and was living with a lady of large fortune in Hyde Park. By this lady and her husband she was treated as a daughter, a carriage and drawing-room were put at her disposal, and she had every external advantage. Mr. Maclean saw and was conquered. He was a grave, silent, spare Scotchman, between thirty and forty, who cared little for poetesses, still less for their fancy or imagination ; but something about this poetess attracted him, and they were soon engaged to be married. He left London shortly afterwards, answered no letters, and when he returned made no apology or excuse for his mysterious silence. Rumour gave out that he had already a native wife in Africa ; but he denied the assertion, and Miss Landon was satisfied. Harriet Martineau mentions meeting her twice ; the first time she found her " very pretty, kind, simple, and agreeable ; " the second time, just before her marriage, " she was listless, absent, melancholy. Nothing seemed to rouse her from her listless gloom."

On the 7th of June, 1838, she was married to Mr. Maclean very privately at St. Mary's, Bryanston Square. Her brother performed the ceremony, and Sir E. Bulwer (as Lord Lytton then was) gave her away. The day of the Queen's coronation (the 20th of June) was the last when L. E. L. was publicly seen. She watched the crowds that filled the streets from Crockford's Club. She wore a plain muslin dress and a white bonnet, and in the evening, amidst cheering and illuminations, a dinner was given at which Sir E. Bulwer proposed the health of " his daughter " in a graceful speech. On setting off to Portsmouth a few days afterwards, she was interested and excited at this her first journey in a railway train. "What will you do without your friends to talk to?" asked her brother at the hotel. "Oh!" she answered, "I will talk to them through my books."

She had planned work which would take her three years to finish. Dinner on board the ship went off cheerfully, and then the brother and sister parted for ever. "My sister," says Mr. Landon, "remained standing on the deck and looking towards us as long as we could see her figure against the sky." During the voyage she composed two of her most finished poems, *The Polar Star*, and *The Night at Sea*. They were her swan songs. On the 25th of June she left England, and on the 15th of August arrived at Cape Coast Castle. The very first experience of this ill-omened spot was unpleasant. Mr. Maclean left the ship in a fishing-boat at two o'clock on a dark foggy night. He returned wet to the skin, and had found his secretary dead. At first the bride did her best to like her new position; then the fact oozed out that she never saw a living soul but the servants from eight in the morning till seven in the evening, and that her husband stayed in a part of the fort to which she was forbidden to enter. She admitted that she thought him strange and reserved, but not actually unkind. He complained of illness, and she went to his room to bring him some arrowroot.

On the 15th of October, 1838, Emma Bailey, who was acting as temporary servant, went into Mrs. Maclean's room. There was a weight against the door; she pushed it, and found the ill-fated L. E. L. lying with her face against the floor, an empty bottle which had contained prussic acid in her hand. There was a slight bruise on one cheek, and Mrs. Bailey thought she heard a faint sigh. The surgeon and Mr. Maclean were called, the body was lifted to the bed, but the spirit had flown. The modern Sappho—the bright, the brilliant, the enthusiastic L. E. L.—had ceased to breathe. A letter lay on the table, the ink scarcely dry. It was a letter to her dearest Maria (Mrs. Fagan), and told how the writer was enacting the part of a feminine Robinson Crusoe :—

"I am in excellent health," she continues. "The solitude, except an occasional dinner, is absolute." Then she tells of a few visits from the Dutch governor, "a most gentlemanlike man, for whom I had to make breakfast, as Mr. Maclean would not get up. On all sides we are surrounded by the sea. I like the perpetual dash upon the rocks ; one wave comes up after another and is for ever dashed to pieces like human hopes that only swell to be disappointed. We advance—up springs the shining froth of love or hope, a moment white and gone for ever. The land view, with its cocoa and palm trees, is very striking ; it is like a scene in the Arabian Nights. Of a night the beauty is very remarkable ; the sea is of a silvery purple, and the moon deserves all that has been said in her favour. I have only been once out of the fort by daylight, and then was delighted. The salt lakes were first dyed of a deep crimson by the setting sun, and as we returned they seemed a faint violet in the twilight, just broken by a thousand stars, while before us was the red beacon-light. Dearest, do not forget me ; write about yourself ; nothing half so much interests your affectionate

"L. E. MACLEAN.
"CAPE COAST CASTLE, *October* 15th."

Such a letter set aside the supposition of suicide. Then it was believed that L. E. L. had taken an overdose of prussic acid by accident, as some thought she was in the habit of taking it to relieve spasms. A verdict was returned to this effect. But her English doctor denied that she had ever suffered from spasms, and no prussic acid had been furnished in the medicine-chest which she had brought out with her. Dark suspicions rested on her husband, or on a little native boy who had brought her a cup of coffee just before her death.   But the boy was not examined, nor were the dregs of the cup analysed.   Inquest, funeral, and all were over six hours after L. E. L. had breathed her last. A cloud of mystery and gloom will always rest over her end.   She died at the age of thirty-six, and was married hardly four months.

In a posthumous novel, *Lady Anne Granard*, which was completed by her friend Emma Roberts, the opening sentence is as follows : " No one dies but some one is glad of it."

The observation is terribly true ; but if any one were glad at L. E. L.'s death, thousands felt a sensation of personal loss at the thought of such a variously-gifted being snatched away just when life was strongest, and her powers were at their prime.   As Elizabeth Barrett said :—

> '' Hers was the hand that played for many a year
> Love's silver phrase for England, smooth and well.'

But the last question that came from her across the solemn sea was not for fame, but for affection : " Do you think of me as I think of you, my friends, my friends ? "

Before the answer could come, a stone lay over her grave in the grim castle-yard, the wind sighed through the palm-trees, and the sullen waves boomed on.

THE HONOURABLE MRS. NORTON.

BORN 1808 ; DIED JUNE 15TH, 1877.

(From a Painting by HAYTER.)

VI.

HONOURABLE MRS. NORTON (LADY STIRLING-MAXWELL).

1808-1877.

Birth—*The Dandies' Rout*—The Three Graces—At a Ball at Almack's—
Sings duets with Moore—Marriage to Hon. George Norton—A bunch
of beautiful creatures—Editor and contributor to Annuals—Her three
sons—*The Undying One*—Unhappy married life—Separation from
Mr. Norton—*The Dream*—*Stuart of Dunleath*—*The Lady of La
Garaye*—*Lost and Saved*—*Old Sir Douglas*—At Lansdowne House—
Second marriage with Sir W. Stirling-Maxwell—Death.

F EW women writers have had such a stormy and eventful life as Mrs. Norton, afterwards Lady Stirling-
Maxwell. We call her by the more familiar name of Mrs.
Norton, as that was the one by which she was best known
to the reading public. Possessed of talent, wit, beauty,
grace, it seemed—to use the simile of the well-known
nursery tale—as if all the good fairies had presided at her
baptism ; but some spiteful one must unfortunately have
been left out, who made the good gifts of the others of no
avail. In spite of them all, Caroline Norton's life was
clouded with sadness and gloom. Married to a man utterly
unworthy of her, she had to contend with the unspeakable
misery of an ill-assorted union ; then came a time of torture
in which her soul was wrung to its very centre, and then
forty years of secret struggles and bitter loneliness of spirit.

After this came a brief space of peace and calm, but the long troublous day was fast ringing to evensong; the once fascinating Caroline Norton was not Lady Stirling-Maxwell for more than three short months, and the close of her life resembled the bright but fleeting sunshine of a November afternoon, which is gone almost as we gaze upon it.

Caroline Elizabeth Sarah Sheridan was born in 1808, and was brought up very quietly at Hampton Court by her mother, the widow of "Tom" Sheridan sometimes known as Dazzle. Mrs. Sheridan was daughter of Colonel and Lady Elizabeth Callander, of Craigforth and Ardkinlas, and had dabbled in authorship herself. The *Critic* of July 1, 1851, gives the names of two of her novels, *Carwell* and *Aims and Ends.* They were reviewed in the *Quarterly Review* for 1832, and are written with ease and grace. Both of them were published anonymously. If little Caroline imbibed some of her literary tastes from her Scotch mother, she inherited a spark of genius from her grandfather, the never-to-be-forgotten Richard Brinsley Sheridan, whom in person she much resembled. The career of the erratic young Irishman, whose speech on the impeachment of Warren Hastings is one of the finest pieces of oratory on record, flits across the annals of the eighteenth century like a flash of lightning. Under-Secretary of State, Secretary to the Treasury, favourite of the Prince Regent, manager of the Drury Lane Theatre, author of two of the wittiest comedies ever written,—*The School for Scandal* and *The Rivals,* both of which keep the stage to the present day,—Richard Brinsley Sheridan was always full of resources, never-failing in repartee, and continually in debt. His smile was so bewitching, his face so expressive, his eyes so brilliant, his manner so captivating, that even his creditors were sometimes silenced and disarmed. But at last the harp was jangled and out of tune ; this friend of an unworthy prince would even have been arrested by the sheriff's officers on his death-bed and carried off to prison in the blankets, if the doctors had not declared that he would certainly die on the way. Then came a magnificent funeral and a grave in Westminster Abbey.

The knowledge that the blood of such an extraordinary genius flowed in her veins had, no doubt, an immense influence on little Caroline's mind. When she was only thirteen, her friends were astonished at the comic talent of *The Dandies' Rout*, a *jeu d'esprit* which she and her sister wrote in ridicule of the foppery of the day, and which was illustrated from her own designs. Some years afterwards she brought out *The Sorrows of Rosalie*, highly praised by Professor Wilson in the *Noctes Ambrosianæ*. The young authoress could not, indeed, complain of want of appreciation, for everything she wrote was hailed as a prodigy of talent. As a child, she showed few traces of the beauty for which she was afterwards so celebrated, and her lovely mother had many misgivings as to the future comeliness of one of the most celebrated belles of her day. Caroline's personal charms developed as she grew older. The fatal gift of beauty came to her by inheritance from her grandmother, the lovely Miss Linley, of Bath, and from her hand-some father and mother. The three Miss Sheridans were often compared to the Three Graces. The eldest, Helen Selina, was married, in 1825, to Captain Blackwood, after-wards Lord Dufferin, and mother of the Marquis of Dufferin. She would have been considered a beauty in every other family, but she was the least beautiful of the three ; she, too, had a gift of song, and her ballads, *Katey's Letter*, *The Bay of Dublin*, and *The Irish Emigrant*, have a simple *näiveté* and sly humour all their own. Next came Caroline, whose dark Southern eyes and queen-like grace and dignity marked her out wherever she went. The youngest, Jane Georgina, afterwards Duchess of Somerset, and Queen of Beauty at the Eglinton Tournament, was fairest of the fair ; but she was probably in the schoolroom when her second sister made her *entrée* into fashionable life. At that time everybody who *was* anybody was sure to go to the balls at Almack's. Moore the poet went, and in his gossiping Diary, dated May 17, 1826, we read how he saw the fancy quadrille "Les Paysannes Provinçiales " danced. " Some pretty girls among them," he adds, approvingly—"a daughter of Lord Talbot's, the Misses Duncombe, &c., Mrs. Sheridan's second daughter, strikingly like old Brinsley, and yet very pretty." A few days later he puts down—" Called at Mrs. Sheridan's, the sky pouring torrents all day. Sung for and with Miss Sheridan, who looked quite as pretty as at night ; promised I would go and see the quadrille of ' The Months ' at Almack's on Wednesday, she being the August of the party." Then on the 31st of May—" Went to Almack's too early, waited till the Seasons arrived, got into their wake as they passed up the room, and saw them dance their quadrille—the twelve without any gentlemen. Rather disappointed in the effect, their headdress (gold baskets full of flowers and fruit) too heavy. Miss Sheridan, the handsomest of any, most of the others pretty."

But the fancy quadrilles at Almack's, and the duets with the gay little poet, were soon to be exchanged for the graver realities of life. When Caroline Sheridan was about sixteen, she attracted the notice of the Honourable George Chapple Norton, brother of Lord Grantley. He proposed for her to her mother, who refused him on account of her daughter's extreme youth ; in three years he proposed again, and at the age of nineteen (July 30, 1827) Caroline Sheridan became the Honourable Mrs. Norton. In the meantime, we are informed, she " had become acquainted with and deeply attached to a gentleman whose early death alone prevented their union." Her destiny had ordained that her married life should be unfortunate. She says herself that she had not exchanged half a dozen serious sentences with her future husband before their marriage, and she soon found him to be selfish and indolent, with

coarse tastes and coarser feelings. He was a poor Honourable,
and a barrister without any "liking or capacity for his profession." His aim now was to make his brilliant wife a
"cat's-paw" by which he might obtain money and position,
for himself. From a notice in the *Athenæum* we learn that
Mr. Norton coaxed his wife into asking the Home Secretary
to make him a police magistrate ; that done, he bullied her
into earning more than his salary by her fluent pen. In
one year she reminded him that she made as much as
£1,400 by this means. Those were the days of "Annuals,"
"Amulets," and "Keepsakes," and half the publishers in
London were imploring tales, sketches, and poems from the
beautiful Mrs. Norton, who was the centre of a brilliant
circle to which outsiders longed in vain to be admitted.
We get an interesting peep at Mrs. Norton in these early
days from Fanny Kemble's *Records of a Girlhood.* She
speaks of Mrs. Norton's "most peculiar soft, contralto voice,
which was, like her beautiful dark face, set to music. The
Nortons then lived at Storey's Gate, at the Westminster end
of the Birdcage Walk. I remember passing an evening with
them there, when a host of distinguished public and literary
men were crowded into the small drawing-room, which was
literally resplendent with their light of Sheridan beauty,
male and female : Mrs. Sheridan, more beautiful than anybody but her daughters ; Lady Grahame, their beautiful
aunt ; Mrs. Norton ; Mrs. Blackwood ; Georgina Sheridan,
the future Duchess of Somerset ; and Charles Sheridan,
their younger brother—a sort of younger brother of the
Apollo Belvedere. Certainly, I never saw such a bunch
of beautiful creatures all growing on one stem. I remarked
it to Mrs. Norton, who looked complacently round her tiny
drawing-room, and said, 'Yes, we are rather good-looking
people.'

"When I first knew Caroline Norton," continues Fanny
Kemble, "she had not long been married to the Honourable George Norton. She was splendidly handsome, of

an un-English type of beauty, her rather large and
heavy head and features recalling the grandest Grecian
and Italian models, to the latter of whom her rich
colouring and blue-black braids of hair gave her an additional resemblance. Though neither as perfectly lovely
as the Duchess of Somerset nor as perfectly charming as
Lady Dufferin, she produced a far more striking impression than either of them. She was extremely epigrammatic
in her talk, and comically dramatic in her manner of
narrating things. I do not know whether she had any
theatrical talent, though she sang pathetic and humorous
songs admirably, and I remember shaking in my shoes
when, soon after I came out, she told me she envied me,
and would give anything to try the stage herself. I
thought, as I looked at her wonderfully beautiful face,
‘ Oh ! if you should, what would become of me ? ’ ”
Not only was she an eloquent and witty talker, but a clever
artist and a delightful singer. Three years after her marriage,
in April, 1830, Moore tells us that he dined at Mr. Baring’s
with the Fazakerleys, Rogers (the poet), and Mrs. Norton,
“ who was at war all dinner-time most amusingly with
Rogers.” “ Sung in the evening,” he adds, “ and so did
Mrs. Norton, some songs full of feeling.”

Fanny Kemble tells us that “ Mrs. Norton was no musician,
but had in singing a deep, sweet, contralto voice, precisely
the same in which she always spoke, and which, combined
with her always lowered eyelids—‘ downy eyelids ’—with
sweeping, silken fringes, gave such incomparably comic
effect to her sharp retorts and ludicrous stories. She sang
with great effect her own and Lady Dufferin’s social satires,
‘ Fanny Grey,’ and ‘ Miss Myrtle,’ &c., and sentimental
songs like *I would I were with thee, I dreamt, ’twas but a
Dream*, &c., of which the words were her own, and the
music, which only amounted to a few chords with the
simplest modulations, was her own too. She used occasionally to convulse her friends by a certain absurd song

called 'The Widow,' to all intents and purposes a broad comedy, the whole story of which (the wooing of a disconsolate widow by a rich lover, whom she first rejects and then accepts) was comprised in a few words, rather spoken than sung, eked out by a ludicruous burthen of ' Rum ti-iddy, iddy-iddy-ido.' " Mrs. Norton seems to have roused her friend's enthusiasm to the highest pitch ; we are told, " Mrs. Norton looks as if she were made of precious stones, diamonds, emeralds, rubies, sapphires—she is radiant with beauty." No wonder that a few verses from her should be pounced upon as a prize by a curious public.

Many years ago a controversy went on in the *Times*, which recalled Mrs. Norton's early literary days. Mrs. Norton accused Mrs. Henry Wood with having borrowed the plot of *East Lynne* from a tale of hers which had appeared in a long-forgotten annual. Mrs. Wood indignantly denied the assertion, and declared that she had never seen the annual in question. Notwithstanding, Mrs. Norton held her ground, maintaining that none of Mrs. Wood's novels had attained such popularity as *East Lynne*, and that the main incidents were identically the same as in her own annual story. The paper war between the two ladies finally dropped, but the strange part was that no one could bring forward the annual which was the great cause of the dispute.

A vast number of Mrs. Norton's minor poems were probably written in the thirties—*The Arab's Farewell to his Steed, Love Not, We have been Friends Together*, and a great many more. The smoothness and ease of Mrs. Norton's verse is remarkable ; her published songs are "most musical, most melancholy ;" they are never humorous, and seldom dramatic. The first years of her married life must have been busy ones indeed. She had often to write under pressure, without the necessary leisure to polish and correct ; and she had, besides, all the cares and anxieties of an affectionate mother on her shoulders. Her eldest son, Fletcher Cavendish, was born in 1829, when she was only twenty-one ; her second son, Thomas Brinsley (afterwards Lord Grantley), two years afterwards ; and her youngest son, William Charles Chapple, in 1833. Mrs. Norton's ardent, impulsive nature, was not one that could *half* feel anything. She was passionate in her loves and hates, passionate in her scorn, passionate in her independence, and deeply passionate in that absorbing sense of motherhood which is one of the keenest instincts in a woman's heart. In *The Lady of La Garaye* she describes how the crippled Countess can never feel—

> " That strange corporeal weakness sweetly blent
> With a delicious dream of full content,
> With pride of motherhood and thankful prayers,
> And a confused glad sense of novel cares,
> And peeps into the future brightly given,
> As though her babe's blue eyes turned earth to heaven."

In *Stuart of Dunleath* she cries with a genuine burst of enthusiasm—

" Children ! They are a sacred happiness. Their place in our hearts is marked out in every page of Holy Writ. Nearer to glory they stand than we in this world and the next. It was a gentle and not unholy fancy that made the Portuguese artist, Siquiera, in one of his sweet pictures, form of millions of infant faces the floor of heaven, dividing it thus from the fiery vault beneath with its groups of lost. For how many women has this image been realised ? How many have been saved from despair by the voice and smile of their unconscious little ones ! The woman who is a mother dwells in the immediate presence of guardian angels. She will bear on for her children's sake. She will toil for them, die for them, *live* for them, which is sometimes harder still. The neglected, miserable, maltreated wife has still one bright spot in her home, in that darkness a watchfire burns—she has her children's love—she will strive for her children. The angry and outraged woman sees in those tiny features a pleading more eloquent than words ; her wrath against her husband melts in the sunshine of their eyes. Idiots are they who in family quarrels seek to punish the mother by parting her from her offspring, for in that blasphemy against Nature they do violence to God's own decrees, and lift away from her heart the consecrated instruments of His power."

With this new joy of motherhood fresh upon her, Mrs. Norton advanced further into the fields of literature. In 1830, three years after her marriage, her poem of *The Undying One* was published. It was a version of the legend of *The Wandering Jew*, and was thought worthy of high praise in the *Edinburgh Review*. In a notice of it in the *New Monthly Magazine* it is said that if one or two poems of equal grace and originality were produced it would go far to recover the public from the apathy into which it had fallen with regard to poetry. The poem is declared to be an honour to modern literature, and the more interesting as being the work of a woman. As time went on Mrs. Norton's fame grew ; her sayings were "extremely noted." Recurring to *Moore's Diary* for April, 1832, we find the following :—

" Called upon Mrs. Norton ; found her preparing to go to Hayter's, who is painting a picture of her, and offered to walk with her. Had accordingly a very brisk and agreeable walk across the two parks, and took her in the highest bloom of beauty to Hayter's, who said he wished that some one would always put her through this process before she came to him. Hayter's picture promises well. Happening to mention that almost everything I wrote was composed in the garden or the fields, 'One would guess that of your poetry,' said Mrs. Norton, ' it quite *smells* of them.' "

Yet all this time there was a skeleton in the closet. Mrs. Norton's domestic life was becoming more and more unhappy every day. In matrimonial differences people generally declare that " there is much to be said on both sides," that "*both* are to blame," &c., &c., but no one has ever been found to say a single word in Mr. Norton's favour. We are told by one authority " that Mr. Norton's barbarity and vindictiveness of disposition bordered on insanity ; that he used physical violence on his wife, who almost supported him by her literary labours, and that he squandered her earnings on his own pleasures." He took her children from her and gave them into the most unworthy guardianship that it is possible to conceive. When *Old Sir Douglas* came out many years afterwards, Mrs. Norton gave us in Kenneth Ross the skilful pen-and-ink portrait of a coarse, selfish, brutal scamp, intent only on his own gratification, no matter at what cost, and utterly incapable of gratitude or any generous feeling. Perhaps, unconsciously, she was reproducing her own early recollections, which had made this type of character but too familiar with her. The incident, in *Stuart of Dunleath* when Sir Stephen Penrhyn clutches his wife by the arm so roughly that he breaks it, may also owe its origin to some of Mrs. Norton's lamentable experiences at this time. The worst, however, was yet to come. To Mrs. Norton's brilliant receptions frequently came Lord Melbourne, who had been a friend and contemporary of her father's ; as such he was welcome and warmly received. Mr. Norton, of course, wished to trade on such a profitable acquaintance. He hastened to ask for a better appointment or a loan of money. Lord Melbourne turned a deaf ear, for he was thoroughly disgusted at the mean-spirited Honourable. Mr. Norton, however, soon finding that no substantial benefits could be gained by fair means, tried something else. He took an action against the Minister whom he had been toadying so long, and laid the damages at £10,000. Mrs. Norton was, of course, the alleged cause, and Mr. Norton did his best to play the part of the injured husband to perfection. But, in legal phrase, he had no case. The jury, without quitting the box (I quote from the *Athenæum* notice), pronounced Mrs. Norton perfectly innocent of the unjust, false, and cruel charges brought against her. The case was *the* great event of 1836 ; to pass it over would be impossible, for all Mrs. Norton's future life is mixed up with it. Before it came off, we are told that Mr. Norton had so worked upon his wife's feelings by remorseful letters, that, in a moment of tenderness, she returned to him. But as she says in her pamphlet, *English Laws for Women in the Nineteenth Century*, she found that this was part of a deeply-laid plot, for after the trial, when she consulted with her lawyers whether a divorce by reason of cruelty could not be pleaded for, and brought forward the many instances of ill-usage which she had suffered, she was told that she could not plead cruelty which she had forgiven, that by returning to Mr. Norton she had condoned all she had complained of. His persecution of her continued. He wanted to raise money settled on her and her sons, and he induced her to give her consent to this in writing. In return he gave her a written contract drawn up by a lawyer and signed by the lawyer and himself. Then he resolved to rescind or withdraw this contract, and when Mrs. Norton resisted, she was informed that, by the law of England, a married woman could not be a party to a contract or have moneys of her own. When she complained, she was punished by a flood of libels published in all the English newspapers—libels for which, though proved falsehoods, she could obtain no redress because they were published by her husband. As to money, even that which she earned by literature was subject to his claims, just as, she proudly adds, the manual labour of the slave is subject to the claims of his master. She says that when she stood at the Westminster County Court with the vain contract in her hand, and when the law was shown to be for her what it was for the slave in Kentucky, the strongest sympathy was given, and when Mr. Norton tried to address the court, his voice was drowned in the groans and hooting of an excited crowd : but sympathy could not, she says, " force open for me the iron gates of the law which barred out justice. It could not prevent libel and fraud, the ripping up of old wounds and the infliction of new."

It is fortunate that by the passing of the Married Women's Property Act no such injustice can be inflicted now.

Mr. and Mrs. Norton were permanently separated in 1840. The bitter scorn, the angry indignation which had burnt and scorched into Caroline Norton's ardent soul soon came out in her writings. The longest of her poems, *The Dream,* was published about this time. It is dedicated to the Duchess of Sutherland, and some of the verses are full of eager gratitude and wounded pride. For example :—

> " When slandered and maligned I stood apart
> From those whose bounded pow'r had wrung, not crushed, my heart,
> Thou, then, when cowards lied away my name,
> And scoffed to see me feebly stem the tide,
> And some forsook on whom my love relied ;
> And some who might have battled for my sake
> Stood off in doubt to see what turn the world would take,
> Thou gav'st me what the poor do give the poor,
> Kind words and holy wishes, and true tears,
> The loved, the near of kin could do no more,
> Thou changed not with the gloom of varying years,
> But clung the closer when I stood forlorn,
> And blunted slander's dart with thine indignant scorn."

The plot of *The Dream* is simply " that of a lovely mother watching over a lovely daughter asleep. The daughter dreams, and when she wakes tells her dream, a vision of first love and domestic bliss. The mother replies by showing the many accidents to which wedded happiness is liable." At times the passion and interest assume a personal hue, and the arrows are dipped in gall; two of the lines run thus :—

> "And learn at length how deep and stern a blow
> Man's hand can strike and yet no pity show."

In a review of *The Dream*, Lockhart says that Mrs. Norton has much of that intense personal passion by which Byron's poetry is distinguished ; he says, too, that she has " Byron's beautiful intervals of tenderness, his strong practical thought, and his forceful expression ; that she feels intensely and utters her thoughts with impassioned energy ; that her thoughts are not the vapourings of a sickly fancy nor the morbid workings of undue self-love, but the strivings of a noble nature abounding in the wealth of its affections, outraged, stamped upon, and turning from its idols to God." Ingenious critic as Lockhart was, he certainly much overrated Mrs. Norton's poetical gifts. She has much of Byron's personality, but she has little of his dramatic instincts or of that stormy and varied power of verse which carries us so irresistibly along. She is often diffuse and long-winded ; her style was formed on that of Rogers, of Mrs. Hemans, and L. E. L. ; she lacks that concentrated strength of expression condensed into a few pregnant lines of which Tennyson has taught us the value. To make poetry alive and bristling with our own personality —our own " selfism "—is in reality a grand mistake, for which Byron has much to answer. As Carlyle says : " The suffering man ought to consume his own smoke ; there is no good in emitting smoke till you have made it into fire." Yes, into fire, pure clear flame, and that can only come with years when the soul is cleansed by suffering !

Mrs. Norton, however, was one who felt compelled to speak out—she *must* speak out or die, and her poems met with immense applause. Another critic, R. H. Horne, in *The New Spirit of the Age*, compares her favourably with Miss

Barrett, afterwards Mrs. Browning. He considers the prominent characteristics of both to be the struggles of women towards happiness, and the struggles of a soul towards heaven. Mrs. Norton, he thinks, is oppressed by a sense of injustice, and feels the need of human love, while Miss Barrett is troubled with a sense of mortality, and tries to identify herself with a higher existence. Mrs. Norton's imagination he considers to be chiefly taken up with domestic feelings and melodious complaints, that of Miss Barrett wanders amidst the supernatural darkness of Calvary. " Both," he says, "are excellent artists ; the one is all womanhood, the other all wings." It was just the wings, the lifting of herself above earth, that Mrs. Norton wanted. As a novelist she is far more successful than as a poet ; in prose, her irony, her sarcasm, her knowledge of life, give variety and effect to that "glow of eloquence" which is one of her highest gifts.

Between 1840 and 1851 she wrote and suffered much. In 1843 she lost her youngest and favourite son, nicknamed " The Emperor " by his brothers, on account of his merry, imperious ways. She says she did not think there was such a fount of love within her as for this child. No doubt she found relief in writing, and at this time she was far from rich, and often had to earn her bread by the hardest literary toil. A poem called *The Child of the Islands* was dedicated to the then infant Prince of Wales, and is a passionate appeal on behalf of the poor and oppressed. Mrs. Norton's warmest sympathies always ran in this direction ; as early as 1836 she published *A Voice from the Factories*, and she wrote many eloquent letters to the *Times* in 1841, in which she took up the cause of the criminal and outcast classes. Her poems, *The Blind Man to his Bride, The Widow to her Son's Betrothed*, and *The Child of Earth* also belong, in all probability, to this period of her life. In 1841 Fanny Kemble began a visit of two years and a half in England,

and renewed her acquaintance with Mrs. Norton. She says
she constantly met her in society. "Mrs. Norton was then
living with her uncle, Charles Sheridan, and still main-
tained her glorious supremacy of beauty and wit in the
great London world. She came often to parties at our
house, and I remember her asking me to dine at her
uncle's, where amongst the people we met were Lord
Lansdowne and Lord Normanby, both then in the
Ministry, whose good will and influence she was exerting
on behalf of a certain shy, silent, rather rustic gentleman
from New Brunswick, Mr. Samuel Cunard, afterwards Sir
Samuel Cunard, of the great mail-packet line of service. I
did not see Mrs. Norton again for several years. The next
time I did so was at an evening party at my sister's house,
when her appearance struck me more than it had ever done.
Her dress had something to do with this effect, no doubt.
She had a rich gold-coloured silk on, shaded and softened
all over with black lace draperies, and her splendid neck
and arms were adorned with magnificently simple Etruscan
gold ornaments which she had brought from Rome,
whence she had just returned. She was still *une beauté
triomphante à faire voir aux ambassadeurs*" (*Records of
a Girlhood*, vol. i. p. 289). A story is told that when she
and her son were looking for lodgings at Brussels, she was
taken for her son's *fiancée*, and the lodging-house woman
whispered to her to be sure and coax him to spend as much
money as possible. Mrs. Shelley speaks of Mrs. Norton's
wonderful charm of manner. "Had I been a man," she
says, "I should certainly have fallen in love with her ; as a
woman, in years ago, I should have been spell-bound, and
had she taken the trouble, she might have wound me round
her finger." She mentions Mrs. Norton dictating a "brilliant
letter" to Lord Melbourne, asking for a pension for the
widow of William Godwin.

It was in 1851 (the Exhibition year) that Mrs. Norton's
first prose work of fiction, *Stuart of Dunleath*, came out.

"Carelessly," she says in her dedication to the Queen of the Netherlands, "no part of this book has been written." Its principal merit lies in its intensity ; she has evidently flung herself heart and soul into every chapter of it. The motto is "Unstable as water, thou shalt not excel," and the lesson intended to be shown is how the instability of one man may ruin the life of another. Eleanor Raymond, the shy Indian-born young heiress, who clings to her attractive guardian, David Stuart, till she believes him drowned in the roaring Linn, interests us at once. Her loss of fortune, her marriage (for her sickly mother's sake) with the rough Scotch baronet, Sir Stephen Penrhyn, and her love for her twin boys, draws us nearer and nearer to her, and few scenes in fiction are so vividly, so terribly described as that when the crazy boat falls asunder, and the strong father swims to shore with his favourite Fred on his back, only to find when, bleeding and exhausted, he reaches land, that his child is dead, that both his children are dead—the child he left behind and the child he tried to save. The vivid reality of the whole, the pale mother waiting at home to "lift the hats from those shining curly heads, and to see those rosy lips quaff from the little silver cups," show us that Mrs. Norton was writing from her heart. As she says herself, "Nothing ever touched the heart of the reader that did not come from the heart of the writer ; your sympathy is the test of our truth."

This very powerful book is melancholy throughout. Tempest-tossed Eleanor cannot obtain a divorce from her brutal husband, she is separated from David Stuart, condemned by her brother with unjust harshness, and dies at length, crushed by sorrow and the intolerance of others. The *Athenæum* objected to the book on this account, and said that the "brightest and best seemed to be marked out exclusively for the discipline of pain." The *Examiner*, however, went into raptures over it, and declared that in comparison with other novels "it was like the crystal

fountain among the other fountains of the Crystal Palace."
Lighter touches certainly relieve the prevailing gloom.
We have Tibbie and her " Airl," and Eleanor's half-brother,
Godfrey Marsden, who " shut the door with a hard, determined clap as though it had been a trap in which he had
just caught a sinner," and we have, too, commonplace
little Emma, his wife. " Nothing frightened Emma like
a scene of any kind. She never understood what was the
cause of dispute or why people were so angry, but she
comprehended that there was what schoolboys called a
' row,' trembled while it lasted, felt relieved when it was
over, and if Godfrey spoke very loud or with unusual
bitterness, generally cried as infants do when grown people
quarrel before them."

In October, 1859, Mrs. Norton had the great grief of
losing her eldest son, Fletcher, when he was only thirty
years of age. He had just been appointed Secretary to
the Legation at Athens, and died at Paris on his way out.
Mrs. Norton alludes to this loss in the poem *The Lady of
La Garaye*, published in 1862, and dedicated to the then
Marquis of Lansdowne. Part of the dedication is as
follows :—

" *Thou* knowest, for *thou* hast proved, the dreary shade
 A firstborn's loss casts over lonely days,
 And gone is now the pale, fond smile that made
 In my dim future yet a path of rays.
 Gone, the dear comfort of a voice whose sound
 Came like a beacon bell, heard close above
 The whirl of violent waters surging round,
 Speaking to shipwrecked ears of help and love.

   .   .   .   .   .

 I weep the eyes that should have wept for me."

The Lady of La Garaye is the best of Mrs. Norton's
poems. The plot is slight, and taken from real life. The
Countess of La Garaye, gay, beautiful, and young, meets

with an accident while hunting which deprives her of the use of her limbs ; she is bowed down by sorrow ; her husband cannot comfort her ; at length, owing to the advice of a Benedictine monk, she devotes herself to the poor and suffering, and founds an hospital for incurables at Dinan, in Brittany. The illustrations are taken from Mrs. Norton's own sketches on the spot, and there are frequent passages of remarkable eloquence and beauty. Though sad, the bitterness so characteristic of former poems has disappeared and has given place to a calm resignation. " Despair is *not* the end of all this woe." " Man believes and *hopes*."

> " Each thinks his own the bitterest trial given,
> Each wonders at the sorrows of his lot,
> But over all our tears God's rainbow bends,
> To all our cries a pitying ear He lends,
> No barren glory circles round His throne ;
> By mercy's errands were His angels known.
> When hearts were heavy and when eyes were dim,
> Then did the brightness radiate from Him.
> God's pity, clothed in an apparent form,
> Starred with a polar light the human storm."

In 1863 *Lost and Saved* came out. The story of Beatrice Brooke, loving, trusting, unsuspicious, entangled in a network of perplexing circumstances, betrayed by false friends, and then having to pay the most bitter penalties, while Montague Treherne escapes scotfree, is extremely painful, but admirably told. In it Mrs. Norton displays her deep knowledge of human nature and of the world in all its various phases. The Marchioness of Updown, fat, rude, and selfish, " stuck over with diamonds as an orange sometimes is with cloves," is a real flesh-and-blood marchioness. We seem to know her, and poor patient Parkes, her much-enduring companion, who " does nothing menial." Those who have a fancy for fashionable rakes would do well to study the character of Montague Treherne, the heartless man of the world, caring only for the fleeting fancy of the hour. What such men really are Mrs. Norton knew only too well. Just as *Juanita* is the best known of her songs, so *Lost and Saved* is the best known of her novels. It went into three editions in a year, and has been brought out in a popular series. *Old Sir Douglas*, which first appeared in *Macmillan's Magazine* in 1867, and was published as a book the following year, though less intense, and perhaps less powerful, is considered by most critics to be Mrs. Norton's masterpiece. Sir Douglas Ross, only called "old" by his scampish nephew, is a vast improvement on the attractive but vacillating David Stuart. Brave, generous, forgiving, we do not wonder that Gertrude Skifton should prefer him to handsome Kenneth, his nephew. As to Ailie Ross, with her stealthy cat-like movements and her fur boa, and Lady Charlotte Skifton, the foolish superannuated coquette, talking of a "pastoral cottage" and "a bachelor of the other sex," these are genuine studies of character. The book, too, ends happily : the good are rewarded, and the cunning plotters come to grief. Mrs. Norton always has a noble aim ; she takes the part of the helpless and oppressed, and fights their battles against the intolerance which condemns, and the prejudice which crushes them. During the last eight years she wrote nothing but a few poems and some anonymous reviews. Fanny Kemble gives us another glimpse of her at this stage of her life. "During one of my last visits to London," she says, "I met Mrs. Norton at Lansdowne House. There was a great assembly there, and she was wandering about the rooms leaning on the arm of her son, her glorious head still crowned with its splendid braids of hair and wreathed with grapes and ivy leaves. This was my last vision of her."

In the autumn of 1870 she was quite old, but undeniably handsome and witty. Her health began to fail, and she was almost entirely confined to her house. In February, 1876, her first husband died, and in March, 1877, she was married in her

own drawing-room (Queen Street, Mayfair) to Sir William
Stirling-Maxwell, of Keir, the cultivated author of *Cloister
Life of the Emperor Charles V., The Artists of Spain,* &c.
She was his second wife, and they had known each other
for many years. Strangely enough, one of Mrs. Norton's
poems, written long before her second marriage, is called
The Great Chestnut-Tree at Keir, and is inscribed to her
future husband. The storm of October, 1860, had swept
over the Stirlingshire valleys, and the chestnut-tree is
supposed to address its master thus :—

> " And I rest, master, I rest,
> Like a strong soul after bitter strife."

The next verses go on to speak of how that ancient house,
like the ancient tree, shall be victor throughout many a
clouded hour, and shall raise a race whose branches shall
o'erspread the land " when I am dead." The last lines are
remarkable : " Young children's voices shall float in at the
silent windows," and "not alone shall *thy* record be perused
on monumental stone," but " 'mongst the men of mark shall
they read in the golden book of lasting fame, the friend and
father's name."

Mrs. Norton had always a love for Scotland. Part of
her girlhood had been spent there. Her mother was a
Scotchwoman ; the scenes of her two best novels are laid
in Scotland ; her heroes are Scotch ; and her second husband was a Scotchman born and bred. We might have
wished for her that her last days (she died the 15th
of June, 1877) could have been spent in Scotland, in
that lovely home of Keir where the sombre yew-trees
lift their dark shade, and the clipped yew hedges quaintly
show from the terraced walks, and make it one of the
most beautiful surroundings of "grey Stirling, with its
towers and town." But it was willed otherwise. It was

enough that Lady Stirling-Maxwell should enjoy for three months the appreciation, the love, and the care which as Mrs. Norton she had so sorely lacked. Life now could hardly be bitter. From her brilliant youth, from her stormy prime, from her sorrowful middle age—idolised, flattered, maligned, insulted, eulogised, loved, and cherished—she passed on to where " beyond these voices there is peace." Who can say it is not well with her ? Calm evening light is sweeter than the glowing and radiant morn : out of suffering comes strength, and—

> " God giveth increase through the coming years,
> And lets us reap in joy, seed that was sown in tears."
>
> *Lady of La Garaye.*

VII.

ELIZABETH BARRETT BROWNING.

(1809–1861.)

Birth—Childhood at Hope End—*The Battle of Marathon*—Death of her
mother—Life in London—Intimacy with Miss Mitford—*A Drama of
Exile*—Her brother is drowned—Illness—Great success of her poems
—*Lady Geraldine's Courtship*—Acquaintance and marriage with
Robert Browning—*Casa Guidi Windows*—Birth of her son—*Aurora
Leigh*—Death.

THE question, What is genius ? is often asked, and not
easily answered in a few words. We may, however,
be tolerably certain that the creative faculty, the power of
striking out new paths, of saying or doing original things in
an original way, is one unfailing proof of the high instinct
of genius. This power is rarely found among women ; they
can follow, but they cannot lead ; they can sing pleasant
songs or write clever novels, but we are often told that the
divine fire of genius is denied them. In answer to this
we may point to Elizabeth Browning, and ask if she did
not strike out a new chord, if she did not sing with her own
individual voice.

What her husband thought of her, we know from a
remark of his given in Mrs. Sutherland Orr's *Life of Robert
Browning.* When a comparison was made between the two
poets to the disadvantage of Mrs. Browning, he eagerly
exclaimed, " You are wrong, quite wrong ; she has genius,
I am only a painstaking fellow. Can't you imagine a clever
sort of angel who plots and plans and tries to build up
something, he wants to make you see it as he sees it, shows
you one point of view, carries you off to another, hammering

ELIZABETH BARRETT BROWNING.

BORN MARCH 4TH, 1809 ; DIED JUNE 29TH, 1861.

into your head the things he wants you to understand ; and while this bother is going on, God Almighty turns you off a little star. That's the difference between us. The true creative power is hers, not mine."

Elizabeth Barrett was born in March, 1809. She was the eldest daughter of Mr. Edward Moulton, a rich West Indian merchant, who, on succeeding to some property, took the name of Barrett. Soon after his daughter's birth he went to live at his country place, Hope End, near Ledbury, in Herefordshire. It was charmingly situated amongst hills, with a well-wooded deer park, and green shaded lakes. The house did not satisfy Mr. Barrett, so it was pulled down, and a large structure with Turkish turrets and a great hall was erected in its stead. "Elizabeth's room," so Mrs. Ritchie tells us, "was a lofty chamber, with a stained-glass window, casting coloured lights across the floor."

Hope End was a few miles from the beautiful scenery of Malvern. "Do you know the Malvern Hills ? " writes Miss Barrett to her unseen correspondent, Mr. R. H. Horne, " the hills of Piers Plowman's visions ? They seem to me my native hills, for although I was born in the county of Durham, I was an infant when I first went into their neighbourhood, and lived there until I had passed twenty by several years. Beautiful, beautiful hills they are I "

At eight years old and earlier, little Elizabeth began to write verses. So have many other juvenile maidens ; but with her, as she says, the early fancy turned into a will, and from that time poetry was a distinct object with her, an object to read, think, and live for. At Hope End she had her fits of Pope, Byron, and Coleridge. She had also the very best surroundings which a precocious child can possibly have. She tells us, in her *Hector in the Garden*, how she

" Had life like flowers and bees
    In betwixt the country trees,
    And the sun the pleasure taught me
    Which he teacheth everything."

We can almost fancy that we see the little elfin child running under the dripping chestnuts and through the wet grass to seek her garden,

> " With the laurel on the mound."

Here there was a " huge giant, wrought of spade," with " eyes of gentianella azure," " nose of gillyflower and box," and

> " A sword of flashing lilies
> Holden ready for the fight."

To her nine-years-old imagination this giant became Hector, the hero of Troy. As she smoothed his brow with her rake an awe came to her, for he seemed to stir with life, as though the spirit of the real Hector were moving within him. Her childish brain was full of visions about Troy and the Greeks ; the Greeks were her demigods, and haunted her out of Pope's *Homer* till she dreamt "more of Agamemnon than of Moses, the black pony." Her grandmother, who came to stay at Hope End, did not approve of so much reading and writing. " She would rather see Elizabeth's hemming more carefully finished than all this Greek."

At eleven or twelve years old her great epic in four books, called by the ambitious title of *The Battle of Marathon,* was not only written, but ushered into the glory of print ; for her father, who was her public and critic, and who, she says, was bent on spoiling her, had fifty copies printed for private circulation. She considered this a curious production for a child ; it showed an imitative faculty and a good deal of reading. " The love of Pope's *Homer* threw me," she wrote, " into Pope on one side and into Greek on the other, and into Latin as a help to Greek." She had the advantage of a first-rate teacher, Hugh Stuart Boyd, who was her brother's tutor, and the author of a work on the Greek Fathers. He had the misfortune to be blind. In one of three sonnets which are dedicated to him she calls him her "beloved, steadfast friend," and remembers how she assisted

"Her dear teacher's soul to unlock
The darkness of his eyes."

With such teaching knowledge became a pleasure. "Because the time was ripe, I chanced upon the poets." Under the trees at Hope End she read Greek as hard as an Oxford student ; she gathered visions from Plato and the dramatists, and "ate and drank Greek and made her head ache with it." She breathed in the music of the classic poets like mountain air ; it broadened and strengthened her mind, it braced her imagination and freed it from weakness and pettiness. It also made her familiar with the alphabet and grammar of her art ; different kinds of verse and metre became easy to her.

An accident which happened when she was fourteen put an end to much out-of-door activity. She was a constant rider, and fond of saddling her pony. One day she overbalanced herself in lifting the saddle and fell backward, inflicting injuries to her head, or rather spine, which caused great suffering, but of which the nature remained for some time undiscovered. Being obliged to stay in the house a great deal, she studied and read more than ever. At seventeen a didactic poem, *An Essay on Mind*, was written and published with other short poems in 1826. It showed a great deal of reading and reflection. Henry Cary (the translator of Dante) said that it contained allusions to books which no young man of his day at Oxford had even looked into. But Elizabeth Barrett herself repented of it as worthy of all repentance. She thought that at times "the bird pecks through the shell," still she mourned over its pedantry and pertness. She would as soon circulate a lampoon or a caricature of herself as this unfortunate essay. Perhaps she

was thinking of it when, many years afterwards, she says in
Aurora Leigh :—

> " For me, I wrote
> False poems, like the rest, and thought them true
> Because myself was true in writing them.
> I, peradventure, have writ true ones since
> With less complacence."

The highest order of minds are often, like good wine, long
in ripening to perfection.   So it was with Elizabeth Barrett;
her real voice had not yet come to her, though her spirit
was stirring restlessly within her, impatient to get out.
She was about twenty when her mother's last illness began,
and at the same time money troubles disturbed Mr. Barrett's
affairs.   He compounded with his creditors, materially de-
creasing his income, so that his wife might not be annoyed.
After Mrs. Barrett's death, the family left Hope End and
its hills, never to return there.

"Not for the world," writes Elizabeth Barrett, " would I
stand in the sunshine of those hills any more.   It would be a
mockery, like the taking back of a broken flower on its stalk."
From Hope End the Barretts went to Sidmouth for two
years, and about this time was published, still anonymously,
Prometheus Bound, translated from the Greek of Æschylus.
The translation was written in only twelve days.   Elizabeth
Barrett calls it, in one of her letters, a blasphemy to Æschylus,
and says it ought to have been thrown into the fire, the only
means for giving it a little warmth.   *Prometheus* was published in 1835, and was afterwards entirely recast.

The next move was to London, to 74, Gloucester Place.
In one of Miss Mitford's delightful letters to her father (May
27, 1836) she tells him how she went to see the giraffes and
the Diorama with Mr. Kenyon.   " A sweet young woman,
whom we called for in Gloucester Place, went with us," she
says, " a Miss Barrett, who reads Greek as I do French, and
has published some translations from Æschylus and some

most striking poems. She is a delightful young creature, shy, and timid, and modest. Nothing but her desire to see me brought her out at all." This delightful young creature is elsewhere described by Miss Mitford as having a " slight delicate figure, with a shower of dark curls falling on each side of a most expressive face, large tender eyes, richly fringed by dark eyelashes, and a smile like a sunbeam." A few days after their first meeting Miss Mitford tells her father how she went to dinner with Mr. Kenyon (Miss Barrett's cousin and friend, to whom *Aurora Leigh* was dedicated). There were present " Wordsworth, whom," says the lively Miss Mitford,

" I *love ;* he is an adorable old man ; Mr. Landor, who is as splendid a person as Mr. Kenyon, but not so full of sweetness and sympathy ; the charming Miss Barrett, and three or four more—one of the most magnificent dinners I ever saw. Miss Barrett has translated the most difficult of the Greek plays (the *Prometheus Bound*), and written most exquisite poems in almost every style. She is so sweet and gentle and so pretty that one looks at her as if she were some bright flower, and she says it is like a dream that she should be talking to one whose works she nearly knows by heart."

The friendship which thus sprang up between the sunshiny elderly lady and the shy young poetess proved not only strong but lasting. Miss Mitford took Elizabeth Barrett into the depths of her warm, capacious heart, she lavished fondness on her, she wrote hundreds of letters to her " beloved," her " precious friend," her " own sweet love."

" My love and ambition for you," she says in one of her letters, " often seems to be more like that of a mother for a son, or a father for a daughter, than the common bonds of even a close friendship between women of different ages and sentiments.   I sit and think of you and of the poems that you will write, and of that strange, brief rainbow crown called Fame, until the vision is before me as vividly as ever a mother's heart hailed the eloquence of a patriot son.   Do you understand this, and do you pardon it ?   You must, my precious, for there is no chance that I should ever unbuild that house of clouds, and the position that I long to see you fill is higher, firmer, prouder than has ever been filled by woman.   God bless you, my sweetest, for the dear love which finds something to like in these jottings.   It is the instinct of the bee that sucks honey from the hedge-flower."

There is something peculiarly touching in these generous words.   They do honour to the woman who could write them and to the woman whose noble nature called them forth.

Elizabeth Barrett not only inspired Miss Mitford's love, she returned it.   She calls her friend a " prose Crabbe." " Who would not go and gather lilies of the valley with her in the Silchester woods ? "

She does not seem at this time of her life to have been at all satisfied with her own literary attempts ; the undiscerning praise which comes from drawing-room friends could not content her ardent genius.   She sent a short poem to Mr. R. H. Horne, the author of *Orion*, with a letter, asking to be frankly told whether the poem could be considered poetry or merely verse.   There was no doubt that it belonged to the former class.   It was forwarded at once to *Colburn's New Monthly Magazine*, then edited by Mr. Bulwer (the late Lord Lytton), when it appeared in the next number.   The second MS. forwarded was *The Dead Pan*, founded on the legend that at the time of our Saviour's crucifixion a voice was heard calling " Pan is dead ! "   The old heathen deity of the woods and forests, the gods of Hellas—Aphrodite, Bacchus, Hermes—are indeed dead, answers the poem, but a new spirit shines forth.

> " God Himself is the best Poet,
> And the Real is His song,
> Sing the truth out fair and full
> And secure His beautiful,
>   Let Pan be dead ! "

Every verse seems to glow with electric sparks ; daring originality and force mark out *The Dead Pan* from the common run of feminine poetry. Compare it with Adelaide Procter's or Christina Rossetti's sweet flowing verses, and we at once see the superiority of its genius. It is like a trumpet blast. Elizabeth Barrett had not studied Æschylus in vain ; now she struck out boldly for herself, and went to the fountain-head for inspiration. *The Dead Pan* is a noble answer to Schiller's *Gods of Greece.* The little girl who had dreamed in the garden at Hope End about Hector and Achilles now called out, all on fire with passion and enthusiasm,

> " O ye poets, keep back nothing,
> Nor mix falsehood with the whole,
> Look up Godward, speak the truth in
> Worthy song from earnest soul."

In 1838 *The Seraphim and other Poems* was published, and this was the first book of hers that Elizabeth Barrett cared to own. Through all its weaknesses and faults she considered that her voice was in it. *The Seraphim* itself is, however, too indistinct and cloudy. The poem consists of a dialogue between two angels, Ador the strong and Zerob the beautiful, who stand outside the heavenly gate during the time of the crucifixion. Though it has much beauty of expression, it has not variety enough to be dramatic ; it wants action and human interest.

Miss Mitford did right when she urged her friend to keep to ballads of human feeling and human life. Elizabeth Barrett never wrote so well as when she descended from the clouds and alighted on the firm, substantial earth ; here she spoke a language which has found an echo in the hearts of thousands. One of her early ballads, *The Romaunt of the Page*, a story of woman's heroism, is worth a hundred *Seraphims*. Lyric poetry is her forte. There is an ease, a ring, a music in her ballads which haunts the ear. *The Romaunt of Margret* is especially exquisite—Margret, who obstinately clings to the love of father, sister, brother, lover, till one by one all fade away under the breath of the shadow which had a voice so calm and slow—

> " It trembled on the grass
> With a low shadowy laughter,
> And the wind did toll as a passing soul
> Was sped by church bell after ;
> And shadows 'stead of light
> Fell from the stars above,
> In flakes of darkness on her face,
> Still bright with trusting love. Margret, Margret."

The unearthliness, the intense spirituality which hover, like air, over this poem, make it only second to Coleridge's *Christabel*.

In the year 1839 Miss Barrett's health, which had never been strong, gave way completely. She broke a bloodvessel in her lungs, and was ordered to spend the winter at Torquay. She went there with fear, grief, and reluctance, too sure a prophecy of what was to follow. Her eldest and favourite brother, Edward Moulton Barrett, accompanied her. On the 11th of July he went out on a yachting trip with two companions. They intended to go only as far as Teignmouth ; but two, three, four days passed, and nothing was heard of them. A report came that a yacht had been seen to go down off Teignmouth with four men on board.

Rewards were offered, and, on the 11th of August, Edward Barrett's body was picked up by a boatman and brought to shore. The shock to the fragile invalid at Torquay was indescribable. "I was struck down," she wrote, "as by a bodily blow, without having time for tears." And again— "During the whole winter the sound of the waves rang in my ears like the moans of the dying." But her faith never broke down. "God's will is so high above humanity," she added, "that its goodness and perfectness cannot be scanned at a glance, and would be very terrible if it were not for His love manifested in Christ Jesus. Only *that* holds our hearts together when He shatters the world."

The frail thread which bound Elizabeth Barrett to life seemed about to be snapped. Once she was kept for weeks in the dark. Often she could not be lifted to her sofa without fainting ; to have the window of her room opened an inch was a wonderful event, and to be wheeled out in a bath-chair in the hot sunshine brought on fits of shivering and weariness all the next day. But the pen was not laid aside. Prose and poetry flowed on as richly as ever in her sick-room. She wrote a series of articles in the *Athenæum* on "The Greek Christian Poets" and on "The Book of the Poets." She busied herself with her *Drama of Exile ;* she studied Hebrew ; she wrote portions of Chaucer modernised, and contributed to an anonymous review, the *New Spirit of the Age,* in which she wrote criticisms of Tennyson, Wordsworth, and Leigh Hunt. Tennyson she was one of the first to appreciate. "If anything were to happen to him," she wrote, "the whole world should go into mourning." She was not one of those writers who are lan- guidly indifferent to everything but their own productions. She admired heartily, and entered into the works of others with an intensity of interest which, perhaps, she did not give to her own after they were finished. Harriet Martineau she considered the noblest female intelligence between the suns, "as sweet as spring, as ocean deep." Her admiration

for Lord Lytton, especially for *Ernest Maltravers* and *Alice,*
was unbounded, and she has even a good word for G. P. R.
James.   But she honestly admits that she cannot read
Lever's novels ; they make her head ache as if she had been
sitting in the next room to an orgie of gentlemen topers.
Victor Hugo's *Trois Jours d'un Condamné* made an immense
impression on her, and George Sand she thought the
greatest female genius the world has ever seen.   She received
criticisms on her own poems with an amusing playfulness.
" Oh ! you are a gnasher of teeth," she writes to Mr. Horne,
who had complained of some of her rhymes in *The Dead
Pan ;* " you are a lion and a tiger in one, and in a most car-
nivorous mood."   Then she gets graver, and goes on to say
that she has *worked* at poetry ; it has not been with her a
reverie, but an art.   " As the physician and lawyer work at
their several professions, so have I, and so do I, apply to
mine."   How such rhyming licences as " silence " and
"islands," " bewildering " and " stilled in," " deep in " and
" leaping " arose, was jocosely accounted for by Miss Mitford,
who tells Mr. Horne that

" Our dear friend never sees anybody but the members of
her own family and one or two others.   She has a high
opinion of the skill in reading as well as the fine taste of
Mr. ——, and she gets him to read her new poems aloud to
her, and so tries them upon him as well as herself.   Mr. ——
stands upon the hearthrug and uplifts his voice, while our
dear friend, folded up in Indian shawls, lies upon her sofa,
her long black tresses streaming over her downbent head, all
attention."

But dear Mr. —— had lost a front tooth, which caused a
defective utterance, a vague softening of syllables, so that
" islands " and " silence " really sounded very like one
another.

This little touch of description calls up a vision of the

spirituelle poetess, with her long drooping ringlets, and her
large brown majestic eyes, shaded by their drooping, silken
lids, eyes in which her "soul was all agaze," and which
were ready to kindle with earnestness and fire. Slight and
fragile in figure, her body seemed all too small to contain
the great heart which throbbed within it. It is hard to
believe that such slender fingers could have written that
passionate *Cry of the Children* in which the poet calls her
brothers to listen to the children "weeping ere the sorrow
comes with years," weeping from factories and mills for
the bright youth that has never dawned on them. *The Lay
of the Human* is another of those earnest songs which seem
to be the outlet of suffering and wrong ; the refrain, " Be
pitiful, O God ! " sounds as if it were wrung out from the
sobs and sighs of a tempest-tossed humanity, and yet it arose
from a sick-room, and was written by a delicate woman
hovering between life and death, whose principal companion
was her pet dog Flush.

Flush was a present from Miss Mitford, and had a very important place in his mistress's heart. She writes of him :—

> " But of *thee* it shall be said,
> This dog watched beside a bed
> Day and night unweary ;
> Watched within a curtained room,
> Where no sunbeam brake the gloom
> Round the sick and dreary."

From her sofa Elizabeth Barrett "heard the nations praising
her far off," while she sat weary and still. Writing in
1843, she says that a bird in a cage would have as good
a story as hers—"most of my events and nearly all my
pleasures have been passed in my *thoughts.*" It was some
time before she was able to leave her enforced exile
at Torquay and to return by easy stages to London,
this time to 50, Wimpole Street. In 1844, two volumes
of her best poems appeared, and established her fame.

An American publisher boldly printed off fifteen hundred copies, and from the remote region of Gutter Lane she received a letter beginning "I thank thee." She had learned much from those tedious six years of pain and loneliness, from that "dreadful dream of an exile, the nightmare of her life." If she had commenced her poet's calling with a blast like a trumpet, the richer tones of an organ had now come to her—anguish, passion, sorrow, suffering alike found an interpreter in her. It was never her aim to be light or amusing; she was too deeply impressed with the solemnity of human life; she was consumed with earnestness, bent on vindicating the ways of God to man. *The Drama of Exile*—the exile being that of Adam and Eve from Paradise—would never, in spite of its fine passages, be a favourite. As usual, the lyrical poems carry away the palm. A meaning lies at the root of each. In *Isabel's Child* a mother prays for her child's life, and then hears a spirit voice complaining that she is "binding and holding" him with her narrow prayers. "Loose me, loose me!" is the cry. She looses him, and he dies. With her submission comes the beautiful thought—

> "This earthly noise is too anear,
> Too loud, and will not let me hear
> The little harp."

In the *Lay of the Brown Rosary* Onora has sworn on the rosary that she will not "thank God in her weal, or seek God in her woe." Conflicting spirits struggle for her soul, the good angels say that "God will draw Onora up the golden stairs of heaven," and yet the evil ones have

> "Power to defer,
> For if she has no need of Him, He has no need of her."

Through loss and agony she is at length brought to throw away her rosary, to acknowledge that it is not wisely done—

" That we who cannot gaze above should walk the earth alone . . .
To choose, perhaps, a lovelit hearth instead of love and heaven,
A single rose for a rose-tree that beareth seven times seven—
A rose that droppeth from the hand, that fadeth from the breast,
Until, in grieving for the worst, we learn what is the best. . . .
We cannot guess Thee in the wood, or hear Thee in the wind ;
Our cedars must fall round us ere we see the light behind.
Ay ! sooth we feel too strong in weal to need Thee on that road,
But woe being come, the soul is dumb that crieth not on God."

The *Rhyme of the Duchess May*, with its mournful burden,
" Toll slowly," brings us back to the days of chivalry when
knights were brave and ladies true. Along with the romantic
surroundings, comes a deep and intense phase of human life.
When the tragic story ends, the noblest faith embodied in
a condensed form of expression speaks out. In spite of
sorrow and gloom

" I smiled to think God's greatness
Flowed around an incompleteness,
Round our restlessness, His rest."

The simple pathos of *Bertha in the Lane* goes at once to
the heart, but in *Lady Geraldine's Courtship* another chord
is touched—a chord of passion and triumph. Miss Mitford
says that the forty-two pages were written in one day, and
we can readily believe it. There is a dash, a swing about it
which carries the reader on like the gallop of a swift horse.
The metre resembles that of *Locksley Hall*, but Lady Geraldine's romance has a nobler ending than that of false-hearted
" cousin Amy." The lowly-born poet-lover wins the earl's
daughter, who smiled her " suitors down imperially as
Venus did the waves." In *Lady Geraldine's Courtship* the
poet-lover reads aloud some classic poem :—

" Or at times a modern volume, Wordsworth's solemn-thoughted idyll,
Howitt's ballad-dew, or Tennyson's enchanted reverie,—
Or from Browning, some ' Pomegranate,' which, if cut deep down the
middle,
Shows a heart within blood-tinctured, of a veined humanity."

She wrote of Browning as a " poet for posterity. I have full faith in him as poet and prophet."

It was natural that Mr. Kenyon, who knew Browning's father, should bring the young poet to be introduced to the author of *Lady Geraldine's Courtship.* The meeting, when it came off, was an era in the lives of both. It was late in the year 1844. Robert Browning was then thirty-two and Elizabeth Barrett thirty-five, though her extreme fragility made her look much younger. " She had so much need of care and protection," he says. " There was so much pity in what I felt for her." Every day they grew closer to each other, every hour they passed together was a revelation. In the *Sonnets from the Portuguese,* which are really sonnets from Elizabeth Barrett's own experience, we are privileged to read the history of her heart, told with a truth, a nobleness, and a purity that every one would do well to study. For revelation of a poet's inner life these sonnets have been compared to *In Memoriam,* and for beauty of construction they have been placed next to those of Wordsworth. One after another the poet gives us these songs of her soul as they rise before her. At first comes the thought of her own unworthiness. She seems

> " An out of tune,
> Worn viol, a good singer would be wroth
> To spoil his song with."

Then, again, she remembers the melancholy years when Death was claiming her for his own, when she lived with visions for her company,

> " And found them gentle mates, nor thought to know
> A sweeter music than they played to me."

But a new day was now dawning—

> " Thou, thou didst come to be,
> Beloved, what they seemed, their shining fronts,

Their songs, their splendour (better, yet the same,
As river water, hallowed into fonts)
Met in thee, and from out thee overcame
My soul with satisfaction of all wants,
Because God's gifts put man's best gifts to shame."

Still the gift seems all too great for what can be given in return. " Go from me."

" The chrism is on thine head, on mine the dew."

At length doubt is vanquished and love is lord of all.

" Thy soul snatched up mine all weak and faint,
And set it by thee on a golden throne."

Then comes the question—

" How do I love thee ? Let me count the ways. . . .
I love thee freely as men strive for right,
I love thee purely as they turn from praise,
I love thee with a passion put to use,
In my old griefs, and with my childhood's faith,
I love thee with a love I seemed to lose
With my lost saints—I love thee, with the breath,
Smiles, tears of all my life, and if God choose
I shall but love thee better after death."

One could almost imagine that these glimpses into the deep heart of a pure woman had grown up of themselves, like some lovely flowers, without speck or flaw.

There were many obstacles to marriage. Not only the extreme delicacy of Elizabeth Barrett's health, but her father's opposition had to be faced. He was devoted to his daughter. " There was no possible husband that he would have accepted for one of his children," Mrs. Sutherland Orr says, " and his will was iron." So the marriage was arranged without consulting him. As a preparatory step, Elizabeth Barrett drove to Regent's Park, and stepped out of the carriage, and felt grass under her feet and air about her.

The sensation, she says, was bewilderingly strange.   On September 12, 1846, she was married to Robert Browning at Marylebone Parish Church, when she was thirty-seven and he was thirty-four.   On the evening of September 19th, attended by her maid and dog, she stole away from her father's house.   The family were at dinner, and as her two sisters, Henrietta and Arabel, were in the secret, there was no difficulty in her escape, except that her dog, Flush, might begin barking.   She took him into her confidence : " Oh, Flush, if you make a sound I am lost ! "   He crept after his mistress in silence.   Her maid joined her, and that night they took the boat to Havre, *en route* for Paris.   From Paris she wrote to a friend on October 2nd : " He loved me for reasons that had helped to weary me of myself, loved me heart to heart persistently, in spite of my own will.   My life seemed to belong to him and no other, and I had no power to speak a word.   Have faith in me, dearest friend, till you know him.   The intellect is so little in comparison to all the rest ; to the womanly tenderness, the inexhaustible goodness, the high and noble aspiration of every hour.   Temper, spirits, manner, there is not a flaw anywhere.   I shut my eyes sometimes, and fancy it is all a dream of my guardian angel.   Only, if it had been a dream, the pain of some parts of it would have wakened me before now—it is not a dream."

While the Barrett and Browning families were thrown into consternation by this unexpected marriage, and while friends were prophesying all sorts of calamities, the married lovers were travelling on from Paris to Pisa.   On the way, they met Mrs. Jameson, who declared that her friend was not only improved, but transformed.   In the sunny south, her health improved so marvellously that she was able to take long walks, to lose herself in chestnut forests, and scramble, on mule-back, up the sources of extinct volcanoes.   Her father was never reconciled to her, and never saw her again, but her love for her husband made up for all.

"Nobody understands him except me," she writes, "who am in the inside of him, and hear him breathe. He thinks aloud with me, and can't stop himself." At another time she writes to his sister : "I think him all beautiful, always." What he thought of her—"his moon of poets"—is shown in his dedication to her of his poem of *Men and Women.* " She is a perfect wife," he says. Mrs. Sutherland Orr tells us that very time he went to London he commemorated his marriage in a way all his own. He went to the church where the marriage had taken place, and kissed the paving stones in front of the door.

At Florence, the city of lilies, where Savonarola had preached and the Medici had plotted, and Dante had sung, the Brownings finally took up their abode, and there, on March 9, 1849, Mrs. Browning's son, her " young Florentine," " her blue-eyed prophet," was born. The old palace of Casa Guidi, gloomy without, has a sombre grandeur of its own. The Americans and English who made pilgrimage to the Browning shrine speak in raptures of the dark shadows and subdued lights which lingered within those favoured walls. First there was the square ante-room, with its great picture and piano, at which the boy Browning spent many an hour ; then came the little dining-room, covered with tapestry and hung with medallions of Carlyle and Tennyson. Last of all was the large drawing-room opening out upon a balcony filled with plants, and looking out on the old grey church of San Felice. Here Mrs. Browning always sat. She usually wore black silk in soft falling flounces, her heavy curls drooped over her face, and a thin gold chain hung round her neck. The tapestry-covered walls, the old pictures of saints in their black, carved wood frames, the bookcases adorned with Florentine carving and filled with priceless books, made a harmonious setting to the delicate figure that was generally to be found in a low arm-chair, with a table strewn with books, papers, and writing materials by her side. " She is a soul of fire enclosed in a shell of pearl," says Mr. Hillard, an American friend. " Her figure is slight, her countenance expressive of genius and sensibility, shaded by a veil of long brown locks, and her tremulous voice often flutters over her words like the flame of a dying candle on a wick." But the best pen-and-ink portrait of the Brownings at home is given by Mrs. Ritchie. She calls up a vivid picture of the peaceful home, " of its fireside, when the logs are burning, and the mistress established on her sofa, with her little boy curled up by her side, the door opening and shutting meanwhile to the quick step of the master of the house, and to the life of the world without, coming to find her in her quiet corner." " We can recall," she says, " the slight figure in its black silk dress, the writing apparatus by the sofa, the tiny inkstand, the quill-nibbed pen-holder, the unpretentious implements of her work. She was a little woman, she liked little things. She had miniature editions of the classics, with her name written in each in her sensitive, fine writing, and always her husband's name added above her own, for she dedicated all her books to him : it was a fancy she had."

Mrs. Browning was not witty or gossipy, but she had a graceful humour of her own, a quaint, playful way of putting things. Though she was ready to enter into the joys and sorrows of others, great deeds, celebrated persons, and the questions which affect humanity at large, touched her most nearly. It was during her happy life at Florence that she wrote *Casa Guidi Windows,* in which she shows how deeply she loved " poor trampled-down Italy that was really groaning its heart out." Austrian tyranny was hateful to her, and she hoped great things from Napoleon III., from Victor Emmanuel, and from Pius IX.

During a visit to Paris, *en route* for England, she gives a graphic account of an interview with George Sand, whom she had addressed in one of her poems as " Thou large-brained woman and large-hearted man ! "

At the first meeting Mrs. Browning was going to kiss her

hand, but George Sand exclaimed, "Non, je ne le veut pas," and, stooping down, kissed her, and again when they parted. The second meeting did not seem so satisfactory. The Brownings found George Sand surrounded by crowds of ill-bred men—"society of the ragged red, diluted with the low theatrical." Mrs. Browning adds : "We couldn't penetrate, couldn't really touch her ; it was all in vain."

During the journey from Italy the box was lost in which part of the MS. of *Aurora Leigh* was packed. Mrs. Ritchie tells us that this same box also contained certain velvet suits and lace collars, in which the boy Browning was to make his appearance to his English relations. Mrs. Browning's chief concern was not for her manuscripts, but for the loss of her little boy's wardrobe. "He is more to me," she says, "than a hundred Auroras." The box fortunately turned up all right. It had been stowed away at Marseilles in one of the custom house cellars.

Aurora Leigh may be called an autobiographical novel in blank verse. Blank verse is generally considered tough reading, but Elizabeth Browning makes it throb with life ; the problems of modern society, the difficulty of bringing the rich in touch with the poor, are fully dwelt on. In unity of plan and sustained dramatic interest it fails, but cameos of thought, pearls of philosophy are scattered richly through it. Aurora is a woman-poet, full of energy and ambition ; she refuses her cousin Romney Leigh, whom she really loves, in order to devote herself to her calling. She does not wish to

> " Make thrusts with a toy-sword,
> To amuse the lads and maidens,"

or to do excellent things indifferently ; she comes to know that her " heart's life must throb in her verse to show it lived." She passes through many experiences. She stands by the outcast, Marian Erle, whom Romney was about to

marry, and who failed to appear when the wedding guests
from east and west filled the church.   At last, when Romney's
schemes for the amelioration of the pair have all failed,
when his house is attacked, and he is blind and helpless,
Aurora flings herself into his arms.   She finds that

> " Art is much, but love is more. . . .
> Art symbolises heaven, but love is God,
> And makes heaven."

Occasionally there is a touch of sarcasm, as, for example,
when Aurora speaks of a good neighbour who

> " Cuts your morning up
> To mincemeat of the very smallest talk,
> Then helps to sugar her bohea at night
> With your reputation."

Though Robert Browning never saw his wife's poems till
they were finished, still his influence can be traced.   Along
with womanly tenderness there is a masculine strength, a
penetrating insight into the heart of things.   *Aurora Leigh*
has many blemishes ; it seems to have been flung off without
much attention to artistic finish ; it is rough and rugged
sometimes, and the expressions verge on coarseness, yet, all
the same, it is the finest poem ever written by a woman.
It was received with enthusiasm, and edition after edition
was called for.   It was the book of the year.

The Brownings soon returned to Italy, and in Nathaniel
Hawthorne's Note Book for 1858 he tells us in his inimitable
way how he paid a visit to Casa Guidi, Mr. Browning, " a
most vivid and quick-thoughted person," having invited
him.

" The street is a narrow one," he says, " but on entering
the palace we found a spacious staircase and ample accom-
modation of vestibule and hall, the latter opening on a balcony, whence we could hear the chanting of priests in a

church close by. Browning came into the ante-room to meet us, as did his little boy, whom they call Pennini for fondness. Mrs. Browning met us at the door of the drawing-room and greeted us most kindly, a pale, small person, scarcely embodied at all, at any rate only substantial enough to put forth her slender fingers to be grasped, and to speak with a shrill, though sweet, tenuity of voice. Really I do not see how Mr. Browning can suppose that he has an earthly wife, any more than an earthly child. Both are of the elfin race, and will flit away from him when he least thinks of it. She is a good, kind fairy, however, and sweetly disposed to the human race, though only remotely akin to it. It is wonderful to see how small she is, how pale her cheek, how bright and dark her eyes. There is not such another figure in the world, and her black ringlets cluster down into her neck, and make her face look all the whiter by their sable profusion. I could not form any judgment about her age. It may range anywhere within the limits of human or elfin life. At Lord Houghton's breakfast-table she did not impress me so singularly, for the morning light is more prosaic than their great tapestried drawing-room, and, besides, sitting next her I was not sensible what a slender voice she had. It is marvellous to me how so extraordinary, so acute, so sensitive a creature can impress us as she does with the certainty of her benevolence. We had tea and strawberries, and spent a pleasant evening."

Mrs. Hawthorne, too, gives her impressions. She describes Mrs. Browning as very small, delicate, dark, and expressive. She looked like a spirit.

" A cloud of hair falls on each side of her face in curls, so as partly to veil her features. But out of the veil look sweet, sad eyes, musing and far-seeing and weird. Her fairy fingers looked too airy to hold, and yet their pressure was very firm and strong. I was never conscious

of so little unredeemed, perishable dust in any human
being. I gave her a bunch of small pink roses, and she
fastened it in her black velvet dress with most lovely
effect. We soon returned to the drawing-room, a lofty,
spacious apartment, hung with gobelin tapestry and pictures,
and filled with carved furniture. Everything harmonised
—poet, poetess, child, house, the rich air, and the starry
night. Pennini was an Ariel flitting about, gentle, tricksy,
and intellectual."

Mrs. Browning was a believer in spiritualism, but her
husband scoffed at it. It was the only subject on which
they differed, and they had many lively arguments about it.

By the death of Mr. Kenyon, Mrs. Browning came in for
£10,000, and it seemed as if many years of peaceful work and
happy calm were in store for her. In the beginning of 1860
she collected her political pieces, and published them as
Poems Before Congress. She spent the winter in Rome, and
after her return to Florence she caught cold ; it became
worse, and congestion of the lungs ensued. She was thought
never to have been so ill before ; then she was better—
she would soon be well. One morning she remained in
bed, but was still well enough to talk of Ricasoli and Italy.
When her boy bade her good-night that evening, she said,
"I am better, dear, much better." But as time wore on,
and her husband watched by her side, the end was seen
to be coming. She seemed to be in a sort of ecstasy, and
spoke faint words of blessing to him whom she loved so
well. But when daylight came she had another morn than
ours. At half-past four on the morning of the 29th of June,
1861, she passed into the region of shadows, in her fifty-
second year. Her husband says, "Always smilingly, happily,
and with a face like a girl's, she died in my arms, her head
on my cheek. Just before her death, when she was asked
how she felt, she answered, 'Beautiful !'"

It was her last word. No dark clouds intervened between
her and heaven ; the clouds were for those who remained

behind. She was buried in the lovely little Protestant cemetery, looking out towards Fiesoli, and a stately marble cenotaph, designed by Sir Frederic Leighton, marks her resting-place. On the wall of Casa Guidi the municipality of Florence placed a white marble slab, and in letters of gold are the words, which may be translated into English as follows :—

> " Here wrote and died
> ELIZABETH BARRETT BROWNING,
> Who in her Woman's heart united
> The wisdom of the sage and the eloquence of the poet
> With her golden verse linking Italy to England.
> Grateful Florence placed
> This Memorial
> A.D. 1861."

The loss of such a spiritual presence, so full of strength and ardour and purity is untold. We want such a woman as Elizabeth Browning to bring us back to the old traditions of those Egerias and priestesses from whom the ancients learned wisdom. To her the whole world was consecrated, as she says herself in *Aurora Leigh* :—

> " Earth's crammed with heaven,
> And every common bush afire with God."

George MacDonald calls her "the princess of poets ; in idea she is noble ; in phrase magnificent." We are continually meeting scraps of her poems in sermons, in essays, in speeches, whenever men wish to stir the hearts of men. Those who learn from her cannot but feel ennobled and elevated by so doing. The "touch of Christ's hand" was upon her. For her life, for her teaching, for her music, for herself, we never can be sufficiently grateful.

VIII.

MRS. GASKELL.

1810–1865.

Birth at Chelsea—A "little motherless bairn"—Is taken to Knutsford
—Early impressions, afterwards reproduced in *Cranford*—School life
at Stratford-on-Avon—Marriage with Mr. Gaskell—Letter to William
Howitt about Clopton Hall—Death of her son—Begins *Mary
Barton*—Success—Admiration of Charles Dickens—Acquaintance with
Charlotte Brontë—*Ruth—Cranford—Life of Charlotte Brontë*—
Manchester distress—*Sylvia's Lovers—Wives and Daughters*—Sudden
death at Holybourne.

TOWARDS the middle of the nineteenth century two
women were busily writing—one in a gloomy Yorkshire
parsonage, the other in the crowded city of Manchester—
one was the daughter of a country clergyman, the other
the wife of a Unitarian minister. One was Charlotte
Brontë, the other Mrs. Gaskell. They were, at that time,
utter strangers to one another. Their lives, their associations
were totally different. Since they became famous, they
have been often compared, and Mrs. Gaskell's novels have
been classed in the school of fiction which Charlotte Brontë
inaugurated. Yet, in reality, the two writers have very
little in common, except sincerity and earnestness.

Mrs. Gaskell had not that passionate, eager intensity
which sweeps on like a hurricane in *Jane Eyre;* she had
none of Charlotte Brontë's burning eloquence, none of her

repressed energy ; she felt deeply and fervently, but her sympathies were wider and broader, less concentrated on herself. Her mind was rather of the objective than the subjective order : she looked outward rather than inward, and in her earlier novels wrote with a distinct moral aim which Charlotte Brontë never had. In *Mary Barton* she tries to justify the poor to the rich ; in *Ruth* she wishes to show that even for the fallen there is a way back to purity and strength. She made common cause with Manchester operatives, factory girls, and mill hands ; she could see with their eyes and hear with their ears. She knew the ties of a true wife, of a tender mother ; they enlarged her range of vision, and filled her with an earnest longing to make others as noble and as pure as she felt they ought to be. Many of her books are sad, just as life is sad ; but we shut them up feeling that there is a meaning in their sadness. They show that

> " Life is not an idle ore,
> Dut iron dug from central gloom,
> And heated hot with burning fears,
> And dipped in baths of hissing tears,
> And batter'd with the shocks of doom
> To shape and use."

We cannot predict what Charlotte Brontë might have been if she had been brought up with Mrs. Gaskell's surroundings ; but we know there is a tender pathos, a wide, all-embracing motherly sympathy in Mrs. Gaskell's books which we do not find in Charlotte Brontë's. One dips her brush in the brilliant crimson of passion ; the other takes the softer hues of love—love pure as snow, and strong as death.

Elizabeth Cleghorn Stevenson was the daughter, by his first marriage, of William Stevenson, a native of Berwick-on-Tweed. Mr. Stevenson's father was a captain in the Royal Navy, and one of his brothers also. It showed great independence of character on the part of William Stevenson to strike out a career for himself. He became, successively, a Unitarian minister, a farmer, and a writer on commercial subjects, finally obtaining the Keepership of Records to the Treasury. His nephew is Father Stevenson, Director of Farm Street, whose interest in historical and antiquarian research is curiously like Mrs. Gaskell's. William Stevenson is spoken of in the *Annual Biography and Obituary* for 1830, as " a man remarkable for the stores of knowledge which he possessed, and for the modesty and simplicity by which his rare attainments were concealed." His modesty was inherited by his daughter, who always remained shy and retiring, with nothing of the noisy blue stocking or literary lioness about her. Her mother was a Miss Holland, of Sandlebridge, Cheshire, a descendant of an ancient Lancashire family. The Stevensons were living at Lindsey Row, now forming part of Cheyne Row, Chelsea, when Elizabeth was born on the 29th of September, 1810. Mrs. Stevenson died a month after little Elizabeth's birth, and the child, after being entrusted to the care of a shopkeeper's wife for a week, was taken down to her aunt, Mrs. Lumb, who lived at Knutsford, in Cheshire, about fifteen miles from Manchester. Mrs. Lumb was poor, and on account of her husband's mental condition was separated from him. She had one crippled daughter, who became Elizabeth's companion.

" The house," says Mrs. Richmond Ritchie, " where Mrs. Gaskell lived, as a little girl, is on the heath, a tall, red house, with a wide-spreading view, and with a pretty carved staircase, and many light windows, back and front. I have heard that Mrs. Gaskell, like many imaginative children, was not always happy. In her hours of childish sorrow and trouble, she used to run away from her aunt's house across the heath, and hide herself in one of the many green hollows, finding comfort in the silence and in the company of birds and insects."

She evidently alludes to herself when, in one of her novels

she compares a child who has lost his mother to a lamb shut out of the sheepfold, or a bird who cannot find its nest. At other times, she had delightful games of play with her cousins in the sweet old family house at Sandlebridge, her mother's home, where so many Hollands in turn had lived. The house was occupied by Peter Holland, Elizabeth's uncle, grandfather of the present Lord Knutsford. Sandlebridge stands lonely in a beautiful position with a view of Alderley Edge against the sky. The forge, the old mill, the blows of the anvil, and the revolving wheel had their part in Elizabeth's dreams. Knutsford itself is a "little town of many oak beams and solid-built walls, slanting gables and latticed windows, so that the High Street looks like a mediæval town. The houses have Chippendale cabinets, old bits of china, prints of George IV., and beautiful oak bannisters. Knutsford is the original of Cranford."

The inhabitants of the little Cheshire town all acknowledged the truth of the portrait. One of them says, "*Cranford* is all about Knutsford. My old mistress, Miss Hawker, is mentioned in it, and our poor cow, she did go to the field in a large flannel waistcoat, because she had burned herself in a lime-pit." The disappearance of Mrs. Gaskell's only brother, John Stevenson, a lieutenant in the merchant navy on his third or fourth voyage, about 1827, suggested an incident in *Cranford;* and surely those graphic word-pictures, fresh with dew, of Hope Farm in *Cousin Phillis*, must have been inspired by the old house of the Hollands, at Sandlebridge. "There was a garden between the house and the shady, grassy lane," says Paul Manning, who tells the story of *Cousin Phillis.* "I afterwards found that the garden was called the court, perhaps because there was a low wall round it with an iron railing on the top of the wall, and two great gates, between pillars crowned with stone balls, for a state entrance. It was not the habit of the place to go in either by the great gates or by the front door ; the gates, indeed, were locked, as I found, though the door stood wide open. I had to go round by a side path, lightly worn on a broad grassy way, which led past a horse-mount, covered with stone-crop, and the little yellow fumitory, to another door—the ' Curate,' as I found it was termed by the master of the house, while the front door, handsome and all for show, was called the Rector.' "

The farmer-minister, the Rev. Ebenezer Holman, sings a hymn with his labourers at the close of his field-work, and what a photograph of country peace is given in the account of " the warm golden air, filled with the murmur of insects near at hand, the more distant sound of voices out in the fields ; the clear, faraway rumble of carts over the stone-paved lane, miles away. The heat was too great for the birds to be singing, only now and then one might hear the wood-pigeons in the trees beyond the ash field. The cattle stood knee-deep in the pond, flicking their tails about to keep off the flies."

Elizabeth Stevenson sometimes paid visits to Chelsea to see her father, who had married again, but as the marriage was not a happy one, these visits must have been more painful than pleasant. When she was fifteen she was sent to a school at Stratford-on-Avon, kept by a Miss Byerley. Here she remained for two years, and learnt something of Latin, as well as French and Italian. It was during these school-days that she was invited to spend a day at Clopton Hall, near Stratford. The weirdness of the place made a great impression on her receptive mind, and later on we shall see how this visit turned out to be her first intro-duction to literature. In April, 1829, her father died, and from that time till her marriage, three years afterwards, she went on visits to her uncle, Swinton Holland, in London, to Newcastle-on-Tyne, with the family of Mr. Turner, a dis-tinguished Unitarian minister, and to Edinburgh.

She is described as a very beautiful young woman. She had a well-shaped head, regular, finely-cut features, brilliant expressive eyes, and perfect hands. At Edinburgh several painters and sculptors asked leave to take her portrait. She was bright, almost joyous, and a delightful companion. In height she was small, being only half a head taller than Charlotte Brontë, who was a perfect pigmy in size. On the 30th of August, 1832, she married, at Knutsford Parish Church—not at the red brick, ivy-grown Unitarian Chapel —the Rev. William Gaskell, minister of Cross Street Chapel, Manchester. She had not then completed her twenty-second year. The marriage turned out most happily. Her husband being intellectual himself, fostered and strengthened the growth of her mind. They lived first at Dover Street, then, in 1842, they moved to Rumford Street, and finally settled at Plymouth Grove. We catch a few glimpses of their happy family life, and of Mrs. Gaskell's daughters, Marianne, Meta, Florence, and Julia. Charlotte Brontë writes : " Could you manage to convey a small kiss to that dear but dangerous little person, Julia ? She surreptitiously possessed herself of a minute fraction of my heart, which has been missing ever since I saw her. That small sprite, Julia, has a great deal of her mamma's nature modified in her. I like what speaks in her movements and what is written in her face."

Mrs. Gaskell prided herself on ruling her house with care and attention. She understood the art of making a home an " earthly paradise," and she had a peculiar tact in training her servants. They felt that in her they had indeed a friend, not a mistress harsh to judge and quick to find fault. Most women find that the household cares of keeping servants and children in order are quite enough to exhaust their energies ; not so Mrs. Gaskell. Her visits among the working classes of Manchester roused a profound interest in all problems connected with their lives : an interest which afterwards brought forth abundant fruit.

For ten years Mrs. Gaskell's married life flowed on un-eventfully. It was in 1838 that William Howitt announced

his new book, *Visits to Remarkable Places*, and Mrs. Gaskell
bethought her of Clopton Hall, and wrote to him, drawing his
attention to it, and describing her girlish impressions. The
letter is so remarkable that it is worth giving here. "I
wonder," she says, "if you know Clopton Hall, about a mile
from Stratford-on-Avon? Will you allow me to tell you of a
very happy day I once spent there? I was at school in the
neighbourhood, and one of my schoolfellows was the daughter
of a Mr. W——, who then lived at Clopton. Mrs. W——
asked a party of the girls to go and spend a long afternoon,
and we set off one beautiful autumn day, full of delight and
wonder at the place we were going to see. We passed
through desolate, half-cultivated fields, till we came in sight
of the house, a large, heavy, compact, square brick building,
of that deep, dead-red almost approaching to purple. In
front was a large formal court, with the massy pillars
surmounted with two grim monsters, but the walls of the
court were broken down and the grass grew as rank and
wild within the enclosure as in the raised avenue walk down
which we had come. The flowers were tangled with nettles,
and it was only as we approached the house that we saw the
single yellow rose and the Austrian briar trained into something like order round the deep-set, diamond-paned windows.
We trooped into the hall, with its tesselated marble floor,
hung round with strange portraits of people who had been
in their graves two hundred years at least, yet the colour
was so fresh, and they were in some instances so life-like,
that, looking merely at the faces, I almost fancied the
originals might be sitting in the parlour beyond. More
completely to carry us back to the days of the civil wars,
there was a sort of military map hung up, well finished with
pen and ink, showing the stations of the respective armies,
and with old-fashioned writing beneath, the names of the
principal towns, setting forth the strength of the garrison,
&c. In this hall we were met by our kind hostess, and told
that we might ramble about where we liked, in the house or

out of the house, taking care to be at the 'recessed parlour' by tea-time. I preferred to wander up the wide, shelving oak staircase with its massy balustrade all crumbling and worm-eaten. The family then residing at the Hall did not occupy one-half—no, not one-third of the rooms, and the old-fashioned furniture was undisturbed in the greater part of them. In one of the bedrooms (said to be haunted), and which, with its close, pent-up atmosphere and the long shadows of evening creeping on, gave me an 'eerie' feeling, hung a portrait so singularly beautiful!—a sweet-looking girl, with pale gold hair combed back from her forehead and falling in wavy ringlets on her neck, and with eyes that looked like violets filled with dew, for there was the glittering of unshed tears in their deep dark blue. That was the likeness of Charlotte Clopton, about whom there was so fearful a legend told at Stratford Church. In the time of some epidemic—the sweating sickness or the plague—this young girl had sickened, and, to all appearance, died. She was buried with fearful haste in the vaults of Clopton Chapel, attached to Stratford Church, but the sickness was not stayed. In a few days another of the Cloptons died, and him they bore to the ancestral vault, but as they descended the gloomy stairs, they saw by the torchlight Charlotte Clopton in her grave-clothes leaning against the wall ; and when they looked nearer, she was indeed dead, but not before, in the agonies of despair and hunger, she had bitten a piece from her round, white shoulder ! Of course she had *walked* ever since. This was 'Charlotte's Chamber,' and beyond Charlotte's Chamber was a state room, carpeted with the dust of many years and darkened by the creepers which had covered up the windows and even forced themselves in luxuriant daring through the broken panes. Beyond, again, there was an old Catholic chapel, with a chaplain's room, which had been walled up and forgotten till within the last few years. I went in on my hands and knees, for the entrance was very low. I recollect little in the chapel, but in the chaplain's room were old, and I should think rare, editions of many books, mostly folios. A large yellow-paper copy of Dryden's *All for Love, or the World Well Lost*, caught my eye, and is the only one I particularly remember. Every here and there, as I wandered, I came upon a fresh branch of a staircase, and so numerous were the crooked, half-lighted passages, that I wondered if I could find my way back again. There was a curious carved old chest in one of these passages, and with girlish curiosity I tried to open it, but the lid was too heavy, till I persuaded one of my companions to help me, and when it was opened, what do you think we saw?—BONES! But whether human, whether the remains of the lost bride, we did not stay to see, but ran off in partly feigned and partly real terror.

" The last of those deserted rooms that I remember, the last, the most deserted and saddest, was the nursery—a nursery without children, without singing voices, without merry, dinning footsteps! A nursery hung round with its once inhabitants, bold, gallant boys, and fair, arch-looking girls, and one or two nurses with round, fat babies in their arms. Who were they all? What was their lot in life? Sunshine or storm? or had they been loved of the gods and died young? The very echoes know not. Behind the house, in a hollow now wild, damp, and overgrown with elder-bushes, was a well called Margaret's Well, for there a maiden of the house of that name drowned herself. I tried to obtain any information I could as to the family of Clopton of Clopton. They had been decaying ever since the civil wars, had for a generation or two been unable to live in the old house of their fathers, but had toiled in London, or abroad, for a livelihood, and the last of the family, a bachelor, eccentric, miserly, old, and of most filthy habits, if report said true, had died at Clopton Hall but a few months before, a sort of boarder in Mrs. W——'s family. He was buried in the gorgeous chapel of the Cloptons in Stratford Church,

where you see the banners waving, and the armour hung
over one or two monuments."

Mary Howitt says that her husband was so struck by the
graphic picturesqueness of this description that he wrote to
Mrs. Gaskell, urging her to "use her pen for the public
benefit." For some time she did not take the advice, but
when her only son, Willie, died at Festiniog, in 1844, of
scarlet fever, Mr. Gaskell, to rouse her from the depression
of her intense grief, urged her to write something. She had
begun a tale of Yorkshire life a century back, but she put
it aside for *Mary Barton*, a tale of Manchester life. A
period of great distress had been sweeping over the manufacturing towns. Chartism and Trades Unionism reigned ;
"men's hearts were failing them for fear." Disraeli, as
Professor Minto has pointed out, saw the question of the
hour, and wrote *Sybil*. Mrs. Gaskell, with real, practical
knowledge of the Manchester artisan, his difficulties and his
wrongs, saw it too ; she wrote *Mary Barton*, and wrote it
from her heart.

"I have often thought," she says, "how deep might be
the romance in the lives of some of those who elbowed me
daily in the streets of Manchester. I had always felt a deep
sympathy with the careworn men who looked as if doomed
to struggle through their lives in strange alternations between
work and want, tossed to and fro by circumstances even in a
greater degree than other men are. A little manifestation
of this sympathy, and a little attention to the expression of
feelings on the part of some of the workpeople with whom I
was acquainted, had laid open to me the hearts of one or
two of the more thoughtful of them. I saw that they were
sore and irritable against the rich."

And again—

"It is a bewildering thing for the poor weaver to see his

employer removing from house to house, each one grander than the last, till he ends in building one more magnificent than all, or buying an estate in the country, while all the time the weaver, who thinks he and his fellows are the real makers of this wealth, is struggling on for bread for his children through all the vicissitudes of lowered wages, short hours, fewer hands employed, &c. And· when he knows trade is bad, he is bewildered to see that all goes on just as usual with the millowners. Carriages still roll through the streets, concerts are still crowded with subscribers, the shops for expensive luxuries still find daily customers, while the workman loiters away his unemployed time in watching these things and thinking of the pale, uncomplaining wife at home, and the wailing children asking in vain for enough of food. The contrast is too great."

The more Mrs. Gaskell pondered on these things the more the fire burned. *Mary Barton* is a " novel with a sob in it." It is not the history of one family ; like *Les Misérables*, it typifies the life of a whole city. The operative, John Barton, sullen and querulous, with his grievances against the rich— his pretty daughter, Mary—the wealthy manufacturer, Mr. Carson, and his son—Job Legh and his granddaughter, the Wilson family, the outcast Esther—all are vivid and distinct. Combinations between masters and men ensue, and the " hands " bind themselves by a solemn oath, the gas is put out, and John Barton draws the lot which pledges him to the murder of young Mr. Carson. The wrong man, Mary's lover, James Wilson, is accused of the crime. Mary's desperate efforts to save her lover ; her journey to Liverpool, to overtake the only witness who can prove the *alibi*—have real dramatic force. We can almost hear the splash of the oars which carries the frail boat all too slowly out to sea ; we can almost see the " gloomy, leaden sky, the cold, flat, yellow shore in the distance," we can almost feel the " nipping, cutting wind " ; but the lights of the *John Cropper* flash, the news of the trial is shouted out to the only witness, and Mary's lover is saved.

Mrs. Gaskell is at home alike in the damp, fœtid, miserable cellar of the Davenports, where the family is laid low with typhus, and in the drawing-room of the Carsons ; while John Barton, brooding over the past, sore, irritable, and yet with a sense of right in all his struggles, has no counterpart in fiction.

The first volume of the novel was finished about 1846, and the book was completed a few months afterwards. For more than a year the MS. was buffeted about between the publishers, and Mrs. Gaskell said she "forgot all about it." Early in 1848 Messrs. Chapman and Hall made an offer for it, and bought the copyright for £100. It was published on October 14, 1848—a year after *Jane Eyre*—without the author's name. It at once aroused universal attention. Carlyle wrote a congratulatory letter, and Landor addressed a poem "to the authoress of *Mary Barton*," which concluded with the words—

> " And thou hast taught me at the fount of Truth
> That none confer God's blessing but the poor."

Some critics admitted Mrs. Gaskell's power, but declared she had a want—"she had no humour." Yet, in reality, she had a great deal of humour ; but there was not much scope for it in *Mary Barton*—in that Rembrandt picture, full of storm and tempest, of the tears, the struggles, and the long-suffering patience of the manufacturing classes.

Miss Edgeworth, just before her death, spoke enthusiastically of the interest of *Mary Barton*, which she sometimes felt to be too harrowing, and George Eliot said, that during a trip up the Rhine one dim, wet day in the spring of the year when she was writing *Adam Bede*, she satisfied herself for the lack of a prospect by reading over the earlier chapters of *Mary Barton*. It has been translated into French,

13

German, and several other languages, including Finnish.
It has been the cause of an immense improvement in the
relations of masters and men. People began to say to each
other, " Can these things be ? " No one welcomed the new
writer more eagerly than Charles Dickens. He was two
years younger than Mrs. Gaskell, but, as an author, he was
many years older. *Pickwick, Oliver Twist,* and *Nicholas
Nickleby* were already written, and he was bracing himself
for new efforts. Mrs. Gaskell's deep sympathies with the
working classes specially appealed to him ; it accorded with
his own. When she came to town in May, 1849, she
was invited to dinner at his house in Devonshire Terrace
to celebrate the beginning of *David Copperfield,* and met
there Carlyle and his wife, Thackeray, Samuel Rogers,
Douglas Jerrold, and Hablot Brown. When Dickens
thought of starting *Household Words,* he wrote to Mrs.
Gaskell, saying there was no living English writer whose aid
he would desire to enlist so much as the authoress of *Mary
Barton.* "I should set a value on your help," he writes,
"which your modesty can hardly imagine, and I am perfectly sure that the least result of your reflection or observation in respect of the life around you, would attract attention
and do good. . . . My great and unaffected admiration of
your book makes me very earnest in all relating to you."
Another notable acquaintance whom Mrs. Gaskell made at
this time was Charlotte Brontë. They met in August, 1850,
at the house of Sir J. K. Shuttleworth, and were mutually
pleased with each other. Mrs. Gaskell soon became fond of
the shy little authoress, and felt deeply for the sorrows of her
private life. In 1851, Charlotte Brontë went on a visit to
Mrs. Gaskell at Manchester, and the visit was returned in
1853. We catch a glimpse of the two friends from Mrs.
Gaskell's *Life of Charlotte Brontë.* They were walking
over the purple moors together, when Charlotte Brontë
observed that she believed some people were appointed to
sorrow and disappointment, that it did not fall to the lot

of all to have their lines in pleasant places. Mrs. Gaskell took a different view ; she thought that human lives were more equal, that to some happiness and misery came in strong patches of light and shadow, while in the lives of others they were equally blended. After they parted, Charlotte Brontë compared Mrs. Gaskell's letters "to the nourishing efficacy of daily bread," or to a page of *Cranford.*

Mrs. Gaskell consented to write for *Household Words,* and the first number (March 30, 1850) contained the beginning of *Lizzie Leigh.* She continued to write short stories for it, and a great part of *Cranford* appeared in it, Dickens himself giving the titles to some of the chapters. Her Christmas story, the *Moorland Cottage,* came out in 1850, illustrated by Birket Foster.

Her next long novel was *Ruth.* Ruth Hilton is a dressmaker's apprentice in a provincial town. She is an orphan, and almost friendless. Sent to the Shire Hall to hand pins to the ladies who attend the county ball, she sees Mr. Bellingham, who is struck by her beauty. Innocent and unsuspicious, she takes Sunday walks with her new acquaintance, and, in the end, he induces her to go to London with him. Her fate is now sealed. In Wales, Mr. Bellingham falls ill ; his mother arrives, and Ruth soon finds herself deserted. Now the lesson of the book begins ; how, even for the fallen, there may be hope and energy ; how—

> " Of our vices we can frame
> A ladder, if we will but tread
> Beneath our feet each deed of shame."

A dissenting minister, Mr. Benson, and his sister, Faith, take pity on Ruth ; they bring her into their house ; by their help, and by the tender love called forth by her child, she is purified and ennobled. When her faithless betrayer turns up and is again attracted by her, she is able to turn from him with loathing ; in the end she dies from a fever caught by nursing the man who has poisoned her life.

Mrs. Gaskell stood forth an enemy of cant and Pharisaism ;
she treated the delicate subject of a girl's fall from virtue
with boldness and truth.   Many women have tried the same
subject, notably Mrs. Norton, in *Lost and Saved,* but Mrs.
Gaskell has touched it with infinitely more power, complete-
ness, and pathos.   There is no quality more marked in her
than her purity ; such a quality was peculiarly necessary
in *Ruth* ; there was every temptation to tinge it with a
lurid and crimson glow, but Mrs. Gaskell did nothing of the
kind.   Ouida generally makes vice prosperous and successful.   Mrs. Gaskell treated it in a sterner spirit.
Ruth tastes the bitter cup of humiliation to the dregs.
When she is turned out of Mr. Bradshaw's house and
called by every shameful name, we feel that full measure
is indeed meted out to her.   " Would to God I had died ! "
she cries in the bitterness of her soul, as she reveals
the secret of his birth to her son.   *Ruth* came out early in
1853, Charlotte Brontë, with characteristic generosity, having
postponed the publication of *Villette,* so that it might not
interfere with Mrs. Gaskell's book.   " Arrange as we may,"
she adds, " we shall not be able wholly to prevent comparisons ; it is the nature of some critics to be invidious, but
we need not care ; we can set them at defiance ; they shall
not make us foes ; they shall not mingle with our mutual
feelings one taint of jealousy ; there is my hand on that.
I know you will give clasp for clasp.   *Villette* has, indeed,
no right to push itself before *Ruth.*   There is a goodness, a
philanthropic purpose, a social use in the latter to which the
former cannot for an instant pretend."

Ruth was not as successful as *Mary Barton.*   Some disliked the subject, though none could deny the sympathy with
which it was treated.   Comparing it with *Mary Barton* M.
Montégut, the French critic, says one is like a frosty winter's
day with the dull wind sweeping through the bare streets
and the icicles hanging on the trees, the other (*Ruth*) is like
a calm day in autumn, when the leaves are turning yellow

and the birds are singing their last songs in the rapidly-
waning sunlight. It is interesting to read George Eliot's
verdict on it. "Of course," she says, writing to Mrs. Taylor,
"you have read *Ruth.* Its style was a great refreshment to
me from its finish and fulness." She goes on to say, "How
pretty and graphic are the touches of description I That little
attic in the minister's house, for example, which, with its pure
white dimity curtains, its bright green walls, and the rich
brown of its stained floor, remind one of a snowdrop spring-
ing out of the soil. Then the rich humour of Sally and the
sly satire in the description of Mr. Bradshaw. Mrs. Gaskell
has certainly a charming mind, and one cannot help loving
her as one reads her books."

Mrs. Gaskell was very sensitive to blame, but suspected
and disliked what she considered over-praise. Dickens told
her she was "always looking for soft sawder in the purest
metal of praise." And writing about *Ruth*, he says, "Forget
that I called these two women my dear friends. Why, if I
told you a fiftieth part of what I have thought about them,
you would write me the most suspicious of notes refusing to
receive the fiftieth part of *that.*"

When the author of *Uncle Tom's Cabin* was the
lioness of the London season, she records, in her *Sunny
Memories,* meeting Mrs. Gaskell. "She has a very lovely,
gentle face," adds Mrs. Stowe, "and looks capable of all the
pathos her writings show. I promised her a visit when I
go to Manchester."

Mrs. Gaskell got into the habit of going abroad whenever
a new work of hers was in the press, that she might be
out of the way of the criticisms that were poured upon it.
In Paris, she had a faithful and original friend—lively,
frank, Madame Mohl (Mary Clarke)—who hated stupid
people, and whose greatest ambition was to *faire un salon.*
Madame Mohl had the gift of making her house pleasant,
and consequently it was crowded with brilliant guests, who
were satisfied to eat biscuits and talk. Madame Mohl loved

and admired " her dear Mrs. Gaskell," who often paid a visit
to the Rue du Bac ; that same house where Madame
Récamier once had her *salon*, and where Châteaubriand died.

In June, 1853, the series of sketches which had appeared in
Household Words, was published under the name of *Cranford.*
It is needless to praise the grace, the tenderness and the delicate humour of these studies of life in a provincial town in the
days when George III. was king. Old maids *were* old maids
then, not emancipated spinsters.

" Cranford was in possession of the Amazons, for all the
holders of houses above a certain rent are women. If a
married couple come to settle in the town, somehow the
gentleman disappears ; he is either fairly frightened to death
by being the only man at the Cranford evening parties, or
he is accounted for by being with his regiment, his ship,
or closely engaged all the week in the great commercial
town of Drumble." " A man," as some one observed once,
" is so in the way in a house."

It was at Cranford (Knutsford) that the Honourable Mrs.
Jamieson lived, and Mrs. Forrester, born a Tyrrell, besides
Miss Pole and the two Miss Jenkyns. They meet at tea-
parties, wear dressy caps, play Preference and Cribbage, and
after the tray of refreshments is brought in, clatter home in
their pattens. They all practise " elegant economies," and are
terribly afraid of robbers. Miss Matty Jenkyns is a wonderful study ; she is so timid, amusing, and pathetic, that we
want to keep her with us. " It is very pleasant dining with
a bachelor," she says, softly (she is fifty-three, and is spending
the day with her old love, Mr. Holbrook) ; " I only hope it
is not improper—*so many pleasant things are.*"

Cranford is described by Lord Houghton as the purest
piece of humouristic description that has been added to
British literature since Charles Lamb. It showed Mrs.
Gaskell's talents in a new light : in *Mary Barton* she
was forcible, dramatic, almost lurid ; in *Cranford* she was
sprightly, arch, and playful.

North and South, after first appearing in *Household Words*, came out as a book in 1855. The heroine, Margaret Hale, is from the South of England, and is full of aristocratic prejudices. Her father gives up his living from conscientious motives, and she is obliged to go, much against her will, to live at Milton, a town in the North of England. Everything and every one is strange and repellent to Margaret, and no one more so than Mr. Thornton the millowner, to whom her father gives Latin lessons. He does not seem to her a gentleman. Yet when the mill-hands, exasperated into rebellion, attack his house, she stands by him, and eventually marries him. So the South is conquered by the North. Margaret loses her Southern prejudices and acknowledges the sturdy strength and independence of the Northern character.

Mrs. Gaskell's men are not women in men's clothes—they are distinctive, strong, often full of faults, but perfectly lifelike. In *North and South* Mrs. Gaskell blended her two styles —her former and her later one. She still keeps to those scenes of Manchester life that had first struck her readers in *Mary Barton ;* but she also brings in the quiet life of a country parsonage, in which Margaret's father, the conscientious clergyman, plays a part. In these chapters there is a foretaste of those delicate touches of middle-class life which delighted so many in *Wives and Daughters.*

When Charlotte Brontë died, in 1855, Mrs. Gaskell was chosen by Mr. Brontë as the fittest person to write her Life, and this Life remains one of the best ever written by a woman of a woman. Mrs. Gaskell viewed her friend from one particular standpoint, and as different lights flow in, this view may be modified or brightened ; but written when it was, it gives a trustworthy portrait of the " firehearted vestal of Haworth," and such a task demanded an immense amount of judgment, patience, and skill. Mrs. Gaskell spared no pains in getting first-hand information about the places connected with her friend. She went to

Brussels to see it for herself, and to ensure accuracy. Yet some of the statements about the Clergy Daughters' school, which she had heard from Charlotte Brontë's lips, were called in question, and brought down so many angry attacks that she was obliged to announce in the later editions that any further letters must come through her attorney.

"We thought it admirable," writes George Eliot; "we cried over it, and felt the better for it. Deeply affecting in the early part, romantic, poetic as one of her own novels ; in the later years tragic, especially to those who know what sickness is. Mrs. Gaskell has done her work admirably, both in the industry and care with which she has gathered her materials, and in the feeling with which she has presented them, except that she puts down Branwell's conduct entirely to remorse. Remorse will not make such a life as Branwell's was in the last three years, unless the germ of vice had sprouted and shot up long before."

This judgment was afterwards confirmed when the truth about Branwell's life came out in the light of subsequent years.

Few biographies contain so little of the writer's self—Mrs. Gaskell kept that formidable " I " in the background, and rarely brought it forward. For some time after the publication of Charlotte Brontë's Life she wrote much less than usual. The discussions and squabbles which it caused gave her a distaste to writing. Early in 1857 she went, with two of her daughters, to Rome, where they were the guests of Mr. W. W. Story. She also spent some time in Paris with lively Madame Mohl. During this visit Prosper Merimée, the celebrated French *littérateur* happened to meet her. "You ask me," he writes to a friend, "what I think of Mrs. Gaskell ? She must have been very pretty, and her daughter gives an idea of what she was. I find the same defect in both of them. It is *un air pleureur*. It is not melancholy, but the expression of some one who

has broken a Sévres porcelain. She took tea at my rooms
the other day with Madame Mohl, and she did not say
three words. I had the blue devils, and we parted *assez
furieux.*"

Mrs. Andrew Crosse, in her *Red Letter Days*, gives
quite a different impression of Mrs. Gaskell. She says :
" There was a genuine warmth and geniality in her manner
—nay more, a fascination about her—that made you regret
the time you had never known her."

Mrs. Gaskell had what Lowell calls a " talent for friendship." She brimmed over with love and sympathy. As
like attracts like, so she drew to her in close intimacy many
good and distinguished women—Susanna Winkworth and her
sister Catherine, to whom we owe the *Lyra Germanica*, Lady
Augusta Stanley, the beautiful and noble-minded Lady
Hatherton, and the two Miss Nightingales. At Manchester
Mrs. Gaskell was sought out by every stranger of distinction
—English, Continental, and American—who passed through
the town, and her house became a centre of intellectual life.
She was called upon for active work with hand and head
when the cotton famine of 1862–3 swept over Lancashire, and
brought with it terrible distress amongst the unemployed.
Her daughter, writing to Madame Mohl, says : " We had
been to London to see the Exhibition of 1862, and had had
the brightest, gayest time possible. We were greeted
directly we got back to Manchester by the terrible news
that, owing to the American war, the cotton supply was failing, and that a famine was beginning to spread over Lancashire. I shall never forget the horror of it. Nobody at first
spoke of organising relief ; and nobody then could have
dreamt that the crisis could have been met and conquered.
I believe that *we* should have just sunk down in despair,
hopelessly watching the incoming tide of misery. But you
know how my mother always sprang to the rescue when
help was needed. She began immediately to think over all
possible plans. Strangely enough, the one that she hit on,

was precisely the one afterwards adopted by the Public Relief Committee, as the best for helping the girls and women, who form such a large proportion of factory hands.

"She planned to gather together as many working women as a large room in our house would hold, and to give them needlework, for which she would pay them, not reckoning the value of the work, but rather paying in proportion to their necessary expenses for food and lodging. Before she had time to carry out this plan, the need for a great public organisation was felt. A committee of ladies was appointed, of whom my mother was one. Sewing-schools, as they were called, were opened ; and my mother worked hard for six or seven hours a day in arranging and superintending them. Her health quite broke down under the excessive strain. One little thing that happened was quite characteristic of her. In one of the sewing-schools, the one to which she went oftenest, there were about five hundred Irishwomen of the lowest class, wild and inclined to resent all control. When the bell for dismissal rang, they always rushed to the door in a regular stampede, eager to escape from the confinement and discipline which they hated. Several really serious accidents occurred. The mistress of the school engaged a soldier as a *commissionaire* to stand at the door, and keep order ; but after one or two days' experience, he was so frightened that he left. He didn't want, he said, to have an arm or leg broken. My mother at once decided to take his post and to try the plan of shaking hands with each woman as she left the room, and wishing her 'good afternoon.' She hoped that this proof of confidence would bring out the innate courtesy of the Irishwomen. She was quite right. Where every one else had failed, she succeeded. Order was re-established. These great, rough women passed through the door, one by one, and stopped, blushing with pleasure, quietly and gently, 'to shake hands with the lady.'"

We are reminded of Elizabeth Fry winning the heart of

a refractory convict by the simple words, "I hope to hear better things of thee."

The cotton-famine crisis over, Mrs. Gaskell returned once more to her pen, and began *Sylvia's Lovers.* She went to Whitby (Monkshaven) and spent some time there, so as to ensure truth in the local colouring. The story is dedicated to her " dear husband, by her who best knows his value." In it we are brought back to the days when George III. was king, to the days of press-gangs and dear bread. Pretty, coy, bewitching Sylvia Robson, a farmer's daughter, near the seaport of Monkshaven, cares little for her solemn cousin, Philip Hepburn, the draper's assistant ; her fancy is taken by brave, daring Charlie Kinraid, the whaler's mate, and she is troth-plighted to him. As he is carried away by a press-gang, he sends her a parting message by Philip, which message Philip never gives. Sylvia believes Kinraid is dead ; but though Philip steps into his place and wins her for his wife, though he is prosperous and successful in outward things, the living lie spoils his household peace. His worst fears are realised. Kinraid comes back and meets Sylvia, who takes a solemn oath against her husband, Philip, for keeping the truth from her. Stung by her reproaches he goes away and enlists, and Sylvia does not see him again till, mangled and heart-broken, he returns to die. *Sylvia's Lovers* is the least popular of Mrs. Gaskell's novels, but it is quite worthy of her genius, though the tragedy is almost painful in its intensity and gloom. Monkshaven, the whalers, Haysterbank Farm, stand out like one of Turner's sea pieces, " while the waves come lapping on the shelving shore."

Mrs. Gaskell's last novel, *Wives and Daughters*, is altogether more cheery and bright. Part of it was written in Madame Mohl's *salon.* Mrs. Gaskell stood by the mantelpiece and used it as a desk. *Wives and Daughters* was for some time the great attraction of the *Cornhill Magazine*, and few guessed that before the story was completed the hand that wrote it would be cold in death. Most of us are acquainted with Molly Gibson, the doctor's daughter, and with Dr. Gibson himself, a trifle cynical but good-hearted and honourable. We see that his second wife, Mrs. Kirkpatrick, is not good enough for him ; she is somewhat deceitful and tricky, accustomed to practise elegant gentilities on small means, and to turn over the greasy pages of a novel with a pair of scissors. His brilliant daughter, Cynthia, we feel will be a formidable rival to good little Molly, and so it turns out, for Roger Hamley, with a man's perverseness, at once falls in love with her. But worldly Cynthia deserts Roger, and Molly is taken at her true value. The story, as far as construction goes, is as commonplace as Mrs. Oliphant could choose, but Mrs. Gaskell's fine touches make it distinctly original. We are sometimes indifferent whether Mrs. Oliphant's heroines marry the right people or not ; but our sympathies with Molly Gibson are as warm as if we had known and loved her all our lives. If Mrs. Gaskell had shown in *Mary Barton* and *Ruth* that she could write exciting and dramatic scenes, in *Wives and Daughters* she accomplished the still more difficult task of making the every-day story of a doctor's daughter as interesting as a romance.

Only a few months before Mrs. Gaskell's death, George Sand observed to Lord Houghton, "Mrs. Gaskell has done what neither I nor any other female writer can accomplish— she has written novels which excite the deepest interest in men of the world, and yet which every girl will be the better for reading." When George Eliot wrote, in 1859, to thank Mrs. Gaskell for her " sweet, encouraging words," she says, " While the question of my powers was still undecided for me, I was conscious that my feeling towards life and art had some affinity with the feelings which had inspired *Cranford*, and the earlier chapters of *Mary Barton*."

Wives and Daughters was not quite finished when Mrs. Gaskell was staying at a country house at Holybourne, near

Alton, in Hampshire, which she had purchased with the proceeds of her last book. She was talking with her daughters on Sunday, November 12, 1865, when she fell back and died suddenly at the age of fifty-five. Success, the love of her friends and family, the admiration of those who might have been her rivals, smiled on her, but the summons came. Surely when she "crossed the bar" there were hands stretched out to greet her, and voices to welcome her.

She was buried in the place she most loved—at Knutsford —in the graveyard of the old Unitarian Chapel, and there, too, her husband was laid to rest beside her, in 1884. Tablets are put up to the memory of both in the Chapel of Cross Street, Manchester.

Mrs. Gaskell did not begin to write till she was thirty-five, so her literary life only lasted about twenty years. Yet what work she gave ! Besides her novels, she wrote *A Dark Night's Work*, and that exquisite idyll *Cousin Phillis*, which is like a delicate water-colour sketch. Only the story of a girl's slighted love, yet how it stirs the heart and touches the fount of tears !

Mrs. Gaskell believed that the art of telling a story is born with some people, and cannot be acquired. We are told by Mrs. Richmond Ritchie that she and her sister were under the same roof with Mrs. Gaskell, at the house of Mr. and Mrs. George Smith at Hampstead, and she says that the remembrance of Mrs. Gaskell's voice comes back to her, harmoniously flowing on and on, " with spirit and intention and delightful emphasis, as we all sat indoors one gusty morning, listening to her ghost stories."

For purity of tone, earnestness of spirit, depth of pathos, and lightness of touch, Mrs. Gaskell has not left her supe-rior in fiction. One who knew her said, " she was what her books show her to have been, a wise, good woman. She was even more than wise or good. She had that true poetic feeling which exalts whatever it touches, and makes nothing common or unclean. She had that clear insight which sees all and believes in the best."

IX.

CHARLOTTE BRONTË.

1816–1855.

Birth—Eccentricities of Mr. Brontë—Cowan Bridge—Round the kitchen fire—At Roe Head—An excursion to Bolton Abbey—A governess—At Brussels—Poems by Ellis, Currer, and Acton Bell—*The Professor*—*Jane Eyre*—Death of Emily—*Shirley*—*Villette*—Marriage—Death.

SOME authors seem like shadows ; their voices interest, amuse, or excite us, but about the owners of those voices we care little or nothing. With other authors the case is different ; soul has spoken to soul, a responsive chord is touched, we feel a strange spiritual kinship with them ; they seem like our brothers, our sisters, our friends. Charlotte Brontë, by virtue of a strong personality and an ardent and vigorous genius, has thus projected herself into the minds of her readers, and made herself one with them. Thus every detail connected with her, whether true or false, is eagerly pounced upon. Years upon years have fled since she was laid in Haworth Churchyard, yet still public interest hovers around her ; and though hundreds of novelists have written hundreds of novels since she has passed away, yet troops of visitors halt at the Haworth station, in order to visit that grim parsonage among the rugged Yorkshire hills with its outlook of graves and its background of moors. Tourists diligently read the long line of inscriptions under the organ-loft of the village church, and

CHARLOTTE BRONTË.

BORN APRIL 21ST, 1816 ; DIED MARCH 31ST, 1855.

bring away some trifling relic of the place—a flower, a pebble, a sprig of heather—to remind them of that lonely little woman, with her projecting forehead, her deep-set eyes, her insignificant figure, and her glowing heart, who lived, and wept, and wrote amidst such uninviting scenes. In addition to Mrs. Gaskell's *Life*, pronounced by Thackeray to be "necessarily incomplete, though most touching and admirable," we have also Mr. Wemyss Reid's *Monograph*, which gives many more interesting particulars of Charlotte Brontë, impossible to be told during her father's lifetime in 1857. Mrs. Gaskell gave us one reading of Charlotte Brontë's character, Mr. Reid another, less gloomy, less morbid, with brighter lights and deeper recesses. Like her own Jane Eyre, Charlotte Brontë laughed rarely, but she could laugh very merrily. Her intimate friend, Miss Ellen Nussey, the "dear Nell" to whom she wrote her last pencilled note, received hundreds of letters, in which every phase of thought and feeling was unfolded. Some of these letters give new peeps into the inner life of the author of *Jane Eyre*.

Not at Haworth, but at Thornton, "an ordinary one-street village, set amongst the shaggy Yorkshire hills," Charlotte Brontë was born on the 21st of April, 1816. Like Maria Edgeworth and Lady Morgan, she had an Irish father and an English mother. The Rev. Patrick Brontë came from Ahaderg in the County Down, and his original name was Prunty. His family was poor and obscure, and the clever handsome Irish lad was patronised by Mr. Tighe, the rector of Drumgooland. Just before the young Irishman left for St. John's College, Cambridge, he changed the name of Prunty, at the request of Mr. Tighe, for the better-sounding one of Brontë. Mr. Brontë obtained a curacy in Yorkshire, and there he met, wooed, and married his Cornish wife, Miss Branwell, a shy, gentle, retiring little woman, who found her husband to be one of those men who are more feared than loved in their own households. His quick eagle eyes, his aquiline nose, his stern dictatorial ways, showed that he was not to be trifled with. Few would imagine that in his youthful days he had published two volumes of poetry, yet such is the case. In after life he appeared to be a scrupulously polite old gentleman, tall and thin, his chin hidden in the folds of his large white neckcloth, who chatted on volubly, boasted of his conquests with the fair sex, and seemed a " mere fribble, gay, conceited, harmless," but there would come a searching glance from the keen deep-set eyes which revealed the secret of what the real man was. When some friend gave his wife a present of a very pretty gay-coloured dress he took affront and resolved that she should never wear it, so he deliberately cut it up and presented her with the pieces. There was a grim irony in the act which marked the character of the man. Though he habitually took his meals alone, yet he would sometimes appear at the breakfast-table and tell his daughters weird Yorkshire legends, or stories of the still wilder life which he had left behind at sea-washed Ahaderg. From this eccentric father, however, the Brontës inherited their great powers of mind, their energy, their courage, and their fervid imagination.

Mr. Brontë's restlessness betrayed itself in a hundred ways ; the story of his carrying loaded pistols in his pockets, and when he was peculiarly excited firing them at the doors of the outhouses, is a well-authenticated fact. He was not, as a rule, outwardly violent to others, but had a particular taste for diplomacy. Once he and Charlotte had a quarrel about one of her friends. He first burst into a passion, " the veins of his forehead swelled, his eyes glared, his voice shook." Charlotte left the house for a few days, and, firm as he was himself, refused to receive any letters in which this friend's name was mentioned. Now came cunning instead of fury. Long and affectionate letters came to Charlotte on general subjects, but also a slip of paper supposed to be from her pet dog Flossy, in which the attacks on the obnoxious person were renewed. Mated to such a stern lord, the gentle wife, nurtured amidst the mild, soft atmosphere of Penzance, drooped and died in her chilly Yorkshire home, and left five girls and one son to grow up with their eccentric but still affectionate father, their rough servant Tabby, and their prim, orderly aunt, Miss Branwell, who clattered about the stone-paved entries and passages on pattens for fear of catching cold. When the little Brontës invited the Sunday-school children to the parsonage and wished to amuse them they were obliged to ask the children to teach them how to play, for they had never learned. Yet their imaginations were briskly at work. Mr. Reid tells us that little Charlotte when she was only six was so moved by the brilliant imagery of the *Pilgrim's Progress* that she resolved to hasten off at once to the Golden City and make her escape from Haworth, which she believed to be the City of Destruction. She had heard the servants speak of Bradford ; it was the only place which seemed to resemble that far-famed city with its golden streets and gates of pearl. So off she set by herself, but when she came to a gloomy spot, overshadowed by trees, her fears overwhelmed her. This must indeed be the Valley of the Shadow of Death. Her knees trembled, her heart failed. Crouching by the roadside, she was found by her nurse and brought back to Haworth. To her things unseen had become as though they were. Her school-days at the Charitable Institution of Cowan Bridge, where she was hardly ever free from the pangs of hunger, have been so accurately reproduced in *Jane Eyre* that any account of them is needless. The early death of the two elder Brontës, the sufferings of Maria (the original of Helen Burns) from illness and tyranny, all worked a deep impression on little Charlotte's sensitive mind. She has made us familiar with the long dreary schoolroom, " its hearth surrounded by a double row of great girls, and behind them the younger

14

children crouched in groups, wrapping their starved arms in their pinafores." The uneaten breakfasts of burnt porridge, the two miles' walk to church on Sunday, when the miserable school-girls "set out cold, arrived at church colder, and during morning service became almost paralysed," are photographed on almost every one's mind.

When Charlotte was nine years old she and Emily were removed from the damp, unwholesome atmosphere of Cowan Bridge, and the old life at Haworth began again. The little party had their own amusements. They read Tory newspapers, wrote tales and plays innumerable, contributed to their own magazine, which came out once a month, and peopled islands with their favourite heroes. Charlotte's island was the Isle of Wight, and her heroes the Duke of Wellington and two sons, Christopher North and Co., and Mr. Abernethy.

How well we can imagine the eager, intent faces of the four Brontë children as they sat before the blazing kitchen fire one December night, when the "cold sleet and stormy fogs of autumn had been succeeded by snowstorms and piercing night winds." A battle with Tabby about lighting a candle had just come off, in which she had been victorious, and amidst these twilight surroundings the islands were peopled. The children in Charlotte Brontë's books, Paulina Home, Jessy and Rose Yorke have an uncanny weirdness about them. They are not real children; they are grown-up people in the form of children, moved by the same passions and interests as their elders. Rose and Jessy talk politics, and Paulina already has a romance. Thus Charlotte Brontë read the nature of children. She and her sisters never had any of the careless joys of youth; they were young, but not youthful; meditative, but not sad.

In January, 1831, Charlotte was sent to school again, this time to Miss Wooler's, at Roe Head, which was a cheerful, roomy mansion, standing in a field. Her friend Mary says she first saw "Charlotte coming out of a covered cart, in very old-fashioned clothes and looking very cold and miserable. She looked like a little old woman, so short-sighted that she always appeared to be seeking something, and moving her head from side to side to catch sight of it. She was very shy and nervous, and spoke with a strong Irish accent."

Her friendship with Miss Nussey (the Caroline Helstone of *Shirley*) now began. "E." took pity on the oddly-dressed, old-looking little girl, and home-sick Charlotte confided to her friendly ear all the secrets of the magazine, and even told her a tale out of it. She used to stand under the trees in the playground and point out the peeps of the skies and the shadows. So, at Cowan Bridge, she used to stand in the burn on a stone to watch the water pass by. But she never wanted to go fishing ; she was too much of a dreamer for that. She was already busy " making out " things. She saw strange moonlight visions, she heard weird voices. Her ardent spirit, which had been temporarily quenched by the dull privation of Cowan Bridge, now began to look through the bars of its prison-house.

In order to illustrate one of the bright spots in Charlotte Brontë's life, Mr. Reid gives us a vivid picture of the three girls and their brother as they drove up, one bright June morning in 1833, to the Devonshire Arms, opposite Bolton Bridge. They were bound for an excursion to Bolton Abbey, and were to meet Miss Nussey, who was waiting for them, with some companions, in a handsome carriage and pair. The Brontës' conveyance was not a handsome carriage, but a " rickety dogcart, unmistakably betraying its neighbourship to the carts and ploughs of some rural farmyard." The horse, freshly taken from the fields, was driven by Branwell, whose shock of red hair hangs about his ears in ragged locks ; as he is a genius and a poet, he has forsworn the use of shears. " Beside him, in a dress of marvellous plainness and ugliness, stamped with the genuine home-made brand, sits Charlotte. She is talking too ; there

are bright smiles on her face.   She is enjoying everything—
the splendid morning, the beauties of leafy trees and fields
and streams.   At seventeen the charm of her brother's
society and the expectation of meeting her friend is enough
to make life pleasant.   The two younger sisters, Anne, a
pretty little girl, with fine complexion and delicate features,
and Emily, a tall, angular figure, clad in a dress exactly
resembling Charlotte's, sit behind."   Emily does not talk
much, but " at times she utters a deep guttural sound, which
those who know her best interpret as the language of a joy
too deep for utterance."   When the dogcart rattles up to
the Devonshire Arms there is silence, " the sisters draw a
long breath, and prepare for that fiercest of all ordeals they
know—a meeting with strangers."   Charlotte's schoolfellow
still remembers how the merry talk and laughter of her
friends were quenched, and how the three girls clung to each
other or to her, scarcely venturing to speak above a whisper,
and betraying in every look and word the positive agony
which filled their hearts when a stranger approached them.
Yet beneath this shrinking exterior what a world of eager,
tumultuous feelings was concealed ; like a hidden volcano,
which only occasionally bursts its crust !

   That " bitter tasting of the cup as it is mixed for the
class called governesses " was peculiarly unpleasant to such
natures as these.   Charlotte's motive for attempting this
distasteful work was to enable her brother (who showed
a taste for painting) to get a thorough artistic training.
She first commenced as a teacher at Miss Wooler's school ;
then she took a situation in the family of a rich Yorkshire manufacturer.   Her mind was torn at this time
with religious difficulties.   She shrank from an austere
Calvinistic creed, and her governess life, " sedentary, solitary, constrained, joyless, toilsome," pressed heavily upon
her.

   " I am miserable," she writes, " when I allow myself to

dwell on the necessity of spending my days as a governess. The chief requisite for that station seems to be the power of taking things easily when they come, and of making oneself comfortable and at home wherever one may chance to be— qualities in which all our family are singularly deficient. I know I cannot live with a person like Mrs. ——, but I hope all women are not like her."

Tasks of all kinds were demanded of her. She was asked to hem yards of muslin, to make nightcaps, even to dress dolls, and was severely reprimanded for her depression of spirits. When one of her pupils put up his face and said, " I love 'ou, Miss Brontë," his mother answered, " Love the *governess*, my dear ! " Such petty slights cut Charlotte's sensitive spirit like a knife. " I see," she says, " that a private governess has no existence, is not considered a rational being except as connected with the wearisome duties she has to fill." One of her mistresses, after treating a person on the most familiar terms for a long time, did not scruple, if anything went wrong, to give way to anger in a most coarse, unladylike way. From such types as these Charlotte gleaned her idea of Mrs. Reed in *Jane Eyre*.

One might have imagined that she would gladly have taken refuge from this uncongenial life in marriage, but she refused two offers, one from an Irish curate, and one from T., a grave, quiet young man. For this last proposal she admitted that there were some things which might have proved a strong temptation ; but, conscientious to the core, she put the following questions to herself : " Do I love T. as a woman ought to love her husband ? Am I the person best qualified to make him happy ? " To both these questions she had to answer " No ! " She had not that intense attachment which would make her willing to die for him. " And if I ever marry," she adds, " it must be in the light of adoration that I will regard my husband."

Life at Haworth was sweet after governess thraldom. The occupations there were certainly not very spirit-stirring. The girls sewed in their aunt's bedroom, then Miss Branwell read aloud to Mr. Brontë from six to nine ; at nine Mr. Brontë, Miss Branwell, and old Tabby were all in bed, and the three sisters were free to pace about the house till midnight. They often busied themselves with household work. Emily did the baking, Charlotte managed the ironing, and sometimes blackleaded the grates, made the beds, and swept the floors.

" To be either a private companion or a governess," says Lucy Snowe, " was unnatural to me. Rather than fill the former post in any great house I would deliberately have taken a housemaid's place, bought a strong pair of gloves, swept bedrooms and staircases, and cleaned stoves and locks in peace and independence. Rather than be a companion I would have made shirts and starved. But I could teach, I could give lessons."

Charlotte and Emily's favourite plan *was* to teach, to set up a school ; Miss Branwell advanced some money, and the two sisters decided on going abroad, before the enterprise was started, to perfect themselves in French and German. Through some friends they had heard of M. and Madame Héger's school at Brussels, and they accordingly set out for the Rue d'Isabelle full of hope and courage. This Brussels period of Charlotte Brontë's life, first as pupil, then as teacher, influenced her books and her character to a surprising extent. Mr. Reid has done good service in marking it out as the turning-point of her life. Her thoughts are perpetually recurring to the Belgian capital, to the episodes of the foreign schoolroom, to the heavy animal Flamandes and the lively superficial French girls who peopled the wooden benches.

" Belgium ! " she cries in *The Professor ;* " name unromantic and unpoetic, yet name that, whenever uttered, has in my heart an echo such as no other assemblage of syllables, however sweet or classic, can produce. Belgium ! I repeat the word now as I sit alone near midnight ; it stirs a world of the past ; like a summons to resurrection, the graves unclose, the dead are raised — thoughts, feelings, memories that slept are seen by me ascending from the clods."

At Brussels Charlotte's mind expanded more than it had ever done. M. Héger's mode of teaching was peculiarly adapted to bring out her powers of analysis and comparison. He would make his pupils read different accounts of the same person or event, and mark the various points of agreement or disagreement between them. For instance, Bossuet's *Discours* on Cromwell, then Guizot's account of him, then Carlyle's, and from these conflicting elements they must compose their *Dévoirs*, and give a many-sided idea of the man. When she had Peter the Hermit for a subject she attacked it *con amore ;* the Old Testament history—so familiar to her—the Grecian myths and legends, all suggested similes and imagery; when she had the "Death of Napoleon " for a theme, all the innate poetry of her nature awoke at the thought of the hero chained to a sandbank ; yet she does not forget to give Wellington, the Tory apostle of law and order, the higher place. These *Dévoirs* became a keen pleasure ; the spreading shoots of her imagination, which might have branched out into wild extravagances, were clipped and pruned by the experienced hand of her tutor. Writing always in French, too, she acquired a freedom and ease of language in a foreign tongue which made her own as plastic as wax. She was no longer kept down, she was appreciated ; beauty and fashion were not at a premium in the Brussels schoolroom ; originality, mental and moral faculties had their innings, and made their influence felt.

"Our likings are regulated by our circumstances," says Mr. Crimsworth, the Professor ; "the toil-worn, fagged, probably irritable tutor, almost blind to beauty, insensible to airs and graces, glories chiefly in certain mental qualities. Application, love of knowledge, natural capacity, docility, truthfulness, gratefulness, are the charms that attract him."

The shy governess-pupil's mind grew rapidly under these congenial influences. In teaching, she felt her power of controlling others ; in being taught by a master she reverenced, her faculties awoke to their full height ; she sought after the best, she was not content with "pretty well," she soared into a wider horizon. Her lines from *The Professor* give a glimpse of how her labours went on :—

> "Obedience was no effort now,
> And labour was no pain ;
> If tired, a word or glance alone
> Would give me strength again ;
> The task he from another took
> From me he did reject,
> He would no slight omission brook,
> And suffer no defect."

It is curious that Frances Henri, Shirley, and Lucy Snowe all write French *Dévoirs*, and these *Dévoirs*, by their sweep and glow of eloquence, show the mark of Charlotte Brontë's early genius ; perhaps she took them, just as they were, from her desk, thrown off in some bright moment of her Brussels life. There were English friends at Brussels, too, relations of some of the pupils, and Charlotte spent pleasant visits with them, which broke the monotony of school routine. For some time she and Emily worked together ; then came the news of Miss Branwell's death, and a summons back to Haworth. At Haworth Emily remained, while Charlotte returned alone to Brussels. This was, doubtless, the *sturm und drang* chapter of her life.

"I returned to Brussels," she says, "after aunt's death, *against my conscience*, prompted by what then seemed an irresistible impulse. I was punished for my selfish folly by a total withdrawal for more than two years of happiness and peace of mind."

The Haworth neighbours remarked that Miss Brontë's future *époux* must live within the sound of the bells of St. Gudule. Such suggestions roused Charlotte's wrath to the utmost. Yet it now seems plain that in the Brussels school-room she had found her real master, not a possible husband, one with whom such a tie could not exist, but one who nevertheless ruled her spirit, the original of Paul Emanuel, irascible, quaint, peremptory, lovable.

When Charlotte Brontë told the tale of Jane Eyre, the obscure governess ; of Caroline Helstone, the penniless clergyman's niece ; of Lucy Snowe, the school-teacher, she made all three suffer from the same cause—the concealment of a troubled, fevered heart under an habitual mask of cold-ness and indifference. What the agony of such a perpetual enforced shutting in of the deepest emotions was, Charlotte Brontë knew but too well. With strong and deep feelings, a glowing imagination and a restless spirit, this "fire-hearted vestal of Haworth" had also a rigid, inflexible sense of duty and a firm, indomitable will. Yet the iron entered deeply into her soul. Mrs. Gaskell made a mistake in attributing the gloom of her life solely to her brother's degradation ; no second-hand grief could have twined its roots so remorse-lessly into her nature. In her books we see her story, written so that he who runs may read. When Lucy Snowe rushes from the great empty schoolroom to the confessional of a Roman Catholic priest, impelled, strict Protestant as she was, to let loose her burdened spirit somehow or some-where, this was a real chapter from the author's own life. Not even to her friend Ellen could Charlotte tell the little odd things, queer and puzzling enough, which she does not like to trust to a letter. "When we find ourselves," she adds, "at Haworth or at B., with our feet on the fender, curling our hair, they may be communicated." With her

spirit shaken to its very centre, her nerves thoroughly un-
strung, and her heart trembling in every fibre, she returned
to the dreary parsonage, that "many-windowed grave."
Things were not improved there—Branwell, once the pride,
was now the disgrace of the family, a burden that could
not be shaken off, drunken and dissolute. He had gone to
be a tutor, had fallen in love with the mother of his pupils,
and had been turned away ; he had been a station-master,
and had neglected his duties ; now there was no hope for
him. Every day he sank lower and lower in moral
degradation. Mr. Brontë's eyesight was becoming affected,
and the school project proved an utter failure, no pupils
turned up, nor could any be expected with such an inmate
as Branwell in the house. "If I could leave home I should
not be at Haworth," writes Charlotte. "I know life is
passing away, and I am doing nothing, earning nothing ;
a very bitter knowledge it is, too, at times, but I see no way
out of the mist." Continual repression of feeling weighed
heavily, dull monotony was worse. "The sea wrought and
was tempestuous, and cast up sand and shingle on the shore."

Charlotte had written a few poems ; she now wrote more.
Emily also produced some verses written in secret, and
Anne also had her little hoard. These were collected into
a small volume "by Currer, Ellis, and Acton Bell," the sisters
paid their money, and the book was given to the public.
But the public did not care about it. Charlotte had not the
gift of song ; she had poetry in abundance, but songfulness,
the natural outbreak of the heart into verse as its proper
vehicle of expression, was not hers. Her verses are com-
mon-sensical, stoical, stern, but they are not poetry, sometimes not better than doggerel. Here, for instance, is a
specimen of one of the best :—

> " There's no use in weeping,
>   Though we are condemned to part,
> There's such a thing as keeping
>   A remembrance in one's heart ;

There's such a thing as dwelling
On the thought ourselves have nursed,
And with scorn and courage telling
The world to do its worst."

No ! Charlotte Brontë, do her best, *could* not sing ; she
could only make what Carlyle calls "a wooden noise," and
her so-called poems showed rather what she could *not* than
what she could do. The next thing was to begin a novel.
Each of the sisters set to work in that business way
characteristic of them. They began simultaneously, after a
long consultation, in which they settled the plots of their
stories and even the names of their characters. Then they
sat round the table of their sitting-room, each busy with her
pen. Charlotte's thoughts naturally turned to the still
recent period of her stay at Brussels. She tried to produce
something sternly true, faithful to the realities of common
life. Her hero, William Ormisworth, was to be a tutor in a
school, he was never to get a shilling that he had not earned,
no sudden windfalls were to lift him in a moment to prosperity, he was not to marry a beautiful girl or a lady of rank,
but Frances Henri, a lacemender, a subordinate school-
teacher. Hampered by the line she had laid down for herself, Charlotte Brontë allowed her imagination small scope,
yet her characters have a distinctness which showed that her
genius had at length found its fitting voice. Mr. Hunsden
is the germ of Edward Rochester, and Frances Henri of
Caroline Helstone.

The Professor was too tame for the London publishers.
This is what the author says of it : " Currer Bell's book
found acceptance nowhere, nor any acknowledgment of
merit, so that something like the chill of despair began to
invade his heart." Back and back again it came, till, at last,
with the rejected MS. came a few words of discriminating
criticism from Messrs. Smith and Elder, and a promise to
examine another work should such be written. These words
were like sparks on tow. Charlotte's soul caught fire. She

had already begun *Jane Eyre*, and during the visit which she had to make to Manchester with her father, who had to undergo an operation for cataract, she wrote busily. When she got her heroine to Thorndale she could not stop ; she was irresistibly carried on by the force of her story. On the 24th of August, 1847, when she. was thirty-one, her novel was finished and sent from Leeds to London. What its fame was, how it even "swept past *Vanity Fair* " and earned for its obscure author a wider circle of readers than even Thackeray could boast—who had been building up his reputation with years of toil and labour—is a twice-told tale.

Jane Eyre was new and startling. No one had ever dared to make a heroine plain, small, and insignificant. Charlotte Brontë had done this. No one had ever dared to hint that the magnetic attraction which draws one soul to another is a stronger bond than mere beauty or grace can be. Charlotte Brontë had done this. Her pages glowed ; her people lived ; her readers were spellbound, held as the wedding guest was by the ancient mariner, and unable to escape from the charm. Thackeray says that with his own work pressing upon him he could not, having once taken the volumes up, lay them down till they had been read through. It was vain for critics to talk of " courtship after the manner of kangaroos," " coarseness of language," " laxity of tone," " horrid taste," and " sheer rudeness and vulgarity " ; blemishes there were, but they were only like smuts on the face of a statue. *Jane Eyre* held its own triumphantly, and, as Mr. Reid says, in two months became famous through two continents. In what does its great merit consist ? Not in the plot ; that is at times clumsy ; and Miss Braddon has now made us so familiar with bigamy that the idea falls dully on our hardened ears. Yet *Jane Eyre* still continues to interest, for its power of interesting mainly consists in the people who stand before. us—living, breathing realities. Rochester — black-browed, square-shouldered, abrupt, rude—has an individuality about him ; Jane Eyre is a distinct person ; they are not put together like bits in a dissecting-map. We do not think it probable that such persons may have been ; we know they *are*. They have been alternately torn with passion and principle ; they stir with glowing life, their speech is sometimes eloquent, sometimes epigrammatic, but never dull or wordy ; they are always dramatic.

Who can speak of the immorality of *Jane Eyre* when the whole drift of the book is the purest morality ?—the victory of duty over inclination. Rochester is, indeed, no saint ; he is an erring man, deeply sinning, deeply punished, and finally saved by the conscientiousness of the woman whom " he suits to the finest fibre of her nature."

In writing *Jane Eyre* Charlotte Brontë had given her soul its natural release. Her poems had been like " dull narcotics lulling pain ; " but this vivid picture of human beings wrestling, struggling, agonising, was a fitting outlet for that " perilous stuff " which had been seething and bubbling in her so long. " Women," she says in *Jane Eyre*, " are supposed to be very calm generally, but women feel just as men feel ; they need exercise for their faculties, and a field for their labours, as much as their brothers do. They suffer from too rigid a restraint, too absolute a stagnation, precisely as men would suffer, and it is narrow-minded in their more privileged fellow-creatures to say that they ought to confine themselves to making puddings and knitting stockings, to playing on the piano and embroidering bags."

As months went on, hundreds of speculations were made as to the author of *Jane Eyre*. Who could the mysterious Currer Bell be ? A man, declared some of the reviewers ; no woman would speak of " trussing game " ; no woman would dress a lady in a morning robe of sky-blue crape, and no woman would " hurry on a frock." Then followed the rumour that the author intended to satirise Thackeray under the name of Rochester, and even to obtrude on his private troubles. If Currer Bell should prove to be a woman, she must be some discarded being, who, according to the *Quarterly Review,* " had, for some sufficient reason, forfeited the society of her own sex." Shocked at such reports, and anxious to contradict the notion that Currer, Ellis, and Acton Bell were one and the same person, and that *Wuthering Heights* and *Agnes Grey* were inferior works by the author of *Jane Eyre,* Charlotte Brontë resolved on a journey to London. She and Anne set off by the night train ; when they arrived, after breakfasting at the station, they walked to Cornhill, and had some difficulty in penetrating to the head of the publishing house. "At last," says Mr. Reid, "he came in, saying, with some annoyance, 'Young woman, what do you want with me?' 'Sir, we have come up from Yorkshire to speak with you privately. I wrote *Jane Eyre.*' '*You* wrote *Jane Eyre!*' cried the delighted publisher, and taking them into his office, he insisted on their coming to the house of his mother, who would take every care of them."

So the mystery was out : Currer Bell was not a man but a woman, small, shy, and shrinking—no bold, brazen Jezebel, but a *ci-devant* governess—a Yorkshire parson's daughter. Introductions followed, and Charlotte often related the strange contrast between the desolate waiting at the station in the early morning and the brilliant assemblage at the Opera House, where the two timid women were taken by their new friends to see the *Barber of Seville,* and to listen to the singing of Jenny Lind.

Though Charlotte never shone in society, still she could talk well in a *tête-à-tête,* and her eyes, now full of fire and now of softness, were so expressive that her large nose and wide mouth were forgotten. Mrs. Gaskell describes her eyes as large and well-shaped, their colour a reddish-brown, but if the iris was closely examined, it appeared to be composed of a great variety of tints. "The usual expression was of quiet, listening intelligence ; but now and then, on some just occasion, for vivid interest or wholesome indignation, a light would shine out as if some spiritual lamp had been kindled. As for the rest of her features, they were plain, large, and ill-set. . . . Her hands and feet were the smallest I ever saw. When one of the former was placed in mine, it was like the soft touch of a bird in the middle of my palm.' The delicate, long fingers had a peculiar fineness of sensation, which was one reason why all her handiwork, of whatever kind, writing, sewing, knitting, was so clear in its minuteness. She was remarkably neat in her whole personal attire, but she was dainty as to the fit of her shoes and gloves."

Family troubles soon darkened the brilliance of literary glory. In September, 1848, Branwell died, without any preliminary warning. "Many," writes Charlotte, "would think our loss rather a relief than otherwise, yet the last earthly separation cannot take place between near relatives without the keenest pangs on the part of the survivors. Every wrong and sin is forgotten then ; pity and grief share the memory and the heart between them."

Death, having found its way into Haworth Parsonage, was not satisfied without another victim. Four months after Branwell died, Emily was snatched, panting, from life. The grim story of her death, her resolute determination to dress herself the morning she died, her refusal to touch medicines or stimulants, or even to own that she was ill, and then the last faint whisper of her exhausted spirit, " I will see a doctor if you send for him now," have a stern pathos which suits the mind that could have originated *Wuthering Heights.* The father, with his two remaining daughters and the fierce old dog Keeper, which Emily had loved better than any human being, followed her to her grave.

We are sometimes told that Emily's genius was of even a higher order than her sister Charlotte's, but *Wuthering Heights*, after all, is more of a prophecy than a performance. It is crude, vigorous, and fragmentary. The flashes of poetry and power which gleam through the darkness, cannot make it what a work of genius ought to be— finished, rounded, and complete.

Emily had not been dead six months when Charlotte and Anne, accompanied by Miss Nussey, set off to Scarborough for the benefit of sea-air. Mild, gentle Anne was rapidly fading away. We are told the sad story how the little party stopped at York, and how Anne made purchases of bonnets and dresses from her bath-chair, and even visited the Minster. Then followed the arrival at Scarborough, Anne's prostration next morning on going to the baths, and her fall at the garden gate. Her end came so gradually that her friend carried her downstairs ; she sat at the breakfast-table and took some bread and milk, and at two o'clock she was dead. "Take courage, Charlotte, take courage," were her last words ; and Charlotte *did* take courage.

When she returned to Haworth alone, and her father met her with "unwonted demonstrations of affection," she tried to be glad to be at home again ; but gladness, never a frequent guest with her, could hardly now be a familiar friend. During the lifetime of her sisters she had written the first two volumes of *Shirley ;* she now began the third, the most brilliant and picturesque of the three ; she slackened the reins of her imagination ; she gave free scope to her fancy—to her descriptive power ; she listened to the voice that spoke to her in secret. There is more variety of character, too, in *Shirley* than in *Jane Eyre ;* instead of having two prominent characters, she fills her canvas with a cluster of vigorous portraits. The three curates, Mr. Malone, Mr. Sweeting, and Mr. Donne, the Yorke family, with their sharply-defined peculiarities, and last, but not least, the old Cossack, Helstone, show a grim humour and an insight into the various contrasts of human nature of which there was little trace in *Jane Eyre.* Mr. Swinburne goes so far as to say that "no more lifelike and memorable portrait than Mr.

Helstone was ever wrought into the composition of an ideal or historic picture. The man's hard, rigid, contemptuous, yet never quite unkindly or unrighteous, force of character, his keen enjoyment of action and struggle, his fierce, imperious relish of resistance, the fine soldierly quality of spirit which made him always less ready to go with Sir Priest than Sir Knight—all these points are relieved and combined with a skill and strength perhaps incomparable in the work of any other woman."

The old Cossack, Helstone, was a portrait of Mr. Brontë. Every novelist must, to a certain extent, copy from life ; the care to be taken is that these copies are not caricatures, in which certain leading traits are exaggerated, while others, which might counterbalance them, are left in the background. This mistake Charlotte Brontë has not made. With the care and pains of a true artist, she has done her subject justice. Mr. Helstone is not an absolute tyrant, but his is a stern, hard nature which brooks no weakness, and asks for none of the sweet amenities of life. He wishes women to be fools ; and though he can enjoy a fencing match with the fearless and fascinating Shirley Keeldar, he will stand no nonsense from the women of his own household. Shirley, " sister to the bright fiery spotted leopard," a " being of fire and air," was Emily Brontë ; but Emily beautified, idealised, glorified, warmed by the sun of prosperity and softened by the purple light of love. Charlotte Brontë may be said to have done for her people what Tennyson describes so well :—

" As when a painter, poring on a face,
Divinely through all hindrance finds the man
Behind it, and so paints him that his face,
The shape and colour of a mind and life,
Lives for his children ever at his best."

Shirley is no Mammon-worshipper. "Small maxims, narrow rules, little prejudices, aversions, dogmas, must be bundled off. She washes her hands of the lot," and " this pantheress, beautiful, forest-born, tameless, fearless," is at length subjugated by the tutor, Louis Moore. He who taught her can alone lead her. The descriptive bits in *Shirley* flash like gleams of light. " The moon reigns glorious, glad of the gale, as glad as if she gave herself to his fierce caress with love," is said by Mr. Swinburne to "paint wind like David Cox, and light like Turner." Charlotte Brontë's inspiration was caught from her beloved purple moors. We can almost see her eyes kindle and her face glow as she looks at them. And out of the Valley of the Shadow of Death came that sob of anguish. " Till break of day she wrestled with God in prayer. Not always do those who dare such Divine conflict prevail."

Through the loneliness that pressed upon her, through weariness and painfulness and illness, she wrote on and on, till *Shirley* was finished in the autumn of 1849. It was greeted with a burst of praise. Those who had murmured at *Jane Eyre* were vanquished by the vigour of *Shirley*.

In December Charlotte Brontë went to London, and found fame waiting for her.

"Ever since I arrived," she says, " I have been in a whirlwind." And then she *naïvely* tells how she has a fire in her bedroom evening and morning, and two wax candles. " Mrs. —— and her daughters seemed at first to look upon me with a mixture of respect and alarm ; but all this is changed. . . . She treats me as if she liked me, and I begin to like her much. Kindness is a potent heart-winner." There was, too, a certain little man, Mr. X. (afterwards a suitor), "who tries to be very kind, and even to express sympathy sometimes, and does not manage it. He has a determined, dreadful nose in the middle of his face, which, when poked into my face, cuts into my soul like iron. He is horribly intelligent, quick, searching, sagacious, and with a memory of relentless tenacity."

On one occasion she met some of her critics who had been her bitter foes in print, but were prodigiously civil face to face. "These gentlemen seemed infinitely grander, more pompous, dashing, showy, than the few authors I saw. Mr. Thackeray, for instance, is a man of very quiet, simple demeanour. His conversation is very peculiar—too perverse to be pleasant." What Thackeray thought of her he has told us in his *Roundabout Papers.* "I remember," he says, "the trembling little frame, the little hand, the great honest eyes. An impetuous honesty seemed to me to characterise the woman. She spoke her mind out ; she jumped too rapidly at conclusions. New to the London world, she entered into it with an independent, indomitable spirit of her own. . . . She was angry with her favourites if their conduct or conversation fell below her ideal. Once about Fielding we had a disputation. She spoke her mind out. . . . Often she seemed to me to be judging the London folk prematurely. . . . I fancied an austere little Joan of Arc marching in upon us, and rebuking our easy lives, our easy morals. She gave me the impression of a very pure and lofty and pure-minded person. A great and holy reverence of right and truth seemed to be with her always."

London society did not suit her, nor did she suit it. George Henry Lewes, with whom she had corresponded, found her "a little plain, provincial, sickly-looking old maid." People were disappointed in her, and things that were popular, such as Macready's acting, did not please her. In the critical faculty she was singularly deficient. She could not appreciate Balzac or Jane Austen. Her remarks on *In Memoriam* are singularly wanting in discernment, and she owns that she cannot admire "a certain wordy intricate obscure style of poetry such as Elizabeth Barrett Browning writes."

One of the strangest episodes of her life was when, during another visit to London, she attended one of Thackeray's lectures. All the London literary world was there, and when it was rumoured that the author of *Jane Eyre* was in the room, all eyes searched for her. She was found, timid and blushing, under the wing of her chaperon.

In the autumn of 1851 she began *Villette*. Here, more even than in her two previous books, her real self comes out. Every sentence, as Mr. Reid says, was wrung from her as though it had been a drop of blood. Lucy Snowe appears cold (she *must* have a cold name), but beneath this frigid exterior is concealed a restless, glowing nature. At first this outwardly unattractive teacher, shut up in the regular routine of foreign school life, gives her heart secretly to the handsome doctor, Graham Bretton, who is constantly thrown in her way. At times Reason remonstrates. " This hag, this Reason, would not let me look up, or smile, or hope. She could not rest unless I was altogether crushed, cowed, broken in and broken down. According to her, I was born only to work for a piece of bread, to await the pains of death, and steadily through life to despond." While this unspoken romance is going on, M. Paul Emanuel, the testy little Professor of Literature, is stamping and storming from the estrade at his pupils. In his ink-stained paletot and bonnet grec, with his close-shaven black head, square forehead, and steel-blue eyes, how imperious, how despotic, how irritable he is ! By degrees we come to know the little man better. He waters the orange-trees, he puts chocolate comfits and interesting books into Lucy Snowe's desk, and though he hisses into her ear sometimes, and is jealous, fitful, and sarcastic, still we are sure he is kindly disposed. She breaks his spectacles, and he does not scold ; he gives a *fête*, and we feel his simple-hearted pleasures and his rare smiles. At length we find the man is a hero. He has been supporting the two helpless women who have wronged him in his youth, and his life has been a series of self-sacrifices. Like Lucy Snowe, we bow our heads and acknowledge ourselves vanquished. Thus it is that people slowly steal upon us in real life. Bit by bit we get to know them. M. Paul is Charlotte Brontë's masterpiece. Surely the quaint, faulty little professor did live and move in the foreign schoolroom, did glare from his " lunettes " at the offending pupils, but to those who soothed or comforted him was as meek as a lamb.

In *Villette* Charlotte Brontë gave her deepest convictions on human life. She is not oppressed with the idea of an overruling Fate ; she assents to it. " I think," says Lucy to Paulina, " it is decreed that you two should live in peace and be happy amongst mortals. Some lives are thus blessed ; it is God's will, it is the attesting trace and lingering evidence of Eden. Other lives run from the first another course. Other travellers encounter weather fitful and gusty, wild and variable, breast adverse winds, are belated and overtaken by the early closing winter night. Neither can this happen without the sanction of God."

Charlotte Brontë was more than a year writing *Villette*. Once her work stood obstinately still. " No spirit moves me," she writes ; "a torpid liver makes a torpid brain." She went for a lonely stay at Filey, which did her inexpressible good, and after a week's visit from her friend Ellen she fell to business ; the " welcome mood came, and her eyes were tired from scribbling." She did not follow Dr. Johnson's advice and sit down doggedly ; she waited till the spirit came. " I have been silent lately," she says, " because I have accumulated nothing since I last wrote." Depression often thrust in his grim visage. "My life," she writes to her friend Ellen, " is a pale blank, and often a very weary burden, the future sometimes appals me."

On the 22nd of November, 1852, her task was finished. She always felt that she had done her very best in *Villette*, and was keenly pained when a small circle of critics found something in the third volume of the MS. which stuck " confoundedly in their throats." Alteration, with her, was impossible. " I must have my own way in the matter of writing," she says. " I must bend as my powers tend."

Even at the request of her father she would not alter the close of *Villette*. Lucy Snowe's romance must have a tragical ending, Paul Emanuel must have a mystery over his fate. Her readers must be satisfied with what is offered. "My palette affords no brighter tints. Were I to deepen the reds or burnish the yellows I should only blotch." She knew the public taste better than her critics. *Villette* was welcomed as a real heart-history, and M. Paul is one of those characters in fiction which stand out from the common herd. Mr. Swinburne goes so far as to compare him with Don Quixote, and to give Charlotte Brontë the highest rank as a novelist, while he places George Eliot in the second place.

It is interesting to see the effect *Villette* had on George Eliot, who at that time had not entered the rank of novelists, and was only Marian Evans, living with her father at Foleshill. She writes: "I have been reading *Villette*, a still more wonderful book than *Jane Eyre*. There is something almost preternatural in its power." And she says again to her friend Miss Hennell: " *Villette*, *Villette*—have you read it ? "

With *Villette* Charlotte Brontë's career as an author ended. We are all tolerably familiar with the closing scenes of her life, with the faithful, long-enduring love of Mr. Nicholls for her, as faithful as that of Jacob for Rachel, with Mr. Brontë's determined resistance ; with Charlotte's hesitating compliance with her father's wishes, with her yearning tenderness towards Mr. Nicholls, and her deep grief as she parted from him at the garden gate, "when she was trembling and miserable." Then came the old Cossack's gradual relenting as his keen eyes rested on the daughter he was so fond and proud of, whose health and spirits now drooped as they had never drooped before. The brilliant novelist was now only a household fairy, attending on sick old Tabby, and with a heavy burden at her heart. Mr. Brontë at last consented that his late curate should be summoned

back to Haworth, and Mr. Nicholls' marriage with Charlotte
Brontë took place June 29, 1854, when she was thirty-eight.
A brief gleam of sunshine came to her hitherto clouded
life. With her husband she visited his native Ireland, and
went to Killarney and Glengariff. She found him always
" reliable, truthful, faithful, affectionate, a little unbending
perhaps, but still persuadable and open to kind influences. I
pray," she says, "to be enabled to repay as I ought the affectionate devotion of a truthful, honourable, unboastful man."
This joy which had come to her so late was as a roadside
flower, not startling or brilliant, but mild and fragrant. "As
far as my experience of matrimony goes," she says, "I think it
tends to draw you out and away from yourself. I think those
married women who indiscriminately urge their acquaintance
to marry much to blame. For my part, I can only with deeper
sincerity and fuller significance what I have always said in
theory—wait God's will." These months of gentle peace and
tender expectation were not fated to last long. Charlotte
Nicholls was only a wife for eight short months. Her friends
thought that all would soon be well, and that her illness would
have a joyful termination, but she grew weaker and weaker.
"I cannot talk," she says, " even to my dear, patient, constant Arthur ! I can only say but few words at a time."

Then came the wild March morning when she spoke no
more words, but passed away and left the two watchers
alone in the dismal parsonage. The blinds were down, the
dog howled, the keen wind swept over the moors, and so
one of the most richly-gifted women of the century went
forth into the land of spirits. " Can you see many long
weeds and nettles among the graves ?" asks sick Caroline
Helstone, " or do they look turfy and leafy ?" "I see
closed daisy-heads," answers Mrs. Pryor, "gleaming like
pearls on some mounds. Thomas has mown down the
dock-leaves and rank grass and cleared all away." So we
may think of Charlotte Brontë's life. The nettles and
docks of turbulence and passion and unrest had been mown
away, that the daisy-heads might show more white.

X.

GEORGE ELIOT (MARY ANNE CROSS).

1819–1880.

Birth at Arbury Farm—Griff House and its surroundings—Brother and sister—Fishing in the canal—At school at Nuneaton and Coventry—Housekeeping—Constant depression—Removes to Foleshill—Intimacy with the Brays—Influence of Miss Hennell—Translates Strauss's *Leben Jesus*—Death of her father—At Geneva—Rosehill—Work on the *Westminster Review*—Meets Mr. Lewes—A winter in Germany—Begins *The Sad Story of the Rev. Amos Barton*—*Janet's Repentance*—*Adam Bede*—*The Mill on the Floss*—*Silas Marner*—*Felix Holt*—*The Spanish Gypsy*—*Middlemarch*—*Daniel Deronda*—Death of Mr. Lewes—Marriage with Mr. Cross—Death.

I WELL remember the short December day in the winter of 1880, when the news came that George Eliot was dead. Nothing had been heard of her illness ; she passed away so suddenly that her death seemed like a translation. The world felt a great deal poorer without her. It was as though a mighty forest tree had been hewn down, and we could no longer rest under the shadow of its greatness. In spite of the joyous bustle of Christmas, in spite of the merry chime of Christmas bells, a feeling of sadness would break in, as we remembered what a vast, sympathetic nature had faded away into that region far beyond our ken.

In her life, as well as in herself, we find many startling contradictions, many unexplained inconsistencies. She was

"GEORGE ELIOT."

BORN 1820 ; DIED DECEMBER 22ND, 1880.

at once diffident and ambitious, nervous, easily depressed, and even hysterical, and yet with a keen, clear vigour of intellect more masculine than feminine. With a clinging, love-demanding nature, she amply abounded in strength for others ; plain in features, she exercised a marvellous personal attraction. Naturally of a religious turn of mind, she shook herself free from all creeds, and, intensely pure in thought and feeling, she yet took a step that drew down upon her the condemnation of many, and even now creates a sort of painful surprise. It is well for us that we are not called upon to pass judgment upon her actions, but only to state facts and to draw our own conclusions as to their motives.

Fortunately, about her merits as an author there are not many differences of opinion. " It reminds us of George Eliot," " As good as anything of George Eliot," are hackneyed phrases, which, though they often mean nothing, are supposed to convey the very maximum of praise.

She was one that all, even Saturday Reviewers, delighted to honour. She has even been classed with Shakespeare and Dante. But such comparisons are more likely to confuse than to enlighten our ideas about her as a writer.

Her novels are immeasurably superior to her poems. She has not the true " bird-note." She wrote poetry because she wished to try that form of expression, not because she *must.* So, though her poetry has many beautiful thoughts and graceful lyrics, though it is always polished and cultured, we miss the fire and inspiration of a born poet. Her greatest power was in her presentment of different varieties of character. She takes us to a country village, or to a small town with its surrounding farmhouses. She brings us from house to house, and we see into the very souls of the various inhabitants—some homely, some aspiring, some humorous, some infinitely sad and pathetic— most of them working out the problems of life under prosaic conditions, and often bruising themselves against the wires of their cage in so doing. We see the faint, ignorant promptings of good in Bob Jakin, and in honest Dolly Winthrop, and then pass on to the soaring aspirations—the passion and the pain that work in the souls of Maggie Tulliver and Dorothea Brooke. Character in her hands was no hard, cast-iron material, but subject to a hundred changes, as shifting and as variable as we find it in real life, where the same man is alternately generous and stingy, wise and foolish, petty and great. To George Eliot the secrets of human nature seemed open. She had a calm mastery over them. Other writers are like knight-errants soiled with dust, stained with blood, and charging blindly and furiously into the very thick of the fray, while she seems to be looking down from some height, able to weigh, to ponder, and to pass judgment on the conflicts that are going on. She takes a place in literature all to herself.

Her Life, told in her letters and journals, and edited by her husband, Mr. Cross, enables us to trace the many phases through which she passed. Mary Anne Evans, was born at Arbury Farm, in Warwickshire, on the 22nd of November, 1819. Her father, Robert Evans, a native of Derbyshire, was a farmer and land agent for the Arbury estate of Mr. Francis Newdigate, and was also employed by Lord Aylesford, Lord Lifford, Mr. Bromley Devonport, and others. Robert Evans is still remembered in the neighbourhood as a worthy, upright man, and suggested more than one character in his daughter's books, especially Caleb Garth in *Middlemarch*. We may remember that Caleb is described as one of those "rare men who are rigid to themselves and indulgent to others." Robert Evans was a man of great physical strength and determination of character. At Griff, one day, while two of the labourers were waiting for a third to help to move the heavy ladder used for thatching ricks, he braced himself for a great effort and carried the ladder alone from one rick to the other, to the astonishment of his men.

In 1801 Robert Evans married Harriet Poynton, and two

children, Robert and Harriet Lucy were born of this marriage. His first wife died in 1809, and on the 8th of February, 1813, he married Christiana Pearson, by whom he had three children—Christiana, born 1814, Isaac, born 1816, and Mary Anne, born on St. Cecilia's Day, 1819. In March, 1820, when the baby girl was only four months old, the Evans family moved to Griff, a comfortable, red-brick, ivy-covered house on the Arbury estate, and here Mary Anne spent the first twenty-one years of her life. There were no railways, no telegraphs, in those days, and the country about Griff was not inspiring, with neither hills nor dales, rivers, forests, or lakes to arouse the imagination. The chief event was the passing of the stage-coach before the gate of Griff House, which lies on the bend of the high road between Nuneaton and Coventry. Little four-year-old Mary Anne and her seven-year-old brother Isaac, so Mr. Cross tells us, " used to wait on bright frosty mornings to hear the far-off ringing trot of the horses' feet on the hard ground, and watch the four greys, with coachman and guard in scarlet, the passengers wrapped up in furs, and baskets of game hanging behind the boot, as his Majesty's mail swung round on its way from Birmingham to Stamford."

The little girl had an abject devotion for her brother. They went to a dame's school together at the gate of Griff House ; and she was continually running after him, wanting to do what he did—to fish with him, to spin tops, and to look for beech-nuts. Griff was a delightful place for children— there was a pond, framed in with willows and tall reeds, to fish in ; a long cow-shed, where Mrs. Evans briskly carried on her butter and cheese making ; a large barn, and a leafy, flowery, bushy " garden with roses and cabbages, gnarled apple-trees, raspberry and currant bushes."

In the poem of *Brother and Sister* we get some peeps of their child-life : "he, the little man of forty inches, bound to show no dread, and she the girl that, puppy-like, now ran,

nor lagged behind his larger tread." It was he who " picked
the fruit too high for her to reach, her doll seemed lifeless,
and no girlish toy had any reason when he came."

> " I knelt with him at marbles, marked his fling
>   Cut the ringed stem, and make the apple drop,
> Or watched him winding close the spiral string
>   That looped the orbits of the humming-top."

*   *   *   *   *

> " If he said ' Hush ! ' I tried to hold my breath,
>   Whenever he said ' Come ! ' I stepped in faith."

The two children wandered toward the far-off stream with
rod and line.

> " Our basket held a store
> Baked for us only, and I thought with joy
> That I should have my share, though he had more,
> Because he was the elder and a boy.
> Our mother bade us keep the trodden ways,
> Stroked down my tippet, set my brother's frill,
> Then, with the benediction of her gaze
> Clung to us, lessening, and pursued us still."

One day, by the brown canal, the brother left the sister in
charge of the line, and she began to muse ; "sky and earth
took a strange new light, and seemed a dream-world, floating
on some tide, a fair pavilioned boat for me alone, bearing
me onward to the great unknown." She was roused by the
coming of the canal boat, nearer and angrier came her
brother's cry, when lo ! upon the imperilled line, suspended
high

> " A silver perch !—
> When all at home were told the wondrous feat
> And how the little sister had fished well
> In secret, though my fortune tasted sweet,
> I wondered why this happiness befell."

Her recollections end with a sigh " at the dim years whose
awful name is Change, grasped our souls in divorce."

> " But were another childhood world my care,
>   I would be still a little sister there ! "

Chrissie, the elder sister, joined in none of the romps that the other two loved. She was prim, neat, and tidy, objected to soiling her pinafores, went quietly to school, and was first favourite with her aunts. There were three of them—Mrs. Everard, Mrs. Johnson, and Mrs. Garner, prototypes of Mrs. Glegg, Mrs. Pullet, and Mrs. Dodson, in the *Mill on the Floss.* They were sisters of Mrs. Evans, who, being of the yeoman class, and " born a Pearson," was on rather a higher rung of the social ladder than her husband. The aunts paid visits to Griff occasionally, and no doubt made uncomplimentary remarks on elfish little Mary Anne, who did not "favour" her mother's family. The queer little girl, with her pale cheeks—compared by her father to a turnip—and her long hair hanging over her eyes, had a great idea that she would be a personage some day. Though she did not know a note of music, she played on the piano one day when she was only four years old, to impress the servant with her superiority. She was her father's pet, Isaac was his mother's. While Mrs. Evans, a pale, sharp-voiced woman, suffering from chonic liver complaint, bustled about, giving vent to her opinions, like Mrs. Poyser, in epigrammatic talk, the " little wench " sat by her father's leather chair looking at pictures. Sometimes she stood between his knees as he drove over the breezy uplands, which, as she says in *Theophrastus Such,* we " used to dignify by the name of hills, along by-roads with broad grassy borders and hedgerows reckless of utility, on our way to outlying hamlets whose groups of inhabitants were as distinctive to my mind as if they belonged to different regions of the globe."

It was in these secluded nooks that Robert Evans and his daughter found the originals of Mrs. Waub, the Pullets, old Mr. Featherstone, and a host of others. Farmhouses *were* farmhouses in those days. Pianos and parlours were unknown, the " kitchen fires were reflected in a bright row of pewter plates and dishes, the sand-scoured deal tables were so clean that you longed to stroke them, the salt-coffer was in one chimney-corner, a three-cornered chair in the other, the walls behind were handsomely tapestried with flitches of bacon, and the ceiling ornamented with pendant hams."

Mary Anne Evans was quite at home in this farmhouse life. She eagerly drank in the racy talk, the pithy answers which she heard flying about. She herself belonged to that sturdy middle-class which is the backbone of England, and which in Warwickshire—Shakespeare's county—seems peculiarly self-reliant, honest, and independent. Robert Evans's "little wench" was no outsider, she was looked upon by the Warwickshire farmers as one of themselves—bone of their bone and flesh of their flesh. Much as she loved the breezy uplands about Griff, still "youth is made up of wants." And she must have been in her early days, as Maggie Tulliver was, a creature "full of eager, passionate longings for all that was beautiful and glad, thirsty for all knowledge, with an ear straining after dreamy music that died away and would not come near her." Like Maggie, she ran away to the gypsies one day, and, like Maggie, she sat poring over Daniel Defoe's *History of the Devil*, or sought refuge in the attic at Griff House after a quarrel with her brother. "This attic was her favourite retreat on a wet day, when the weather was not too cold. There she fretted out all her ill-humours and talked aloud to the worm-eaten floors and the worm-eaten shelves, and the dark rafters festooned with cobwebs, and here she kept a fetish which she punished for all her misfortunes. This was the trunk of a large wooden doll which once stared with the roundest of eyes above the reddest of cheeks, but was now entirely defaced by a long career of vicarious suffering. Three nails driven into the head commemorated as many crises in Maggie's nine years of earthly struggle, that luxury of vengeance having been suggested to her by the picture of Jael destroying Sisera, in the Bible." When her brother Isaac was eight years old he was sent to school at Coventry, and little Mary Anne, then five, went to join her sister at Miss Lathom's school at

Attleboro', where they continued as boarders for three or four years, coming back to Griff on Saturdays. She was naturally of a chilly temperament, and remembered the difficulty of getting near enough to the fire in winter, the elder girls forming a circle round it. But she had the delight of welcoming her brother home from school, and hearing all he had to tell her, and she had a little trip to Staffordshire and Derbyshire with her father and mother, and passed through Lichfield, sleeping at the "Swan." As her brother grew older he had a pony given to him, and, to her great mortification, cared less and less for playing with her. She was sent, at the age of nine, to Miss Wallington's school, at Nuneaton, with her sister. There were thirty girls here, all boarders. The principal governess, Miss Lewis, became Mary Anne Evans's friend and correspondent, and being an ardent Evangelical Churchwoman influenced her religious life. The little thirteen-year-old girl was now an eager devourer of all books that came in her way. So great was her admiration of *Waverley*, that when it was taken away from her before she had finished it, she began to write it out for herself from memory. Years afterwards she says, " It is a personal grief, a heart-wound to me when I hear a slighting or depreciatory word about Scott."

In her thirteenth year she was removed to the Miss Franklins' school at Coventry. They were daughters of a Baptist minister who had preached at Coventry for many years, and who bore some likeness to Rufus Lyon in *Felix Holt.* From the time of her entering the school at Coventry she was far beyond the other girls in English composition. Her teacher rarely found anything to correct in them. In music, too, she took the first place, and her master soon said he had nothing more to teach her. As the best performer in the school she was sometimes called into the parlour to play for visitors. Though suffering tortures from shyness she obeyed, but the moment the ordeal was over she flung herself on the floor in an agony of tears. One of her schoolfellows says that a source of great interest to the girls and of envy to those who lived further from home, was the weekly cart which brought Miss Evans new-laid eggs and other things from her father's farm.

As schools went in those days, the Miss Franklins' establishment was a very fair one, and they took pains to get good teachers of French and Italian. Mary Anne Evans was much looked up to by her companions, and became the leader of prayer-meetings. One lively lady objected to send her daughters to the Miss Franklins' school, because "that saint, Mary Anne Evans, had been there." Some years afterwards, when the Evanses went to live at Coventry, the Miss Franklins introduced Mary Anne to their friends, not only as a very clever girl, but as a person sure to get up something in the way of a clothing club or other charitable undertaking. In fact, she bade fair to be a capable, intelligent woman of a serious turn of mind, and with strictly Evangelical principles.

At Christmas, 1835, when she was just sixteen, her last half at school was over. She returned to Griff, where her time was taken up nursing her mother, who, after a long, painful illness, died in the summer of 1836. It was the first break in the family, and was soon followed by another ; her sister Chrissie was married in the spring of the next year to Mr. Edward Clarke, a surgeon, living at Meridan, in Warwickshire. Mr. Isaac Evans remembered on the day after the bride's departure that he and his younger sister had a good cry together over the breaking up of their old home-life. The two sisters were so widely apart that there could not have been much sympathy between them, yet George Eliot writes, after twenty-three years' separation, that she had a very special feeling for Chrissie. In the description of Celia, in *Middlemarch,* she told Mr. Cross that she had Chrissie continually in her mind. Celia was a woman who made no great demands on life, she was quite contented to take things as they came, and found commonplace Sir Robert Chettam an eminently satisfactory husband —one even to be proud of.

The whole management of the Griff household now fell upon Mary Anne. She took up the reins of housekeeping and held them well, she worked with hand as well as with head. One day she wrote to Miss Lewis that her hand was tremulous from boiling currant-jelly ; another, she is stupid from "standing sentinel over damson-cheese and a warm stove ;" at Christmas, she was about to begin making mince-pies. The dairy, too, with its bright red milk-pans and polished vessels, had to be attended to, and she had a practical acquaintance with butter and cheese making. With all these multifarious regulations, she found time to visit the poor, as well as to study Italian and German, and to play to her father in the evenings. Her letters to Miss Lewis show how ultra-Calvinistic her views were at this time.

She "highly enjoyed Hannah More's letters. The contemplation of so blessed a character as hers," she adds, "is very salutary." She promises herself a rich treat from reading the *Life of Wilberforce.* "May the Lord give me such an insight into what is truly good," she writes, "that I may not rest contented with making Christianity a mere addendum to my pursuits, or with tacking it as a fringe to my garments. May I be sanctified wholly ! "

At another time she felt herself to be a mere cumberer of the ground, and laments that her soul seems completely benumbed. "The weapons of the Christian warfare," she writes, " were never sharpened at the forge of romance." She disliked religious novels, and domestic fiction seemed even more dangerous. "Of music," she writes, "it would cost me no great regret if the only music heard in our land was that of strict worship." "I used to go about like an owl," she said afterwards, "to the great disgust of my brother, and I would have denied him what I now see to have been quite lawful amusements." When she was twenty she

16

wrote some verses, what she calls doggerel lines, which came
out in the *Christian Observer.* They begin :—

> " As o'er the fields by ev'ning's light I stray
> I hear a still, small whisper—' Come away,
> Thou must to this bright lovely world soon say
> 　　　　　Farewell ! ' "

Every verse ends with "Farewell ! "—farewell to the sun,
to the song of birds ; the Bible is the only exception—

> " To thee I say not of earth's gifts alone,
> 　　　　　Farewell ! "

She still continued her visits to the poor, who used to say,
" There never will be another Mary Anne Evans ; " but the
apparent union of religious feeling with a low sense of
morality amongst the Methodists about Griff, struck her as
being inconsistent, and Scott's novels had shown her that
there are good, pleasant, and noble lives amongst those who
cannot be called strictly religious people. All this unsettled
and disturbed her—the strict Calvinism which she was
trying to force on herself was gradually becoming a burden
too great to be borne. She spoke afterwards of the "absolute despair she suffered from ever being able to achieve
anything." This despair seems to infect her style of writing ;
her letters are stiff and laboured, there is not a vestige of
humour or brightness in them, no vivid touches of description such as might be expected from her. A gloomy pall
hangs over everything.

A change came to her life when she was not quite twenty-
one. Her brother Isaac married Miss Rawlins ; he had
been assisting in the land agency business, and it was
arranged that he should take on the establishment at Griff,
and that his father and sister should remove to a house near
Coventry, on the Foleshill Road. The move took place in
March, 1841. The house is semi-detached, with a good

garden and a wide view. It is town rather than country—town with a vista of long chimneys and ribbon manufactories. It so happened that next door to the Evans's lived a Mrs. Pears ; there had been some acquaintance between her and the Griff family, so she visited them in their new house, and they soon became friends. Mrs. Pears's brother, Mr. Bray, was a ribbon manufacturer, and had a charming house, called Rosehill, in the suburbs of Coventry. He had written several philosophical works, and by his marriage with Miss Caroline Hennell, he was related to her brother, Mr. Charles Hennell, the author of *An Inquiry Concerning the Origin of Christianity*, which had been translated into German, with a preface by Strauss. An acquaintance between Mary Anne, or Marian Evans—as she was then called—and the Brays soon ripened into friendship. Both the Brays and Hennells were freethinkers on religion, and their opinions soon worked a complete change in Marian Evans. Her former Calvinistic views fell from her gradually bit by bit, till none were left. Those who believe in the sanctities of religion, who rest on the Fatherhood of God and the loving Brotherhood of Christ, must deeply regret that she did not

" Cleave to the sunnier side of doubt,
And cling to faith beyond the forms of faith."

But unhappily she did not. The swing of the pendulum was too strong. She left off going to church—a great offence to her father, who was a thoroughgoing Tory Churchman of the old school. He was so much annoyed that he was about to give up his house at Foleshill, and she proposed taking lodgings at Leamington and supporting herself by teaching. Both plans, however, fell through. After a three weeks' stay with her brother at Griff a reconciliation was patched up, her father received her again, and she resumed going to church as before. A lifelong friendship began in

1842 with Miss Sara Hennell, Mrs. Bray's sister. With Mrs. Bray she found affectionate companionship, but with Miss Hennell she found intellectual sympathy. "You are the only friend," she writes, "who has an animating influence over me." Of these two clever, intellectual young women, Sara Hennell seemed to be the one most likely to make a mark in the world.

Marian Evans took various excursions with the Brays to Stratford and Malvern, and in July, 1843, they went to Tenby, accompanied by Miss Brabant, who was engaged to be married to Mr. Charles Hennell. Miss Brabant had undertaken to translate from the German Strauss's *Life of Christ.* On her marriage she handed over the work to Marian Evans, who set about it zealously, turning off six pages a day. At one time there was a doubt if her "soul-stupefying labours" would ever see the glory of print, but a subscription was got up, and £300 was collected to pay for the publication. The work was often very tough. "My leathery brain must work at leathery Strauss," writes Marian Evans to Miss Hennell, "before my butterfly days come ; I am never pained when I think Strauss right, but in some cases I think him wrong." Once she wrote that she was Strauss-sick. A trip to Scotland with the Brays and Miss Hennell made a short break ; and in April, 1846, Mrs. Bray writes to her sister to say that "Marian Evans is as happy as you may imagine at her work being done. She means to come and read Shakespeare through to me as her chief enjoyment."

The translation was considered faithful, elegant, and scholar-like ; the English style easy, perspicuous, and idiomatic. One advantage certainly came from it, her letters became freer and more easy, though the gloom of her spirit still continued. Once she writes : "My address is Grief Castle, on the River of Gloom, in the Valley of Despair." Mrs. Cash, of Coventry, who read German with her, mentions that one day she placed the volumes of

Schiller together, and said, "Oh, if *I* had given these to the world how happy I should be!"

Her religious opinions, too, seem to have slightly changed. She considered Jesus Christ as the embodiment of perfect love, and appeared to be leaning to the doctrines of Carlyle and Emerson. She told Mrs. Cash she considered the Bible a revelation in a certain sense, as she considered herself a revelation of the mind of the Deity, &c. She attended the opening of a new church at Foleshill with her father, and remarked to Mrs. Cash, as she looked at the gaily-dressed people, how much easier life would be to her, and how much better she would stand in the estimation of her neighbours, if she could only take things as they did—be satisfied with outside pleasures, and conform to popular beliefs. There were occasional gleams of sunshine in her life. She went to London with the Brays, and heard the first performance of Mendelssohn's *Elijah*, at Exeter Hall. And on her return from a visit to St. Leonard's with her father, she spent a day with Emerson at Rosehill. "I have seen Emerson," she writes; "the first *man* I have ever seen." His verdict on her was, "That young lady has a calm, clear spirit."

Her father's health had been gradually failing, and much of her time was spent reading Scott's novels to him. She did all the nursing herself, and was with him when he died on the 31st of May, 1849.

After his death she needed a change, and, fortunately, at this time the Brays were going to the Continent, and she went with them. They went by Paris and Lyons to the Italian Lakes, and arrived at Geneva in July. During this trip Marian Evans says she was "peevish, wretched, utterly morbid, given to fits of hysterical sobbing, her nerves and spirits quite unhinged." She had been left a small independence, between £80 and £100 a year, and when her friends went back to England she decided to remain at a Pension in the Campagne Plongeon. It was a good-sized, gleaming white house, with a look-out on meadows sloping down to the blue lake. Here she stayed several months, and enjoyed the variety of foreign life.

She was very anxious to get a certain black velvet dress. "The people dress and think about dressing here," she says, "more even than in England." "You would not know me," she writes to Mrs. Bray, " if you saw me. The Marquise took on her the office of a *femme-de-chambre*, and dressed my hair one day. She has abolished all my curls, and made two things stick out on each side of my head like those on the head of a sphinx. All the world says I look infinitely better, though to myself I seem uglier than ever." "There is a certain Madame Ludwigsdorff, " who is so good to me," she writes, "petting me in all sorts of ways ; she sends me tea when I wake in the morning, orange-flower water when I go to bed, grapes, and her maid to wait on me. She is tall and handsome, dresses exquisitely—in fact, is all that I am not." " Miss F. tells me that the first day she sat by my side at dinner she looked at me, and thought, ' That is a very grave lady. I do not think I shall like her much.' As soon as I spoke to her, and she looked into my eyes, she felt she could love me." This was a very usual experience with those who knew Marian Evans : her features were large and irregular, but her grey-blue eyes, though small and narrow, had a wonderful amount of expression in them. At thirty or thirty-five she was more attractive than at twenty.

Her next move was to the house of M. D'Albert, a clever Swiss artist, and with him and his wife a lifelong friendship began. He painted the portrait of which, by the kind permission of Mr. Cross, I am enabled to give a reproduction. With music and conversation the days passed pleasantly at Geneva. "Madame brings up her boys admirably," writes Miss Evans, " and I love M. D'Albert as if he were father and brother both."

She looked with a shudder at the thought of returning to England—" a land of gloom, of *ennui*, of platitudes ; "

but the wish to see her friends at Rosehill prevailed, and she
and M. D'Albert started, crossing the Jura in sledges. She
arrived at Rosehill on the 20th of March, after a long, cold
journey. She felt the wintry flat acutely after the brilliant
blue skies of Switzerland. For sixteen months she remained
with her friends the Brays, writing occasional reviews. A
new series of the *Westminster Review* was projected. Mr.
Chapman, the publisher, paid three visits to Rosehill about
it ; and it was finally settled that Miss Evans should be
the assistant editor. At the end of September, 1851, she
came to London to stay at the Chapmans' house in the
Strand, as a boarder, and to enter on her arduous work.
Article reading, proof correcting, and scrap-work of all kinds
often proved wearisome, and brought on depression and
nervous headaches ; but there were literary *soirées* and
concerts, and now and then a fortnight's stay at Broadstairs
and St. Leonard's. Marian Evans's connection with the
Westminster brought her in contact with the most celebrated
literary men of the day, amongst them Herbert Spencer,
with whom she speaks of having a " deliciously calm new
friendship." He brought George Henry Lewes to see her ;
her first casual impression of Lewes had not been favourable—
she calls him a " miniature Mirabeau "—but as she grew to
know him better her interest in him increased. He was
at this time literary editor of the *Leader* newspaper ; a small,
slight man, with very bright eyes ; he was a brilliant talker,
and so amazingly versatile that it was said of him, "Lewes
can do everything in the world except paint, and he could
do that, too, after a week's study." He had travelled a
great deal, had been a medical student, an actor, a lecturer,
a novelist, a critic, and the author of a *Biographical
History of Philosophy*. Thackeray said it would never surprise him to see Lewes riding up Piccadilly on a white
elephant. He was compared to the Wandering Jew, as you
could never tell where he was going to, or what he would
do next.

Yet with all his varied gifts, Mr. Lewes had not yet made a distinct or permanent mark in literature. His novels—*Runthorpe* and *Rose, Blanche, and Violet*—had fallen flat. He was married, and had three sons, but his marriage, too, had been a failure. For two years, Mr. Cross tells us, his family life had been irretrievably spoiled and his home broken up. He was separated from his wife, and could not obtain a divorce. Such was the man who was now thrown into daily contact with Marian Evans, a noble, high-souled woman, full of strength and unselfishness, longing for some possibility of "devoting herself where she might see a daily result of pure calm blessedness in the life of another."

In October, 1853, she left the Chapmans, and went into lodgings at 21, Cambridge Street, Hyde Park, where she remained till the following July, when the most important step of her life was taken. This step—her union with Mr. Lewes—is beset with so many difficulties that I dread to say anything about it. We, who hold the sanctity of marriage, cannot excuse such a union, but we can suggest reasons why it took place. Marian Evans was now thirty-five, Mr. Lewes was two years older ; at this time of life the early passions of youth have cooled down, but the desire for intellectual sympathy and companionship become more intense. Mr. Lewes was in delicate health ("his poor head, his only fortune, is not well yet ") ; he appealed to Marian Evans's always strong feeling of pity—that tender pity which is akin to love—and then he seemed to be lapsing into stagnation and idleness, from want of a powerful stimulating influence ; this influence she could supply. And then she was bound by no religious scruples, neither was Mr. Lewes. Law, as we define it, had no meaning for them. "All sacrifice," she says, writing of *Jane Eyre*, "is good, but one would like it to be in a somewhat nobler cause than that of a diabolical law which chains a man, soul and body, to a putrefying carcass." The claims of others were not interfered with ; her altruism, her ardent wish to benefit and to bless, urged her to sacrifice everything

for Mr. Lewes, and she did so. The desertion of many of
her friends startled and wounded her. She always considered
herself as Mr. Lewes's wife, she adopted his sons as her own,
and they treated her as their mother. She was spoken of
and written to as " Mrs. Lewes," the manuscripts of all her
books are dedicated to her "dear, every day dearer, husband," and she seems to have no thought apart from him.

"Being happy in each other," she writes, "we find everything easy." He, on his part, writes in his journal, "To
know her was to love her ; since then my life has been a new
birth. To her I owe all my prosperity and all my happiness." One thing is certain, if her intellect stimulated his,
his, in its turn, stimulated hers. Without him her books
would never have been written.

In July, 1854, she went to Germany with him to collect
materials for his *Life of Goethe,* which he was rewriting.
They spent some time at Weimar, visited Goethe's house,
breakfasted with Liszt, and heard him play. The winter
was spent at Berlin : visiting, theatre-going, and opera-going,
alternated with quiet evenings of reading and writing. A
translation of Feuerbach's *Essence of Christianity* had been
published in 1854, and in the following March, after returning to England, George Eliot finished translating and
revising Spinoza's *Ethics*, and wrote articles for the
Westminster Review and the *Leader.* Translating may be
said to repress rather than to encourage originality, yet
nothing teaches better the use of words. At every page the
tough leather of language becomes more pliant, and sentences arrange themselves without effort.

It was not till September, 1856, that a new era—the
fiction-writing era of George Eliot's life—began. She was
then thirty-seven, and had never gone further in writing a
novel than an introductory chapter, describing a Staffordshire village and the life of the neighbouring farmhouses.
She read it to Mr. Lewes in Germany, and he thought it a
good bit of description ; but he, as well as George Eliot
herself, doubted her dramatic power.

In the summer of 1856, which they spent at Ilfracombe and Tenby, Mr. Lewes said positively, "You must try and write a story." One morning George Eliot's thoughts merged themselves in a dreamy doze, and she imagined herself writing a story, of which the title was, *The Sad Fortunes of the Reverend Amos Barton.* She awoke, and told Mr. Lewes, who said, "Oh, what a capital title!"—and from that time it was settled that this should be the first story. There was some doubt as to how it would turn out. Mr. Lewes said, "It may be a failure, it may be that you are unable to write fiction, or perhaps it may be just good enough to warrant your trying again, or you may write a *chef d'œuvre* at once; there's no telling."

They settled in lodgings at Park Shot, Richmond, and at first there was an article to write on "Silly Novels by Lady Novelists," and a review of contemporary literature for the *Westminster,* so the story was not begun till September 22nd. One night Mr. Lewes went to town, so as to give George Eliot a quiet evening for *Amos.* The chapter which concludes with Amos being dragged from the bedside of Milly was read to Mr. Lewes when he came home. "We both cried over it," writes George Eliot in her journal, "and then he came up to me and kissed me, saying, 'I think your pathos is better than your fun.'"

Amos Barton was sent by Mr. Lewes to Blackwood, who wrote back in a few days to say, "I think your friend's reminiscence of clerical life will do. *Amos Barton* is unquestionably very pleasant reading, the descriptions humorous and good, the death of Milly powerfully done," &c., &c. The tone of the letter was not enthusiastic, and Mr. Lewes wrote back that his clerical friend was discouraged at it—"He is afraid of failure. I tell you this that you may understand the shy, shrinking, ambitious nature you have to deal with." *Amos Barton* made its appearance in *Blackwood* in January, 1857. Fifty guineas was paid for it, and the publisher grew more lavish in praise, and said it was long since he had read anything so fresh, so humorous, and so touching. It was in answer to this letter that the writer for the first time signed herself "George Eliot"—George because it was Mr. Lewes's name, and Eliot because it was a good mouth-filling, easily-pronounced word. When Mr. Lewes read *Amos* to a party at Sir Arthur Help's, they all came to the conclusion that he must be a clergyman—a Cambridge man. No one except Charles Dickens guessed that the author was a woman. Mrs. Carlyle thought he was a " middle-aged man, with a wife, from whom he has got these beautiful feminine touches, a good many children, and a dog that he has as much fondness for as I have for my little Nero. For the rest, not just a clergyman, but brother or first cousin to a clergyman."

We are all familiar with Milly Barton, who salted bacon, ironed shirts and cravats, put patches on patches, and re-darned darns. Gentle and uncomplaining, with a profound admiration for her husband, who has dull grey eyes, and is not worthy of her, she brings her basket of stockings to bed, so that she may begin darning at four in the morning, while he sleeps undisturbed by her side. Poor Milly, that lovely worn-out body must be laid to rest in Shepperton Church, where the key-bugle and bassoon sounded every Sunday ; yet there is something in these commonplace troubles and homely cares that seem almost divine !

Mr. Gilfil's Love-Story was begun on Christmas Day, 1856, and the epilogue was written from the Scilly Isles, where Mr. Lewes went to gather notes for his *Seaside Studies*. His *Life of Goethe* had come out, and was his first genuine success. From the Scilly Isles they went to Jersey, to lodgings at 13s. a week, and Mr. Lewes, who was now a "zoological maniac," was in all the bliss, George Eliot writes, of discovering "a parasitic worm in a cuttle-fish." When they returned to Richmond *Janet's Repentance* was finished, which, strange to say, Blackwood did not like as well as the other stories. It is really the gem of the whole. A deeper chord is touched in it. Janet Dempster, the slighted wife, shut out at night from her husband's door, and on the verge of becoming the slave of drink, is saved by that very Mr. Tryan, the Evangelical curate, whom she once ridiculed and despised. It is like drinking in pure air or gazing into the blue sky to read this master sketch, full of the deepest and truest teaching and instinct, with that quaint humour which is one of the true signs of genius. We can well believe what George Eliot says, that " her sketches of both Churchmen and Dissenters are drawn from close observation in real life, and not at all from hearsay or from descriptions of novelists." The *Scenes of Clerical Life* were reprinted in a volume, and £120 was given for the first edition of 750 copies. Just at the threshold of her great success, George Eliot wrote in her journal at the end of 1857 : " My life has deepened unspeakably during the last year, the blessedness of a perfect love and union grows daily. Few women have had such reason as I have to think the long sad years of youth were worth living for the sake of middle age. Our prospects are very bright. I am writing my new novel."

The new novel was *Adam Bede*, one of the greatest novels of the century. It was written slowly ; part of it was shown to Mr. John Blackwood when he came to Richmond. He read the first page, and said, " This will do ! " We may remember that it begins with that graphic picture of the carpenter's shop and the five workmen, busy upon doors and window-frames. A scent of pine-wood from a tent-like pile of planks outside the open door mingled with the scent of the elder branches, which were spreading their summer snow close to the open window. Adam's voice begins—

> " Awake my soul and with the sun
> Thy daily stage of duty run."

The note of reality which is then struck goes on to the

last page. It is impossible not to believe in the intense yet calm realism of *Adam Bede*. The grand figure of Dinah Morris, the Methodist preacher, is unique in fiction. " Dinah's first sermon," George Eliot tells us, " was written with streaming eyes out of a full heart." We remember how Marian Evans used to lead the prayer-meetings at school—this sermon was probably a chapter out of her own experience.

As to Mrs. Poyser, she is as immortal as Sancho Panza, her cut and dry sayings and pungent retorts have become household words. What can be more biting than her reproof to Bartle ?—"Say ! why, I say as some folks' tongues are like the clocks as run on striking, not to tell the time o' the day, but because there's summat wrong with their own insides." And Hetty Sorrel, the farmhouse coquette, "her cheek like a rose-petal, dimples playing about her pouting lips, her large, dark eyes, with a soft roguishness under their long lashes, and her curly hair pushed back under her round cap," we know that she cannot turn out well, yet with what fascina-· tion do we follow her entanglement with Arthur Donni-thorne. Her childish vanity, her delight in her own beauty, her passion for fine dress and gay ribbons, are touched with a woman's delicate hand. How true it is to nature that Adam, upright and God-fearing as he is, should at first love pretty, provoking Hetty rather than Dinah, that saintly picture of unselfish womanhood. The germ of the book, George Eliot tells us, arose from a story which her Methodist aunt—a very small, black-eyed woman, very vehement in her style of preaching—had told her at Griff. Elizabeth Evans had gone to see a condemned criminal who had murdered her child and refused to confess. She stayed with her praying through the night, till at last the poor creature confessed her crime.

This incident made a great impression on Marian Evans when she heard it, but she never spoke of it till many years had passed, when she mentioned it to Mr. Lewes, after the

Scenes of Clerical Life came out. He thought the scene in the prison would make a fine element in a story, and so, under the transforming touch of genius, Elizabeth Evans became Dinah Morris, and the poor, ignorant girl, pretty provoking Hetty. The character of Adam was suggested by Robert Evans—"but he is not my father," adds George Eliot, "any more than Dinah Morris is my aunt." She says, in a letter to the Brays : "There is not a single portrait in the book, nor will there be in any future book of mine. There are portraits in the *Clerical Scenes,* but that was my first bit of art, and my hand was not well in."

Adam Bede was finished on the 16th of November, 1858. The second volume was begun at Munich : the fight in the wood between Arthur and Adam came to George Eliot, she says, as a necessity one night at the Munich opera, when she was listening to "William Tell." She wrote on uninterruptedly and with great enjoyment at Dresden, and finished the second volume at Richmond. The third volume was written in six weeks without the slightest alteration from the first draught. "It was written under a stress of emotion," she says, "which first volumes cannot be." While uncertain what the public verdict of the book might be, George Eliot wrote, "I love it very much, and am very thankful to have written it."

Blackwood wrote in warm admiration and offered £800 for four years' copyright, which was accepted. With the first-fruits of *Adam Bede,* a new house—Holly Lodge, Wandsworth—was taken, and very soon the book was landed, high and dry, on the *terra firma* of success. Though only published in February, by March 16th 2,090 copies were sold, in April it went into a second edition, and in a year 16,000 copies were sold. One of Mrs. Poyser's sayings, "It must be hatched again, and hatched different," was quoted in the House of Commons. Charles Reade said *Adam Bede* was the finest thing since Shakespeare ; John

Murray, the publisher, said, "there has never been such a book"; and Mrs. Gaskell wrote that she had read it and the *Scenes of Clerical Life* again, and "must tell you how earnestly, fully, and *humbly* I admire them. I never read anything so complete or so beautiful in my life before." Such testimony as this gave George Eliot, as she says, "reason for gladness that such an unpromising woman-child was born into the world." She had at last found out her true vocation, after which her nature had been "feeling and striving uneasily without finding it." "I sing my Magnificat," she says, "in a quiet way, and have a great deal of deep, silent joy."

The money part was not less satisfactory. Blackwood gave an additional £400, as an acknowledgment of the success of *Adam Bede*, making £1,200 in the year. In writing to acknowledge this liberality George Eliot says : "I don't know which of those two things I care for most—that people should act nobly towards me, or that I should get honest money. I certainly care a great deal for the money, as I suppose all anxious minds do that love independence, and have been brought up to think debt and begging the two deepest dishonours short of crime."

A great annoyance arose from a Warwickshire man of the name of Liggins, who claimed to be the author of *Adam Bede*, and induced many people to believe in him and even to give subscriptions for his support. It took some trouble to dispel this myth.

Meanwhile George Eliot was meditating another novel, and says, almost in despair, "Shall I ever write a book as true as *Adam Bede* ?" There were many discussions as to what the title should be. *The Tullivers, or Life on the Floss*, was proposed, but finally *The Mill on the Floss* was adopted. It was finished on the 21st of March, 1859, and was a new revelation of George Eliot's genius. It is hard to believe that while she was writing it Giant Despair was whispering in her ear that " *The Mill on the Floss* is detestable, and that the last volume will be the climax of the general detestableness."

It requires a great gift of sympathy and insight to understand the nature of children, the slow growth of their minds, their fears, their loves, and their hates. Amongst the few who are thoroughly successful in doing this, George Eliot stands pre-eminent. As we read of the childhood of Maggie and Tom Tulliver, we seem to be looking through a microscope into their souls. Maggie running away to the gypsies, because Tom has given her an unkind word ; Maggie, gazing at us with love-needy, beseeching eyes, and defying her aunt—even formidable Mrs. Glegg—is a most vivid picture of a child. We know that the real Marian Evans was what Maggie was, eager for knowledge, impetuous, hard to manage, and full of sympathy and pity for others. It is no wonder that commonplace Tom cannot understand Maggie's generous nature. When the supreme moment of her life comes, after she has drifted down the river with Stephen Guest, she will not purchase happiness at the expense of others. "I have never said they shall suffer that I may have joy." She cannot take "a good that is wrung from their misery," and so she resolutely puts it from her, and walks on in darkness, till at length she is drowned in the Floss along with the brother who had disbelieved in her truth and purity. *The Mill on the Floss* is one of those finished pictures which makes ordinary novels look like coarse, vulgar daubs beside it. The comedy is supplied by the Gleggs, the Pullets, and the Dodsons, and the humour with which these immortal families are drawn is inimitable. "Many people," says George Eliot, "prefer *The Mill* to *Adam Bede,* but *Adam* is more complete and better balanced. My love of the childhood scenes made me linger over them, so that I could not develop as fully as I wished the concluding book in which the tragedy occurs."

After *The Mill on the Floss* was finished, a journey to Italy was undertaken. Rome, with its churches and picture galleries and catacombs, roused George Eliot from her depression. One spot which moved her deeply was Shelley's grave, " at rest," she writes, " from the unloving carelessness of this world, whether or no he may have entered on other purifying struggles in some world unseen by us."

It was during a visit to Florence that she first thought of writing an historical romance, but she put it off to begin *Silas Marner, the Weaver of Raveloe.* At this time she and Mr. Lewes had left Holly Lodge, and were living first at Harwood Square, and afterwards at Blandford Square. " *Silas,*" writes George Eliot, " came to me quite suddenly, suggested by my recollection of having seen in early childhood, a linen weaver, with a bag on his back." Of all her books, it is the most rounded and complete. It is a prose-poem—the story of the evolution of a soul. Silas, the cataleptic, near-sighted weaver, shunned by every one, solely intent on his beloved sovereigns, and in despair at their loss, is awakened to new life by the little golden-haired child whom he finds in the snow. The group at " The Rainbow "—Macey, tailor and parish clerk, at their head—is a master-study of village life. From it we might imagine that George Eliot had spent her days watching the village philosophers as they drank their beer, smoked their long pipes, and delivered their sentiments on things in general, from " red Durhams " upwards. We do not find that George Eliot was depressed after *Silas.* " My books," she writes, " don't seem to belong to me after I have once written them, and I feel myself delivering opinions as if I had nothing to do with them. I could no more live through one of my books a second time than I can live through next year again."

Her favourite amusement was going to the Monday Popular Concerts, where, she says, " I go in my bonnet. We sit in the shilling places in the body of the hall, and hear to perfection."

Her historical romance was still seething in her brain. She had shown what she could do with the middle-class life

17

of the Midlands—with millers and farmers, with clergymen
and parish clerks, with Wesleyan preachers and class leaders
—but how would it be if she attempted new scenes in other
countries than her own ? This question she was going to
answer in *Romola.* In April, 1861, after *Silas Marner* was
finished, she and Mr. Lewes took another journey to Italy.
She spent most of her time at Florence, looking at streets
and buildings and pictures, and hunting up old books. In
August, 1861, she writes : "Got into a state of so much
wretchedness in attempting to concentrate my thoughts on
the construction of my story that I became desperate, and
suddenly burst my bonds, saying, 'I will not think of
writing.'" At another time she was "bitterly despondent
about her book, trying to write, trying to construct, and
unable." "I almost resolved to give up my Italian novel."
And again, "Flashes of hope are succeeded by long intervals
of dim distrust."

Mr. Cross tells us that the writing of *Romola* ploughed
into her more than any of her other books. To use her
own words, "I began it a young woman, I finished it an old
woman." On the first page she wrote, "To the husband
whose perfect love has been the best source of her insight
and strength, this manuscript is given by his devoted wife."
Romola first appeared in the *Cornhill Magazine,* and the
highest price ever given for a serial—*i.e.,* £7,000 was paid
for it.

George Eliot's novels have been divided into two classes.
In the first are *Adam Bede, The Mill on the Floss,* and
Silas Marner, to which *Felix Holt* and *Middlemarch* were
afterwards added. The novels which belong to the first
class have more of George Eliot's self in them, they are
mostly reproductions of what she has seen or known.
Those in the second class show her imaginative powers
best. *Romola* is perhaps the least popular of her novels,
partly because most readers prefer stories that relate to the
present day and do not care to transfer their attention

to bygone ages, and partly because the scene is laid in a
foreign country, and English people always love to read
about themselves. Yet to those who look on fiction as
an art—to critics and writers—*Romola* seems a triumph of
genius. The Florentine citizens talk almost as naturally as
Warwickshire peasants, and Tito, in his strength and weakness, gradually slipping down the slope of egoism and selfishness, beautiful as day but false at heart, not intending at
first to rob his benefactor, but gradually yielding as circumstances draw their coils around him, is a profound study in
moral anatomy. Romola herself is the type of George
Eliot's favourite woman, calmer than Maggie Tulliver, but
just as eager for knowledge, noble, aspiring, full of faith in
others. When she discovers what her husband, Tito, really
is, when the veil falls from her eyes, and she finds that he
has saved himself while others are ruined, she turns to him
with that terrible, " And you . . . *you* are safe ? " Words
which are so full of withering contempt, and yet have an
under-current of sobbing anguish behind them. The monk,
Savonarola (to whom George Eliot is said to have borne a
strong personal resemblance), is a stronger, loftier, more
ascetic Mr. Tryan ; just as bruised, sorely-smitten Janet
Dempster pours out her soul to the Evangelical curate in
her passionate desire for help and sympathy, so Romola
goes to the Heaven-sent guide, to unfold those terrible
conflicts which rend her asunder and sap her faith in
others.

Writing of *Romola*, George Eliot says that her feeling is
not that she has achieved anything, but that " great facts
have struggled to find a voice through her, and have only
been able to speak brokenly." Nothing is more noteworthy
of her than her great humility. She was glad when Herbert
Spencer wrote that he felt better for reading *Adam Bede*,
and when Hermann Adler gave a lecture on *Daniel
Deronda ;* but she had no feverish craving for praise. She
had not even, like Harriet Martineau, a calm consciousness

of her own superiority. In a chapter on the "Diseases of Small Authorship" in *Theophrastus Such,* she says that "whenever she sees a failing in others, she immediately looks for it in herself."

In November, 1863, a house—The Priory, North Bank, Regent's Park—was bought, and George Eliot writes that the "fringing away of precious life, thinking of tables and chairs, is an affliction to her." The house-warming took place on Mr. Charles Lewes' twenty-first birthday, and in a letter to Mrs. Congreve, she says, "You would perhaps have been amused to see an affectionate but dowdy friend of yours splendid in a grey moire antique, the consequence of a severe lecture from Mr. Owen Jones on her general neglect of personal adornment."

The first act of *The Spanish Gypsy* was commenced in September, 1864, but was laid aside for *Felix Holt the Radical,* which was begun on the 29th of March, 1865. George Eliot writes that she is going doggedly to work at it, that it is "growing like a sickly child, and she can't move till it is done." When she reached the end she was in a state of nervous exhaustion, throbbing, and palpitation. Blackwood offered £5,000 for it, which was accepted. *Felix Holt* does not rank as high as *Adam Bede* or *The Mill on the Floss.* It gives a picture of Dissenting life in the Midlands when the glory had not departed from the old coach-roads and the horn of the mail was still heard ; but we miss the picturesqueness and the intensity of the earlier novels. The pithy talk of Mrs. Holt, and her reproaches at her son's refusal "to sell the pills which suited people's insides, and when folks can never have boxes enough to swallow, I should think you have a right to sell," are as distinctive as anything of Mrs. Poyser's ; yet the story drags ; Esther Lyon does not live as Dinah Morris does, nor Felix as Adam Bede. Mrs. Transome, handsome and haughty, reaping the fruits of her early sin to the dregs, is one of the best characters. But there is an effort throughout. It seems laboured, and the closing scenes are not effective.

After *Felix Holt* was finished, George Eliot and Mr. Lewes went for a trip to Holland and the Rhine, and soon afterwards *The Spanish Gypsy* was again taken up. In a note given by Mr. Cross we are told that the subject was suggested by a picture which hangs in the Scuoto de San Rocco at Venice. A young maiden on the eve of marriage suddenly hears the announcement that she is chosen to fulfil a great destiny involving a totally different experience from that of ordinary womanhood. She is chosen not from momentary arbitrariness, but as a result of foregoing hereditary conditions. On Fedalma's submission and Silva's rebellion, George Eliot spent infinite labour and care. At one time she writes that "she is swimming in a sea of Spanish literature and history." It was rewritten throughout, and a journey to Spain—to Alicante and Seville and Cordova—was undertaken solely for the purpose of gathering materials and of studying the country. Mr. Lewes was in an unprecedented state of delight with the poem, and was astonished that he could not find more faults. It gave him a deeper joy than any work George Eliot had done before. It was published in May, 1868, and awakened a storm of criticism, favourable and the reverse. George Eliot's poems have never gone home to the bulk of the reading public as her novels have done. They are read, admired, criticised, even quoted, yet they seem more studied, less spontaneous. There is the same power of dramatic presentment, but we miss the racy humour. Still she enjoyed writing verse, for which she only got hundreds, while her novels brought her thousands. She says, "I seem to have gained a new organ, a new medium that my nature had languished for."

The Spanish Gypsy was followed by *Agatha*, which was sold to the *Atlantic Monthly* for £300. *The Legend of Jubal* and *Armgart* came out first in *Macmillan's Magazine*, and were published along with *Agatha* and other short poems in volume form in 1874. *The Legend of Jubal* and *Armgart* are both intensely dramatic, and have found more favour with many readers than *The Spanish Gypsy*. Armgart is a singer who loses her voice, and is obliged to be contented with humble work. She will not " feed on doing great tasks ill " ; she will not

> "' Dull the world's sense with mediocrity
> And live by trash that smothers excellence."

In *Armgart* and in a later poem, *Stradivarius*, we see George Eliot's love of work for work's sake. The old violin-maker " winced at false work and loved the true." He says :

> "' 'Tis God gives skill,
> But not without man's hands ;
> He could not make
> Antonio Stradivari's violins without Antonio."

George Eliot calls it the deepest disgrace to do work of any sort badly. She did not despise the commonest things, she was excellent at her needle, wrote a clear, distinct hand, and was a first-rate housekeeper. The idea of women despising household affairs because they had great intellectual gifts, was abhorrent to her.

Mr. Rudolf Lehmann lately contributed to the *Cornhill Magazine* some valuable pages from the note-book of his father, Mr. Frederick Lehmann, who became acquainted with George Eliot through Mr. Lewes, and at one time saw a great deal of her. " What first struck me about her," he says, " was the strange contrast between the large head, the masculine Dantesque features, and the soft, melodious voice, which always cast a spell over me. One might almost have forgotten she was a woman, so profound was her insight, but I, at least, could never forget while in her company that I was with an exceptional being. In the autumn and winter of 1866, my wife and family were at Pau, while I was alone in London. George Eliot was a very fair pianist, not gifted, but enthusiastic and very painstaking. During a great part of that time I used to go to her every Monday evening at her house in North Bank, Regent's Park, always taking my violin with me. We played together every piano and violin sonata of Beethoven and Mozart. I knew the traditions of the best players, and was able to give her some hints, which she received eagerly and thankfully. Our audience consisted of George Lewes only, and he used to groan with delight whenever we were rather successful in playing some beautiful passage."

It was during a visit to Rome in 1869 that Mr. Cross saw George Eliot for the first time. She was sitting on a sofa, talking, and he also mentions "the low, earnest, deep, musical tones of her voice, the fine brows with the abundant auburn brown hair framing them, the long head broadening at the back, the grey blue eyes constantly changing in expression, the finely-formed, thin, transparent hands."

It was early in the following spring that she began to think of writing *Middlemarch*. *The Vincys* and *The Feather-stones* were the first parts actually written, *Miss Brooke*, which now stands first, was not written till November, 1870, three months afterwards. On the 1st of December, 1870, the opening part appeared, and each monthly instalment was a literary event.

Dorothea Brooke interests us at once; she is the fore-shadowing of the intellectual aspiring woman who now betakes herself to Newnham or Girton. But Dorothea is more than intellectual, she is a modern St. Theresa. She does not want to deck herself with knowledge, but to use it for the good of mankind. She hails Mr. Casaubon, believing him to be a treasury of wisdom, a contrast to commonplace Sir James Chettam. She is influenced by Ladislaw, who is very much inferior to herself, just as Romola throws away her love on Tito, and Maggie gives hers to Stephen Guest. The secret may be found in George Eliot's own lofty nature;

her great desire was to give, not to get ; to spend herself for others, not to take anything from them. If she could bless the life of any one, that was the greatest joy she could feel.

The wonderful series of pictures in *Middlemarch* are all linked with one another. At one time we are at the deathbed of old Featherstone with the grasping relations outside, waiting for what they will get ; at another we are with Dorothea, puzzling how to bring her feelings to-wards her fossil of a husband into any kind of order ; at another, we are following the gradual spoiling of Lydgate's life by the selfishness and egoism of Rosamund. In all George Eliot's best writings, says Mr. Cross, " there was a ' not herself ' which took possession of her, she felt her own personality to be merely the instrument through which the spirit acted. This was specially the case in the scene between Dorothea and Rosamund. She always knew they would have to come together, but she kept the idea resolutely out of her mind, until Dorothea was in Rosamund's drawing-room. Then abandoning herself to the inspiration of the moment, she wrote the whole scene exactly as it stands, without erasure or correction, in an intense state of agitation and excitement. She felt Rosamund's character the most difficult to sustain." The impression that *Middlemarch* leaves behind it is that it is better to strive and struggle after the best, even if we do not attain it. To desire high things, to feel generously, to have noble earnest aims for ourselves and others, is worth living for.

The usual despondency and self-distrust—only kept in check by Mr. Lewes's buoyancy—set in during the writing of *Middlemarch*. George Eliot says, " I can't help wondering at the high estimate made of *Middlemarch*, compared with my other books." Not only was her health ailing—she calls herself and Mr. Lewes " two nervous dyspeptic creatures "—but she was too anxious to finish her book to look at it in mental sunshine. " I shudder," she says, "to think what a long book it will be." Sometimes she was afraid of breaking down before it was finished.

A cottage at Shottermill, in Surrey, was taken in May, 1871, and she speaks of "the ravishing country round, per-petual undulation of heath and copse, and clear views of harrying water, with here and there a grand pine-wood, steep wood-dotted promontories, and gleaming pools. . . ." "Tennyson, who is one of the hill-folk about here," she adds, "has found us out." "There is sunshine over our fields now," she writes, "and in the warmest part of the day, I, having a talent for being cold, sit shivering, some-times, even with a warm water-bottle at my feet." She occa-sionally took walks amongst the fields, and paid visits to a farmer's wife, to whom she would talk about vegetables and butter. The old lady commented much on the "sight of green peas she sent down to that gentleman and lady every week."

When *Middlemarch* was finished she was thoroughly at peace about it. She felt terribly until a subject wrought itself out, afterwards it seemed to take wing and go away from her. "*That* thing is not to be done again, that life has been lived."

Soon after it was finished she paid a visit to Oxford, and two ladies came up to her at a dinner-party, and said, "How could you let Dorothea marry *that* Casaubon?" The other, "Oh! I understand her doing that, but why did you let her marry that other fellow, whom I can't bear?" To use George Eliot's own words : "On religion and novels, every ignorant person feels competent to give an opinion."

The reception given to *Middlemarch* surprised her. No former book of hers was received with more enthusiasm— not even *Adam Bede*. In a year 20,000 copies were sold. "Is it not wonderful," she writes to Blackwood, "that the world can absorb so much *Middlemarch* at a guinea a copy? She was encouraged the following year to "brew" another novel, which was also to appear in monthly parts. In

December, 1875, the two first volumes of *Daniel Deronda* were in print. "I have thought very poorly of it throughout," writes George Éliot in her journal; "but George and the Blackwoods are full of satisfaction about it." The sale exceeded that of *Middlemarch*, and much interest, curiosity, and discussion was created by the Jewish part. It is this Judaism, together with the long involved sentences and scientific words, which prevent *Deronda* from being quite as popular with ordinary readers as *Middlemarch*, yet what studies of character are to be found in it ! Mordecai, wearying for a deliverer, who never seems to come, looking out with earnest, imploring eyes, is like a painting by Rembrandt, that gazes at us from the canvas. Gwendolen Harleth is a creature quite apart from Dorothea Brooke, she is vain, confident, full of self, yet the bitter teaching of her life, and her marriage with Grandcourt, make her abhor what she is. Deronda is a perpetual conscience to her, his influence disturbs, irritates, and fascinates her. For a proud woman to acknowledge her love, and then to be cast out in the cold, is a hard beginning for a nobler life, and yet we feel that it is better for Gwendolen to have been brought down that she may rise.

George Eliot was never a lover of towns; she revelled in the "sweet peace of the country." "Climate," she says, "enters into my life. Sunlight and sweet air make a new creature of me." After the publication of *Daniel Deronda*, she bought a large country house—The Heights, Witley, near Godalming, in Surrey. Green fields undulate up to Haslemere, and pine-woods, copses, village greens, and red-brick cottages abound. For neighbours there were the Tennysons, Du Mauriers, and Allinghams. Between The Heights and The Priory the next four years were spent.

The Sunday receptions at The Priory attracted the best literary society in London. George Eliot, Mr. Cross tells us, was not a typical mistress of a *salon*. Her talk was most enjoyable *à deux*. She found it difficult to take her mind off from one person to another; but Mr. Lewes, being a brilliant talker and *raconteur*, made these gatherings a social success. George Eliot "generally sat on a low armchair, on the left-hand side of the fire. On entering a visitor was at once struck by her massive head ; her abundant hair, then streaked with grey, was draped with lace arranged in mantilla fashion and coming to the front of the head. She had a great dislike to raising her voice, and often became so absorbed in conversation that she did not look up ; but the moment the eyes were lifted, they smiled a rare welcome."

One of her greatest gifts was her sympathy with others. As Mr. Lewes said to Mrs. Cash, "She forgets nothing that ever came within the curl of her eyelash, no one who ever spoke to her a kind word." She hated *obligato* reading and *obligato* talk about her books ; she never sent them to any one and never wished to be spoken to about them, except by an unpremeditated prompting. "It is the better for us all to hear as little about ourselves as possible, to do our work faithfully, and be satisfied with the certainty that if it touches many minds, it cannot touch them in a way quite aloof from our intention and our hope."

Every one was struck by the admiration she and Mr. Lewes had for each other. "How I worship," she writes, "his good humour, his good sense, his affectionate care for every one who has claims on him."

After one of the little dinners at The Priory, Tennyson read aloud a great part of *Maud* and the *Northern Farmer*. It must indeed have been interesting, as Mr. Cross says it was, to see these two representatives of English literature sitting side by side. There was often music at The Priory receptions ; music was more than a love with George Eliot, it was a necessity. We feel that she is speaking her own feelings when Maggie Tulliver says, "I think I should have no other mortal wants if I could always have plenty of music. It seems to infuse strength into my limbs and ideas

into my brain. Life seems to go on without any effort when
I am filled with music."

Of contemporary fiction George Eliot read little, she took
only a languid interest in Trollope and Dickens, but says
she can never resist Miss Thackeray's stories when they
come near her ; and she writes to Madame Bodichon, "If
you want delightful reading get Lowell's *My Study Windows*, and read the essays called "My Garden Acquaintances,"
and "Winter."

Towards the close of 1878 Mr. Lewes' health, always
fragile, began to fail even more ; but his natural buoyancy
still kept up, and he occasionally wrote an article for the
Pall Mall Gazette, and brought out his admirable book on
The Art of Acting, together with other articles and essays.
His death, which took place at The Priory on the 28th of
November, 1878, shook George Eliot to the very centre of
her being. She calls herself " a bruised creature. I shrink
from the tenderest touch. Here I and sorrow sit."

Madame Bodichou, who went to see her, said she looked,
in her long, loose, black dress, like the black shadow of
herself. And yet her vigour was not gone : she said she
had so much to do that she must keep well. "Life was so
intensely interesting."

She founded a scholarship of Physiology at Cambridge in
memory of George Henry Lewes, and revised the proofs of
Theophrastus Such, which had been written before Mr.
Lewes' death. Her intimacy with Mr. Cross became closer
by their reading Dante together. A bond of mutual dependence, he says, was formed between them, and when he
offered to devote his life to her, she consented. He was
many years younger than she was, but that did not seem
any bar to their affection. The marriage took place at St.
George's, Hanover Square, on the 6th of May, 1880, Mr.
Lewes' son giving her away.

Under the sunny skies of Italy George Eliot revived,
and when she returned with Mr. Cross to Witley, it seemed

as if some peaceful years were before her. She very much enjoyed reading aloud from the Bible, "which was a very precious and sacred book to her, and suited the organ-like tones of her voice." Whatever her religious opinions were, she never obtruded them in her books ; never do we find a slighting or disparaging word against the beliefs of others. Reverence, she considered the most precious thing in the world, and toleration one of the great lessons of life. On December 4th she and Mr. Cross came up to his town house, 4, Cheyne Walk, Chelsea. About a fortnight afterwards she caught a chill at one of the Monday Popular Concerts, alarming symptoms set in, and on the 22nd of December, 1880, she breathed her last.

The funeral at Highgate Cemetery that day week was attended by many of the literary men who had known her —Oscar Browning, Herbert Spencer, and others. After the funeral service, amidst a thick drizzling rain, Dr. Sadler, the Unitarian minister, delivered an address. He spoke of George Eliot as one of the immortal dead who "live again in minds made better by their presence."

Her noble aspiration has been fulfilled ; she has joined "the choir invisible." Her life presents many difficulties to those who admire and love her writings, but there are no "miserable aims that end with self." She *has* been to other souls "the cup of strength in some great agony, she *has* fed pure love and begotten the smiles that have no cruelty," and so let us leave her in silence to God.

XI.

ADELAIDE ANNE PROCTER.

1825–1864.

Birth at Bedford Square—"Barry Cornwall"—"Golden-tressèd Adelaide"
—Contributor to *Household Words* as "Miss Mary Berwick"—Goes
to Italy—The truth comes out—Two voices—*Legends and Lyrics*—
"A little changeling spirit"—*Victoria Regia*—Illness and death.

IS it possible for a shy, sensitive girl, living principally
in her father's drawing-room, going little into the
busy world, and unfitted for rough and stormy paths—is it
possible for her to "make her life sublime"? This is the
problem which many women have to solve, and often with
little success; often, dispirited and cast down, they give up the
attempt in despair, and content themselves with busy idleness,
and with gossip which generally degenerates into scandal and
mischief-making. But, fortunately, this was not the case
with Adelaide Procter; her life, short though it was, only
reaching to thirty-eight years, was a fruitful one, and left
behind it some "footprints on the sands of time" which
may give many of her shipwrecked sisters "courage to take
heart again."

Her success stole upon her gradually—unlooked for and
unexpected. The demand for her poems is said to have
been "far in excess of any poetry, except Tennyson's."
In America her popularity is equally great, one of the

ADELAIDE ANNE PROCTOR.

BORN OCTOBER 30TH, 1825; DIED FEBRUARY 2ND, 1864.

(From a Painting exhibited at South Kensington.)

prettiest one-volume editions of her poems being printed at Boston.. They have also been translated into German and other languages. Not only do young ladies shed tears over her melodious and touching verses, learned men and shrewd critics also acknowledge their charm, and musical composers have pounced eagerly upon them as treasures which are not to be found every day.

Adelaide Procter did not write songs for the people ; she did not, like Lady Nairn and Lady Anne Barnard, give us ballads of homely life which touch chords that are common to all. She dealt rather with the lessons which come from loss and disappointment, of the beauty of resignation, patience, and self-sacrifice ; and in doing this she brought out those delicate shades of feeling—what the French call *nuances*—which are so difficult to express in words. She knew exactly when and how to leave off, she knew how to give the atmosphere of a thought : we breathe it in rather than read it ; and this is the gift of a true poet. As Hawthorne says, " The element of poetry is air ; we know the poet by his atmospheric effects, by the blue of his distances, by the softening of every hard outline, by the silver mist in which he veils deformity and clothes what is common, so that it changes to awe-inspiring mystery."

It is this " element of air," this delicate spirituality, which has made Adelaide Procter's poems suitable for music. They are peculiarly songful. Wherever we live, whether amongst acres of brick and mortar or buried in the depths of country villages, we are sure to find pianos, and wherever there are pianos there are piles of music, and amongst this music we are certain to find *The Lost Chord* or *The Message*, *The Doubting Heart* or *Cleansing Fires*. Blumenthal and Sullivan have married their music to Adelaide Procter's suggestive words, and so these songs have been handed down from London concert-halls till they have received the stamp of popularity—that magical hall-mark which so many have yearned for in vain. One

of the most impressive of modern songs is *The Storm,*
with its refrain of *Miserere Domini,* which some of our best
contralto singers have made so popular.

Several of her sacred songs have taken their places in our
hymn-books.   One of them—

> " The shadows of the evening hours
> Fall from the dark'ning sky "—

may be heard through the grey arches of Westminster
Abbey as well as in the humblest dissenting chapel.   Professional and amateur reciters are largely indebted to
Adelaide Procter.   She has given them one of their most
popular pieces—*The Story of a Faithful Soul;* and the
Legend of Provence, with a musical accompaniment, is one
of Clifford Harrison's favourite selections.   As I listened to
him at sunny Montreux, the thought of Adelaide Procter
came to me, sitting, " with the lights extinguished, by the
hearth, the flickering giant-shadows closing round, all dull,
all dark, save when the leaping flame lit up a picture's
ancient frame."

Adelaide Anne Procter was born at 25, Bedford Square,
London, on the 30th of October, 1825.   She was the eldest
daughter of Bryan Waller Procter, the author of many
poems and dramatic pieces, one of which, *Mirandola,* was
acted sixteen times at Covent Garden, and produced the
considerable sum of £630.   Mr. Procter always wrote under
the name of Barry Cornwall.   It is under this name that he
gave us the song of *The Sea! the Sea! the Open Sea!* but
the only time this enthusiastic sea-lover was on the watery
element he was grievously sea-sick, so he allowed himself a
good deal of poetical license.   Miss Martineau says that his
favourite method was to compose alone in a crowd, and he
said he did his best when walking the London streets.   He
had an odd habit of running into a shop to secure his verses,
often carrying them away on scraps of crumpled paper in
which cheese or sugar had been wrapped.   He was quite a

young man when he was introduced to Mr. and Mrs. Basil
Montagu, and to Miss Anne Skepper, his future wife, the
daughter of Mrs. Montagu by her first marriage. It was said
of Mrs. Montagu that " to know her was a liberal education."
There was something noble and exalted in her beauty,
which she preserved to a great age. The year after Mr.
Procter's introduction to the Montagus, he became engaged
to Miss Skepper, and dedicated one of his poems, *The Flood
of Thessaly* to her. After his marriage, on the 7th of October,
1824, he returned to the legal profession, and began as a con-
veyancer. The home of the young couple was first in the
upper part of a house in Southampton Row. Work rapidly
increased, and Mr. Procter used to sit up two entire nights in
a week. He took pupils, of whom he had between thirty and
forty ; amongst them were Kingslake and Eliot Warburton,
who continued his faithful friends. In 1825, the Procters
went to live with the Basil Montagus at Bedford Square,
and here Adelaide was born. Their house was the centre
of literary society, they had troops of friends, a fair com-
petence and no history.

The birth of "golden-tressèd Adelaide" roused her
father's poetical gifts. Just a month afterwards—November,
1825—he celebrated her in a sonnet, now disinterred from
an old musty annual :—

> "Child of my heart I my sweet beloved first-born,
> Thou dove that tidings bring'st of calmer hours !
> Thou rainbow, that dost shine when all the showers
> Are past or passing ! Rose, which hath no thorn,
> No spot, no blemish, pure, and unforlorn,
> Untouched, untainted I O my flower of flowers I
> More welcome than to bees are summer bowers,
> To stranded seamen, life-assuring morn.
> Welcome, a thousand welcomes ! Care, which clings
> Round all, seems loosening now its serpent fold.
> New hope springs upward, and the bright world seems
> Cast back into a youth of endless springs.
> Sweet mother, is it so, or grow I old
> Bewildered in divine Elysian dreams ? "

18

In a lighter mood he celebrated his baby daughter as
follows :—

"Sing, I pray, a little song
Mother, dear,
Neither sad nor very long
It is for a little maid,
Golden-tressèd Adelaide
Therefore let it suit a merry, merry ear,
Mother, dear ! "

Fanny Kemble in her *Records of a Girlhood* notes that
she went up "to see Mrs. Procter and found baby Adelaide
at dinner. That child looks like a poet's child and a poet.
It has something doomed—(what the Germans call fatal—in
its appearance), such a preternaturally thoughtful, mournful
expression for a little child, such a marked brow over the
heavy blue eyes, such a transparent skin, such pale golden
hair. John says the little creature is an elf-child. I think
it is the prophecy of a poet. Talked a great deal about the
little Adelaide, who seems a most wonderful creature."

Poets' daughters are not often gifted with sparks of the
divine fire. Mrs. Clarke, wife of the Spitalfields weaver,
though she read Greek to Milton, her father, imbibed
nothing of his genius ; but not so with Adelaide Procter,
she inherited all "Barry Cornwall's" poetical instincts
and sense of melody. Yet she was never a show child.
Modest and reserved, her nature resembled one of those
mountain streams, covered over with tangled heather and
ferns, which hardly reveals its existence, and yet which
never dries up, and is always fresh and pure. Golden-
haired Adelaide's love of poetry was so great that Charles
Dickens, in his memoir of her, tells us that she had a tiny album
made of small notepaper, into which her favourite passages
were copied by her mother before she herself could write.
It looks, he says, "as if she had carried it about as another
little girl might have carried a doll." Her father never had
an idea that she could turn a rhyme till he saw her first little
poem in print in a Book of Beauty.

Naturally very quick, she had also a remarkable memory, and could solve several problems in Euclid when she was quite a child ; she soon learnt French, Italian, and German, could play well on the piano, and showed great taste for drawing. But as soon as she had gone into any branch of study, she lost interest in it, and passed on to another. She was always a great reader, and read on industriously, as her fancy dictated. Her home was always in London ; first in a little Gothic cottage opposite to the house of Sir Edwin Landseer—5, Grove End Road, St. John's Wood—then 13, Upper Harley Street, Cavendish Square, a house which will be long remembered as the meeting-place of all the celebrities of the time — Landor, Leigh Hunt, Dickens, Carlyle, Hazlitt, and Thackeray—for Barry Cornwall was a man of many friends, and his wife was a perfect hostess. Amongst the most frequent *habitués* of the house was Thackeray, who dedicated *Vanity Fair* to his good friend, Procter. In a letter to Mrs. Brookfield, dated July, 1849, he says, " Adelaide Procter has sent me the most elegant velvet purse, embroidered with my initials and forget-me-nots on the other side. I received this peace-offering with a gentle heart." We are not told what prompted this "peace-offering" from the shy girl of twenty-four to the mature author of thirty-eight.

Mr. Procter was called to the Bar in 1831, and was made Commisioner of Lunacy in the same year. There were six children, of whom one, a son, died early.

Mr. Fields, the American publisher, says, "I distinctly recall Adelaide Procter as I first saw her in one of my early visits to her father's house at Upper Harley Street. She was a shy, bright girl, and her father drew my attention to her as she sat reading in a corner of the library. . . . Her father told me what a comfort Adelaide had always been to his household. He described a visit Wordsworth made, and how gentle the old man's aspect was when he looked at the children.

"' He took the hand of my dear Adelaide in his,' said Procter, 'and spoke some words to her, the recollection of which helped, perhaps, with other things, to incline her to poetry.'"

Charles Dickens has related how in the spring of 1853 a short poem was sent in to *Household Words*, very different and much superior to the ordinary run of verses which editors have to wade through. The authoress's name was given as "Miss Mary Berwick," and she was to be addressed by letter—if addressed at all— at a circulating library in the west district of London. The poem was accepted, and Miss Berwick became a constant contributor to *Household Words*. She herself was never seen, and the Dickens family settled that she was a governess, who had been long in the same situation. She proved "business-like, punctual, self-reliant, and reliable." In 1851, when she was twenty-five, she became a Roman Catholic. Those who study the different tendencies of character will have little difficulty in finding out the attraction which the gorgeous pageantry and the mysterious awe which the Church of Rome has for certain minds. Adelaide Procter loved to muse on the picturesque and dreamy aspects of things ; therefore the charm of the Roman Catholic religion was irresistible to her, and out of her three sisters two followed her example. This change of faith, says the editor of *Procter's Autobiographical Fragment*, "does not appear to have even ruffled the family peace and affection." Few traces of it can be found in Adelaide Procter's poems. Most of them belong to that wider Church which includes all creeds. For instance, who cannot join her when she cries :—

"My God, I thank Thee Thou hast made
The earth so bright,
So full of splendour, and of joy,
Beauty, and light.
So many glorious things are here,
Noble and right."

In 1853 Adelaide Procter went to Italy and spent some
time at Turin with an aunt, who was a Roman Catholic,
like herself. She found great pleasure in studying the
Piedmontese peasantry, their dialect, habits, and customs.
From her letters, which are given in the short memoir
prefixed to *Legends and Lyrics*, we see that she not only
observed well, but had a sense of humour which does
not appear in her poems. She is describing a betrothal
ball. First of all a band is heard, and she is told "that
band is playing at the farmer's near here. The daughter
is *fiancé* to-day, and they have a ball." Says Adelaide,
"I wish I was going." Then it comes out, "the farmer's
wife did call to invite us." So it was settled that the whole
party should go, and, after putting off every shred of black,
they started.

"We were placed on a bench against the wall, and the
people went on dancing. The room was a large, white-
washed kitchen, with several large pictures in black frames,
and very smoky. I distinguished the 'Martyrdom of St.
Sebastian,' and the others appeared equally lively and ap-
propriate subjects. The band was seated opposite us—five
men with wind instruments. They really played admirably,
and I began to be afraid that some idea of our dignity would
prevent my getting a partner, so, by Madame B——'s advice,
I went up to the bride and offered to dance with her. Such
a handsome young woman ! very dark, with a quantity of
black hair, and on an immense scale. After we came to
the end of our dance, a polka mazurka, I saw the bride
trying to screw up the courage of her *fiancé* to ask me to
dance, which, after a little hesitation, he did ; and admirably
he danced, as indeed they all did, in excellent time, and
with a little more spirit than one sees in a ball-room. In
fact, they were very like one's ordinary partners, except
that they wore earrings and were in their shirt-sleeves, and
truth compels me to state that they smelt decidedly of garlic.

Some of them had been smoking, but threw away their cigars when we came in. . . . The musicians played a 'Monferrino,' which is a Piedmontese dance. It was very fatiguing, like a Scotch reel ; my partner was a little man, very proud of his dancing. He cut in the air and twisted about till I was out of breath, though my attempts to imitate him were feeble in the extreme. At length after seven or eight dances I was obliged to sit down. We stayed till nine, and I was so dead beat with the heat that I could hardly crawl about the house and in an agony with the cramp, it is so long since I have danced."

The marriage feast, when it came off, is also capitally described.

"The bride was dressed in a shot silk, with a yellow handkerchief, and rows of large beads. On our arrival we found them all dancing out of doors, and a most melancholy affair it was—all the bride's sisters were not to be recognised, they had cried so. The mother sat in the house and could not appear ; and the bride was sobbing so, she could hardly stand. The most melancholy spectacle of all was that the bridegroom was decidedly tipsy. We danced a ' Monferrino '—I with the bridegroom, and the bride crying the whole time. . . . As she lives quite near, makes an excellent match, and is one of nine children, it really was a most desirable marriage, in spite of all this show of distress. . . . In a couple of days we had some rolls of the bride's first baking, which they call Madonnas. My wrath against the bridegroom is somewhat calmed by finding that it is considered bad luck if he does not get tipsy at his wedding."

There is so much fun about these letters that it is difficult to reconcile them with the subdued tone of Adelaide Procter's poems. It was after her return from Italy that the secret of " Miss Mary Berwick " came out. In December, 1854, when the Christmas number of *Household Words—*

The Seven Poor Travellers—was printed, Dickens happened to be going to dine with the Procters, and took the proof with him. He remarked, as he laid it on the table, that it contained a very pretty poem by a Miss Berwick. Adelaide Procter was in the room at the time, and next day Dickens was told by her mother that he had no such correspondent as " Miss Mary Berwick," that the name had been assumed by Adelaide Procter, who had been anxious that her poems should be accepted on their own merits, and not because the editor happened to be an old friend of her father. The praise given by Dickens brought tears of joy to Mrs. Procter's eyes.

Adelaide was now twenty-nine, and her name soon began to be known. In 1861, the family removed to 32, Weymouth Street, and the friendly receptions were still kept up, but on a more limited scale.

Meanwhile Adelaide Procter looked into her heart and wrote. Two voices appear to be speaking within her, especially as years went on—one which expresses the intense sadness of life, the other which exclaims against it. Outwardly she was cheerful, and in her laugh, we are told, there was "unusual vivacity, enjoyment, and sense of drollery." She is indignant at that morbid spirit which wails out incessant complaints. She cries :—

> " Why wilt thou make bright music
> Give forth a sound of pain ?
> Why wilt thou weave fair flowers
> Into a weary chain ?
> Why turn each cool, grey shadow
> Into a world of fears ?
> Why say the winds are wailing?
> Why call the dew-drops tears ?
>
> The voices of happy Nature,
> And the heavens' sunny gleam
> Reprove thy sick heart's fancies,
> Upbraid the foolish dream.

Listen, and I will tell thee
  The song creation sings,
From the humming of bees in the heather
  To the flutter of angels' wings.

.   .   .   .   .

Above thy peevish wailing
  Rises that holy song,
Above Earth's foolish clamour,
  Above the voice of wrong.
So leave thy sick heart's fancies,
  And lend thy little voice
To the silver song of glory,
  That bids the world rejoice."

Again we see the struggle coming in, the desperate desire
to conquer despondency, at all hazards. She tells herself :—

" Raise up thine eyes, be strong,
    Nor cast away
  The crown that God has given
    Thy soul this day."

Yet through this desperate resolve we see that there *is* an
effort, the imprisoned spirit *is* suffering, the iron which
binds it is pressing in deeply. Now and then the burden
seems almost too great. Sometimes she strives to reconcile
the ways of God to man, so in *Give Me thy Heart* she
brings out the upward tendency of life's teaching, till at last
the soul cries :—

" Send down, O Lord, the sacred fire,
    Consume and cleanse the sin
  That lingers still within its depths—
    Let heavenly love begin.
  That sacred flame Thy saints have known,
    Kindle, O Lord, in me ;
  Thou, above all, the rest for ever,
    And all the rest in Thee."

The same spirit which breathes in her poems, we see in her
refined face—deep pathos, tender sympathy, and love ; those

large, yearning, steadfast eyes, "true windows of the soul,"
know how to weep with those who weep as well as to rejoice
with those who rejoice. It is not known if she had any
romance in her life, probably she had, but the public knew
nothing of it ; it was buried in her heart. For little
children she had a passionate affection ; there is real
motherliness in her *Links from Heaven*, which first appeared in the *Victoria Regia*, a gorgeous volume, edited
by the Society for the Industrial Employment of Women.
Mothers of dead children seem to her to have more grace,
for they give angels to their God and heaven :—

> " How can a mother's heart feel cold or weary,
>   Knowing her dearer self safe, happy, warm ?
> How can she feel her road too dark or dreary
>   Who knows her treasure sheltered from the storm? "

It is strange that one of the most touching attempts to
console the hearts of mothers who, like Rachel, are " mourning for their children, and refuse to be comforted, because
they are not," has been written by one who never knew the
joys or sorrows of a mother, except in imagination.

In 1860, when Thackeray gathered round him all the first
names in literature, as contributors to the *Cornhill Magazine*, Adelaide Procter was amongst the select band, and
her poem beginning *A Little Changeling Spirit* appeared
in one of the first numbers. Though she wrote a few
ballads, such as *The Legend of Bregenz*, *The Wayside Inn*,
and *The Tomb of Ghent*, yet her shorter pieces are decidedly
her best, and few of us are not familiar with *Spinning* and
One by One. How many of us have cause to remember that
simple, but often disregarded, truth—

> " One by one, thy griefs shall meet thee,
>   Do not fear an armèd band ;
> One will fade as others greet thee,
>   Shadows passing through the land."

The faults of Adelaide Procter's *Legends and Lyrics* are diffusiveness, want of power—they have at times a sort of soft, sweet, amiable weakness.

She was very generous about her literary earnings ; the poor and the suffering always had a claim upon her. In her *Chaplet of Verses*, which was published for the benefit of a night refuge in London, she makes the following eloquent appeal :—

" There is scarcely any charitable institution which should excite such universal, such unhesitating sympathy as a Night Refuge for the Homeless Poor. A shelter through the bleak winter nights, leave to rest in some poor shed instead of wandering through the pitiless streets, is a boon we could hardly deny to a starving dog. And yet we have known that in this country, in this town, many of our miserable fellow-creatures are pacing the streets through the long weary nights, without a roof to shelter them, without food to eat, with their poor rags soaked in rain, and only the bitter winds of heaven for companions ; women and children utterly forlorn and helpless, either wandering about all night or crouching under a miserable archway, or, worse than all, seeking in death or sin the refuge denied them elsewhere. It is a marvel that we can sleep in our warm comfortable homes with this horror at our very door."

Adelaide Procter's energy was not confined to talk ; she suited the action to the word, and wore herself out visiting the sick, teaching the young, and raising the fallen. She worked, we are told, with a flushed earnestness that disregarded season, weather, time of day or night, food or rest. The active mind gradually wore out the feeble body ; she was up and about till she could move no longer. At length she took to her bed, where she lay, patiently and uncomplainingly, for fifteen long months. Spring blossomed into summer, summer flushed into autumn, autumn faded into winter, and life still lingered. She had never been ambitious or vain, or spiteful or envious; but any earthly alloy which clung to her, had indeed been purified away by " cleansing fires," before her spirit left the world. At midnight, on the 2nd of February, 1864, she turned down the leaf of a little book she was reading, and shut it up. As the clock struck one, she said to her mother, "Do you think I am dying, mamma ? "

" I think you are very, very ill to-night, my dear."

" Send for my sister—my feet are so cold. Lift me up ! "

As her sister came in, she said, " It has come at last ! " And, with a bright and happy smile, she looked upward and departed.

These are very nearly the words in which Charles Dickens tells us of her last moments ; and when he, too, in his turn, had passed into the land of spirits, and his life, too, had to be written, his friend, John Forster, says, " My mention of these pleasures of editorship shall close with what, I think, to him was the greatest. He gave to the world, while yet the name of the writer was unknown to him, the pure and pathetic verses of Adelaide Procter."

" Pure and pathetic ! " these words express Adelaide Procter's life as well as her poems. She did not attempt lofty things. Simple feelings, simple thoughts, simple lessons, were her province, and so well has she accomplished her life's mission, that we ask for nothing more. There is a place in God's earth for the dove as well as for the eagle —for the violet as well as for the rose. When " Friend Death," as she once called him, came to her, she could meet him with a smile:

XII

LOUISA MAY ALCOTT.

1832–1888.

Birth at Germantown—Boston—A birthday party—A friendly dog—A cottage at Concord—Plays in the barn—Fruitlands—Concord again —*Flower Fables*—A room in a Boston attic—Hospital nursing— *Hospital Sketches*—*Moods*—The Pathetic Family—*Little Women*— *Good Wives*—*Little Men*—*Eight Cousins*—*Rose in Bloom*—Death of Mrs. Alcott—*Under the Lilacs*—"My baby"—*Lulu's Library*—Death.

WHAT girl has not read *Little Women?* The story of the four sisters—Meg, Jo, Beth, and Amy—is as familiar to most of us as household words. It seems so real, and much of it *is* real, for Louisa Alcott took her stories from her own experience. "The nearer I keep to nature," she says, "the better my work is." Her creative powers were not of a high order, her range was limited, but she has infinite fun and drollery, some pathos, and a shrewd, if not a deep, insight into character. Her novels of *Moods*, and *A Modern Mephistopheles*, are disappointing and feeble, but her girls' stories are admirable, and will always take a very high place in that department of literature. They have been sold by hundreds of thousands, and the demand for them still continues. In Holland there is hardly a girl who has not read *Little Women*, and *Good Wives*—in the

LOUISA M. ALCOTT.

BORN NOVEMBER 29TH, 1832; DIED MARCH 6TH, 1888.

Dutch translation—*Under Mother's Wings,* and *With Their Own Wings,* so that the name of Louisa Alcott is as well known in the marshes of the Netherlands as in the crowded cities of America and England.

Her life, especially the earlier part of it, was a perpetual struggle with poverty—not the semi-genteel poverty that has to be contented with one pair of gloves a month, but poverty that has to do without new gloves at all. Her wardrobe was made up of " old clothes from cousins and friends." She had to battle her way to independence inch by inch. Finally, she became the good fairy of her family. Hers might be called an heroic life—full of noble self-sacrifice and labour for others. It was well for her that before the end came she was able to enter into the fruits of her labours ; she saw her work crowned with success, and, through her, benefits poured in on those she loved in no stinted measure.

Louisa May Alcott was born at Germantown, in Pennsylvania, on her father's birthday, November 29, 1832. She was, like Jo, the second daughter, and is described as the " prettiest, best little thing in the world, with a fair complexion, dark bright eyes, long dark hair, a high forehead, and a countenance of more than ordinary intelligence."

Her father, Amos Bronson Alcott, was an idealist—a philosopher so full of lofty theories for the good of mankind, that earning money to support his family was quite a secondary consideration. Mrs. Alcott was a large-hearted, energetic woman, and her love for her husband was so great that, in spite of the failure of his schemes, she never lost confidence or trust in him. At the time of Louisa's birth he was taking charge of a school, but he soon gave it up, and the earliest anecdote that is told of her is during the journey from Philadelphia to Boston by steamer. She and her elder sister, Anna, were nicely dressed in clean nankeen frocks, but they had not been long on board before lively little Louisa was missing, and was finally brought up from the engine-room, where she was having a "beautiful time with plenty of dirt."

Mr. Alcott opened a school at Boston in 1834, and here a third little girl, Elizabeth, was born. Mr. Alcott was a strict vegetarian, and, in deference to his wishes, all the family were put on vegetarian diet, and none of his daughters tasted meat till they were grown up. They were fed on boiled rice without sugar, and graham meal without butter or treacle. A friend who lived at an hotel used to save pieces of pie or cake, and bring them to the Alcott children in a band-box. Years afterwards, when she met Louisa, she was eagerly greeted by her.

"Why, I did not think you would remember me!" exclaimed the friend.

"Do you think I could ever forget that band-box?" was Louisa's reply.

From her *Recollections of My Childhood's Days* we learn that one of her earliest memories was playing with books in her father's study, "building houses and bridges of the big dictionaries, looking at pictures, pretending to read, and scribbling on blank pages whenever pen or pencil could be found."

Another memory is told in a sketch of her childhood given in her Life by E. M. Cheney. Her fourth birthday was celebrated at her father's schoolroom in Masonic Temple. "All the children were there. I wore a crown of flowers, and stood upon a table to dispense cakes to each child as the procession marched past. By some oversight the cakes fell short, and I saw that if I gave away the last one I should have none. As I was queen of the revel, I felt that I ought to have it, and held on to it tightly till mother said, 'It is always better to give away than to keep the nice things, so I know my Louey will not let the little friend go without.' The little friend received the dear plummy cake, and I my first lesson in self-denial—a lesson

which my dear mother beautifully illustrated all her long
and noble life."

Running away is one of the chief events of an active
child's life. So it was with Louisa. She says : " Being
born on the birthday of Columbus, I seem to have something of his spirit of adventure, and running away was one
of the delights of my childhood. Many a social lunch have
I shared with hospitable Irish beggar children as we ate our
crusts, cold potatoes, and salt fish on voyages of discovery
among the ash-heaps of the waste land that then lay where
the Albany station now stands."

On one of these occasions a trip to the common cheered
the afternoon, but as dusk set in " I felt that home was a
nice place, and longed to find it. I sat down to rest on
a doorstep, where a big Newfoundland dog welcomed me
so kindly that I fell asleep with my head pillowed on his
curly head, and was found by the town-crier, whom my
distracted parents had sent in search of me. His bell, and
the proclamation of the loss of a little girl, six years old, in
a pink frock, white hat, and new green shoes, woke me up,
and a small voice answered out of the darkness, ' Why, dat's
me ! ' I was carried to the crier's house, and feasted sump-
tuously on bread and treacle. But my fun ended next day
when I was tied to the arm of the sofa to repent at leisure."

Another adventure was when, running after her hoop,
she fell into the Frog Pond, and was rescued by a black
boy, which incident made her a friend to the coloured race
ever afterwards.

At first the little Alcotts were taught in their father's
school, but the school proved a failure, and in 1840 the
family removed to Concord, and took a cottage with a
garden full of trees and a large barn. Here the youngest
daughter, May, was born—the " Amy " of *Little Women.*
The children were taught by their father in that wise way
which unfolds what lies in the child's nature, and brings out
rather than puts in. The lessons were generally given in

the garden, and Mr. Alcott taught them from nature, and used little symbolical pictures to illustrate his teaching. Sometimes he invented leaflets and drawings for each child. Louisa's was—

> "Louisa loves—
> What?
> Fun.
> Have some, then, father says."

Louisa never liked arithmetic or grammar, and dodged these branches on all occasions, but reading, composition, history, and geography she enjoyed, as well as the stories read aloud " with a skill which made the dullest charming and useful."

The Pilgrim's Progress, Krummacher's *Parables*, Miss Edgeworth, and the dear old fairy tales, made that hour the pleasantest of the day. " On Sundays," she says, " we had a simple service of Bible stories, hymns, and conversation about the state of our little consciences and the conduct of our childish lives, which will never be forgotten. . . . Needle-work began early, and at ten my skilful sister made a linen shirt beautifully, while at twelve I set up as a doll's dress-maker, with my sign out, and wonderful models in my window. All the children employed me, and my turbans were the rage at one time, to the great dismay of my neighbour's hens, who were hotly hunted down that I might tweak their downiest feathers to adorn the dolls' head-gear. Active exercise was my delight from the time when, a child of six, I drove my hoop round the common without stopping to the days when I did my twenty miles in five hours and went to a party in the evening. . . . No boy could be my friend till I had beaten him in a race, and no girl if she refused to climb trees, leap fences, and be a tomboy " (*Recollections of My Childhood's Days*, p. 11).

These Concord days were the happiest of Louisa's life ; she had charming playmates in the little Emersons, Channings, and Hawthornes, with the illustrious parents and their friends to enjoy their pranks and share their excursions.

Plays in the barn were their great amusement, and they dramatised all their favourite fairy tales. "Our giant came tumbling off a loft when Jack cut down the squash-vine to represent the immortal bean. Cinderella rolled away in a vast pumpkin, and a long black pudding was lowered by invisible hands to fasten itself on the nose of the woman who wasted her three wishes. . . . Little pilgrims journeyed over the hills with scrip and staff, and cockle-shells in their hats, lords and ladies haunted the garden, and mermaids splashed in the bath-house of woven willows over the brook."

One day Emerson and Margaret Fuller paid a visit to the Alcotts, and, the conversation having turned on education, Miss Fuller said, "Well, Mr. Alcott, you have been able to carry out your methods in your own family, and I should like to see your model children." Just then a wild uproar was heard, and round a corner of the house came a wheelbarrow, holding baby May arrayed as a queen ; Louisa was the horse, bitted and bridled, and driven by Anna, while Lizzie played dog, and barked as loud as her gentle voice permitted. All were shouting and wild with fun when Louisa's foot tripped, and down they all went in a laughing heap, while Mrs. Alcott, with a dramatic wave of her hand, said, "Here are the model children, Miss Fuller !"

In 1841, Colonel May, Mrs. Alcott's father, died and left her a small legacy. She decided to purchase with this a house in Concord, and, with the addition of five hundred dollars from Mr. Emerson, a place called Hillside was bought. The dates given are rather confusing, and it is hard to settle the exact time when the Alcott family lived at Hillside, and how long they remained there. It seems certain that Mr. Alcott left America for England in 1842. He was full of plans for organising a great social reform, and he found English friends like-minded with himself, who gave him their encouragement and support. Some of

19

them accompanied him back to America the following year,
and they agreed to join in taking a farm in the town of
Harvard, near Concord, which they called Fruitlands.
Louisa has described this expedition so inimitably in her
sketch, *Transcendental Wild Oats*, that some extracts from
it may be given here. She saw the scheme in its ridiculous
light, and yet there is a touch of reverence for the dreams
of these idealists. She may well call it a "chapter from an
unwritten romance."

"On the first day of June, 1843, a large waggon, drawn
by a small horse, and containing a motley load, went
lumbering over certain New England hills, with the
pleasing accompaniments of wind, rain, and hail. A serene
man, with a serene child upon his knee, was driving, or rather
being driven, for the small horse had it all his own way.
. . . Behind them was an energetic-looking woman, with a
benevolent brow, satirical mouth, and eyes brimful of hope
and courage. A baby reposed on her lap, a mirror leaned
against her knee, and a basket of provisions danced at her
feet, as she struggled with a large, unruly umbrella. Two
blue-eyed little girls, with hands full of childish treasures,
sat under one old shawl, chatting happily together. In
front of this lively party stalked a tall, sharp-featured man
in a long blue cloak, and a fourth small girl trudged along
beside him through the mud as if she rather enjoyed it.
The wind whistled over the bleak hills, the rain fell in a
despondent drizzle, and twilight began to fall. But the
calm man gazed as tranquilly into the fog as if he beheld
a radiant bow of promise spanning the grey sky. The
cheery woman tried to cover every one but herself with
the big umbrella. . . . The little girls sang lullabies to their
dolls in soft maternal murmurs. The sharp-nosed pedes-
trian marched steadily on, with the blue cloak streaming
out behind him like a banner ; and the lively infant
splashed through the puddles with a duck-like satisfaction

pleasant to behold. Thus these modern pilgrims journeyed out of the old world to found a new one in the wilderness. . . . The prospective Eden at present consisted of an old red farmhouse, a dilapidated barn, many acres of meadow land, and a grove."

Ten ancient apple-trees were all the chaste supply for the bodily needs " which the place afforded as yet, but in the firm belief that plenteous orchards would soon be evoked from their inner consciousness, these sanguine founders had christened their domain Fruitlands. Here Abel Lamb" (Mr. Alcott), " with the devoutest faith in the high ideal which was to him a living truth, desired to plant a Paradise, where Beauty, Virtue, Justice, and Love might live happily together, without the possibility of a serpent entering in. And here his wife, unconverted but faithful to the end, hoped, after many wanderings over the face of the earth, to find rest for herself and a home for her children. . . . The new-comers were welcomed by one of the elect-precious, whose idea of reform consisted chiefly in wearing white cotton raiment and shoes of untanned leather. . . . The goods and chattels of the Society not having arrived, the weary family reposed before the fire on blocks of wood, while Brother Amos regaled them with roasted potatoes, brown bread, and water. His table service was limited to two plates, a tin pan, and one mug. Having cast the forms and vanities of a depraved world behind them, the elders welcomed hardship with the enthusiasm of pioneers, and the children heartily enjoyed this foretaste of what they believed to be a sort of perpetual picnic." .

Their programme was that each member should perform the work for which experience, strength, and taste, best fitted him. "We shall rise at dawn, begin the day by bathing, followed by music, and then a chaste repast of bread and fruit. Each one finds congenial occupation till the meridian meal, when some deep-searching conversation gives rest to the body and development to the mind. Healthful labour again engages us till the next meal, when we assemble in social communion, prolonged till sunset; we retire to sweet repose, ready for the next day's activity."

Mrs. Alcott's sense of the ludicrous supported her through many trying scenes. She took possession of a large dilapidated kitchen, containing an old stove and the stores out of which food was to be provided for the family of eleven, brethren included. "They had cakes of maple sugar, dried peas and beans, barley and hominy, meal of all sorts, potatoes and dried fruit. No milk, butter, cheese, tea, or meat. Even salt was considered a useless luxury, and spice was strictly forbidden by these lovers of Spartan simplicity. Unleavened bread, porridge, and water for breakfast; bread, vegetables, and water for dinner; bread, fruit, and water for supper, was the bill of fare ordained by the elders. No teapot profaned that sacred stove, no gory steak cried aloud for vengeance from that chaste gridiron."

The Alcott children lived a healthy out-of-doors life at Fruitlands. They were let to run wild. Louisa says she remembers running over the hills just at dawn one summer morning, and, pausing to rest in the silent woods, she saw, through an arch of trees, the sun rise over river, hill, and wide, green meadows as she had never seen it before. "Something born of the lovely hour, a happy mood, and the unfolding aspiration of a child's soul seemed to bring me very near to God, and, in the hush of that morning hour, I always felt that I had 'got religion,' as the phrase goes. A new and vital sense of His presence, tender and sustaining as a father's arms, came to me then, never to change through forty years of life's vicissitudes, but to grow stronger for the sharp discipline of poverty and pain, sorrow and success."

She began to keep a diary at Fruitlands, in which all her doings are noted. The first entry—September 1, 1843 —is as follows :—

"I rose at five, and had my bath. I love cold water! Then we had our singing lesson with Mr. Lane. After breakfast I washed dishes, and ran on the hill till nine, and had some thoughts ; it was so beautiful up there. Did my lessons, wrote and spelt and did sums, and Mr. Lane read a story—'The Judicious Father.' . . . I liked it very much, and I shall be kind to poor people. Father asked us what was God's noblest work. Anna said *men*, but I said *babies :* men are often bad, babies never are. We had a long talk, and I felt better after it, and cleared up. We had bread and fruit for dinner. I read and walked and played till supper-time. We sang in the evening. As I went to bed, the moon came up very brightly and looked at me. I felt sad because I have been cross to-day and did not mind mother. I cried and then I felt better. . . . I got to sleep saying poetry : I know a good deal.

"October 8th. When I woke up, the first thought I got was, 'It's mother's birthday ; I must be very good.' I ran and wished her a happy birthday. After breakfast we gave her our presents. I had a moss-cross and a piece of poetry for her. We did not have any school, and played in the wood and got red leaves. In the evening we danced and sung. I wish I was rich, I was good, and we were all a happy family together.

"Tuesday, 12th. After lessons I ironed. We all went to the barn and husked corn. It was good fun. . . . I made a verse about sunset."

She had begun verse-making at Concord, and it now continued at Fruitlands. One of her pieces, written at fourteen, *My Kingdom*, is good and true :—

> " A little kingdom I possess
> Where thoughts and feelings dwell,
> And very hard I find the task
> Of governing it well ;

For passion tempts and troubles me,
A wayward will misleads,
And selfishness its shadow casts
On all my words and deeds.

* * *

Dear Father, help me with the love
That casteth out my fear;
Teach me to lean on Thee, and feel
That Thou art very near.

* * * *

I do not ask for any crown,
But that which all may win,
Nor seek to conquer any world
Except the one within."

The diary goes on for three years. Louisa washes dishes and irons; she reads the *Vicar of Wakefield*, the *Heart of Mid Lothian*, and Miss Bremer's *Home;* she runs, and jumps, and climbs; she is very anxious to have a little room all to herself, and at last, in March, 1846, she got it.

But the social experiment at Fruitlands was falling to pieces; the brethren gradually deserted—one joined the Shakers, another had a call from the Oversoul elsewhere, and at last Mr. Alcott was left alone with his faithful wife and his four little girls. Winter was coming on, and he was in the depths of despair. Mrs. Alcott, whose motto was "Trust in God and keep busy," sustained him. She said, "I can sew, and you can chop wood." She engaged four rooms at a neighbour's house in Concord, and so, one bleak December day in 1846, the Alcotts packed their few possessions on an ox-sled, the rosy children were perched on the top, and the exiles left their Eden and faced the world again. They struggled on as best they could. It is not quite plain when they went to Hillside. Probably the year after leaving Fruitlands. The intimacy with Emerson was certainly renewed, for he gave Louisa Goethe's works, and she was fired with a desire to be a second Bettina. She wrote letters to him, but never sent them, left wild flowers on the doorstep of her "Master," and sung Mignon's song under his windows.

"Goethe is still my favourite author," writes Louisa in her
Recollections of My Childhood, " and Emerson remained my
beloved ' Master,' doing more for me, as for many another
young soul, than he ever knew, by the simple beauty of
his life, the truth and wisdom of his books, the example of
a great good man untempted and unspoiled by the world
which he made nobler while in it, and left the richer when
he went."

Her thoughts naturally turned to teaching, and she had a
little school in the barn at Hillside for Emerson's children,
and began to write her *Flower Fables* for them. The
burden and cares of her family weighed on Mrs. Alcott
heavily. A friend passing through Concord found her in
tears, and after hearing her struggles and sufferings said,
"Come to Boston, and I will find you employment." So
the little family left Concord for Boston in November, 1848.
Louisa was then sixteen. Just before she left the home of
her girlhood, she sat on a cart-wheel, half hidden in the
grass, and said, shaking her fist at a crow that cawed
defiantly, "I *will* do something by and by. Don't care
what : teach, sew, act, write, anything to help the family,
and I'll be rich and famous and happy before I die, see if
I wont ! "

The leafless trees, sere grass, leaden sky, and frosty air
could not daunt the resolute spirit that beat under the old
red shawl.· When the sisters found themselves in a small
house at the south end of Boston with not a tree in sight,
only a back yard to play in, and no money to buy any of
the splendours before them, they all longed for the country
again. Anna soon found little pupils, and trudged away
each morning to her daily task. Mr. Alcott went to his
classes down town, Mrs. Alcott to her city missionary work,
the little girls to school, and Louisa kept house, feeling, as
she says, " like a caged seagull, as she washed dishes, and
cooked in the basement kitchen, when her prospect was
limited to a procession of muddy boots." Sometimes she

stood at the wash-tub and sang her *Song From the Suds—*

> " Queen of my tub, I merrily sing,
>   While the white foam rises high,
> And sturdily wash, and rinse, and wring,
>   And fasten the clothes to dry.
>
>   *   *   *   *
>
> I am glad a task to me is given
>   To labour at, day by day,
> For it brings me health, and strength, and hope,
>   And I cheerfully learn to say,
> ' Head, you may think ; heart, you may feel ;
>   But hand you shall work alway ! ' "

In the evening the family met. Anna related her teaching experiences, Mr. Alcott brought news from the upper world and the wise people who adorned it, and afterwards, Louisa says, " we adjourned to the kitchen for our fun, which usually consisted of writing, dressing, and acting plays. We recited pages without a fault, and made every sort of property from a harp to a fairy's spangled wings. Later, we acted Shakespeare, and Hamlet was my favourite hero, played with a gloomy glare and a tragic stalk which I have never seen surpassed." She was attacked by a mania for the stage, and in her diary for 1850, which she resumed at Boston, she says, " Anna wants to be an actress and so do I. Mother says we are too young and must wait. I like tragic plays, and shall be a Siddons if I can. We get up fine ones, and make harps, castles, armour, dresses, waterfalls, and thunder, and have great fun." While Louisa was washing and sewing, her thoughts were busy constructing plays— one of them, *The Captive of Castille ; or, the Moorish Maiden's Vow,* is still preserved. Another, the *Rival Prima Donnas,* was offered to Mr. Barry of the Boston Theatre, who promised to bring it out ; but from some difficulty in the arrangements it was never produced. Mr. Barry, however, gave Louisa a free pass for the Theatre, which was a source of great delight to her. It was not till some years afterwards, in 1860, that a farce of hers, *Ned Bachelor's Pleasure Trip ; or, the Trials of a Good-natured Man,* was acted at the Howard Athenæum at Boston with success. The disappointments about these plays gave Louisa many a bitter hour.

At this time of her life she was a tall girl, with brown hair a yard and a half long, a well-shaped head, a good nose, and at times an expression of uncontrollable fun and drollery. "A wilful, moody girl," she calls herself in her diary ; "my tongue is always getting me into mischief and my moodiness makes it hard to be cheerful when I think how poor we are, how much worry it is to live, and how many things I long to do I never can."

The Alcott family had a "small-pox summer" in 1852, and they afterwards removed to a house in High Street. Here Mrs. Alcott opened an intelligence office which grew out of her city missionary work. A gentleman came one day to look for a companion for his father and sister who was only to do light work. Ever-ready Louisa said, "Why can't I go, mother ? " So she went, and her two months' experience is given in her story, *How I went out to Service.*

In 1852, her first tale was printed and 5 dollars (about £1) given for it. "It was written at Concord," she remarks in her diary, "when I was sixteen. Great rubbish ! Read it aloud to sisters, and when they praised it, not knowing the author, I proudly announced her name."

In January, 1853, she started a little school of about a dozen pupils. Lizzie was the little housekeeper—"an angel in a cellar kitchen." May went to school, Anna was teaching at Syracuse, and Mr. Alcott wrote and talked, when he could get classes, "so poor, so hopeful, so serene." Louisa's apprenticeship to life was going on in good earnest. Teaching she tried most, but it is probable that she was too impulsive and impatient for the routine of a school. Sewing she worked hard at, stitching at shirts for hours.

"I have 11 dollars" (about £2 5s.); she writes to Anna
at Syracuse, "all my own earnings—five for a story, and
four for the pile of sewing I did for the ladies of Dr. Gray's
society, to give him a present." With part of her small
earnings she bought a crimson ribbon for May's bonnet.
"She is so graceful and pretty, and loves beauty so much
that it is hard for her to wear other people's ugly things.
I long to dash out and buy the finest hat the limited sum
of ten dollars can procure. I hope I shall live to see the
dear child in silk and lace." It was at this time that her
eyes were opening to see "the strong contrasts and the fun
and follies of every-day life." Yet her first book, *Flower
Fables*, which came out in December, 1854, deals with
woodland fancies, not realities. The little tales in prose and
verse, which are told of Violet, Clover-Blossom, Lily Bell,
and Thistle-down are pretty in their way, but do not show
Louisa Alcott's real powers. There is no individuality
about them. They are reminiscences of Hans Andersen
and other story-tellers. Each contains a lesson—the frost-
king's palace melts under the sun of love; Thistle-down
has to do deeds of kindness before he can win Lily Bell, and
so on throughout the book. It was written for Emerson's
daughter Ellen, and is dedicated to her. Miss Stevens paid
for the book, and Louisa received 32 dollars (about
£6). "It has sold very well," she remarks, "and people
seem to like it." In a letter to her mother, with the
Christmas present of her "first-born," Louisa writes, "I
hope to pass on in time from fairies and fancies to men
and realities."

Topsy-turvy Louisa would amount to something, after
all. Up in the garret at Pinckney Street, with her papers
round her and a pile of apples to eat, she planned
her stories, and listened to the patter of rain on the roof.
It was here she found peace and quiet. Sewing, school, and
house-work took up most of her day. Her winter's earnings
amounted to: "School, one quarter, 50 dollars (about

£10) ; sewing, 50 dollars ; stories, 20 dollars (about £4)—
if I am ever paid," adds Louisa, sapiently.

She thoroughly enjoyed a run in the country, at Walpole,
New Hampshire, where she stayed in June, 1855, with
some friends. "So glad to run and skip in the wood and up
the splendid ravine. Shall write here, I know." In July
the Alcott family all came to live in a house at Walpole,
which was lent to them rent free. They had plays and
picnics, pleasant people and good neighbours. Fanny
Kemble came up, and "we acted *The Jacobite, Rivals,* and
Bonnycastles, to a hundred people, and were noticed in
the Boston papers. Anna was the star, I did Mrs.
Malaprop, Widow Pottle, and the old ladies."

Louisa had written another fairy book, *Christmas Elves,*
and she decided to take it to Boston herself and seek her
fortune. So, with a little trunk of home-made clothes, 20
dollars earned by stories sent to the *Gazette,* and her MSS.,
she set out by herself from Walpole one rainy day in
November, 1855. It was her birth-month, and always a
memorable one to her.

It was too late to do anything with her book, so she
wrote poems and tales for which she got about £2 a-piece,
and sewed industriously, one job consisting of a dozen
pillow-cases, one dozen sheets, six fine cambric neckties,
and two dozen handkerchiefs. She sat up all one night to
finish them, and 4 dollars (about 16s.), was all she got for
them. An outbreak of scarlet fever called her back to
Walpole to nurse her two sisters, but in November, 1856, she
set out for Boston a second time with her little old trunk,
25 dollars (about £5) in her pocket and much resolution in
her soul. "I said to the Lord, 'Help us all and keep us
for each other !' as I had never said it before."

She had a little room in an attic, and found a house full
of boarders very amusing to study. Her principal variety
was going to Theodore Parker's Sunday evening receptions.
Large, bashful Louisa sat in her corner weekly, staring and

enjoying herself. Mr. Parker said, " God bless you, Louisa ; come again ! " and the grasp of his hand gave her courage to face another anxious week. " He is like a great fire," she says, " where all can come and be warmed and comforted." In May she had done what she had planned—supported herself, taught four months, written eight stories, and earned 100 dollars (£20).

A great shadow was coming to her in the long illness of her sister Elizabeth—the " Beth " of *Little Women.* The Alcotts returned to Concord in October, 1857, and lived a few months in part of a house which they hired, till Orchard House, which they had bought, was ready for them. Louisa came to nurse her sister, who gradually faded away, " so sweet and patient and so worn that my heart is broken to see the change." At last, in March, 1858, with one last look of her beautiful eyes, Beth was gone. " Death," says Louisa, " never seemed terrible to me, and now is beautiful, so I cannot fear it, but find it friendly and wonderful."

Another family break happened soon afterwards, when Anna came walking in to announce her engagement with John Pratt. Louisa moaned in private over her loss, for Anna was her special friend and comforter—her second self. She notes in her diary, " Another sister gone ! " In July, 1858, the Alcott family settled into Orchard House. " Father is happy," writes Louisa ; " mother is glad to be at rest. Anna is in bliss with her gentle John, and May busy over her pictures. I have plans simmering, but must sweep, and dust, and wash my dish-pans a while longer." She worked off an attack of stage fever by writing a story, and felt better ; also a moral tale, and got 25 dollars (£5) for it.

The desire to get in amongst the haunts of men soon set in again in full force. Life was her college, and in October, 1858, she was back at Boston in search of work. She said resolutely, " There is work for me, and I'll have it." She was on the point of taking a place at the Girls' Reform School at Winchester, to sew for ten hours a day, make and mend, when unexpectedly one of her former pupils wanted her, and she went away to her little girl with a bright heart. One of her stories, *Mark Field's Mistake*, was accepted for the *Atlantic Monthly*, and Mr. Lowell asked if it were not translated from the German, it was so unlike other tales. Publishers were now eager for her stories, and went on writing for them. The year 1860 was "a year of good luck." Mr. Alcott was appointed superintendent of schools in Concord, Louisa's farce was acted, she was writing for the *Atlantic Monthly*, and getting better pay, and in May, Anna was happily married to her John. Louisa went to see the young couple in their honeymoon home, a little cottage in a blooming apple orchard. "Very sweet and pretty," she writes ; " but I'd rather be a free spinster and paddle my own canoe." She characteristically jokes about her own love-affairs. "Had a funny lover," she writes in her diary, " who met me on the cars, and said he had lost his heart at once. A Southerner, and very demonstrative and gushing. He called and wished to pay his addresses, and being told I didn't wish to see him, retired to write letters, and haunt the road with his hat off. He went at last and peace reigned. My adorers are all queer."

She laughingly said that she always got tired of everybody, and felt sure that she should of her husband. And yet in *Work* we find a yearning after the might-have-been, when Louisa says, "Her eyes followed some humble pair, longing to bless and be blessed by the Divine Presence, whose magic beautifies the little milliner and her lad with the same grace as the poet and his mistress. . . . I shall be solitary all my life perhaps, so the sooner I make up my mind to it the better."

Her last teaching experiment was in 1862, when she opened a Kindergarten school, but it was not successful, and she returned to her pen, and wrote some chapters of *Moods* and *Success*—afterwards called *Work*. A friend said to her, "Stick to your teaching, you can't write." She answered, "I won't teach, and I *can* write, and I'll prove it."

The American war was now sweeping over the States ; every man was eager to be a soldier, every woman was eager to be a nurse. Louisa soon caught the infection ; the Alcotts were all Abolitionists, and sided with the North against the South. One of Louisa's early recollections was seeing her mother hide a runaway slave in the oven. She volunteered her services, which were accepted, and she was sent off to the Union Hospital at George Town in December, 1862. She was just thirty, and from a photograph done at this time we see that along with the drollery in her face, her somewhat protruding under-lip, firm chin, and steadfast eyes, gave her an expression of resolution and force. She needed all her courage for her new life. She was up at six, and ran through her ward and opened the windows, for the house, she says, was a perfect pestilence-box, cold, damp, dirty, full of vile odours from wounds, laundry, and stables. Then to breakfast of fried beef, salt butter, husky bread, and washy coffee. After breakfast, dressing wounds, dusting tables, sewing bandages, and rushing up and down stairs for pillows, bed-linen, sponges, books, and directions. At twelve the big bell rang, and dinner of soup, meat, and potatoes came. After dinner some slept, many read, and others wanted letters written. This part of the business Louisa thoroughly enjoyed, her big babies put in such odd things, and expressed their ideas so comically that she had " great fun interiorally, while as grave as possible exteriorally." Supper at five set every one running, and when that flurry was over, all settled down to their evening's amusements, newspapers, gossip, the doctor's last round and final doses for such as needed them. At nine the bell rang, gas was turned out, the day nurses went to bed, the night nurses went on duty, and " sleep and death had the house between them."

After six weeks, Louisa's strength gave way and she was prostrate in typhoid fever. Her father came for her, and she was brought back to Concord more dead than alive. She says she had never been ill before, and was never well afterwards. She had three weeks of delirium, and when she looked in the glass, she saw a " queer, thin, big-eyed face." All her hair had been cut off, and she " felt badly " at the loss of her one beauty. She never sold her hair as Jo did in *Little Women*, but it was always looked upon as a possible resource, and she said in her journal, "I will pay my debts, if I have to sell my hair to do it."

Her hospital life had done much for her. She had now a wider experience of life in its intense phases; she had been brought face to face with deeper realities than she had found in Boston boarding-houses. Her letters, hastily written home to her family, were so graphic and interesting that she was prevailed on to publish them in the *Commonwealth* newspaper. These *Hospital Sketches* were soon republished in a book by James Redpath, who gave 200 dollars (£40) for them. They brought more than money to Louisa Alcott—they showed her her style, and were the first step towards fame. In the first few months after her illness her thoughts were principally taken up by her first nephew, Anna's boy, and by the work of launching her novel, *Moods*, into the world. *Moods* had been tossed about from publisher to publisher : Redpath found it too long ; Ticknor could not use it ; Loring liked it, but wanted it shorter ; so it was thrown into a spidery cupboard. Louisa at length saw a way to shorten it ; she took out ten chapters, and wrote—wrote like a thinking machine in full operation. In this condensed form " poor old *Moods* " came out at last. There is no doubt that the publishers were right. *Moods* is not a good novel ; none of the characters live, and it leaves no distinct impression on the mind. *Hospital Sketches*, however, made the public interested in *Moods*, and it was fairly floated. Louisa Alcott received a handsome sum for the copyright, and the year closed free of debt, with the family comfortable and happy. The following year, 1865, she paid her first visit to Europe, as companion to an invalid friend. At Vevay, she made the acquaintance of a young Pole, who suggested the character of Laurie in *Little Women*. He played beautifully, and Louisa found him very interesting. " Boys are always jolly," she observes ; " even princes."

At Nice, she left her companion and went off to Paris alone, feeling as happy as a freed bird. She passed a fortnight at Wimbledon with the Conways. Of all the London sights none, she thought, was lovelier " than the old thatched house, the common of golden gorse, nightingales flying at night, hawthorn everywhere, and Richmond Park full of deer close by." She had a free and jolly time, *à l'Américaine*, roaming about London all day, dining late, and resting, chatting, music, or fun in the evening. She visited Furnival's Inn, where Dickens wrote *Pickwick*, the Charterhouse, where Thackeray went to school, and the Saracen's Head. St. Paul's she liked better than Notre Dame.

After " fourteen dull, stormy, long, sick days," she reached home in July, 1866, " to find father at the station, Nan and babies at the gate, May flying round the lawn, and Marmie crying at the door. Into her arms I went, and was at home at last." She found plenty of work waiting for her. One editor wanted a long story in twenty-four chapters, which she wrote—a hundred and eighty-five pages—in a fortnight.

Of her method of work she says : " I never had a study. Any pen and paper do, and an old atlas on my knee is all I want. Carry a dozen plots in my head, and think them over when in the mood. Sometimes keep one for years, and suddenly find it all ready to write. Often lie awake and plan whole chapters, word for word, then merely scribble them down as if copying. Used to sit fourteen hours a day at one time, eating little and unable to stir till a certain amount was done." The next three years was her busiest time; she was " sick from too hard work." She spent the winter of 1866–67 in her little room—" Gamp's garret"—in Boston. She had editorial work for *Merry's Museum*, which included reading manuscripts, writing one story each month, and an editorial, and when Mr. Niles, of Roberts Brothers, asked her, in September, 1867, to write a girls' story, she answered, "I'll try, sir." She had often thought of describing her own and her sisters' early lives under the title of the Pathetic Family, and this thought was in her mind when she began *Little Women*—the story of "when we were girls." Her book was begun in May, 1868, and finished in July, when Louisa Alcott was thirty-six. The publisher thought the first chapters dull; "so," adds Louisa, "do I"; but the girls who read it in MS. declared that it was "splendid," and their verdict has been amply verified by hundreds of thousands of other girls who have laughed and wept over it in all parts of the world. "It reads better than I expected," says Louisa; "we really lived most of it, and if it succeeds that will be the reason of it." The facts in the book, which are literally true, though often changed as to time and place, are, we are told by Louisa Alcott herself: "the early plays and experiences, Beth's death, Jo's literary and Amy's artistic experience, Meg's happy home. Mr. March did not go to the war, but Jo did. Mrs. March is all true, only not half good enough. Laurie is not an American boy; he was a Polish boy, met abroad in 1865. Mr. Lawrence is my grandfather, Colonel Joseph May; Aunt March is no one."

What Fredrika Bremer has done for Swedish girls in *The President's Daughter*, what Charlotte Yonge has done for English girls in the *Daisy Chain*, Louisa Alcott has done for American girls in *Little Women*. She has photographed the four sisters : they are independent, rollicking, fun-loving, aspiring, ambitious. We know them all as well, or better, than our next-door neighbours.

The success of the book was complete, and the copyright, which Louisa Alcott kept in her own hands, made her fortune. "The dull book," she adds, "was the first golden egg for the ugly duckling." There was such a clamour amongst the girl-readers of *Little Women* to know what became of Meg, Jo, and Amy, if they married, and who their husbands were, that Louisa Alcott had to write a sequel to it. She was not fond of love-scenes, and did not wish her prototype, Jo, to marry at all, but the publishers and the public insisted on it, and so the German Professor Bhaer had to be created. The book is sometimes called *Good Wives* and sometimes *Little Women Wedded*, and was quite as great a success as its predecessor. It was commenced November 1, 1868, and Louisa was so full of her work that she could not eat or sleep. On New Year's Day, 1869, it was finished ; she paid up all her debts, and felt that she could die in peace. In a letter to her publishers she says : "After toiling so many years along the uphill road—always a hard one to women-writers—it is peculiarly grateful to me to find the way growing easier at last, with pleasant little surprises blossoming on either side, and the rough places made smooth by courtesy and kindness."

After two years of incessant work came the reaction, and during the summer at Concord, in 1869, Louisa Alcott was ill and tired. Her *Hospital Sketches* were republished by Roberts Brothers, with the addition of six *Camp and Fireside Stories*, and two thousand copies of the book in its new form were sold the first week. Literary celebrity was rather a burden than a delight. Louisa Alcott remarks, "People begin to come and stare at the Alcotts ; reporters haunt the place to look at the authoress, who dodges into the woods *à la* Hawthorne, and won't be even a very small lion. Refreshed my soul with Goethe, ever strong and fine and alive." She was not like some Americans whom she had met at Frank- fort looking at Goethe's house. They asked, " Who was Goethe to fuss about ? "

In 1870 she got well enough to write a little, and finished her *Old-fashioned Girl*, a delightfully fresh and breezy story. Polly is a wholesome, natural girl, with no nonsense about her, and every one who reads her adventures must be the better for them. And yet Louisa Alcott wrote it with her left hand in a sling, one foot up, head aching, and no voice. As the book is funny, people used to say to her, " Didn't you enjoy doing it ? " She wrote in her journal, "I often think of poor Tom Hood as I scribble. I certainly earn my bread by the sweat of my brow."

Strangely enough, she seems to have enjoyed writing her novel of *Moods*, which is dull, laboured, and stiff, much more than her girls' stories, which are all bright, humorous, and delightful. But in *Moods* she was learning her art, she had not found it.

Another trip to Europe was projected in 1870. Louisa Alcott was now not only in a position to pay her own expenses, but to bring her sister May with her. May was not only the beauty, but the artist of the family—"our little Raphael "—and Louisa's darling and pride. She calls her in *Little Women* a " regular snow-maiden, with blue eyes and yellow hair curling on her shoulders, pale and slender, and always carrying herself like a young lady mindful of her manners." As the sisters were on their way to New York, a newspaper boy in the train put *An Old-fashioned Girl* into Louisa's lap, saying, "Bully book, ma'am. Sell a lot. Better have it." When Mr. Pratt, Louisa's brother-in-law, told the boy that the lady had written it, his " chuckle, stare, and astonished ' No I ' was great fun."

The account of the second voyage across the Atlantic, and the weeks spent at Morlaix, Dinan, Tours, Geneva, Vevay, and Bex, are graphically related in *Shawl Straps*, and in Louisa's chatty letters to her people. She has no reverence for cathedrals, ruins, or priests, but enjoys human life immensely. She gets enthusiastic about the pine forests of Brieg, the white mountain-top of the Simplon, and the heavenly Lake of Como, but at Rome, she is oppressed with a general sense of sin, dirt, and a universal decay of all things.

While in Rome the news came of the death of her brother-

in-law, Mr. Pratt.   Her first thought was how her sister and
the dear little boys could be helped, and with this object she
began her story of *Little Men.*   " In writing and thinking
of the little lads, to whom I must be a father now," she says
in her journal, " I found comfort for my sorrow."

She always loved boys, and she wanted to do for them
what she had done for girls in *Little Women.*   The school
at Plumstead, with Denis, John, Nat, Franz, Emil, and
Tommy Bangs, the dog Christopher Columbus and the
two pups, Castor and Pollux, is certainly a very odd school.
In Mrs. Jo and her husband Louisa embodies some of her
father's theories about school-life.   "Latin, Greek, and
mathematics were all very well, but in Professor Bhaer's
opinion, self-knowledge, self-help, and self-control were more
important."

Little Men was out the day Louisa Alcott arrived at
New York.   Fifty thousand copies had been sold before it
was out, and her father came to meet her with a great red
placard pinned up in the carriage.   Her New Year's gift
from her publisher was four thousand and forty dollars,
(about £808).

She had not been at home much more than a year when
Mr. Beecher sent one of the editors of the *Christian Union*
to ask for a serial story, and she got out her old manuscript
of *Success* and called it *Work.*   Three thousand dollars
(about £600) was offered for the serial, and she had to
write three pages at once on impression paper as Beecher,
Roberts, and Low of London all wanted copies.   *Work* is a
story of experience, and Christie is another revelation of
Louisa Alcott herself.   When Christie tries the stage, when
she is about to end her own existence by plunging into the
river, we know that these are phases of life with which
Louisa Alcott was familiar.   If she did not actually do these
things, she was in the state of mind that prepared her for
doing them.   *Work* is far better than *Moods,* but it is not a
good novel.   The best thing about it are bright sayings, full

of quaint philosophy and fresh from the Alcott mint. Such, for instance, as :—

"She was one of those who could find little bits of happiness for herself, and enjoy them heartily."

"Religion cannot be given or bought, but must grow as trees grow, needing frost and snow, rain and wind, to strengthen it before it is deep-rooted in the soul."

"You've had bread and water long enough now, you want meat and wine a spell, and when it's time for milk and honey some one will fetch 'em. The Lord feeds us right, it's we that quarrel with our vittles."

" As if the Great Sculptor had blocked out a statue, and left the man's own soul to finish it."

It was a great pleasure to Louisa Alcott that her sister May had also a wish to be busy and independent. May worked hard at her art, living for some time in London and copying Turner's pictures at the National Gallery. She came home with a " portfolio full of fine work," and Louisa had leisure to finish her story of *Eight Cousins*, to which a sequel—*Rose in Bloom*—was afterwards added. In October, 1875, she attended the Women's Congress at Syracuse and saw Niagara. She says she had a funny time with the girls. " Write loads of autographs, dodge at the theatre, and am kissed to death by gushing damsels. . . . This, this is fame ! " She enjoyed a winter at New York, and was specially interested in a visit to the Newsboys' Home. During the winter of 1877 she devoted herself to a novel for the *No Name* series. It was called *A Modern Mephisto-pheles*, and she evidently took a great deal of pains with it. The plot somewhat resembles Mr. Anstey's *Giant's Robe*. A young poet, Canaris, is induced to publish as his own the work of his friend Halwyze, who in reality is a Mephistopheles, and tries to drag down Canaris to the lowest level, from which he is saved by the trusting love of his young wife. It is a sad story, and Gladys dies in the end. Louisa Alcott attempted in it to sound a depth for which she was quite unfitted ; we miss the lightness of touch, the ease and fun of her girls' books. She reminds us of the comic actor, who was always wanting to act tragedy. No wonder her friends said, " I know *you* did not write it, you can't hide your peculiar style." She *did* hide it, but the result was not a success.

There were many long, quiet days of watching by Mrs. Alcott's bedside, and as Louisa watched, she wrote some short stories and finished *Under the Lilacs*. She had the nursing all to herself, for she had sent her sister off to London and Paris to go on with her art studies. There was great joy in the family when May had a study of still life in the Paris *Salon*, and she was very proud to see her six months' labours bear fruit. In November, 1877, the brave, faithful mother, "the Marmie," so tenderly loved and cared for, passed away. She used to say, " Stay by me, Louey, and help me if I suffer much." And Louey *did* stay by her to the end.

" We thought to weep, but sing for joy instead,"

cries Louisa in her beautiful *In Memoriam* poem on the death of her mother.

That "Spartan spirit that made life so grand, teaching us how to seek the highest goal, to earn the true success," had always been to Louisa one of the highest influences in her literary career. And this blow was followed by another. Her sister May married a young Swiss, M. Nieriker, and they were very happy in their Paris nest. In December, 1879, a little girl was born—Louisa May—but the mother died unexpectedly two weeks afterwards. Her last wish was that the child should be sent to Aunt Louisa, and the little princess arrived in September, 1880, and was received with smiles and tears. Every one came to see Miss Alcott's baby. " My life," writes Louisa, " is absorbed in my baby." It was for this child that *Lulu's Library*, a collection of short stories, was written. The first volume was published in 1885, the second in 1887, and the third in 1889. *Jack and Jill* was written while May was dying, and Louisa Alcott seemed to shrink from it.

The busy pen was gradually getting weary. Mr. Alcott had an attack of paralysis, which left him almost speechless. At the age of eighty-six he was not likely to rally, and Louisa herself, the strong, the capable, the inexhaustible one, suffered from rheumatism and vertigo, and had often to be left quite alone. She had taken a house at Boston, in Louisburg Square, and felt that she must grind away providing for others. "I don't want to live," she said, " if I can't be of use." To a young man who wrote to her asking if he should devote himself to authorship, she said, " Not if you can do anything else. Even dig ditches."

She still went on planning stories. *Jo's Boys* was the last long one, and *Spinning Wheel Stories* came tumbling into her mind so fast that she pinned a few down while "genius burned." Any excitement brought on violent headache. Her nervous system had completely broken down from long years of incessant work. She found rest and quiet at Dr. Lawrence's house at Roxburg. Here she wrote very little, and busied herself with fancy work, making pen-wipers in various colours for her friends. The last thing she made was a flannel garment for a poor child.

In March, 1888, she drove in from the country to see her father, and as the day was warm she forgot her fur cloak. She caught a chill, and had violent pain in her head. The pain went on, she gradually became unconscious, and died at half-past three March 6, 1888, in her fifty-sixth year. She did not know that her father had passed away a day or two before her. When his friends came to his funeral, they were met at the door by the news, "Louisa Alcott is dead !" Her remains were brought to Concord and buried in the cemetery at Sleepy Hollow. Her mother, father, and her sister Beth, were laid there before her, those dear ones whom she had loved so well and served so faithfully.

America has given us many famous women-writers—Mrs. Stowe, Elizabeth Wetherell, Adeline Whitney, Elizabeth Stuart Phelps, Louisa Chandler, Mary Wilkins, and others —but none will leave a brighter, purer, or more sunshiny memory than Lousia Alcott. Her humour has a flavour of its own. It is boisterous rather than delicate, racy rather than refined; her simplest letters are full of it, so are her girls' stories, but when she writes novels, and creates a crowd of mature characters, it deserts her. George Eliot's letters, on the contrary, are utterly devoid of humour, but her characters, such as Mrs. Poyser, Mrs. Glegg, and dozens of others, are rich in it. The reason is not far to seek. George Eliot had a strong dramatic faculty; Louisa Alcott had very little of it. And yet her personality is so vivid that we cannot do without her. We seem to see her, her eyes twinkling with drollery, laughing with the girls, joking with the boys, full of hope and courage, thoroughly believing in the gospel of work, and never losing trust in God even in the darkest days.

THE END.